S0-ATK-963

Behind him William heard the clash of steel on steel. His friend Haakon roaring.

Throughout the inn, doors were slamming. William leapt for the door, stumbled over his rifle propped at the foot of the bed, and fell headlong.

Haakon hauled him to his feet, and they burst into the hall and raced for the stairs. Laying a hand on the banister, William vaulted over the rail. The attacker lunged and slashed, and the wind of the falling blade ruffled his hair. He never saw Haakon barreling down the stairs like a charging bull. The Norwegian hit him low, propelling him halfway across the room. A table cracked and collapsed. With a groan the thug fell back among the splintered wood and lay still.

Haakon and William got their backs together, their blades weaving a net of steel in the air before them. Two men ran down the stairs and into the taproom. Another man emerged from the shadows.

William dodged an overhand cut. "Help! For the love of God, help!" he screamed.

♦ ♦ ♦ ♦

Also by Melinda M. Snodgrass

Runespear
(with Victor Milán)

Published by
POPULAR LIBRARY

QUEEN'S GAMBIT DECLINED

MELINDA M. SNODGRASS

POPULAR LIBRARY

An Imprint of Warner Books, Inc.

A Warner Communications Company

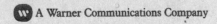

DEDICATION

This book is for my editor and dear friend Brian Thomsen. Not many editors would be willing to take a risk on a fantasy that is really an antifantasy. Thank you, Brian, for letting me realize a dream. This book is also dedicated to the work of outstanding men and women throughout history—the Huygens, Newtons, Curies, and Einsteins who have challenged the limits to human endeavor.

ACKNOWLEDGMENTS

Two gentlemen were very helpful in the creation of this book—Victor Milán and Walter Jon Williams. They discussed sword fighting techniques of the latter seventeenth century with me, they loaned me books on cavalry warfare, they encouraged me to include some of the more outré stories about Louis the XIV—in short, they listened patiently while I fumed and rambled. Thanks, fellows, for all the help. I'd like to mention several biographies of William of Orange which were instrumental in the writing of this work: *William and Mary*, by Henri and Barbara van der Zee; *William of Orange: A Personal Portrait*, by Nesca A. Robb; and *William III and the Defense of European Liberty*, by Stephen B. Baxter. Thanks also to Robert Graves and his epic work *The White Goddess*. The chapter headings are drawn from the ancient Celtic calendar-alphabet the *Song of Amergin* reproduced in that volume.

For those authorities on the seventeenth century, allow me to offer an apology in advance. In the interest of dramatic storytelling I have substantially compressed time. The invasion of the United Provinces took place on June 1, 1672, and the war lasted until August 1678. My war begins on June 1, 1670, and ends in August 1671 with William's invasion of France. And as knowledgeable historians will tell you William of Orange in fact never invaded France. It was discussed more than a few times during the thirty years that William resisted French expansion and the threat of a universal monarchy, but never attempted. In fact I doubt William would ever have approved such a step. He was a great admirer of all things French. His ballet, his clothes, his bed, his palaces, and indeed his language, was French.

I also hope that this book will in some small way offset the consistently bad press to which William of Orange has been subjected. If he knew of the atrocities currently committed in his name in Northern Ireland he would undoubtedly be devastated. To quote Baxter, "Although he (William) secured the political and religious freedom of Europe, he was never an enemy of France or of the Catholic church so long as they stayed within their proper boundaries. Nor was William III an enemy of Catholicism as such; the Mass was said daily in the chapel of his château at Orange, his personal attorneys in the Dutch Republic were Catholics, toleration was extended to the Catholic minority there. It is much more accurate to think of William III as the leader of a struggle for liberty and toleration. . . ."

Behold, . . . I am come. . . . I am she that is the natural mother of all things, mistress and governess of all the elements, the initial progeny of worlds, chief of the powers divine, queen of all that are in Hell, the principal of them that dwell in Heaven, manifested alone and under one form of all the gods and goddesses. At my will the planets of the sky, the wholesome winds of the seas, and the lamentable silences of hell be disposed. . . .

The White Goddess by Robert Graves

Prologue

**I am a wizard: _who but I sets the
cool head aflame with smoke?_**

A man of God lay like a carven effigy upon the embroidered coverlet. His cardinal's red was a livid slash against the green brocade. Fine, dark Italianate eyes stared rigidly at nothing, and drool ran from slack lips, wetting a neatly trimmed spade beard and luxuriant mustache.

A six-foot-tall concave mirror reflected and distorted the bed and its occupant. Then its silvery surface was dimmed by boiling clouds of oily gray. Mist oozed from the mirror, and now it took on a dull and angry fire, and a shape that was arguably human. Suddenly it collapsed again, and lay like black, evil water on the parquet floor.

Flowing across the room it climbed the hem of the coverlet and vanished, like water absorbed into thirsty ground, into the limp body of the cardinal.

The man sat up and straightened his hat.

"Damn the bitch," he said, enunciating each syllable as if he would like to bite through the word.

His soutane rustled as he swung from the bed and crossed

swiftly to an elaborate chess table. The pieces were carved from white onyx and garnets, and the board was marble.

Slowly he studied the game laid out before him. A white pawn was one square from the final rank. If it succeeded it would be promoted, and could become any piece desired—a knight, a queen . . . or a king.

The cardinal swept up the hapless pawn. His long white fingers tightened, and white powder dribbled from his fist.

One

I am an infant: *who but I Peeps*
from the unhewn dolmen arch?

"He who would distinguish the true from the false must have an adequate idea of what is true and false."

Baruch Spinoza laid a hand on the slender shoulder of his student and watched the words flow smoothly from the nib of the quill pen.

"You think it's worth writing down?" His usually somber black eyes were alight with self-mockery.

William Henry, Prince of Orange, glanced up. His large, expressive dark eyes held their usual cautious aloofness. "The words of a philosopher should always be treasured, don't you think?"

"Prettily said, Your Highness, but is it true? I don't think you like me very much."

"Ah, no, Heer Spinoza, I *try* not to like you, but find that despite my every effort I do."

"Johan de Witt seeks only the best for his country." It was gently spoken.

"First, Heer Spinoza, this is *my* country." There was a brief struggle, reflected upon William's thin face, but when he re-

3

sumed it was in his customary dry, level tone. "And as for de
Witt . . . I do not impugn evil intent to the man. No doubt he
does as he thinks best."

"He has given us peace, a thing not lightly to be despised,"
reminded Spinoza.

"Are you an advocate of peace at any price?"

"I prefer it to king's glory."

"Louis is a king, too, and France might not always be content
with the Netherlands as a lickspittle on her eastern flank. Someday Louis will stretch out his hand and take us, and what then
will become of honor and liberty . . . of men like you, Heer
Spinoza, by birth a Jew, by reputation an atheist?"

The older man flinched, for where else in Europe in this year
of our Lord 1668 could Jews live and worship free from fear
and oppression? But peace was not a thing to be lightly cast
aside, and Jan de Witt and his Loevenstein party preserved the
peace, and thus far the only cost had been the loss of the Stadholderate by this slender boy. Spinoza looked down at the curly
chestnut head bent once more over the notebook—at the narrow profile and aquiline nose silhouetted against the ice-pat-
terned window—and wondered what was going on in that
secretive mind.

"Well, Your Highness, I will pray—"

"Will you now?" A flash of humor lit that usually humorless
face.

"All right, I *hope* that peace can be maintained, and Johan de
Witt will rule this tiny republic with wisdom for many more
years."

The door to the small sitting room crashed open, and Jan van
Gent strode into the room. William, drawing the feathers of the
quill lightly through his fingers, tensed at this discourteous in-
trusion. The slim white fingers tightened on the pen, and with a
tiny snap the fragile feather broke.

William pinned his governor with a frigid, haughty gaze. "It
is customary to knock before entering, Heer van Gent."

"Ah, yes, quite so. My apologies, Your Highness."

Spinoza could see that the use of the honorific did little to
mollify the prince. William rose, walked to one of the long
windows, and said with an irritated hunch of one shoulder.
"You interrupted me at my studies."

"God's blood, young William!" said van Gent in a horrible

parody of bonhomie. "You're always at it! Drudge, drudge, drudge. Best have a care lest all this study fret you into a brain fever."

"I should think you and Johan de Witt would hope for such an eventuality," said William with sweet malice.

But van Gent was inclined to be patient. He cast an indulgent glance at the prince, then rolled an eye toward Spinoza.

"In the hips, eh? Bad weather will do that. Makes for a sour stomach, and fills the head with humors."

Spinoza's mouth quirked. "Quite so."

Van Gent plowed across the room. "So what are you studying?"

"Heer Spinoza and I began with natural science, but having tired of that we touch briefly upon philosophy."

Van Gent fingered a lens which Baruch had brought to replace the broken eyepiece in William's microscope. "Gazing at tiny creatures were you?"

"Yes." William bit off the word.

"Worrisome, those golliwogs in the water." Van Gent's fat face folded into mirth lines. "More reason to drink only good Holland schnapps, eh?"

He began idly turning the pages of the leather-bound notebook. Cat quick, William crossed and flipped shut the cover. Pacing to the bellpull, he laid a hand on the velvet cord and cocked an inquiring brow at van Gent.

"Will you take wine, sir?"

"Damn, but I will, boy." With a screech and a scrape van Gent dragged a chair across the hardwood floor, deposited it by the fire, and sank wheezing onto its embroidered seat. He then pinned William with a glance from which all jocularity had been leached. "Are you hiding something from me in yon book?"

"Just a few notes on Caesar's expeditions into Gaul."

Van Gent grunted. "Still dreaming of military glory? Well, put it from your mind. There will be no war. That great, just king, Louis XIV, will keep us safely protected beneath the mantle of his glory."

William grimaced and turned away. Curious over his student's caution, Spinoza slid into a chair by the desk and opened the journal.

It is said that all the Stuarts are Powerful Magic users, but if Mother knew the way of it before she died, she did not pass it on to me. My Father's Line may also have carried the ancient Powers, but this too has been denied to me since he was so disobliging as to Die a scant week before my birth. I suspicion that he at least had the Tendency, for a Prince of Orange rode in the train of Charlemagne, and much has been written of the Power of those great knights.

But this is all mere idle Speculation on my part, for it seems that what remains of my family have Abandoned Me, and I am left to struggle on without hope, without support, and in fear of my Life, for my great enemy grows ever stronger while I sit alone, frightened and ravaged by the paroxysms brought on by the weakness of my Blood. Is there no one to guide and help me?

Here a spatter of ink across the page betrayed the writer's agitation. The passage reeked of self-pity, and Spinoza was not surprised to see that the entire page had been crossed out. There were many things William Henry would endure—his headaches, his fainting spells, his weak lungs—but whining and self-pity were not among them. But the wildness of the words! Prating of magic and ancient powers. Could it be the prince's mind was as weak as his frail body?

Spinoza rejected the notion. After months with the Dutch heir he knew the power of that mind. Of all the princes in Christendom, William was the brightest and the best educated: he was possessed of a working knowledge of seven languages, drilled in military tactics and strategy both ancient and modern, an talented amateur scientist and mathematician, accomplished on the lute, a connoisseur of art and music.

The boy was speaking again, and Baruch wrenched back his wayward attention.

"I do not think of glory, sir. I am grateful to my most noble cousin Louis for his interest in my little country, and I am also pleased to bide by the wishes and desires of my guardians." William made a slight bow.

Spinoza, looking sharply up, wondered that van Gent could have missed the bitter irony in those proper words.

The governor seemed nervous, his blunt, thick fingers going to his throat to fiddle with his falling band with its lace trimming. Silence lay like dust while van Gent pushed his lips in and out and seemed to be tasting, weighing, and discarding words.

"Excuse me, sir, but why have you sought me out?" William finally asked, irritation sharpening the words.

"Come to invite you hunting," van Gent blurted.

William's slim, chestnut brows flew up, and he gave a regretful shake of the head, the heavy chestnut curls tumbling on his shoulders.

"I thank you, sir, but I must decline. Pastor Grundek expects me for lessons."

Van Gent brushed aside the objection with an airy wave of his hand. It was an odd and curiously jarring gesture. The motion seemed so light and graceful, while the member chosen to execute the maneuver was a great, broad, spadelike hand with a smattering of coarse curling hairs across the back of the knuckles.

"Come, come, boy. You study too hard. All these books will turn you into an old woman or—God forbid—a monk." His lips stretched back in a wide grin revealing the pale pink of his gums. "'Tis a beautiful day, come hunting."

Both William and Spinoza looked through the window to where thick white clouds hung like thick icing above the slate gray of the canals, and the empty fields looked nude and vulnerable stripped of their summer verdure. "Nay, sir, I cannot give such insult to Pastor Grundek, especially not in pursuit of such frivolous pleasure. Though riding in such inclement weather would bring little joy and, more like, an attack of asthma or gripe."

Van Gent rested his hands on his knees and leaned intently forward. His belly sagged forward onto his thighs. "Don't be a whiner, boy." The prince's small white teeth closed hard on his lower lip, and his nostrils, like tiny porcelain cups, tightened in fury. "And I've already spoken to Grundek about our little outing." Van Gent rose and placed a heavy, companionable arm about William's shoulders. "He says his bones are aching, and he would be just as pleased to sit by the fire and drink ale as grill you on the Prophets. So what say you? Will you come?"

His arm tightened, the fingers digging into the muscles of the prince's upper arm as he leaned in close. William recoiled and, dodging nimbly away, placed a chair between himself and his governor. Baruch was not surprised at the young man's reaction. In the months he had tutored William he had seen the prince's distaste of casual physical contact. It had gained him a reputation of coldness. Spinoza wondered if it hid in fact other, more passionate emotions.

"Very well, sir, I will ride."

The older man gave a gusting laugh which seemed to hold a shade of relief, and clapped his hands together in delight and anticipation.

"Good, good. It will be fine sport, you'll see."

"Indeed, sir, I hope so." William held the door. "If you will grant me but a few minutes indulgence, sir, I shall change for riding."

"Take as long as you need, as long as you need. You are the *prince,* Your Highness, we wait upon *your* pleasure."

The archness of the remark once more stiffened William with outrage. Fingers tensing whitely on the edge of the heavy door, he slammed it shut and raged, "My great-grandfather died to free this country from the Spanish, and now *he*"—a furious thrust of his arm after the departed van Gent—"and his kind give it meekly over to the French a scant hundred years later. God's blood, my grandsire must be spinning. And *you* approve of them."

Spinoza had never before seen William in the company of his guardians, and he was disturbed by the evident lack of respect accorded to the young man. Cautiously he asked, "Are they always so discourteous to you?"

"Yes, but what right have I to object?" William shrugged. "It's simply one more discourtesy in the long line of discourtesies that make up my life." He gripped the back of a chair and leaned toward the philosopher. "Heer Spinoza, consider this when you think so approvingly upon the rule of Johan de Witt and the Loevensteiners. I am called a ward of the state. In fact I am a prisoner, and I exist on a knife's edge. If I show too much spirit—any hint of desire for my throne—this carefully disguised imprisonment will become imprisonment in fact. And given my infirmities I would not last two months in some dungeon in Enschede." He folded his hands at his breast. "So I am docile and meek, and thus have saved——" He pressed his lips together.

"What?"

"You'll carry tales to your great good friend."

"I will not!" Spinoza drew himself up and threw back his long black hair. "What an insult you have offered me! I, like you, Your Highness, care for you despite myself. I'm not a spy set upon you."

"Such heat." A small grim smile. "I wonder if you'll believe me."

"You can't know until you try."

"Very well—there have been two half-hearted and bungled attempts upon my life. The next time I don't think they'll bungle."

"Who? Why? . . . You're right, I don't believe you."

"To give your precious Loevensteiners the benefit of the doubt . . . I don't think they are entirely comfortable with this course. But Louis is pushing them, and so terrified of war are they that I think they consider the death of one man small price to pay to maintain the peace."

"Johan de Witt would never countenance it."

"He might not have to. All he would need do is wring his hands over a corpse."

"You talk as if you expect another attempt. Have you any proof to support these fantasies?"

"Circumstantial at best, but enough to place me on my guard." William tapped his forefinger nervously on the journal. "Louis has raised taxes yet again, and I don't think it's to pour more money into his pleasure palace in the swamp. Also, there has been a new conscription order."

"How came you by this information?"

"Travelers talk."

Spinoza took an agitated turn about the room. "The government must be informed."

"The government has greater sources of information than I. I assume they have received this intelligence, but are choosing to ignore it."

"Spain. He must be intending to strike west?"

"Why? Louis's married to a Spanish princess. It's through her that he lays claim to my country. No, Heer Spinoza, you must resign yourself to it—our time as a vassal state is past."

William crossed to the door, the dismissal clear. Baruch gathered his books.

"Young William, I have a confession to make."

"Yes?"

"I trespassed upon your privacy. I scanned your journal."

Blazing anger brought color to William's pale cheeks, then he shook his head at Spinoza's contrite expression. "Your detractors would say that comes from being a Jew."

"No, Your Highness, it comes from being as curious as a cat, and just as amoral."

That drew a chuckle. "Well, I absolve you."

"I am curious—"

"Ah ah!"

"You write of magic, and as if you accept the possibility."

"Someday when I am less pressed I will tell you of the Stuarts, and the legends surrounding the Order of the Garter, and the coven that is said to guard England. But take this assurance—I admit to being curious but I remain skeptical. That passage represents the ravings of a man driven nearly to distraction."

Spinoza bowed and left, and William leaned against the closed door. A shivering ran down his nerves and settled in his thighs and groin, and nausea filled the back of his throat.

"How I hate them," he whispered to the silent room.

The sick spell was passing, the anger fading, but a nagging concern remained. Never since his formal education had begun at age four had he been allowed to forgo devotional instruction. But now he was to frolic, not pray. And he was afraid, though he couldn't say why.

An icy finger traced a line down his spine. With a shiver William shook off the sensation and walked swiftly to his bedchamber.

Before he could even touch the bellpull, Hans William Bentinck, his personal page, came bouncing through a wainscoted door. Bentinck was a solid, upstanding youth of nineteen, with reddish blond hair and an open, ingenuous face that would have looked more appropriate on a happy burger than on the third son of a count. Like all members of the personal household he was dressed in blue satin with gold and silver trimmings, white silk stockings, and crimson laces in the sleeves and shoes. The rich colors suited him well.

But William was less interested in Bentinck's beauty than in the rich and spicy scent of baked cinnamon apples which accompanied him. Saliva filled the prince's mouth and he burst out, "You greedy pig. Eating, and leaving none for me?"

Bentinck rose red-faced and laughing from his bow, and pulled a covered dish from behind his back. "Baked apples with walnuts and cream, stolen from the kitchen a scant half hour ago and kept warm by the fire. The chess game is waiting, and this time—"

William raised a hand. "I can't."

"Tell old Grundek you've got a bellyache."

With a hard kick William sent a high-tongued shoe flying into the far wall. "It's not Grundek. Van Gent has set up a hunting party for my pleasure."

"In this weather?" Bentinck ran a blunt hand through his hair. He stared at the swirling snow pecking against the frosted glass of the mullioned windows.

"Seemed plaguy odd to me too, but he was not to be denied, so I shall ride out."

"Eat while I pull out your clothes," ordered Hans.

William savored both the flavor and the texture of the snack: the mealy flesh of the apple, the sharper crunch of the nuts, the rich flavor of the cream. With a shock he realized that he was eating like a prisoner enjoying his last meal. The page eased down William's breeches, and the prince shivered again. But Bentinck didn't notice—he was pulling a seal-brown coat and breeches from the closet. Ten minutes later William was dressed for riding, in high leather boots with broad tops, and embroidered gauntlets. Placing a plumed hat on his thick curls he buckled his small sword about his waist, and at Bentinck's urging threw a heavy cloak about his shoulders.

They made their way through the rabbit warren of The Hague, and encountered few of the prince's household. Most were in the various offices and sitting rooms conducting business or merely trying to keep warm. For some reason William found this walk through the palace to be unbearably sweet and somehow melancholy. His eye was caught by every detail, from the wainscoting that decorated the whitewashed walls to the cleanly scrubbed floorboards beneath his feet. The smell of cooking blended with the scent of the sachet that had been rubbed into the draperies and hangings to sweeten the scent of stale indoor winter air. William threw back his head and drank in the odor. He suddenly realized that despite pain and loss and suffering he had been happy in this place, and that he counted it his home.

A large outer door loomed before him, and the man-at-arms who had been seated by the door leaped to his feet preparatory to opening it for his prince. William stopped abruptly, and Bentinck trod on his heels. A feeling of intense dread had fallen like a smothering cloak, and William felt as if his breath had caught somewhere between his lungs and his mouth. His heart was hammering, and waves of faintness were washing up, threatening to blot out his view of the anteroom and carry him unconscious to the floor.

He whirled, his cloak swinging about him. Behind him the man-at-arms, unprepared for his prince's sudden retreat, had thrown open the outer door. A gust of cold air, bearing a few large, wet snow flakes, came whistling into the room. It also carried the sound of van Gent's voice, pursuing William like an invisible snare.

"Ah, Your Highness. And here is my surprise—Monsieur de Coulan from the court in Paris, come to see how you are getting on."

William froze, and hunched his shoulders as if expecting a blow. There were some representatives of the French court that he could abide, but de Coulan did not fall among their number. The man was a preening, strutting popinjay who seemed to be of the opinion that his king's glory shone through him like light through a lens. He came to the Netherlands only rarely, and then only to carry instructions and demands from Louis XIV which were likely to be burdensome or irksome to the Dutch people. It seemed to give him keen pleasure to be the bearer of such communications, and his contempt for the Dutch state and the Dutch people was undisguised.

Somehow William swallowed his anger, though it felt like eating glass, and when he turned he was able to present a placid face to de Coulan. Giving a slight bow he extended a gloved hand. De Coulan's round, overfed face reddened at this reminder of their differing ranks. His outthrust chest and belly expanded, giving him the look of an outraged pigeon, and his pudgy fingers tapped irritably at the pearl buttons of his jacket. Moments lengthened to minutes.

"Monsieur de Coulan," William prodded. He felt a fool with his hand outstretched, but it had now become a point of honor.

"Your . . . Highness." There was an infinitesimal pause between the words, and William's brows snapped together in a sharp frown.

Van Gent stepped in, and a glance passed between the two older men. Stiffly de Coulan touched his lips to the gloved fingers.

"Ah, Highness," boomed van Gent. "It was monsieur who suggested this outing, knowing your pleasure in the hunt, and wishing to give you a treat."

"I am obliged to monsieur." William edged the words with fine aristocratic ice.

Van Gent rubbed his hands together. "Well then, shall we to saddle?"

William nodded and swept past his governor. De Coulan tried to proceed him through the door, but Bentinck was too quick. He quickly interposed himself between the Frenchman and the door, allowing his prince to exit first.

"*Salaud!*" de Coulan hissed. Bentinck smiled sweetly back at him.

Outside, organized chaos held sway. A pack of brown and white spotted hounds, a gift from William's uncle, Charles II of England, were winding about their handlers and through the legs of the waiting horses, whining with anxiety and anticipation. Narrow streams of mist gusted from their noses and mingled with the heavier white clouds that ringed the horses' muzzles.

Grooms stood shivering at the sides of their charges, and William sympathized with them. It was bitterly cold for the middle of November. On the other hand, they would be able to retreat to the warmth of the stable once their noble patrons had ridden away, while William would have to suffer through three or four icy hours in the saddle. Hans trailed after him as he made his way across the cobblestone courtyard to his mount. Through the broad, arching double gates set in the southeast wall he could see flat fields and forests. A sudden gust of wind went howling through the courtyard and pulled a white curtain of snow across William's view. Digging his heels into the slick cobbles the prince fought the wind to his horse's side.

His groom had saddled Barbarossa, the great bay Hanoverian who had been a gift from yet another of his innumerable relatives—his cousin Frederick William, the Elector of Brandenburg. The great horse was a deep mahogany bay with a thick, black mane and tail, and four black stockings. The animal stood a full seventeen hands, effectively dwarfing his small master, but William knew that Barbarossa loved him with a passion bordering on the obsessive. The emotion was reciprocated. The stallion stretched down his head, pressing his nose against William's chest.

The prince fished in his pocket and found that Bentinck had not forgotten. A handful of sweetmeats lined the bottom. He fed a piece of the hard candy to Barbarossa, noticing how the stiff whiskers on the horse's muzzle were rimmed with frost. He rubbed the sensitive spot above the horse's right eye and murmured, "I wish you could have stayed safe and warm in your stall, but with luck these fools will become chilled before too long, and you can return to your hay."

Barbarossa blew on his hand, no doubt searching for more candy, but it sounded as if he were answering and reassuring his master that it really didn't matter and that a run across the fallow fields of Holland was just what he wanted. William stepped to the horse's side, rolled his boots above the knee, gathered up the reins, and prepared to mount. Bentinck waved back the groom and, lacing his hands beneath his master's knee, boosted him into the saddle.

Leaning over, William positioned his foot in the stirrup, checked the girth, and drew the double reins through his gauntleted fingers. Barbarossa began to dance with impatience, arching his neck and shaking his head. William allowed him to play with the bit for several minutes, then with a touch of his legs collected him. Johann, the elderly Master of the Hunt, trod in stately dignity to Barbarossa's side and reverently handed up William's Nuremberg wheel-lock rifle.

It was a piece of exquisite workmanship. The long barrel was chased with embossed silver, while the walnut stock had been appliquéd with carved ebony and staghorn panels. William gripped the leather sling and swung the rifle with practiced ease over his shoulder to let it hang comfortably across his back.

One of the junior huntsmen would carry an extra rifle, and stand ready to reload whenever William discharged his weapon. William relaxed back into the saddle. He was ready.

There was a babble of conversation and shouted commands as the gentlemen of William's small court, and his household, mounted. De Coulan required both a mounting block and the aid of a groom to drag himself into the saddle of his placid brown mare. William watched the horse's ears droop disconsolately to either side, and her back sway, as de Coulan landed like an unwieldy sack in the saddle. The prince and Bentinck exchanged grins and winks.

De Coulan clucked to his horse, urging her to William's side. The prince looked inquiringly down at him from beneath the broad brim of his hat.

The Frenchman gestured to someone in the crowd, then asked, "Will you drink the stirrup cup with me?"

It was an effort for William to pull back his lips in even a semblance of a smile. The usual courtly phrases spun like maddened moths through his head, but for the life of him, he could not utter a single one of the platitudes. His fingers tightened on the reins, and Barbarossa danced.

"I don't drink with my enemies, Monsieur de Coulan," William said in a low tone.

A man was wending his way through the crowd bearing two cups on a silver tray. One was of simple silver while the other was of carved rock crystal with a row of garnets set in the base. William's eyes widened at the sight of the cup.

"Yes, *Highness*, I have done you the courtesy of bringing you a princely gift. And I get brag and rudeness in return. You really are a nation of cheesemongers."

"I'll match my manners against those of your kind anytime, *sir!*"

William snatched up the crystal goblet, and suddenly a piercing whinny came floating down the wind. It was a wild, lonely, and challenging sound, carried as if it was on the ragged edges of the coming storm. William jerked about in the saddle just as Barbarossa threw up his head. The goblet spun from the prince's hand, and shattered in a spray of crystal and wine on the cobbles. A spasm of fury twisted de Coulan's face, and he slashed his whip across the servant's face. Blood welled from the wound, and clutching at his bleeding face the man staggered back into the crowd.

William barely noticed, for he was staring in wonder and amazement at the pure white horse who had appeared, as if from the very heart of the snow, and was rearing and plunging in a nearby meadow. Trees marched down either side, creating a cathedrallike effect above the billowing mane of the white horse. A strange, eerie light, like that of a full moon just breaking through the clouds, seemed to curl about the animal's feet, and there was a glint of silver each time the horse pranced and reared. Far and faint came a sound of ringing like ice bells.

Abruptly the creature froze, becoming a milk-white statue posed against a backdrop of naked silver birches. Once more its haunting call rang out, and William was unable to resist the challenge contained in that cry. Never had he seen a more beautiful animal, and he had to possess it. Lifting the reins he drove his heels into Barbarossa's sides. The great bay hunter leapt through the gates.

Baruch Spinoza, taking the long way round so that he could see the hunt depart, stared in amazement after the running bay horse. The white ghost horse had already vanished into the snow. A knot of horsemen, led by van Gent, galloped for the gates, but suddenly the wind tore screaming about the buildings with demonic force. The great double gates were seized in its powerful grip and slammed shut in the faces of the pursuing courtiers. Horses trumpeted in confusion, plunging back onto their hocks. Riders tumbled to the cobbled pavement.

De Coulan, shaking his crop furiously in the air over his head, was cursing and bouncing in the saddle as he stared at the blank barrier of the closed gates. The page Bentinck stood stunned in the center of the milling confusion, staring at a hound creeping from the rest of the pack to lap at the spilled wine. Spinoza also watched, and reflected that among all these maddened humans this simple beast had the proper attitude. But as he watched the animal suddenly began to froth at the mouth. Its eyes rolled back until only the whites remained, and then it fell onto its side. Several severe convulsions shook the brown and white form; then it lay still.

Bentinck's blue eyes widened in terror, and he pressed a hand to his mouth. He ran forward, knelt, and cradled the dead beast in his arms. He opened his mouth to call, but Baruch slipped an arm around him, and gave a hard squeeze.

"Hush!"

"But someone's . . . the prince . . . poison."

"Yes."

Spinoza glanced at de Coulan, who was screaming at Van Gent, who was bellowing back. There were flecks of spittle on the Frenchman's lips, and his face was suffused with an unhealthy purple mottling.

The young page followed Spinoza's gaze, then began to shake. He dropped the dog to the pavement, then gaped as Spinoza tossed his cloak casually over the body and lifted it in his arms.

"Wha . . ."

"Watch and learn, Heer Page."

"But we must tell them, show them the hound."

"And who among them will you trust?" Almost inaudibly, he added, "God forgive me, William, I didn't believe you."

"Beg pardon?"

"I wasn't speaking to you. Be rid of the hound." He thrust the limp bundle into the boy's arms. "Then stand ready to catch your master when he returns. He must be warned."

"And you, what will you do?"

"Consider how best to smuggle him from the city."

"But why should we trust you? You . . . you . . . Jew."

"Possibly because you've no one else."

The page opened and closed his mouth several times, shook his head in confusion, and hurried away. Spinoza walked thoughtfully toward his house, wondering how best to smuggle one small prince from a guarded palace. As a people the Jews had become masters at the art of flight. Spinoza only hoped the art would prove to be a race memory.

Two

I am a wonder: *among flowers*

Barbarossa plunged across the open parkland in pursuit of the white mare. A low hedge separated the palace grounds from the neighboring meadow. William felt the great bay stallion's muscles bunch beneath his knees, and then they were over with scarcely a lengthening of stride. The mare, her silvery tail foaming like a waterfall behind her, continued to draw away. Her speed was incredible, and William, leaning low over Barbarossa's powerful neck and riding high in his stirrups, asked the bay for all he had. The horse responded, surging with his powerful hindquarters, and they went thundering across the frozen grass after their elusive quarry.

The ghost horse's hooves rang like falling icicles as she galloped across the bridge spanning one of the innumerable canals which surrounded The Hague. William felt the stallion struggle for purchase on the slippery snow and wet wood, and he shifted well back in the saddle trying to help Barbarossa keep his footing. A fall now would be disastrous. William's skin seemed to recoil as he contemplated the smash through the railing, the fall to the ice-covered canal, the splintering ice, and the touch of black water. Then they were across, his visions had become mere nightmares, and they were racing east with the moon.

Moon.

It was scarce past noon on a snow-filled day. There could be no moon. William lifted his face from Barbarossa's whipping black mane, and took a cautious peep. It was still there, its radiance riming the horse's ears with silver.

Panic lay like jagged glass in the center of his chest. Desperately William hauled on the reins, but the stallion had gone mad. He fought the pressure of the bit, throwing his head until

18

the prince felt as if his shoulders were being wrenched from
their sockets. Sharp knives seemed to drive into his knees as he
clung grimly to the saddle. His breaths emerged in labored
pants in time to the rocking of the powerful body beneath him.

They were galloping through a fantastic forest. Birches, wil-
lows, oaks grew from tiny sapling to ruinous age as horse and
rider flew past. A vast field of wheat lay rippling before them.
Barbarossa plunged in, the heads of wheat hissing as they
brushed against his sides and knees. Suddenly the grain burst
from the heads with a sound of bells, and became stars.

William and Barbarossa were on a roadway of stars. Comets
rocketed past them, and the sound of their passing was a like a
screaming of tormented strings and flutes. William risked a
glance over his shoulder. His cloak streamed out behind him,
but it seemed to have no end. The dark material faded into a
reddish light that stretched into infinity. He knew he had
screamed, for it formed a raw memory in his throat, but no
sound emerged. He was insignificant to the cosmos.

William became aware of other presences racing with them.
Stars tangled in their manes and tails and lay like crowning
jewels between their liquid eyes. He and Barbarossa were
shadow creatures in a world of light. Cold burned through his
veins. Desperately William tightened his numbed fingers about
the stiff leather of the reins, and bending forward buried his
face in Barbarossa's whipping black mane.

He remembered the touch of his mother's hand on his hair
when as a child he had knelt at bedside, lisping gravely through
the Lord's Prayer.

"Our Father which art in Heaven." Coarse strands of mane
caught on his cracked lips.

Suddenly Barbarossa bucked. It was too much for William's
weakened knees and shaky seat. He parted company with the
saddle, and landed hard on a sandy shore. The boom and hiss of
the breaking and retreating waves was loud in his ringing ears.
With a groan he slid away into a haven of unconsciousness.

He awoke as if from sleep. Before him lay a billowing silver
sea, and out of the phosphorescent spume appeared a woman's
face. William pushed to his knees, but he was shaking so hard
he couldn't gain his feet. Wrapping his arms about his body, he
rocked forward and back in misery and terror.

But terror can only be sustained for so long. Dread still filled him, but there was within him a growing kernel of anger. Lifting his head he faced the woman who now stood before him on the edge of an ageless sea. Seven white mares surrounded her. On her forehead rested a crescent moon, and the circlet was formed by coiling serpents. In her arms she cradled a sheaf of corn. Golden hair billowed like a cloak and fell in waves to the ground.

"Behold, William, I am come. I am present to take pity on thy fortune. Behold, I am present to favor and aid thee." Her voice was deep, carrying the memory of wind in the pines, and the murmur of brooks on a summer evening.

"I accept no power save that of Jesus Christ, my Lord."

"Then you are a fool. Accept reality as you find it, William Henry. Such is the strength of a practical Dutchman."

"Who are you?"

"Many names and diverse forms—Cecropian Minerva, Paphian Venus, Dictynnian Diana, Proserpine, Ceres, Juno, Bellona, Hecate."

William tried to bring her face into focus, but it was difficult to concentrate on her features. They seemed to blend and shift even as he watched. One moment he saw a young girl, fresh and gay as at kermis time, while the next moment his mother's eyes gazed out at him, and behind it all lay a fearsome face, as cold and stern as death. He knew a little of the isolated pagan cults which still dotted the Germanies—there were rumors of men and women who served a white-horned goddess. He shivered, remembering tales of satanic rites, and blood sacrifices.

"This means nothing to me. What is it you wish, if you be real, and not merely the fantasies of a disordered mind."

"That you may see glory, little princeling. And in so doing, serve me as well. Would that suit you?"

"Not if I must sell my soul for earthly reward."

Her voice sharpened. "I have not asked for your soul. It is your blood I require. The promise of your patrimony, the blood of your ancestors which runs into the dim past, and carries the power to serve me."

"And pray what form would this service take?"

Her arm lifted in a sweeping circle. "A great evil is rising in the west. In time it will spread like a choking mist over the face of the earth, and nothingness will replace the life of the world.

The Christian god cannot withstand it. Already they have twisted and altered the rituals of the Christians, turning them to their own purposes. Now they seek to despoil and destroy me, but my roots go deeper, for I am a part of all living things, and the evil ones will find their task much harder. Still, in time they will succeed, and I will fall—last as I was first—and cold, sucking death will envelop the cosmos. Men are being used to open the gateway to this evil, and men must be used to close it. You alone of all your blood are open to my power. You must stop the evil, drive it back, and forever bar the doorway into this dimension."

"Madam, I am a cautious Dutchman. If I am to risk life and sanity and soul, what, pray, is in this for me?"

"Service to a goddess," came the dry reply.

"Then I must decline. I serve only my God and my people."

"You are a stubborn and difficult little man. I offer to you what I have offered to few mortals."

"I think, Lady, that you need me more than I need you."

Thunder growled from sky and earth, and William felt his belly turn to water. You're a prince, and a Stuart and a Dutchman, he reminded himself. *And a fool*, added a small voice. *This is a* deity!

"If you do not act the world dies, and *you* with it. Surely survival is worth a little effort? Unless you are so eager to retire to that dismal heaven of your Christian god?"

"An excellent point. But, Lady, I cannot help you. I am a captive prince without armies or power. And I know nothing of magic. I am only a man."

"Under my tutelage you will surpass mortal limitations. You will gather to yourself talismans which will help you to focus these newly awakened powers and use them in my service. Companions will be provided to you, and one of my own will come to train and guide you. Do not fail me, young William. I have risked much interfering so directly in your plane and bringing you here. Henceforth only my servants will guide and aid you. I shall not come again . . . again . . . again . . . again. . . ."

The words echoed in the recesses of his mind as sleep took him.

His toes, nose, and fingers were burning. *Damn Hans for putting so much wood on the fire*. William became aware of the irritating scratch of sand down his breeches and filling his shirt. The waves pounded on the nearby shore, sea birds screamed overhead, and the smell of seaweed was strong in his nostrils.

For a long time the prince sat supporting his aching head in his hands. *No wonder they call her the Night Mare*, he thought bitterly as he reviewed his situation. The sun was sinking in the west, fog was rolling in off the ocean, he was miles from The Hague, and riding boots were not made for walking.

With a sigh he settled his sword more comfortably on his hip, reslung his rifle, and slogged off, his heavy riding boots sinking into the deep sand between the grass. Then from over a dune he heard an inquiring whinny.

Pulling off a gauntlet, he thrust two fingers into his mouth and gave a shrill whistle. Barbarossa came plunging over the dune flinging sand from his hooves, mouth still working vigorously as he chewed a mouthful of grass past the encumbering bit.

William whooped with joy and relief, and ran to meet the horse. Pressing his forehead against Barbarossa's glossy neck, he straightened the long black mane.

"Oh fellow, my dear old fellow. I feared you lost or stolen while I was away in that other world. Thank God you are here."

He pulled a few loose twigs from the bay's mane and tail, tightened the girth, and, gathering up his reins, swung into the saddle.

"Shall we go home, old fellow, and see if any of our old comrades are living still? I would like to believe that I am a man touched by destiny, but. . . ."

Now that he was back in the gray dreary winter of the world, he had begun to doubt that the events of the past hours had ever taken place. Conflicting emotions warred within him. On the one hand he wanted to believe, desperately needed to think that he had been chosen for this high and noble purpose, and that his years of helplessness and uncertainty were about to end. On the other side stood the warm and comforting familiarity of his life—The Hague, the lovely old house at Leyden where he had passed so many happy summers, days spent in hunting or in study, and nights in pleasant companionship with his pages— could he trade all that to face foes of such power and evil that even deities quailed?

Deities.
What ever would God think of his disloyalty?

The canal lapping at the foot of The Hague shone like a black mirror as William rode across the bridge and toward the welcoming lights of the palace. Cold hours spent on the road had done little to resolve his confusion. *A great evil is rising in the west*. But who? And where? And why? He tried to recall his occult lore. That the Order of the Garter was in truth a witches' coven. *Merry Charles as a focus for world-devouring evil?* Absurd.

Well, then why not Louis XIV? There had been whispered rumors which had persisted for fifty years that Richelieu had been a black sorcerer, and that his mantle of evil had passed to Mazarin, current advisor to the young French king.

Someone out of the French court was trying to kill him . . . but did that necessarily make his enemy a demon?

So maybe it had been a mere dream, or a passing fit of madness. William rubbed hard at his burning eyes and growled in vexation. Was crazy really preferable to the revelation of an occult world?

Hysteria greeted his return. Grooms led Barbarossa, head hanging with exhaustion, to his stall. Van Gent fairly danced about William, demanding and scolding.

But the prince's eyes were fixed on the tall stooping figure waiting in the doorway. "Enough," he ordered curtly.

Thrusting his rifle into his governor's hands he trod up the stairs to greet his guardian the Raadspensionary of the United Provinces, Johan De Witt. The older man's dark, piercing eyes were leveled on him, and William forced himself to keep his chin up and his gaze equally as level as his guardian's.

"You have behaved in a most irresponsible manner, William Henry. You have thrown this household into disorder, and sent good men on long cold and fruitless rides searching for you. It was not well done of you to cause such worry to your guardians."

"Sir, I beg pardon for any alarm which may have been caused by my precipitous departure, but in truth I was carried for miles by my mount. I lost control of him."

De Witt's brows twitched together. William's skill in the saddle was well-known, and the older man never doubted for a moment that the lad was lying to him.

William continued, "That is not a lie, sir, and further, I must take offense at the tone you have seen fit to adopt toward me. I am neither child nor imbecile. In three days I turn eighteen and come of age."

De Witt indicated the door, and William preceded him into the hall. "Not so, William Henry. In this matter we have adopted Roman law, and you will not reach your majority until your twenty-fifth birthday."

"If you think I'm to be kept in leading strings—" William folded his lips, cutting off the hot words. He resumed in a more moderate tone. "It would be unfortunate if this matter had to come before the courts for settlement. In this case, *I* contend, Heer de Witt, that the English law applies, and that at eighteen a prince is deemed fit to rule."

The lines to either side of the Raadspensionary's mouth deepened. "You are not a hereditary prince, sir. And the Stadholderate has been placed forever beyond your grasp."

"That remains to be seen, and so long as I hold Orange I am indeed a hereditary prince." His voice had gone shrill, and William cursed himself for sounding like a sulky child.

"Go to bed, William, you are tired and overwrought."

The prince gaped after that tall, lanky form retreating quickly down the narrow passageway, and with an inarticulate sound William shot through the door to his chambers and slammed it hard behind him.

Bentinck tackled him with a cry of joy, and William went tottering across the room under the assault.

"God's teeth, we had feared you killed," cried Hans with a catch in his voice.

"'Struth! Are you trying to kill me?" gasped William, wrenching free from Bentinck's choking hold. "I had a ride in the cold. I won't break—"

William pulled up short, startled to find Spinoza curled in an armchair by the fire, his pipe forming wreaths of smoke about his dark head.

"What are you doing here?" asked William, shooting his jaw forward belligerently. "If you think to continue Heer de Witt's lecture you've got another—"

"Hush. Tell him, Hans."

"Oh, my dearest prince, they seek to kill you!" burst out the page, who fell once more on William.

"What?"

"Poison, Highness—I'm afraid it's true," said Spinoza.

Then, in an impassioned, rambling discourse, Bentinck poured out the tale of the poisoned cup and the dog. Spinoza's hand was a welcome support beneath William's arm as the philosopher eased him down on the bed.

"Mull him some wine and bring food," the older man ordered Bentinck. "He's fagged nigh unto death."

"Nay, I'm better now. A momentary faintness."

"We have important matters to discuss, Highness, but first allow me to make apology. Forgive me for disbelieving you. There are parties who seek your death. We must now find a way to thwart them."

Bentinck craned around from the fire where he was thrusting a hot poker into a mug of wine. "He must flee! He must leave at once!"

Spinoza made a rude noise. "Your passion and loyalty do you credit, Hans, but they do little to convince me that you also possess a brain. He is a prince. He cannot ride pell-mell from the palace and into the night. First, they will be keeping watch, so we must deceive them. And second, His Highness must have a destination. A sanctuary."

The shock which seemed to have frozen his brain and sapped his will relaxed its hold, and William said slowly. "I could tell them I'm going to Breda to visit my grandmother, then make my way to the coast and seek refuge with my Uncle Charles."

A funny, twisted smile touched Spinoza's lips. "If you are bound for the sea why not travel by a route which will do you the most good."

"I beg your pardon?"

"You'll soon be eighteen, Highness."

"Yes. So?"

"You will be an adult, so why not assume those rights by beginning with your hereditary titles."

"Zeeland," breathed William with dawning wonder.

"Good, I haven't trained a lackwit. This will kill a number of birds with a single stone. It takes you out of The Hague, and it establishes that you are a man grown. It would be ridiculous for the First Noble of Zeeland to have guardians in Holland. Thus you are free of Johan de Witt, and, most important, it puts you on the coast."

"They'll never allow him to go," objected Bentinck.

"But His Highness is correct. They *will* allow him to visit the Princess Dowager Amelia."

William rose, crossed to the desk, and pulled a sheet of paper to him. "I will tell her what we are planning and instruct her to have her yacht waiting to carry me to Zeeland."

"And from thence to England," said the page.

"Hans, you must carry this letter. I dare trust no other."

The young man dropped to one knee and pressed a kiss onto the prince's hand. "I will serve you 'til death and beyond! I swear this on my mother's life."

William laid a hand on the curly head bent before him. "Make no rash vows. It is possible such passionate words will be remembered, and acted upon."

With a clatter of heels Bentinck was gone. Spinoza stroked his chin and contemplated his student. "You are strange this night, young William. What meant you by that?" He jerked his head toward the door.

"I . . . I have seen things . . . this day."

Spinoza caught the prince as he pitched forward in a dead faint. The older man's arms tightened about the slender form, and he murmured a prayer to the God in which he did not totally believe.

"Protect him, Father, and keep him safe. Make an effort to prove to me your presence."

"A duel."

"Indeed?"

"'Tis sad. Such a pretty gentleman."

The gossip went skittering and tittering around the corners of the overheated rooms at the Count of Bergenhof's monthly gaming salon in his Copenhagon townhouse, and Lord Haakon Sverhardt Lindel, a grin curving his lips, tried to eavesdrop on the whispers. Dropping his gaze to his cards he listened to dice clattering noisily onto inlaid tables. The sound was as dry and heartless as bones rattling in stone crypts, and Haakon with a sudden spurt of graveyard humor thought it was like to be *his* bones rattling mournfully in the grave, and far too soon.

"I'd thought Magnus past that." A sudden lull in the conversation carried the man's voice clearly through the room. "He hasn't killed a man in two years."

"What's the fight over?" asked someone else.

"Does Magnus need a reason to quarrel?"

"True, but 'tis said that the ward is at the *heart* of the matter." There was a titter.

Einer Rynning gave a grunt of disgust, his plump face folding in on itself like a colicky baby about to cry.

"To think you are fool enough to fight over an overhot little bitch with the roundest heels in Copenhagen," he said to Haakon. "By gad, it's a joke that Magnus fights to defend her honor."

Haakon shrugged. "I had the pleasure, now the piper must be paid." He grinned, his teeth very white against his dark tan. "Besides, I like to fight."

"You don't fight Tyge Magnus, you *die* when you face him."

"Don't underestimate my skills."

"This has nothing to do with skill, and a great deal to do with being a blackguard," Einer burst out. "Magnus keeps servants ready to hand, to shoot or stab any man who seems like to prevail over the duke."

Haakon threw down his cards with a laugh, and many eyes were drawn by the merry sound. "Then I'll cheat too, but I'll by God not run."

"You *are* a Norse barbarian, just as Tyge said."

"Took you this long to notice? My father fought dragons with the Black Captain during the religious wars. I'm not afraid of a strutting fool, no matter how blue his blood or dishonorable his intent."

"You'll die, and it's such a waste," grumbled Einer, studying the handsome face across from him: deep blue eyes so intense against dark skin, heavy gold curls falling to broad powerful shoulders, that jutting blade of a nose.

Haakon reached out with one large hand and stroked the other man's round cheek. "You'll find another, prettier, and more amenable lad to enjoy. One who may actually be willing to share your bed. And speaking of, I must to bed."

"You shouldn't have come at all on the eve of a duel."

"Nag, nag, nag. God's blood, you're like a fishmonger—or worse, a wife. No need for you to come," added Haakon as Einer rose.

"The thought of your death has quite spoiled my appetite for play or supper. I may as well go home."

They collected their wraps from the footman in the lower hall. Then, cloaked, hatted, and their hands tucked firmly into heavy fur muffs, the two men stepped out into the dark, snow-packed street. The wind, racing between the buildings, struck them like a great fist, and Einer staggered back a few steps under the onslaught. Haakon merely planted his feet and threw back his head, reveling in the icy attack, daring the wind to move him. They paused at the intersection of three crooked streets.

"Well, then, this is farewell. I'll not see you again in this life."

"We'll both no doubt meet again in Hell," came Haakon's unruffled reply.

Einer gripped him urgently by the forearms. "Go home, Haakon. Flee this fight."

"No. There's nothing at home but a small estate, and five older brothers and six sisters to be provided for, and my mother praying for an end to suffering, and an old grandmother ruling like the beldam she is, and seeing to it we *all* suffer. Thank you, I'd rather fight Tyge."

Einer flung up his hands. Haakon laughed, embraced him, and strode away through the deserted streets toward his mean rented lodgings. He fondled the hilt of his rapier as he walked, keeping a close and hopeful eye out for footpads.

The wind increased in fury. It had become a blizzard, and with a curse Haakon wiped snow from his eyes. A figure loomed out of the darkness. The Norwegian leaped back, rapier hissing from its scabbard, and dropped into a defensive *en garde*. There came a low and decidedly feminine laugh, and from out of the heart of a cyclone of blowing snow stepped a woman.

She was everyman's dream of youth and beauty. Her black hair seemed tipped with a crown of ice crystals, and her skin glowed white and pure above the laced bodice of her gown. Her dress was made of shades of blue and silver, and it was caught up to display her shapely ankles. The cold seemed to disconcert her not at all. In fact, she had the look of a girl gone a-Maying. Her cheeks were touched with rose, and her lips were as red as fresh rowanberries.

That she was a whore there could be no doubt. As Haakon gaped at her, she planted her hands on her hips and thrust her pelvis forward in a quick and suggestive movement.

"Put up that sword, young man, and draw another." Her voice was low and throaty like her laugh, and Haakon shivered.

"What the hell are you?"

"Cold. Warm me. My room is nearby."

He debated . . . reminded himself of the duel . . . shrugged and grinned and held out his hand.

Her room lay at the back and on the third floor of a row of rickety wooden buildings whose upper stories overhung the street. Haakon's nostrils pinched fastidiously at the smells emanating from the lower floors, but the smell of rancid grease and human sweat and excrement vanished beneath the fresh odor of new-cut pine as she pushed open the door to her quarters. His eyes widened in surprise at the bower which met his gaze.

Pine boughs lay on the dingy gray floor and were twined about the posts of the sagging bed. Flowers—tulips, hyacinths, and lilies, arranged in white porcelain pots—nodded and swayed from the blast of wind which swirled through the door.

Haakon knew on some deep and intuitive level that he was in the presence of magic, but the thought gave him no fear. His people were among the last to take to the Christian god, and he himself had no interest in gods of any form. He eyed the world with a cynical and humorous rationality which offended his more temperamental and intuitive grandmother. The fact that he seemed to have stepped out of the known world held only a curious interest to him. Of far greater import were the white globes of the whore's breasts straining at her loosely laced bodice. The woman led him to the bed and began opening his breeches.

"Forgive me, this may be an inopportune moment, but I doubt we'll find a better one. If I poke it in am I like to have it bit off?"

She reached up and patted him on the cheek. "No, sweet one."

"Bewitched then."

"No, bewitching you would take more effort and energy than I am willing to expend."

"Fine."

"So incurious?"

"My grandmother says I have a head like a block," he said with a touch of pride as he kicked off his high-tongued shoes. "Griffins could dance beneath my window and I would notice naught."

"No, you would complain only of the noise." She had his cock in her hand now, and he sucked in a quick breath.

"I have need of a man who neither walks with nor fears the unseen worlds."

"To do what?"

"Later," she whispered.

Much later he woke with a snort, and pulled his arm across his sleep-dulled eyes. His body felt heavy and languid with the aftermath of love. Beyond the small leaded-glass window he could see the new moon sinking rapidly in the west. The storm was past. A star seemed to be trembling on the low horn of the moon. Haakon sensed someone watching him in the darkness, and he glanced to his left.

The woman was leaning against the headboard, her knees drawn up to her chest, and her long black hair tumbling over her shoulders and breasts. The sight of those luminous white globes revived his passion, and he reached for her.

"No." Her hand caught his and held it in the air between them. "Now is the time for talk."

"Not for long I hope." He leered.

"And then it shall be time for you to go." His brows snapped together in a frown. "What do you want, Haakon Lindel?" the woman asked.

"What? Now? Well, right now I bloody well want—"

"For your life, not your cock."

"Passion, wealth, romance, adventure, and to die in bed at eighty . . . killed by a jealous husband."

"I can give you the first four."

"How?"

"There is a young man. He will be fleeing danger, and riding into danger. I wish you to find him, and help him."

"That only describes half of Europe. I'll be eighty by the time I find him."

She gripped his chin, her nails digging into the skin. "Do you think I arrange things so badly? You will find him, and you will recognize him because *I* say you will."

"What's so important about this young man?"

"He is the hope of the world."

"Right. Well, that's it." He swung out of the bed, fished his purse from his breeches, and tossed it to her. She caught it easily while it was still in the air, then threw it back—and Haakon staggered under the weight. Suspicious, he opened it, and goggled down at the gold glinting there.

"I'm supposed to pay *you.*" He forced himself to speak lightly, mockingly.

"Will you serve me for money, Haakon Lindel?"

"Naturally."

"Later you will serve me for love."

"Whatever you say. You're paying for my agreement."

She rose, her naked body a figure of ivory and alabaster in the moonlight. "And now you must go. The night is waning." She stretched out her hands toward the window, and it seemed that stars danced on her fingertips like diamonds. "You will prevail in your duel this day. That far I can see. From thence you must trust to your destiny."

He tucked in the knee-length tails of his shirt. "Of course I'm going to prevail. I'm going to blow the brains out of his servants before they can blow out mine."

Her laugh was like bells. "So practical. You will serve my prince well."

"Thank God this wandering young fool is a prince. I should get something out of this."

Three

I am a breaker: *threatening doom*

Father Armand du Lac, tossing on his hard pallet, moaned and plucked restlessly at his scratchy blanket. He was in that distressing state partway between sleep and waking, and he felt as if ants were crawling beneath his skin. Through the muffling stone walls of the Abbey de la Tour Courbette he heard the chanting of monks, but the sound (which he usually found so soothing) brought him no comfort. In fact, the deep male voices sounded ominous as they echoed through the icy halls. The sound seemed a dark, forbidding chant, summoning ancient evils and leaving men writhing in horror at their approach.

He knew he was on the verge of another of *those* dreams, and he fought the onslaught of sound and sight the way a drowning man fights the water seeking to choke him. It had been the dreams that had brought him to this bleak and isolated abbey on the windswept plains of Normandy. His bishop in Paris had found du Lac a disruptive element. One preferred to have one's saints safely dead, not disturbing the peace of a major cathedral with visions. A bishop must be politician as well as shepherd, and to have one of his priests ranting about the evil in the palace . . . well, clearly du Lac was seeing signs sent by Satan, not by God. He ordered the young priest into retreat to seek answers, and preferably an end to these disturbing visions. If he failed there always remained the Inquisition as a final inducement.

The sound of the chanting faded and Armand spiraled into the heart of his nightmare. *A vast empty plain. Scattered across the sand massive standing stones; some upright, some lying haphazardly in the wind-rippled sand. A deep groaning rising from the earth beneath his feet. The gray, flat sky overhead.*

Suddenly the very air writhed and shivered, and creatures appeared. A harsh red light illuminated them as they came creeping and crawling across the sands. A high-pitched wailing stabbed Armand's ears. One of the stones burst apart in a violent explosion. Splinters of rock lacerated his face. He felt blood flowing down his forehead and into his eyes. Through the film of gore he saw in the heart of the riven rock the handsome, arrogant face of the king—Le Roi Soleil. The creatures seized the stones, and built a great gateway. Through that leaning portal Armand saw the fertile plains of the Île-de-France. Louis stepped through the gate, and his minions melted into a flowing miasma of gray death. And followed him through.

Armand staggered after them, his feet kicking up clouds of ash—all that remained of sweet grass and rich grain. A numbing cold crept into heaven, and the stars themselves were extinguished. After a time there was nothing. And the priest, the final spark of life and awareness in a lifeless universe, screamed out his fear and loss and loneliness.

Du Lac started up on his hard pallet, reaching desperately to steady himself. The touch of cool stone beneath his fingers reassured him. He was in the abbey, he still lived, and the slow, choking destruction he had witnessed in his dream had not yet come to pass.

He pulled his knees up to his chest, and huddled deeper into his thin blanket. It was inadequate protection against the freezing cold which seemed to be exhaled by the stone walls, and which laid a rime of ice about the window of his cell. The abbey was silent. The monks had finished Compline, and had returned to their cells to seize what sleep they could before Lauds.

Rising, Armand pulled on his soutane and a pair of high fleece-lined boots, picked up his rosary, and slipped silently through the deserted corridors of the abbey. Outside the wind howled like a maddened animal, shaking even the thick walls of the ancient building.

In the chapel, the crimson vigil lamp was burning, and votive candles threw their flickering light across the front pews. The pews huddled like hunched beasts in the darkness, and the stained glass windows were merely gray holes, sightless eyes in blind walls. A sudden gust of wind sent snow rattling against the lancet windows. Du Lac froze, and held his breath as he cowered behind one of the supporting pillars that marched the length of the chapel. He sensed other presences in the darkness with him, and they were not benign.

He scuttled quickly across the flagstone floor until he reached the transept, and hurried down the western arm. At the far end was a small altar at the top of three marble steps. In a niche above stood a delicate fifteenth-century statue of the Virgin. Her white marble face seemed young and very vulnerable, and its pale beauty was heightened by the rich blue of the carved robe which fell about her. The tendrils of hair which escaped from beneath her veil were painted pale gold, and the candles flickering at her feet made her appear to be floating in a golden sea.

Armand knelt slowly and reverently at the base of the altar and, stretching his arms to either side, prayed for guidance. He had always felt a great affinity for the gentle mother, the slender young virgin who had carried the Son of God beneath her bosom, and he felt now that she would not fail him. His prayers increased in intensity, and he began to feel that exaltation which often lifted him when he was at his devotions. The painful pressure of the cold marble beneath his knees faded. The shadowed room began to spin about him, and he pitched forward on his face before the altar.

A brilliant light filled the miniature chapel, and his Lady stepped down from her narrow niche and laid a gentle hand upon his hair. He pushed himself to his knees and stared reverently up at her as she smiled down on him. Like a young girl she seemed, and there was the radiance of a full moon emanating from her garments and milk-white skin.

"There is a rider from the sea who will combat the evil which you have witnessed. Seek him out. Give him your strength and the power which burns within you, and guide him on his way. Go quickly now, and carry my blessing with you."

"But, Lady," he cried aloud, and his voice shook from the trembling of his body. "How shall I know him?"

"By the power which is within you. It will call to him, and he to you."

His Lady was receding from him, floating away on a golden light back into her niche where she would once more become only cold stone. He cried out in his distress and reached up for her. There was a crescendo of what seemed like music, but it matched no instrument he had ever heard, and then she was gone. The light vanished as abruptly as a candle being blown. out, and he fainted.

"Father du Lac, Father du Lac! Wake up! What nonsense is this?" The harsh voice of Abbé le Blanc cut through his pleasant dreaming. In the background Armand could hear the murmurings of many people, and lantern light forced its way past his eyelids. Slowly he opened his eyes, and he gazed wildly about.

"Ah, my Lady, my Lady!" He clutched at le Blanc's hand. "Did you see her?"

"See what? I see nothing. I was awakened by a cry from the chapel, and when I come I find you unconscious on the steps, and murmuring nonsense about the evil in Paris, and the one who shall rise to combat it. You have been sent here to clear your mind of such fantasies, Father, not to augment them."

"But it is true, the Blessed Virgin herself appeared to me. My visions are true! Evil surrounds the King!"

Le Blanc's face closed down, his eyes becoming narrow slits through which Armand could see only the gleam of his black eyes. The Abbé whirled and pointed at two of the larger, burlier monks.

"Take Father du Lac to his cell, and see that he stays there." He laid a large iron key in the palm of the larger of the two brown-frocked monks. "I must send to Paris for instructions."

Armand gaped up at le Blanc as he was pulled roughly to his feet by his two holy jailers. He struggled futilely in the grip of his keepers. It was a useless attempt, for he was a small, plump man whose strength was not great.

"Abbé! Mon père! You must not do this!" he shouted back over his shoulder as he was dragged down the aisle. "Something dreadful is about to happen. We must try to prevent it! If the Church retreats in the face of evil, who then shall the people look to for guidance?"

He wailed out the final words, trying to reach le Blanc's heart and convince him before his words were cut off by the stone walls. It was no use. Le Blanc stood like a black statue before the Virgin's altar and gazed impassively after him. The look was all the more frightening and horrifying because of its lack of expression.

Armand's captors dragged him through the halls of the abbey, then flung him into his cell. The door fell shut with a bang, and he heard the key grate in the lock. Wrapping his arms about his body Armand huddled against the wall beneath the window. The wall seemed to be exhaling cold, dank air into the center of his back, and for the first time Armand began to fear that imprisonment would not be the worst he would suffer. Death loomed like a living possibility in the center of the dark cell.

His thoughts fluttered like frightened birds, and he seemed incapable of movement. Despair took him. *But his Lady had told him that this young savior needed his help.* He raised his head. *She had also told him to go and go quickly.* He pushed to his feet, using the wall for support. There could be no further delay.

He stood on tiptoes, and peered out the narrow, high-set window. On this side of the abbey the ground dropped abruptly away toward the orchards, so it would be a rather long fall. He placed his back to the wall and gazed about the tiny stone room. His eye fell upon the blanket. It had done him little good during the bitter nights, but it would serve him now. He gathered his cloak from a peg on the wall and threw it about his shoulders. Next he dragged the small stand, which held his missal and the few toilet items he was allowed, beneath the window.

Wrapping the blanket about his hand he broke out the thin glass window pane, then held his breath, praying that no one had heard. The abbey remained silent. He climbed onto the wooden stand and peered nervously down.

It seemed a very long drop in the darkness. Also, the window was very narrow. There was not as much of him as there had been, though—three weeks of cold, prayer, and privation at the abbey had pared away some of his flesh. Still, it would be a tight fit. Gritting his teeth, he placed his hands on the rough stone sill and boosted himself up onto the ledge. There were a few heart-stopping moments while he tried to shift around on his narrow perch.

He swung his legs through the narrow opening. The rough stone scraped at his hips and ribs, and then his shoulders stuck tight. His legs were swinging free over the hard stony ground while his shoulders were wedged painfully into the window. He gave a hard kick with his legs, and twisted violently in the window. It hurt—horribly—but it worked. His shoulders slipped free, and he tumbled to the ground. Rising, he rubbed at his bruised rump, then went trotting down the slope of the garden, heading for the orchard. The trees, even though winter bare, would give him some cover and allow him to reach the road before his escape was discovered. Then, north and east to the sea, and only his priest's black and his cross to protect him from evil. It would be enough.

The streets of Middelburg were nearly impassable, and roofs, windows, and even trees and the masts of ships in the harbor were black with spectators. When William appeared at the windows of his apartment in the ancient Gothic abbey a great roar shook the crowd. A salvo boomed out, fired by the militia. William, now installed as the First Noble of Zeeland, bowed. Spinoza, slumped in an armchair, called out:

"A little less dignity, there, Your Highness. A little less dignity. A prince needs the love as well as the loyalty of his subjects."

Blushing slightly, the young man pulled off his hat and waved it over his head. Another great shout arose. From beneath the balcony a pretty peasant girl, her skirt hiked high on either side, flung up a bouquet of holly and mistletoe. William caught it, kissed it, and threw it back.

"*Love*, not *lust*," the tutor grumped.

"What's wrong with you, old bear?" asked Hans Bentinck, offering a cup of wine.

"I'm too old for this. Plots and alarms. I'm a lazy old Jew—" William turned from the window. "And my dearest friend."

Spinoza hurrumphed, and took a long swallow of wine. "Enough of that. Greet your subjects, Highness."

Two hours later the fireworks display began, and William retreated from the window. William frowned when he saw the hot meal laid out on the table.

"I've eaten enough at that banquet to founder a dray horse."

Spinoza jerked his head toward the window, where the rockets were exploding like colorful stars and reflecting their fire in the black waters of the harbor.

"It's cold out there, and you'll feel the cold less with some ballast in your belly."

Grumbling, the prince seated himself and nibbled at a chicken wing as he completed a letter.

"You're still determined to go alone?" asked the tutor.

"Yes. My Hans would ride into Hell for me, but with luck that won't be necessary on this leg of the journey."

Sand pattered on the paper, and, tipping the candle, William sealed the missive and imprinted the wax with his ring.

"Have you everything you need, child? Money? Warm clothes? Weapons?"

"My Hans has seen to everything. I also have this." William reached inside his waistcoat and pulled out a miniature of Mary Henrietta, Princess of Orange, enameled on the back with a spray of violets and the motto *J'aime un seul.* "She will keep me from harm."

Spinoza gazed down at the chestnut head bent tenderly over the portrait, and felt a surge of pity for the boy. The Princess of Orange had been dead these eight years, and she had died in England, cavorting at the court of her brother, Charles II of England. Had she even spared a thought for the lonely little boy waiting for her back in Holland? Probably not. From everything Spinoza knew of the prince's mother it was likely that she had gone to her grave still loving her brother more than her son.

A clock chimed the quarter hour, and William pushed back from the table. "It is time." He gripped his tutor's hand. "Go with God, Heer Spinoza."

"And you, young William, though I think you would do just as well to trust to your own power. What is it? What have I said to make you jump so?"

"I had forgot . . . begun to believe it was only a dream. God grant it may be so."

A cluster burst overhead, showering sparks across the face of the ancient abbey. The explosion threw William's thin face into sharp relief, and what Spinoza saw reflected there sent a shiver down his back.

"All ready," sang out Bentinck as he came stumping through the door. He had two packs slung over his shoulder, a pair of rifles, and a brace of wheel-lock pistols. William laughed.

"You look like a cherubic mercenary. The *enfant terrible* of the Black Company."

"Sir!"

"I'm glad to see you are packed. I have this letter which must reach Amelia—"

"No, sir! Begging your pardon, sir, but no. I'm coming with you."

"No, Hans, it is more important that you reach my grandmother, and that she bring my minority to an end. If this is not done, de Witt might have me dragged home like an errant schoolboy."

"But you will have no one to guard you! To care for you!"

"I'm not glass. I can manage to dress myself for the few days it will take for me to reach London. And what's the worse that can happen? Seasickness?"

The page's lower lip was trembling, and his blue eyes swam with tears. "Please, sir, don't send me from your side."

William drew his hand down Bentinck's cheek, felt the rasp of stubble, and the moisture of his tears. "Hans, I must. For your own protection, and for mine."

"But, sir."

"Hans! Do not argue with me. You're sworn to serve me, now do so!" William folded his arms and presented his shoulder to the miserable Bentinck.

The page fell to one knee, tugged William's hand free, and pressed a frenzied kiss onto the back. "I will obey. Farewell!"

Seizing the letter he fled from the room. Spinoza and William listened to his retreating footfalls as he ran down the stairs.

"Such heat. Ah, you young people . . ."

"Do not mock his pain!"

Baruch laid a hand on his student's heaving shoulder. "I do not mock. I envy. Come, it is time. You must away while those drunken fools at the gate are gaping skyward."

"No need for you to accompany me. Then you can truthfully say you did not see me leave."

"Humor me."

They slipped down the back stairs. William was soberly dressed in gray and crimson. Spinoza carried the prince's pistols cradled awkwardly in his arms. The butt of the rifle clinked against the wall, and William stifled a curse.

"I didn't know you knew words like that, Highness," teased Spinoza.

And the older man reflected that in truth no monk had lived more cloistered than this boy walking at his side. William had been raised in a predominately male household. His tutors had for the most part been Calvinist ministers such as Trigland. The standing rules of the household had been that no immoderate language was to be uttered in the prince's hearing. There had been some disapproval that he had been taught to dance, and that he had musicians for his personal pleasure. A new thought intruded, and Spinoza shot William a sharp glance.

"Lad, have you ever. . ."

"Yes?"

"Well . . . have you lain with a woman yet?" The sudden wash of blood into those pale cheeks gave Spinoza all the answer he needed. He sighed, laid a hand on the boy's shoulder. "You are going into the world. For at least a few days you will be alone, and the heady delight of such freedom might tempt you—"

"I hope my faith in God will defend me from such lapses," came the stiff reply.

"Yes, well, God is a good thing, but less immediate than a plump armful nestled against your chest in some cozy inn. Only be aware that you have such drives, and the fact that you possess them is not a sin. You are, after all, only a man."

They pushed open the outer door and crossed the cobbled yard to the stable. As hoped, the grooms were all out rollicking in the street and viewing the fireworks. While William saddled Barbarossa his tutor gave him a final lecture on choosing whores, getting value for his money, avoiding the pox, and guarding against footpads.

"I know this seems far removed from our usual topics, but I would send you forth prepared."

William led out the big charger, and, with a flash of that rare and bubbling wit which he usually kept so carefully confined, he said, "On the contrary, my dear teacher, I think it has a great deal to do with the natural sciences."

Spinoza cuffed the prince lightly, then laced his hands beneath William's knee and boosted him into the saddle. "With that saucy tongue you should do well enough. Go with God, and write me when you reach London."

The prince's gloved hand closed about the Jew's. "Thank you. I owe you my life."

The sudden prick of tears at his eyelids embarrassed Spinoza. Gruffly, he said, "Begone, begone with you. Long farewells are as irritating as overlong sermons. Go."

William clapped heels to the horse's sides, and galloped for the gate. The steel shoes struck sparks from the cobbles, and overhead a great rocket exploded in a white glare. For an instant horse and rider seemed suspended against a net of stars.

There was something eerie about the moment, as if the unseen were pressing close to the seen, and Spinoza breathed a quick prayer. It did no harm to observe the rituals. Especially in the face of uncanny happenings.

The creature had been beyond the mirror. Fire, running like lightning from cloud to cloud, played and flickered through the mist form. Eyes like holes in eternity stared sadly back at the turgidly swirling nothingness that lay on the other side of the glass. The creature extruded a piece of itself and drew an intricate pattern across the mirror. The vision faded, to be replaced by the ordinary silver sheen of glass. Of the creature, there was no trace. Slowly it turned and regarded the discarded human husk that sprawled across the elaborate desk.

Mazarin lay with his right cheek pillowed on a stack of papers, and his expression was gentle, comtemplative. That changed once the creature had again taken up residence. Rising quickly, the cardinal crossed to the mirror and studied his image. He rubbed thoughtfully at his belly, then coughed twice —hard, wracking spasms that shook the slim frame—and forced from his throat and lips a knot of maggots.

Grinning, he plucked them from the floor and dropped them one by one into a candle flame. There was a sharp rap on the door, and Mazarin froze, the final maggot undulating between his fingers.

"A moment." Swiftly he swept up the charred remains, and along with the one living maggot, flung the entire mess into the fireplace. "Enter."

The messenger knelt briefly with his hand on the hilt of his sword. "Your Eminence, I regret to inform you that de Coulan has failed. His letter was garbled and I destroyed it after reading it, as you instructed, but it ran thus—the prince was on the verge of drinking the wine when suddenly a white horse appeared and lured him away. When van Gent and others attempted to follow, the gates were mysteriously shut in their faces, allowing the prince to escape."

"You distress me." The cardinal stroked thoughtfully at his beard. His expression betrayed neither pleasure nor displeasure at the tidings he had just received. It was a death mask riding on a living man. "And a white horse, you say?"

"Yes, Eminence."

Mazarin turned and took a few steps toward the mirror. "Damn the slut."

"Pardon, Eminence?"

He turned back and stared at the still kneeling messenger.

"I trust that de Coulan and van Gent are seeking a way to rectify this oversight?"

"Alas, my lord, the Prince of Orange has vanished from Middelburg, and has not been seen for two days."

"Middelburg?"

"He tricked his guardians. He was supposed to join his governor at Breda to go hunting. There de Coulan would have tried again. But instead of joining them at the lodge he fled on his grandmother's yacht to Zeeland, where he was installed as the First Noble."

There was a flash of red deep within the cardinal's dark eyes, but it was quickly dampened. "Indeed?"

"Yes, Your Eminence."

"I think that de Coulan has failed us for the last time. See that he is suitably rewarded for this latest failure."

The messenger smiled, a thin, predatory expression. "Yes, my lord. Shall I instruct him to return to Paris?"

"Yes, it will be my pleasure to personally deliver the punishment." The messenger's tongue flicked out, pale and wet, to moisten his thin lips. "Spread the word that the Prince of Orange is to be found and killed. Give warrants and money to any willing to undertake the hunt. We will worry no more with subtlety. If he's abroad on the roads he will merely be one more vagabond soldier of fortune who died in a tavern brawl. No need to make it appear a sudden illness to appease that nation of cheesemongers."

"Yes, my lord. Will you tell the King, my lord?"

"His Highness has planned a masque for this evening. I would not wish to spoil his pleasure in the event. Tomorrow will be soon enough, and I trust I will soon be able to report our success?" He looked significantly at the kneeling courtier. The man blanched under the inhuman threat that lurked behind those eyes.

"Y-yes, my lord."

"Excellent. Now go, quickly, and implement my will. It would distress me to think that this aggravating princeling might continue to inhabit the same world with our glorious King for an instant longer than is necessary."

The man bowed his way from the room.

Mazarin smiled thinly, and moved to stand before the mirror. With its odd concave shape it threw a distorted image of the face. It was no matter. The creature had worn another body before this, and it too had been clothed in the cardinal's red. The face did not matter. Only the vessel mattered, to give form to the creature's nothingness so that it might carry out its Master's work. And soon, if all went according to plan, it could put aside these crude, fleshy envelopes forever, and revel once more in the restful silence of nothingness.

Four

I am the shield: *for every head*

The wallowing old tub had put into port at Flushing. Haakon, perched glumly on the rail, picked his teeth and eyed the stinking, bustling harbor with disfavor. The duel had gone as planned. He had shot the Duke's servants, Einer had had the vapors at the sight of the blood, Tyge's second had screamed like a scalded cat, and he and the Duke had gotten down to the serious business of trying to kill one another. The Duke had managed to slide his blade between skin and ribs, a painful but not serious wound, and Haakon had pierced Tyge's lung. When he left Denmark the Duke was still breathing. But the Duke's friends hadn't seemed to appreciate Haakon's magnanimity. A lynch mob had come hunting him, and he had taken to his heels.

His belly was rumbling, but there was no point in leaving the old merchantman. He had managed to lose all the Lady's money in a dice game with a poxy Spanish bastard—may he burn in hell—who cheated better than he did. At least he'd had the sense to pay for his passage in advance. He might starve, but he'd make it to England.

A shrill whinny cut the air and roused Haakon from his moody reverie. A big bay stallion was taking umbrage at a crate full of geese, and had reared to his full height. A young gentleman dangled from the headstall.

"Whoa, dammit," the young man screamed shrilly. "You've seen geese before you big booby! Whoa!"

The horse dropped back to all fours and nuzzled his diminutive master—and got roundly cuffed on the muzzle for his pains. They started up the gangplank, and Haakon straightened. He studied the young gentleman's elegant suit, the fine harness on the warhorse.

"What ho, what ho, a pigeon ripe for plucking," he murmured, and pulling his dice from one capacious pocket he began to juggle with the ivories.

The coast was a gray line before Haakon actually approached his pigeon. The gentleman was wrapped in his cloak, head pillowed on his saddle, and he was an alarming shade of green.

Haakon squatted on his haunches. "Seasick?" he asked sympathetically in German.

The young man looked puzzled for an instant, then curtly replied. "Yes."

"It will pass."

"I hope so or I'll be dead 'ere I reach England," said the lad, switching to French.

"I've always found that it helps if you take your mind off it."

"Oh?" The young gentleman brightened a bit.

"It's warmer below decks, and we can have a friendly game."

"Oh?" Now suspicion laced the words. "I haven't much money."

"Then we're even for neither have I. My luck's been shockingly bad recently."

The young man flatly refused to dice, so they settled on a game of cards. Playing rashly for the first few hands Haakon managed to lose more than he won, and he was gratified to see a touch of color in his opponent's pale cheeks. Haakon called for a bottle from the ship's captain, and toasted his companion.

"Here's to newfound friends."

"Chance-met companions," agreed the young gentleman, and they drained their glasses.

"Haakon Lindel at your service."

"William Nassau."

"What say you to higher stakes?"

The lad's winged brows shot up in surprise. "But you're losing."

"Sometimes plunging makes the luck change."

"As you will. It's your money."

Haakon, with judicious use of the cards up his sleeve, won the next five hands decisively. There was dismay in William's dark eyes as he stared at the pile of coins by Haakon's left elbow. Then the youth's chin stiffened.

"Again," William ordered curtly. "Winner takes all."

"You're not shy, I'll grant you that," said Haakon, infusing his voice with admiration. He shuffled the cards, and dealt in a blur of motion. Play began.

Suddenly William flung himself across the table and pinned Haakon's wrist. There was a knife in his right hand, and before the Norwegian could twist free the young man had slashed his sleeve. An ace, king, and queen tumbled out. William drove his knife through the king's eye, skewering him on the scarred wood, and Haakon winced.

"Not only am I not shy, I'm not a fool. You're a cheat and a blackguard, Haakon Lindel. I'll take my money now, and yours too for punishment, and you should be glad I left you with your life." Sweeping up his winnings the young man stalked to the ladder leading to the deck. "And you were right. I'm quite over my seasickness."

Haakon spent a long time cursing in several different languages, and never repeated himself once.

The North Sea was doing its damnedest to tear apart the wallowing old merchantman. Waves like gray dikes crowned with flying snow crashed onto the deck. Water ran foaming between the barrels of pork and wine, soaking the bales of wool and linen, and chuckled toward the scuppers. Spindrift writhed like lost souls about the masts. Haakon's gelding screamed with terror, pulling an echoing cry from William's bay tethered next to him.

"Do you think we will sink?" came the familiar accented voice.

Haakon glanced down. William's long hair was plastered

across his cheeks and shoulders, and his lips were blue with cold. His eyes had become two dark hollows in a white face. The ship swooped down one side of a monstrous wave, and the youth doubled over the rail retching. For an instant the tub lay shuddering in the trough, the sails flapping against the masts.

"Jesus God, we'll be knocked down!" screamed Haakon.

On the quarter deck the captain and helmsman fought the wheel while sailors swarmed up the rigging to adjust the sails. Slowly, laboriously, the old ship came around so that the on-coming wave caught her on the bow rather than amidships. There was a desperate cry, and William was torn from the rail. Cursing, Haakon tackled him, and they both went rolling across the deck. The grating over the hold met his scrabbling hand, and Haakon made a desperate grab, locking his fingers through the holes. The shock threatened to rip his arm from its socket, but somehow he kept a grip on the young man.

There was a shout from the helmsman. Haakon fought to his feet, pulling his companion with him. Dashing away the spray and rain which threatened to blind him he peered forward. A line of low dunes marched down to meet the sea. Waves pounded against the sand like teeth tearing at the body of the land.

He bellowed over the scream of the wind. "We're going to run aground. Somewhere near Dieppe I'd guess."

"But I have to get to England!"

"Well, you aren't going to make it, are you? Come." The young man held back, tugging at Haakon's hand like a recalcitrant foal.

"Where?"

"To our horses. They may just be our salvation."

"Ride them off the bow when we first strike, and swim to shore."

"Correct."

It was difficult to get their packs tightened on the plunging animals, much less mounted, but eventually it was done. The youth was light and wiry, and Haakon decided after watching him quiet the terrified stallion that he was also a masterful horseman. A desperate sailor grabbed Haakon's boot. Haakon kicked him away.

"Grip the horses' tails," the young man called down to the sailor. "Else you will pull us down with you."

"You're mad!" bellowed Haakon.

"It's only a few hundred yards. These good men have fought to save us. Can we do less?"

"Wonderful," groaned Haakon. "Not only must I fall in with a man who possesses eyes in the back of his head, he must needs be a saint as well."

The captain remained grimly at the wheel, guiding them straight in for shore. William looked to the burly old man, but the captain simply shook his head. The boy had pulled a seaman up behind him. With a sigh Haakon followed suit.

A long shudder ran the length of the ship. The masts groaned like dying men then cracked and fell in a welter of canvas and rigging. A sailor was dragged kicking and screaming over the rail by the trailing ropes. There was a sudden settling at the center.

"She's broken her back!" roared Haakon. "No time to lose!"

For an instant William's big bay danced and shied at the rail, his hooves scrabbling for purchase on the soaking deck. The boy drove home his spurs, and the warhorse lurched in an awkward jump off his hocks, over the rail, and into the boiling water.

Thunderer, Haakon's mount, not eager to be left alone, went plunging after. Sometimes swimming, sometimes lumbering on the sandy bottom, the horses fought for shore. With desperate thrusts of their powerful hindquarters they climbed free of the water. A bedraggled sailor released his grip on the black tail of the bay horse and fell sobbing to the sand, crying, praying, kissing the earth. Haakon glanced back and noted he had lost his bit of human flotsam. Only the cabin boy clinging to his waist remained.

Silently they all watched as the waves beat the *Queen of Dunkirk* to bits. Then over the dunes came a new wave, surging like a carpet of black ants—villagers drawn by the wreck. They were soon fighting over the barrels and boxes washing ashore.

The sailors had already joined the mob of scavengers. So much for loyalty, thought Haakon sourly as he spurred up the dune. A man rose up out of the marsh grass reaching for his reins. Haakon knocked him sprawling with a blow from the flat side of his rapier's blade.

"Shall we run?" inquired William calmly.

"Let us run."

They galloped for some two miles, until they reached a road. Glancing down its rutted length Haakon asked, "East or west?"

The young man shrugged. "Either direction leads to danger and trouble for me."

"Wonderful. A saint, eyes like a hawk, *and* a thatchgallows."

"I am *not* a thatchgallows. I have merely run away from home. By the by, allow me to thank you for saving my life. I shall forgive you for attempting to cheat me."

Haakon was half-amused, half-angered by the arrogance and authority in the young voice.

"So happy to have been of service," he murmured, a little ironically. "By the by, I'm a lord."

The lad's large, dark eyes rested speculatively upon him. "One can scarce credit it."

"Charming."

"Well, come or not. I'm riding."

Gazing after that slender figure swaying easily in the saddle, Haakon wrung water from his cloak and muttered aloud:

"Is any amount of glory worth this? Nursemaid to an impudent pup. And, by the way, I doubt the existence of this great prince. *You were nothing but a poxy whore!*"

"Do stop bellowing on the roadside like a village lackwit, and come along." The youth flashed a sudden shy smile. "I'll buy you supper since I've taken all your money."

Haakon eyed the gray, weathered walls of the inn with disfavor.

"It'll like as not be better on the inside," William offered.

"And how many country inns have you stayed in?"

"None."

"Dear God, a fledgling as well as a pup. Now I must needs guard against your plucking as well."

"You're a fine one to talk. The man who tried to pluck me."

"High ho, so proud, but I seem to recall a certain youngster heading over the side of a dirty old merchantman had it not been for the intervention of a certain Norse gentleman."

William bit his lower lip. "I beg your pardon."

"Oh, stow the gabble." Haakon dismounted with a grunt, and twitched the reins over Thunderer's pricked black ears. "Are there no ostlers at this pestilential inn? *Ho, keeper, ho there!*"

"My God, what a noise you make."

"I'll make more until my horse is tended to." Haakon strode to the door and hammered on the heavy panel with the butt of his crop. A startled ostler thrust his head out and gaped at the man on the step. "Stable the horses, and be quick about it," commanded the Norwegian.

The air in the taproom was thick with the effluvia of unwashed bodies, the malty odor of beer, the more pungent scent of spilled wine. Smoke from white clay pipes trailed like wraiths among the rafters. The only light was provided by a heavy wooden chandelier in whose branching arms guttered fifteen tallow candles. They were not enough to dispel the gloom that clung in the corners like cats to draperies. A more hopeful sign was the ten or so capons roasting on a spit in the enormous fireplace.

The innkeeper, a massive man with a heavily pockmarked face and a completely bald head, frowned at them.

"We're full to the bursting from the storm."

"One room and pallet will do, I'm nigh to dropping with fatigue," replied William, again with that flash of arrogance.

The innkeeper's small eyes peered out from rolls of fat, and he took a long look at the slender youth before him. Even stained, and stiff from the salt in its folds, William's long *justaucorps* coat showed the quality of his tailor, his hands, when he stripped off his gloves, were white and soft, and his speech bespoke the gentleman. The host revised his opinion of the quality of his guests, and bowed low.

"I have but this moment recalled. A small room beneath the eaves. Insufficient to monsieurs' needs, but if they will deign to look. . . ."

" 'Twill do," said William impatiently.

They followed their host up the stairs. Halfway up, William lost his grip on his canvas-wrapped rifle, and the material fell away. Several of the men looked up from their tankards and gasped at the sight of the chiseled gilt barrel and the walnut stock appliquéd with carved ebony and staghorn panels. Haakon too stared. Not even among the highest-born in Copenhagen had he seen such a weapon.

"Did you neglect to mention that when you ran away from home you also snaffled up a king's rifle?" muttered the soldier from the side of his mouth. "Well, we're sure to be robbed now."

William eyed him with disfavor, and followed the innkeeper into a cramped room set high beneath the eaves. An old, sagging, bedstead squatted in the center of the room. William threw back the coverlet and inspected the gray sheets. He shuddered.

"We shall be eaten alive."

"Most likely."

Returning to the taproom, they found a corner table and slid onto the hard wooden benches. Haakon settled with his back to the wall, assuring himself an unobstructed view of the room and the door. William's brows climbed toward his hairline at these precautions.

"Perhaps I am a fledgling, and perhaps it is of benefit to me that I fell in with a man of your experience," he admitted with a small smile.

"How old are you, lad?"

"Eighteen."

"Hmm."

"And you?"

"Twenty-nine."

"You seem to have seen much."

"Some. Soldiering gives you a rough if limited education. I fought for the Russians against the Poles, but the Peace of Andrusovo left me flat."

"How I envy you. I was supposed to be a soldier."

"So what are you then?"

A wary look filled the dark eyes. "A schoolboy."

A buxom serving girl sashayed to the table and leaned in on Haakon. He grinned and slapped her on the rump. William blushed, and the girl tickled his chin with a plump finger. Haakon pinched her and, eyes dancing, she glanced down at him.

"What will you, sir?"

"For now, wench, we'll each have a glass of mulled wine, followed by dinner. Are yonder fowl fresh?"

"Oh, aye, sir, shot just yesterday." She caught her full lower lip between her teeth. "Very . . . fresh." She wet her lips, and ran a finger around the low bodice of her dress. William stared in fascination at the swelling mounds of her breasts, lightly shining with sweat.

"Go on with you." Haakon slapped her firmly on the rump and sent her on her way. He noted how William's eyes rested on the suggestive sway of her hips and, grinning, he warned, "You'd have the pox, brat."

"I wasn't thinking . . . I'd never . . . with such a creature."

Haakon listened with only half an ear to William's sputtering denials, for his attention was riveted on the front door where four men had entered. They were lean and harsh, and their faces wore the lines and creases of too many summer suns and too many winters unprotected from the icy winds. Their clothes were drab and soiled, but one man wore an elaborate hat complete with no fewer than three plumes. Haakon felt certain that hat had never been purchased. Most likely it had graced the head of some poor fool who had fallen prey to these ill-favored rogues.

The man with the hat turned to survey the taproom, and Haakon saw that the left side of his face was twisted by a livid scar that ran from his temple to the corner of his mouth. That they were mercenaries there could be little doubt. That they were also closer in spirit to those packs of ravening wolves who had roamed across Europe during the Thirty Years War there could again be no doubt. They wore insolence like a badge, and danger followed in their footsteps. The locals quickly gave way before their entrance and moved mumbling to the corners.

Haakon leaned over the table, nipped William on the arm, and nodded toward the door.

"What make you of them?"

"God's blood, they're rough-looking customers, aren't they?"

"Yes, and not at all what I'd expect to see on the road this time of year."

"True, the summer campaigns are long finished. Perhaps they're heading east to be in position for the next round of recruitment."

"Unlikely. Such types usually hole up in the cities where there are women to fuck and men to rob."

The scar-faced man glanced at William, and touched the sleeve of one of his companions, and nodded toward the youth. Haakon tensed, and fondled the basket hilt of his rapier.

The serving wench came wending her way through the throng with a loaded tray. She bent to place the tray, and her breasts hung exactly at eye level, blocking Haakon's view of the room. He had twisted, trying to peer past her, when suddenly Scar Face slammed into her, sending the glasses crashing from the tray, the contents of the beaker splashing across Haakon's shirt front, and one of the capons leaping into William's lap. With an oath Haakon leaped up from the bench, wiping futilely at the spreading stain.

William carefully returned the roast duckling to the table, and rocked back in his chair, his hand thrust into his coat pocket. The mercenary leaned languidly on the table, grinning challengingly down at the young man.

"You great clumsy oaf!" Haakon raged. "If you fight like you walk 'tis no wonder your face looks as it does."

"So the boys object to having their finery ruined," the man drawled, with a scornful glance at William's expensive coat.

"Show him what it's like to have his skin ruined as well," one of Scar Face's companions urged as he drifted over to join the argument.

The innkeeper waddled across the room, hands waving agitatedly in the air over his head. "Monsieurs, I beg you, this is a peaceful inn. No brawling, I implore you."

"Innkeeper, this man has ruined our dinner. Place it on their tab, and be kind enough to bring us another," William snapped.

Command crackled in the clear young voice, and even the mercenaries were affected, for they drew back momentarily from the flash in the smaller man's dark eyes.

"At once, sir." The innkeeper bowed.

"By God, we'll not pay to feed your puling faces! You'll dine all right, but on cold steel!"

Scar Face grabbed for his sword. The front legs of William's chair crashed to the floor and the man suddenly found himself staring down the barrel of a pistol, which was pressed uncomfortably against his left nostril.

"This is how a gentleman fights!" raged William. "Do you think I would cross steel with a low-born ruffian like you? Now get you gone before I summon the authorities!"

The foursome retreated with ill grace, and settled at a table on the far side of the room. The crowd relaxed and conversations resumed, along with the click of utensils on china and the rattle of dice boxes. A plump priest who sat huddled by the fire loosened his grip on his elaborate silver cross, and sank back in his chair.

A new meal was brought, and Haakon and William fell to work. The Norwegian was a stout trencherman, while the younger man merely toyed with his food, satisfying himself with the merest sliver of duck and a piece of bread.

"Girl!" called William.

She simpered. "My name is Lisette, monsieur."

"Er . . . well, yes, Lisette. The good father seems hungry. Pray offer him what remains of this duck with my compliments."

"You're generous," mumbled Haakon around a mouthful.

"His eyes have been following every mouthful like a starving starling. And it's good to honor men of God."

Haakon grunted. The priest turned soft brown eyes on William and, rising, he bowed and blessed him. William nodded in reply, then sipped at his wine until Haakon had gnawed down to the bones.

Pulling out a pipe, the Norwegian tamped in tobacco and leaned back with his long legs stretched out before him. He gave a deep sigh of repletion. "Join me in blowing a cloud?"

"Thank you, no. I've yet to develop a taste for it. I'm for bed."

"Don't steal all the covers."

"You'll doubtless simply steal them back."

"Aye. Good night, brat."

The prince had never been the best of sleepers, and now—with Haakon's large frame listing the bed to starboard and inexorably working the scratchy, sour-smelling old blanket away from William's shivering form—he was not enjoying a restful night.

Furious, he threw out a hand—then froze at the soft intake of breath and scrape of boot on wood. Muttering, he dug his cheek into the pillow, drew his cloak closer about his body, and tried to still his racing heart and quick breaths. With his eyes opened to slits he strained into the darkness until a shadow resolved itself from shadows—the head and shoulders of a man creeping toward the bed.

He tried to wait until the man drew nearer, but his flesh was cringing, expecting the bite of steel at any moment. The tension snapped his control, and with a shout he yanked his pistol from beneath his pillow, spun the wheel and fired. The room lit to the red glare of discharging powder, and a deafening roar assaulted his ears.

Snorting and bellowing curses, Haakon came out of the bed like a breaching whale. Spots swam before William's eyes, and, cursing himself for looking directly into the muzzle flash, he blinked, and groped for his small sword. His hand closed about the hilt of the sword, and he slitered for the foot of the bed, then gasped as a blade sank into the mattress near his ear. Cat quick, he landed on his feet and lunged for his shadowy assailant. The man bellowed as the blade pinked him, and he fell back. Behind him William heard the clash of steel on steel, and Haakon roaring:

"*Ho, thief, thief!*"

Throughout the inn, doors were slamming. William leapt for the door, stumbled over his rifle propped at the foot of the bed, and fell headlong. A hand closed around his arm, and he slammed the hilt of his sword into the man's face.

"Ow! *Scheisse*! It's me!"

Haakon hauled him to his feet, and they burst into the hall and raced for the stairs. On the stairs, William realized that the Norwegian had checked his headlong flight and was proceeding step by cautious step down the steps, guarding their retreat. William pulled up, and so did not run full into the waiting blade of the man in the taproom. Laying a hand on the banister, he leaped over the rail. The man lunged and slashed, and the wind of the falling blade ruffled William's hair. Whirling, he took his guard and, coming in under the man's arm, stabbed him in the biceps.

The attacker's attention was on William, and on his own sluggishly bleeding arm. He never saw Haakon barreling down the stairs like a charging bull. The Norwegian hit him low, driving his shoulder into the man's belly and propelling him halfway across the room. A table cracked and collapsed. With a groan the thug struggled onto his elbows, then fell back among the splintered wood and lay still.

Haakon and William pressed their backs together, their blades weaving a net of steel in the air before them. Two men leaped down the stairs and into the taproom. Another man emerged from the shadows.

A crowd was gathering. The landlord, a bulky white figure in his shirt, lumbered through the gaping spectators.

"No fighting! I forbid—"

One of the mercenaries whirled and drove his blade into the

keeper's fat belly. He fell back, his mouth working, hands supporting his paunch as if trying to hold back the blood.

"Help! For the love of God, help!" screamed William, dodging an overhand cut from his opponent.

The crowd, having seen what happened to the innkeeper, were none too anxious to intervene. They hung back like spectators at a bullfight as the five men circled, feinted, thrust.

"Light, at least give us light! In Mercy's name!" cried Haakon, parrying blows from his two opponents. ˙

The plump priest raced forward and lit candles. He then pressed his back to the wall, fingering his beads, his lips moving in silent prayer.

With a roar, Haakon swept up a beer stein and went wading in. He feinted, thrust, and getting in close bashed one of the men in the side of the head with the stein.

William spared no more thought for his companion, for Scar Face beckoned him in with a slight wiggle of the fingers of his left hand. Taking the guard, the prince evaluated his foe, who was four inches taller and outweighed him by perhaps forty pounds. The mercenary's rapier added to his reach. Scar Face chuckled, nodded at William's small sword.

"Where came you by that? From a lady's pincushion?"

William leaped in a quick glide down the length of his opponent's blade. Scar Face threw the slender blade aside with a quick beat, and followed with a riposte which would have spitted William like a pig had he not leaped inelegantly aside. Still, the rapier's point scraped down his forearm, tearing the fine lawn sleeve and leaving a burning trail that blossomed with blood. Panting from the exertion and a sudden flare of fear, the prince realized that courtly lessons from his fencing master counted for little here. This was fighting in deadly earnest. His foe would not oblige him by taking the sixth guard to William's high-outside.

Face's greater reach and heavier weapon were going to settle this affair unless William's skill exceeded that of his foe. The youth's only hope was to run him, stay virtually disengaged, and wait for an error, an opening. The maze of tables, stools, and benches was not helping. Darting through the furniture, William danced in, feinted, disengaged. A bellow from Haakon distracted him momentarily. His eyes flicked back to his foe, and he saw the point coming for him as Scar Face leaped for-

ward, blade extended. Seizing a chair he flung it into his opponent's path. It cracked him on the shins, pulling a curse from
the mercenary and ruining his thrust. William prayed for him to
fall (he had no compunction about stabbing the man while he
was down), but God saw fit to do otherwise. The man recovered his balance and charged. The chase began anew.

Sweat ran in the youth's eyes, but that first flash of terror was
past. Coolly, now, he watched, anticipating blows, noting
weaknesses, measuring the rise and fall of his opponent's chest
as he gulped down air. A frown puckered the skin between Scar
Face's eyes. He has trusted to strength and reach and a bull-like
attack to dispose of this gadfly, and had failed. It was clear that
the young man was a master swordsman.

But William was almost spent. His fragile lungs were betraying him, making each breath an agony. This had to end, and end
quickly. He allowed his sword to droop in his hand . . . stumbled
once . . . left his breast exposed. Scar Face committed everything he had in a long *flèche*. William swept off his cloak and
enveloped his opponent's blade in the smothering folds, twisting it aside and lunging. His back leg shaking with the strain,
he drove his blade almost to the hilt into the man's chest.

Scar Face's eyes widened in surprise. He let fall his weapon,
touched hand to breast, and inspected the blood. He began to
collapse in discrete sections—to his knees, chin falling forward
as his neck folded like a·broken flower, hand to the floor to
support him, finally pitching onto his face at William's feet.

Haakon had dispatched one ruffian, and now held the other at
bay, the tip of his rapier at the man's throat. He had watched the
fight between his young companion and the mercenary leader,
ready to intervene had William ever seemed truly in danger.
Foolish perhaps, but he sensed that William's pride would be
sorely wounded had Haakon come to his rescue. Best to let a
young hawk taste first blood unaided.

Conversations stuttered into life, running about the room like
leaves in a whirlwind. Suddenly an icy wind swept through the
dimly lit taproom. The candles guttered and died. There were
confused and frightened cries from the darkness. Haakon felt
the hair on the back of his neck rise as three circles of spectral
light appeared over William's head. Dumbly he stared, the rapier hanging limply from his hand. His prisoner bolted. Haakon
started in pursuit, but was drawn back by a moan from the

watchers. He whirled in time to see William pitch forward in a dead faint.

Cradling the unconscious youth, Haakon muttered, "God's teeth, you weren't a whore. But must needs be a display of magic portents? You're not making this very easy for me," he added, as if answering the Lady's command that he protect this small princeling.

"'Struth, are you babbling to yourself again?" William said thickly.

"Highness."

Five

I am a lure: *from paradise*

Haakon had stopped talking to himself, but he was again bellowing in William's ear.

"Brandy! Ho, some brandy here!"

William winced, then yelped slightly as Haakon slammed the rim of a glass against his front teeth. He gasped in pain, sucked in a lungful of cognac, and began to cough. A cool hand was laid on his forehead, and a strange voice asked.

"Will he be all right?"

"Minor cuts is all, Father. Nerves most likely."

Haakon tried to pour another mouthful of brandy down his throat. William batted the glass away. "Damn your eyes," he croaked. "I'm fine! Or I would be if you stopped trying to drown me in brandy. I fainted. No more. Pray, stop discussing me as if I weren't present."

"Do you remember what happened?"

"I killed a man."

Haakon grasped William by the wrist and pulled him to his feet. "Not that. The wind. The lights."

"*What?*"

"Highness, I am Father Armand du Lac, and my Lady has led me to seek you across half of France." The priest was still on his knees, gazing intently up at William. He had a sweet plump face with pink cheeks, velvet brown eyes, and a fall of jet black hair which blended with the black of his soutane. A silver and amethyst cross glowed on his breast. "Command me, and I will obey."

"This is perhaps neither the time nor the place for such vows of lifelong devotion," muttered Haakon from the side of his mouth. "The provost marshal will be here soon enough. And His Highness better have his royal ass miles away."

William flushed, then paled. "I resent your tone."

"Willy, my lad, I, like yon father, have been sent in search of a wayward prince. But unlike the good father I've had direct experience of princes, and I'm none too impressed." Haakon crossed to one of the unconscious ruffians and nudged him with a toe. "These men were no mere robbers."

"How so?" demanded William, somewhat belligerently.

"They stayed to fight. Have you ever heard of such a thing from mere footpads?"

"This is all very fascinating, but I have reasons for not wishing to come to the attention of the authorities of France, so if you please—now what are you about?" asked William testily.

"Satisfying a curiosity."

Haakon rolled the scar-faced ruffian onto his back and rifled through his pockets. Removing a grimy and many-times-folded piece of paper, he opened and scanned it, then tossed it at William.

"Unquestionably you. There can't be two such noses in all of Europe."

William flushed and snatched the fluttering paper from the air. He studied the rough sketch, then read aloud, "By my hand, the bearer has done what he has done for the good of the crown, and in service to France. Louis's seal, and Mazarin's signature." Thoughtfully he refolded it, and thrust it into the breast of his shirt.

"I don't understand," said the priest.

"A subtle way to issue a death warrant without doing anything so gauche as naming the victim," explained Haakon as he continued his search. One of the large coat pockets yielded a fat and very heavy purse. Loosening the draw string the soldier shook several louis d'or into the palm of his hand.

"'Struth!"

"They were paid well to assure my death." It was said in a flat, emotionless tone, and Haakon shot the prince a quick glance, wondering how long this unnatural reserve could last, and dreading the hysterical outburst when it broke. "Call for the horses, we must be gone."

"And me, sire?"

"Pray ride with me, good Father. I would welcome your presence."

"Why is the king of France seeking to kill you?" asked Haakon.

"'Tis none of your concern."

"A whore in Copenhagen told me I'd run into a prince. The good father here obviously thinks you are a prince. Personally I think you're a troublesome brat with your lights and magics, and murderers stalking your trail, and I think I'm entitled to a few answers."

"Later."

"At least tell me who you are."

"William Henry, Prince of Orange, Count of Nassau." William beckoned to Lisette. "How is the landlord?"

She fidgeted and bobbed like a fisherman's float. "They think he will live, sir."

"Praise God. Please give him this." He laid three gold louis in her hand. "And tell him I deeply regret that the peace of his house has been disturbed." He paused again at the foot of the stairs. "Lindel, are you still gawping? The horses, man!"

"Yes, sir, Your Majesty, sir! Nothing is worth this abuse," Haakon grumbled as he stomped out the door. Then, glancing down, he watched the snow wetting his stockings and let out a roar of fury.

"A cunning Lady, egad!" Haakon snorted. "She appears in a separate guise to each of us, but the good father here gets the Virgin, and I get a whore. Wonder what that says about me?"

"I could hazard a guess," drawled William.

The priest gazed in bewilderment from the Norwegian to the prince and back again. William laughed and waved dismissingly toward Haakon.

"Take no heed of him, Father."

The door to the private parlor flew open with a crash propelled by a kick from the proprietress's small foot. Rotund and motherly, she smiled at the eagerness with which the three young men surrounded her. Steam rose from covered dishes on her laden tray. The trio had ridden through the night toward Dunkirk. Early that morning, stiff, sore, hungry, and tired, they had stopped in a village whose tiny jewellike inn had beckoned them, and instinct had served them well. Madame Bonnard had welcomed them, clucked over their muddy boots and frostbitten noses, and ensconced them in the small parlor with mugs of mulled wine warming their chilled fingers, and their feet outstretched toward a roaring fire.

Haakon and Father Armand piled their plates high, and set to with a will. William poured out a glass of milk, broke off a piece of bread, and sat nibbling.

"Rot your insides," mumbled Haakon around a mouthful of ham. "That pap."

William ignored him. "We were about to hear Father Armand's story."

Armand sucked down a spoonful of thick barley soup, and began. "For many months I have been disturbed by dreams of destruction, of a terrifying, freezing death creeping out from Paris. I reported these to my bishop, and was ordered to Normandy and into retreat. It is not wise to impugn evil to a king. At the abbey the Blessed Lady appeared to me, and ordered me to seek a prince who would stand against the evil."

"I too was sent looking for a prince." Haakon suddenly leaned forward and twitched the grimy warrant from the inner pocket of William's open jacket. "A prince who was in trouble."

"But a whore?" asked Father Armand. "I don't understand."

"Haakon is right, she appears in the guise most agreeable to us," said William.

"This sounds dangerously close to heresy." Armand frowned down at his plate.

"Father, believe me, though we do not share the same religion our God remains the same. I would do nothing to endanger my immortal soul."

Haakon shook a peremptory finger at the other men. "But we are in a web of magic. That cannot be denied."

"It must be. Denied and rejected," said the priest.

William rose from the table and paced the room, his coat swinging about his knees. "I am a practical man. Yet I cannot deny the events of the past days. I have been saved from death. I have seen a vision who seemed a spirit to me. I have been told that companions would be provided me, and, lo, here you are. I have been told I must stand against a great evil rising in the west. You, Father, have had visions of evil in Paris."

"Mayhap we are enemies then, sire. You are a Dutchman. I, a Frenchman."

"Whatever this woman is—ancient goddess or Queen of Heaven—she has said that the evil which threatens us threatens all mankind. Is it not perhaps right and proper that we set aside national and religious differences?" asked William.

Haakon set aside his flagon. "So what are we to do? Where were you bound when I plucked you from the waves?"

"England. I had thought to seek refuge with my Uncle Charles."

"The garter star. That explains it," muttered Haakon.

"And how came you to know of that?"

"I snooped while you were sleeping last night."

"The Devil!"

"I feared I'd fallen in with a thief."

"And I know I have fallen in with a rogue!"

"Perhaps the good father will have a moderating effect upon me." Haakon grinned. "But I put the question again. What are we to do now?"

"Continue my original plan. Make for England." William yawned and stretched. "The Lady said something about a guide to teach me, and talismans to aid me, but clearly you are not he . . . or they . . . or whatever. God, I'm tired."

The priest raised troubled eyes. "If this apparition is the Blessed Mother then I am at peace. But if not . . . witchcraft, magic." He shook his head.

William knelt before the priest's chair and lifted the cross in his hands. "Father, I do not think I am any more evil than any other man born of woman."

Armand ran his fingers through the boy's tumbled curls. "Very well, I am satisfied. What I have seen in my dreams is evil. You are not." He lifted William's chin with a forefinger.

"But you must guard against the temptations of power, my son."

"Yes, Father, I will. Though it's not too hard at this point. I have no power."

"Wonderful," muttered Haakon.

William grinned. "But I do have a purpose—to protect the world against an all-consuming evil." He rose and laid a hand on the soldier's shoulder. "And friends to help me achieve that purpose."

"*Scheisse!*"

They were sitting on the crest of a hill gazing out over a misty landscape of rolling hills, naked leafless woods, and evergreens sparkling with a dusting of new snow. Somewhere beyond the mist lay Dunkirk.

"God's blood, it's colder than a witch's tit," grumbled Haakon.

"Then let us gallop, and start the blood flowing." William laughed, and spurred Barbarossa down the hill.

Father Armand tried desperately to hold his newly purchased chestnut mare to a sedate trot, but seeing Thunderer's and Barbarossa's churning hindquarters she flung up her head and bolted after them. The trio drew up gasping beneath the eaves of the forest.

"You're mad, both of you," panted the priest. "In this cold you can fair break your buttocks."

"Ride a little lighter, Father, and spare the poor cheeks." Haakon chuckled, slapping Thunderer on the neck.

"I meant to ask this morning and completely forgot," said William. "What did happen when I fainted at the inn? You mentioned lights and winds."

"A great wind blew through the inn extinguishing all the candles, and then three glowing balls of light appeared above your head, sire," replied Armand.

"Oh."

"This means something?" asked Haakon, at the prince's peculiar expression.

"It's happened once before. At the moment of my birth, or so my old nurse claims. The lights in my mother's chamber were extinguished, and three lights appeared above my head."

"Meaning what?"

"Take your pick. The people of Holland claim that I am destined to wear three crowns. I would settle for one."

His voice seemed to echo in the snowy wood, and William fell silent.

"Holy Mother, 'tis uncommon quiet," whispered Father Armand, and quickly crossed himself. "Our voices seem as strident as crows."

"Speaking of crows I haven't seen a single beast. Not even a track," said Haakon, frowning down at the fresh snow. "More uncanniness. Damn."

"Let us ride," William ordered shortly.

The iron-shod hooves of the horses crushed the thick flooring of fallen pine needles beneath their coverlet of snow and sent up a crisp clean scent that tickled the nostrils. Wind sighed and rushed through the pines, a low, deep-throated sound like the murmur of an organ. A cascade of snow sloughed off a branch to land with a soft thud in the center of the trail.

Never had William been so aware of the life around him. He removed a gauntlet and laid his hand on Barbarossa's glossy neck. The life of the great horse seemed to run up through his fingers and set his body to tingling in sympathetic resonance. He half-closed his eyes and imagined he could see threads of silver energy linking the trees to the horse, to his companions, to himself. For an instant he had the bizarre and very disquieting notion that if he just gave a twist he could leave his body, and his spirit would go soaring along those lines of power.

Wrapping his hand in Barbarossa's thick black mane he struggled against the phenomenon. A sensation like a long-legged insect stalking up the length of his back set his skin to prickling, and William glanced nervously from side to side. His heart began to labor, his breath coming in short gasps. Through the trees he caught a glimpse of silver white hide. He swept a sleeve across his eyes and looked again. A milk white mare was pacing them.

"Look," he whispered.

"At what," Haakon mumbled around a gigantic yawn.

"I see nothing save a pattern of light on the snow," said Armand.

Floating on the wind came the sound of a flute. Haakon straightened in his saddle.

The horses stopped, and gazed with pricked ears and flared

nostrils down the path. The trees, slender birches and powerful oaks, hung over the trail and intertwined their branches in a vaulting roof above the riders' heads. The sunlight filtering through the canopy of ice-hung branches broke into prismatic fire and patterned the snow with dancing streaks of red, green, and blue.

"Oh, mercy," whispered Haakon.

Armand raised his hand to cross himself, but completed only half the gesture before freezing like a man enthralled. William felt a growing pressure that seemed to center behind his eyes. He longed to scream, shout, drum his heels on Barbarossa's sides, anything to break this tightening circle that held him helpless at its center.

There was a flash of color at the bend of the trail, and a power lay revealed. And in that moment the forest came to life. Birds broke into abrupt and riotous song, there was the patter of small animals running over the fallen leaves and needles on the forest floor, and a breeze went sighing through the trees as if the very forest itself had released a long pent-up breath. The girl strolling casually down the trail removed the flute from her lips and regarded them with wide, curious eyes.

She was dressed in a blue riding habit heavily embroidered with silver thread, and a large pistol was thrust through her belt. She held the flute loosely between the long fingers of her right hand, and with her left she fondled the butt of the pistol. Haakon shifted nervously in his saddle. The stirrup leather creaked beneath his weight, and he cleared his throat—a startling explosion of sound that sent several birds soaring skyward with a clap of wings. Armand completed his aborted self-blessing, and the gesture seemed to amuse the musician, for she smiled and pushed her plumed hat a bit further back on her white blond curls.

William sat silent, warily watching. The unbearable sense of encircling power had faded, but there was still a prickling down all his nerve endings, and everything around him, the leaves on a nearby bush, the rough crinkled bark of a tree, his own hand, and Barbarossa's pricked ears, seemed to be edged in a soft silver light.

He narrowed his eyes, and took a long look at the solitary troubadour. A beautiful face with its wide white brow, delicate pointed chin, eyes fringed with dark lashes, a startling contrast to the white blond brows. The prince's brow furrowed in a sharp frown.

Anger filled him, and he swung abruptly from Barbarossa's back, needing the release of physical movement. Resting his forehead against the horse's warm neck he ran his fingers agitatedly across the buckles of the girth. He had no doubt of the identity of this apparition. God's teeth, he had been imagining a potent guide and teacher: wise, old, and powerful. Instead he was to be placed in the hands of a female who looked to be even younger than himself.

An aching lump had settled into the base of his throat. He swallowed convulsively several times. A gentle hand touched his shoulder, and a flask was thrust beneath his nose. The rich scent of wine tickled his nostrils, bringing back memories of lazy autumn days filled with the hum of bees and the sweet smell of mowed grass and ripening grapes.

"My lord, will you drink?"

His head jerked up at the respectful tone and formal address, and he read only sincerity in the girl's wide eyes. They were a deep, midnight blue flecked with points of gold and silver light, and it was those eyes which began to mollify him as to her sex and her presence. They were deep and shadowed, as if mysteries beyond count lay hidden in their blue gold depths. He seemed to be falling, spiraling down into an endless blue sea flecked with the light of stars, and a sense of vast age washed through his soul. Then suddenly he was free, seeing only the surface of those amazing eyes, and the past and the future were gone, and she was only a slender girl offering him a flask of wine.

"You know each other?" Haakon inquired sweetly.

William took a pull of the wine. It went down smooth and mild, and sent out a small burst of warmth when it hit his stomach. "No, but I've been expecting her."

Father Armand spurred his mare forward. "'Tis dangerous, child, for one of your sex to be wandering alone with no male companions to protect you."

She cocked her head, an enchanting little gesture, and looked up at the priest. "Ah, but my good Father, I am no ordinary woman." Her lips curved into a merry smile, and she swept him a glance from beneath her lashes. "Besides, do I not now have male companions?"

Armand gaped at her, and his hand executed a jerky circle in the air before him. "You . . . you remind me of someone, a statue back in the abbey—"

She curtsied. "I am but her messenger, Father." The priest crossed himself.

William handed back the silver wine flask. "Am I correct in assuming that the Lady of the Wood has sent you?"

"Yes."

"I am bound for England, lady. Does that suit you?"

"It does not. We must travel east."

"East! After I've been half-drowned, nearly killed by assassins, and have ridden 'til I'm raw? Why didn't you contact me in Zeeland or better still at The Hague, and save us all this waste of time?"

"Consider nothing a waste of your time until it has been shown to be so. It was necessary for you to travel west. How else were you to find your companions?" She looked less like a seventeen-year-old girl, and more like an indignant mother faced with a particularly witless and irritating child.

"Forgive me." William bowed. "So, pray, where are we bound?"

"Nuremberg."

"Why, for God's sake?"

"You are becoming tiresome, my lord. You say you have been expecting me, yet you resist me. You say I have wasted your time, yet you seem determined to waste more time in useless argument. There are strong and valid reasons for our journey, none of which I am going to discuss with you while we stand in the middle of a trail deep within the heart of our enemy's territory."

"It will be a wearisome, long, and cold journey in winter," said Haakon.

"Such will simply have to be our fate. The prince is not ready to test his strength against his enemies." She returned her attention to William. "In fact, you are not even ready to grasp the first talisman. That, however, will be corrected by the time we reach Nuremberg."

"Talisman?"

"Patience! All will be revealed to you when you are ready. It takes time to master any new skill, Highness," she said in a gentler tone. "You must trust me a little in this."

"All I know is that we're going to end up with sore bottoms," muttered Haakon to Father Armand. "Nuremberg. Jesus!"

"I think you will find this trip far more useful than that, Lord Lindel," she said sharply. "Now, we have tarried as long as we dare. Let us ride and make camp somewhat closer to the boundaries of this inhospitable land."

"Lady, it will be a very slow journey if you intend to walk while the rest of us ride," Haakon said.

"I have a mount, good sir. He is grazing among the trees, but he will come when I call."

Haakon leaned forward with his arm across the pommel of his saddle. "So, you have a horse and a flute, and a pistol, but have you a name also?"

She smiled—a shy, girlish expression. "Indeed, yes. I am Sagitta."

"I suppose it's a waste of time to introduce ourselves?" grumbled William.

"Yes, I know you all."

"Witchcraft," Armand muttered. He had been sinking into deeper and deeper silence as the conversations flowed about him, and now he seemed to shrink down within the black folds of his soutane, like a turtle retreating into its shell.

Sagitta stepped up and laid her hand on his booted foot. He shrank back from her.

"Dear Father, I promise you there is nothing to fear."

"There is much to fear when a man travels in company which may endanger his immortal soul."

"Then you must find some way to leave your very self behind, for you carry the power as surely as William and I do, and as surely as Haakon does not."

"Thank you so much," muttered the Norwegian. "Puts me right in my place—"

"Hush," said William automatically, as Haakon began another of his monologues.

The priest's plump face was wan, and his eyes blinked rapidly for several moments. "Perhaps it were best if I returned to the abbey," he whispered. "I am not comfortable in this company."

"I must warn you they are searching for you, and once found you would be forced to reveal all you know of our plans and destination."

"I would not betray you."

"You would not *wish* to," Sagitta corrected gently.

"I wish none of this had occurred. I wish I were safely back in Paris!"

"Father, we need you, need your gifts of farseeing to keep us from harm. What better purpose for a priest to serve? Is that not your calling? I promise you, we will do no evil, even though we will not work in the name of your god."

"I have seen great evil," he said, in a little boy's voice.

"Yes, and William will combat it."

He stared intently down at her. "They say evil is masked by a beautiful face."

"What does your heart tell you?"

He slid his eyes cautiously toward William. "To ride with the prince."

"Then let us ride."

Raising two fingers to her lips, she let loose a piercing whistle. Far off in the woods there was a startled nicker, and the other horses threw up their heads, jaws working, ears pricked. Moments later the riders heard the swish and crash as a large form forced its way through the branches and brambles. William peered intently through the screening pine trees, certain of what he would see. But it was not a white horse that emerged onto the trail. Instead it was a piebald old gelding whose red spots formed a leopardlike pattern across his rotund white body. Two of the spots circled his dark eyes, giving him a perpetually startled expression, and his muzzle was a bright pink.

"Dear God," Haakon breathed. "Small children shall pursue us hooting through each and every village. Couldn't you find anything less . . ." He paused, searching for a tactful word. "Startling? But then, so far the Lady hasn't done anything discreetly. Suspending crowns over the babe's head—"

"Haakon. Please."

"Sorry, Highness."

Sagitta slapped the old horse on his thick neck. He gave a grunt of pleasure. Gripping a fistful of mane she swung herself onto his broad, flat back.

"No tack?" William asked.

"I'll purchase some in the next village."

"They'll think you stole the horse."

"No they won't," Haakon corrected. "*No one* would steal that horse."

They laughed, and the last vestiges of unseen mystery seemed to blow away. William tried to recapture the feelings of anticipation and power he had felt when he first faced Sagitta, but they were gone. She seemed no more than a slender girl mounted on an absurd horse. He focused on the fall of hair which bounced up and down on her back as she trotted ahead, leading them eastward and even deeper into the sheltering woods. Haakon was humming tunelessly as he rode, and even Armand seemed to have relaxed. His hands were clasped loosely about the reins, his eyes closed and his lips moving. William fancied that he was praying, but it didn't seem to be the desperate prayers of a man who feels himself among enemies. Instead it seemed like a priest who had suddenly realized that a day had passed without him properly executing his religious duties.

William too closed his eyes and prayed, but his world had lost its anchor. The Calvinist code which had dominated and supported him throughout his life seemed unequal to his present confusion. It was now apparent that predestination was a meaningless concept—certainly to one who had been told that his actions would directly affect the outcome of history for all time. But did that necessarily negate his faith entirely? Copernicus established that the earth orbited about the sun. Did God die in that moment?

Or did man merely understand a little better?

Six

I am a tear:
the Sun lets fall

Barbarossa gave a grunt as he dropped to his knees, eased over on his side, and rolled vigorously among the fallen needles. Lurching to his feet, he shook—a long shudder that began at his muzzle and ended at his tail and pulled a deep groaning sigh from his big body.

"Wish I could do that, and it would feel as good," remarked Haakon, pulling the saddle from Thunderer's back.

"I wish I could have a bath. Gallons of hot water, and a body servant to scrub my back," sighed William.

"Bath?" Haakon lifted an arm and sniffed at his armpit. "What the devil do you need a bath for?"

"Because I stink. You stink, and the Father stinks."

"That's why God created perfume."

"I'm accustomed to bathing every week," said William repressively.

"God's blood, no wonder you're sickly."

Haakon slouched away to where Sagitta was striking sparks from her flint lighter. Father Armand sat on the ground like a forgotten black sack, shifting occasionally as he tried to find a softer spot for his sore buttocks.

Their camp was in a deep hollow surrounded by ancient spruce trees. The blue green needles formed an impenetrable wall about the dell, but Sagitta had known exactly where to push through the stiff branches. The floor of the hollow was carpeted with a layer of fallen needles and dead grass. They would at least sleep soft if not warm this night. And if they were not to sleep empty as well as cold, someone would have to hunt.

Ignoring his aching back William unlimbered his rifle, climbed the steep side of the dell, and pushed through the evergreens. The pungent scent filled his nostrils. The forest was starting to stir with awakening animals. There was the distant cough of a buck, the frantic patter of small feet on the mold and leaves, then a squeak of pain and fear as an owl slid silently out of the dusk and scooped up some small creature.

Thick tendrils of white fog rose like phantom dervishes from the moist loam to whirl about the boles of the trees. A rabbit bounded into view. Man and animal regarded one another in sudden bewilderment, then a stone came flying from over William's shoulder and hit the beast squarely in the head. It toppled, its hind legs twitching as if it were still trying to flee from the death that had come unseen out of the darkness.

Sagitta emerged from the mist, a sling held negligently in one hand. Kneeling by the dead rabbit she softly stroked the silky fur, bowed her head as if in benediction, then gripped the animal by its hind legs and rose to face William.

"I thought you might have come hunting, and it's easy to become lost when the fog rises."

"Thank you, but I'm not a child. You're quick," he then added, fearing he had been churlish.

She shrugged. "Stones are cheaper than balls, and make less noise." They walked for several yards in silence, then she said. "We have little time, so I think we should begin your instruction tonight." William froze. "Are you frightened?"

"Yes."

"Good. What we do is dangerous."

"Living is dangerous."

"You're very cool for one so young."

"And you, are you so old?"

She lightly touched his cheek. "Oh yes. Women always are. So much older than men, that is."

They walked on in silence. Abruptly the forest ended at the foot of a rounded hill. They climbed to the top, and Sagitta's hand swept out.

"What do you see?" she asked.

An icy wind hissed through the dead grass and moaned about the gray bulk of the standing stones which surmounted the hill like a broken crown. The mist whipped like the tattered clothing of disconsolate ghosts about the pitted stones, and overhead stars glittered diamond-hard against the black vault of the sky. Miles away the lights of a village flickered in a fold in the hills.

William shrugged. "Stones."

"Be more precise."

Narrowing his eyes, he dropped his chin into his cloak and studied what lay before him.

"Thirteen gray stones. Seven are standing, the remaining six have fallen. One stands in the exact center of the circle." He walked forward and inspected the pitted surface of one. "Someone has carved a cross on this one."

"As a ward against evil," said Sagitta.

William backed away, then turned so that he and the girl were face to face, the white puffs of their breaths mingling. "*Is* this place evil?"

"No, merely old, and it is a focus for power, so that the ignorant, the Christians, have feared it. Now look again, and this time really *look*."

Drawing in several slow breaths, he ignored his shivering body and concentrated. There was a sensation like the lick of flames at the base of his spine, and he saw faint silver lines weaving an intricate pattern between the stones. Beads of crystal hung from each line like dew on cobwebs, and shimmered in the starlight. They seemed to hum as if holding some perfect celestial note. He felt his body beginning to vibrate in sympathetic resonance with that soul-aching sound.

Sagitta nodded with satisfaction and, raising her left hand, emitted a pure soprano tone that joined with the singing beads and formed a chord. It stretched beyond the range of human hearing, becoming a pain like an ice needle driven into the mind. William staggered and fell to his hands and knees. He shuddered as Sagitta withdrew a white-handled knife from beneath her coat. He steeled himself for the blow, wanting to resist but too weak. Then she stepped into the ring of stones, and his terror receded.

Three times she circled the central stone, chanting softly in an unknown tongue and cutting the air in an intricate pattern with the clear crystal blade. Starlight flickered along the blade. Watching it brought on a twisting nausea. William looked away, concentrating on the frozen blades of grass beneath his hands and trying to quiet his heaving stomach.

"Come." He looked up as Sagitta cut a doorway in the air with the knife. "But leave your weapons outside."

"Why?"

"This modern steel and gunpowder destroys the purity, the harmony of the circle. Leave it."

"All right." He unbuckled his sword and dropped his pistols next to it, laid aside the rifle. Unencumbered, he stepped through the unseen doorway. And felt a prickling across his forehead and in the tips of his fingers. He shivered, for it was an uncomfortable sensation.

A slab of rock lay on the ground before the center stone like an altar before a headstone.

"Lie down."

His thoughts of headstones had brought to mind visions of unwilling sacrifices and black rituals. He started for the circle's edge.

"Wait! Where are you going?"

"To get Haakon."

"Why?"

"I want him to guard me."

"I will not harm you."

"How can I know that?"

"It is not given to us to know. You must be guided by your heart, your feelings."

"Forgive me, madam, but I prefer something a touch more tangible."

"All right, be *logical* then. I have been sent into this world at great effort to guide and teach you. The Lady has walked among men in order to save you, and to send you companions. You are our last great hope. Why then should we harm you?" She gave a sudden shy, sly, wicked, and merry laugh. "Besides, you might find this pleasurable."

"Plea . . . pleasurable?"

"Pleasurable," she whispered.

She stepped in and kissed him full on the mouth, the tip of her tongue playing tantalizingly across his lips. Her fingers were wrapped tightly about his wrist, and the gold and silver flecks in her strange eyes were glowing in the darkness. Something seemed to explode behind his eyes, and the prince pulled her close. Images of violent death receded. This was merely sin. Sin was acceptable.

Still kissing, his hands groping awkwardly at her bodice, they stumbled toward the stone and fell in a tangled heap on its cold, hard surface. Even through the thick skirt of her habit he could feel her thigh pressing against his. His cock was a tumescent bulge in his breeches, and William flushed with embarrassment.

She pushed him away, and began lecturing in a dry, precise voice while she pulled from her pocket a cup, a flask, a packet of herbs, and a small stone jar.

"The powers we use are like a great ocean lapping endlessly at the edges of consciousness, but before you can use these powers you must find the path to the source. Usually a person learns slowly, through years of meditation, and a careful opening of the centers. But time we do not have, so I am going to take you there."

"And these . . . centers?" he asked, stumbling over the strange word.

"Will be opened tonight by rather drastic means." He shrank away. "But pleasurable, very pleasurable," she hastened to assure him.

She mixed a pinch of the herbs with the wine, removed the lid of the jar. Several sharp, pungent odors assailed him, and William pinched his nostrils fastidiously. Sagitta laughed, and gave him an open-mouth kiss that stopped the breath in his throat. With one hand she unbuttoned his *justaucorps* and the waistcoat beneath, unlaced his shirt, and rubbed the sharp-smelling unguent across his breast. The catch of her fingertips in his chest hair was an exciting sensation.

A tug and her bodice fell open, breasts swinging tantalizingly before his hungry, embarrassed gaze. "Now me."

He thrust his hands beneath his back, blood flaming in his cheeks. "I can't."

She pulled his hand free, dipped his fingers in the unguent, and drew them across her breasts. William felt the nipples tightening and crinkling beneath his touch. Doubt and embarrassment died in an explosion of lust. He eagerly took over the massage.

"Drink." She thrust the cup into his hands, and he drained it in one long swallow. There was an explosion of heat in the pit of his stomach, and the bitter taste of gall on the back of his tongue. His hand flailed in protest, and Sagitta rescued the cup.

She pushed him back, and he lay heavy and inert on the stone. His erection was a painful presence, and with a groan he tried to touch himself, but his hand refused to move. Owlishly he blinked up at the delicate, beautiful face hanging over him. She rose and slithered from her clothes . . . opened his breeches, and drew him out. Her palms were icy against the burning skin of his penis.

He gave a cry, and then another of outrage and pain as she drew the crystal blade across his chest. A thin line of blood marked the path. Sagitta reversed the blade and made a quick slash across her own breast. Seizing William by the shoulders she yanked him up and pressed her lips against the cut on his chest. Her mouth was warm, and the cut stung slightly as saliva entered the wound. She pulled his mouth to her, and he tasted the salty, coppery taste of blood overlaid with the sour flavor of the unguent. He realized he was spinning, floating, rising above the surface of the stone, and he clutched wildly at Sagitta's shoulders.

"Hush, it's all right. You're almost free."

He sank back, aware of the thunderous song of the crystal beads. Sagitta stroked and fondled him, straddled him, and impaled herself on his cock. Wildly he rocked and bucked, clutching at her hips and breasts. Just as he was about to come, she slipped free and thrust her finger against the root of his penis. The orgasm raced back along his spine, white-hot power exploding in his soul.

Darkness took him.

He became aware of voices—the murmuring thoughts and hopes and dreams of the people who slept in the village. The voices rose like smoke from a chimney, to touch his heart and mind.

"Good, good," crooned Sagitta. "You're ready. Come with me."

He stared at her hand, which glowed with an intense white light like the fire of the sun at the edge of a cloud. Their fingers twined, and she pulled him to his feet. Looking down at his body sprawled on the stone he felt another flare of fear. But Sagitta lay beside him, her white gold hair forming a coverlet across his chest. Perversely he was reassured by the two seemingly dead bodies. Silver lines bound him to his discarded body. He touched them gently, listening to their harmony.

"Break them and the body dies," said Sagitta softly.

"I understand."

"Now come and play." She beckoned, and with a diving, sweeping motion they left the dimness of the physical plane and entered a glowing, silver dimension lying above the world he knew. They paused and she pressed her lips to his cheek, whispering:

"Find the power."

Find it? How to avoid it? It beat on him like sunlight on the face of a blind man.

He turned and a silver sea lay before him. A fairylike mist rose above the surface of the phosphorescence-kissed waves, and the break and hiss of those waves on the crystal beach gripped his heart like fine music. He stepped forward, ready to enter the bosom of this power and never emerge.

Sagitta pulled him back.

"Careful. Enter there, and William, the individual, will be lost forever."

"I can't bear to leave it."

"You don't have to. You now know where it lies. You can reach out and draw from it as needs be. It is endless and eternal. It will always be with you. Now let us go. You should learn the advantages of this mode of travel." Her smile was youthful and mischievous. He laid his hand in hers and smiled back.

With William clinging like the tail of a swift-flying kite they flashed across the darkened surface of the earth. He saw the familiar inlets and canals of The Hague, and with a cry of joy and loneliness he raced down and through the insubstantial walls of the palace. In quick succession he searched through the rooms: servants nodding in the kitchen, Hans Bentinck agitatedly pacing in his quarters. He reached out to stroke the young page's hair and reassure him that he was safe and well, but his hand passed through, and Hans gave no indication that he was aware of his prince's presence.

"He cannot sense you," Sagitta said, joining him in the firelit room.

"Can I make him?"

"Yes, but it would take more effort than it's worth. Magic is only useful against those with an affinity to magic."

He was reluctant to leave the comforting warmth of home, but there was an insistent tugging, a voice calling—sirenlike and luring, eyes that searched the silver mist. He was drawn, curious despite a faint nervous trembling. Somewhere, far behind him, he heard a despairing cry. The silver mist receded, took on physical form, and William fell back with a murmur of disgust. Leprous white fungus covered the walls of a cavern and spilled across the damp floor like an obscene tide.

Voices chanted in the firelight. William beheld a circle of black-robed figures. He stepped between them and stared down at de Coulan, lying naked on a stained altar stone. The French envoy's eyes were wide with fear and pain. A red-robed figure loomed above him, knife in hand. A flash of obsidian, a falling knife, and William's hand shot out and caught the master magician by the wrist. But unlike with Bentinck, he *connected*. Foul breath hissed into his face, and William gagged. Captor became prisoner as the magician gripped the prince's hand with his free one and forced down the polished stone blade. De Coulan screamed in agony. Blood coursed down his thighs. The master of ceremonies of this macabre ceremony raised high the severed penis, then spun like a graceful dancer on his heel and thrust the disgusting member straight at William's face, smearing him with blood. The prince struggled to free himself, sobbing in horror.

The man's strength was incredible, and aching cold seemed to flow from his fingertips. William groped in his pockets, his hand closed about the miniature of his mother, the filigreed frame cut into his palm. Like a striking snake he ripped the edge across his enemy's eyes. The man screamed, a sound like escaping steam. His grip relaxed, William jerked free and fled as grasping, red-stained hands reached for him.

Shooting out of the cave he sought the clean purity of his silver overworld, but he couldn't find it. He was lost in a tangled labyrinth of shifting gray corridors. Like a bird indoors he flung himself against the icy walls of his prison, maddened with terror and despair. Suddenly he became aware of a presence, bloated, devouring, and deadly cold. Worse, he knew it had become aware of *him*. He froze. For a brief instant he saw himself as an interlocking network of energy, fire flickering along each line. Then even this illusion of a body passed away, and he was a collection of spinning particles.

"Democritus—all matter is composed of tiny atomic particles, the word 'atom' meaning unbreakable or indivisible.

Nothing which exists can be reduced to nothing. Nothing can come out of nothing."

Spinoza's voice.

You were wrong, dear teacher, you and old Democritus. Nothing can come out of nothing. Something . . . Nothing is coming for me now.

It closed in, shambling slowly and uncertainly toward him, attracted by the light and fire of his spirit.

Cold like gripping claws reached out and crawled up his legs. Whimpering in terror, William curled in on himself, forming a shivering, paralyzed ball. The cold advanced and he felt a distant sadness over his impending death. There was an insistent tugging, and he stared down down at the silver cords drawn out taut from his body.

Lifelines.

Break them and die. Follow them and . . . live?

Power washed through him warming body, heart, and mind. He glowed like a spark of sun-fire as he flew along lines of power. The cold grayness retreated, and he fell toward his supine body where it rested on a stone on a hilltop in France. There was a jarring snap of joining. Nausea and faintness washed through him. He rolled onto his belly and vomited the meager contents of his stomach onto the ground.

"William! William!"

Sagitta ran to him and enfolded him in her arms. She was sobbing and murmuring, rocking him like a baby. He lay limply against her bare breast and gasped for air. The taste of vomit was sour in his mouth.

"What in the *hell* was *that*?"

"It was the end of all things," she sobbed.

"That is *not* an answer," he said, and fainted dead away.

Seven

I am the queen: *of every hive*

"God's teeth, what a dump."

"Would you prefer another rat-and-bug-infested inn?" asked William with awful politeness.

Haakon tipped the prince's hat over his eyes with his crop as he rode by. "What a prickly infant. Will you never learn when I'm joking? But if such is the state of all your houses, H.H., you're in trouble."

"This is a hunting lodge, not a palace."

They dismounted in the great courtyard. Haakon saw a curious head thrust from one of the windows.

"Highness! Highness! Highness!"

"An excited blackamoor," grunted the Norwegian, loosening Thunderer's girth.

"Jan, here? Wonderful," cried William, and ran for the principal lodge.

The prince and his African page collided on the stone stairs. "Oh Lord be praised! We had heard you were drowned, and shot, and stabbed and killed."

"What, all at the same time?" William chuckled, both at the absurdity of the remark, and the expression on the dark face of Jan the Moor. "But Jan, I beg you, hold your tongue, I come in secret, and must be gone ere tomorrow's eve."

"But Highness, you were to go to England."

"A small change in plans. I'm bound for the Germanies."

"But—"

William laid a hand across the boy's mouth. "Jan, there are four of us, we are butt-weary, travel-stained, and hungry."

"Baths, dinner, bed."

"Excellent." The other travelers had joined them, and William drew Jan forward. "Sagitta, Haakon, Father Armand, this is Jan, one of my pages, and it is good fortune that allows us to find him at Dieren."

Greetings were exchanged, and the boy hurried away to see to their accommodations. Sagitta pivoted slowly in the center of the great hall, studying the hundreds of antlers which adorned the whitewashed walls. There was a strange little smile on her lips which for some reason disturbed William. He stretched out on a bench, trying to ease his aching back.

"Is he a slave?" asked Armand.

"I own animals, Father, I don't own people. Jan was given to me by the Bishop of Münster, and I freed him. He takes instruction with my chaplain."

"God bless you, my son, for your charity."

"Thank you, Father."

The page returned and led them to their bedchambers.

"Why are you not at the Noordeinde?" asked William, as the boy helped him from his boots.

"Heer Bentinck thought it best if servants loyal to Your Highness were placed at your various residences in case you returned."

"Noble Hans! What would I do without him," cried William. "How I wish I could see him."

Rocking back to sit on his heels, Jan asked, "Can you not return home, Highness?"

"No, not yet. My journey is only beginning."

A sharp crash brought him to quivering wakefulness. William groped for his pistol and, sliding from the bed, ran to the door. Spots danced before his eyes, and he realized he was holding his breath. Sheepishly he exhaled, then breathed deeply of the lingering scent of wood smoke, roast venison, and beeswax.

Returning to the bed, the prince gathered up a candle and lit it from a taper in the hall. Then, with pistol in hand and candle in the other, he made his way into the great hall.

Haakon was already there, staring bemusedly at a pair of antlers which had fallen from the wall. William thrust his burdens into the soldier's hands and picked up the trophy.

"All hail, lord," called Sagitta from the darkness.

"*Scheisse!*" gasped Haakon. "Damn you, chit. I nearly blew a hole—"

"Hush," whispered William, for *that* feeling had come over him again.

The room faded, and suddenly it seemed that the two men stood upon a rock ledge. Before them rose a cliff's face. High among the rock clefts was a nest woven of feathers and white horse hair. William still clutched the stag's antlers.

"Saints preserve us from all nightmares."

"Especially from waking ones," William forced past stiff lips.

She came to them riding on a white mare. Her lips were like blood against her pale, pale face.

"And so it begins, and scarce soon enough. You, Haakon, be thou the shield that thou art. And you, prince, king, gentle roebuck, learn well, and serve me better. Three talismans of power you will gather unto yourselves. You, William, are the focus, the hand to wield the sword. Give yourself into the care of my handmaiden, and obey her. Spare not the body. Each day the gateway between the worlds opens wider, and death strives to enter.

"You were less mystic in Copenhagen," remarked the soldier.

"*Haakon,*" moaned William. "This is a *goddess.*"

"All I'm asking for is a little plain speaking."

The White Lady laughed. "Then you shall have it. The three objects of power will serve to focus and augment William's power. Our enemies will seek to deny you the talismans. Be prepared to fight."

"Fine. Fighting I understand."

"And once I have these objects?" asked William.

"You will strive with the demon Mazarin and close the gate."

"Another question—you said at our first meeting that men were being used to open this gate. If Mazarin is a demon then who is his human?"

"Have you not guessed yet? Your cousin Louis of France."

William was thunderstruck. "Good God."

"Why couldn't it be a simple swineherd in Languedoc," muttered Haakon. "Why is nothing ever simple or easy?"

"Stop blathering," ordered William. "Lady, I am disturbed. You send me companions, and then exclude two."

"My handmaiden is with us."

William's eyes jerked to the white mare. "You are quick, William, very quick," said the Lady.

"But Father Armand," the prince persisted stubbornly.

"William, Armand is the infidel."

He flung out a hand, indicating the Norwegian. "Haakon is an infidel. The father—"

"Is a man of misguided faith. I will take the man of no faith, for he will accept the evidence of his eyes and not seek to twist the truth."

"Lady, what is truth?"

"Would you have me answer the riddle of the ages? Accept me and serve, William Henry, and leave such questions to the philosophers."

"Damn it! Listen to me!" Haakon gripped Sagitta's arm and swung her around. Fury flamed in her eyes, and she ripped free. "He can't take much more of this."

"He must."

"And if you kill him? What about your great quest then? Who then will save the world? If indeed this refuse heap is worth saving." The Norwegian spun away and stared out the ice-rimed window of their inn in Heidelberg.

The touch of her hand was like a butterfly's kiss. "You're bitter."

"Yes. It's a hell of a world." Haakon faced her. "Where boys are driven past their strength to attain . . . Christ, I don't know what."

"He must learn these things if he is ever to stand against Louis and Mazarin. You were present when my Lady explained all."

"She explained nothing! She ordered and commanded, and now he's gasping his life out in there." His out-thrust arm quivered with strain.

"We are wasting time."

"A day. What can it hurt?"

"More than you know, Lord Lindel. More than you can possibly understand." She swept from the room with a rustle of skirts.

With an oath he swept the breakfast setting from the table. The pewter plates rang on the stone-flagged floor, the beer mug shattering. He walked into the small bedchamber where Father

Armand sat in quiet vigil by the prince's bedside. The priest closed his missal and regarded the soldier.

"How is he, Father?"

"Not good."

Lindel knelt by the bed, noted the white, waxy quality of the prince's skin, the shadows hung like cobwebs beneath his eyes, touched one feverish cheek.

"Thank God for the river. If we'd had to ride this distance..."

"He'd be in a box," replied the Norwegian harshly. Armand crossed himself. "But now she says we must ride, and that I'm a blockhead for opposing her."

"Lindel, I think...do you think...could it be that she is a demon, a succubus?"

"I don't know anymore."

"She lies with him."

"Not an uncommon occurrence in this sinful world, Father. If every woman who laid down with a man not her husband were a succubus we'd be up to our asses in demons."

"God forgive your levity."

Haakon ignored him and touched William lightly on the shoulder. "Highness."

"What? Time...already?"

"I'm afraid so. *She* says we must ride."

"She's right. Each day the gateway opens a little farther. It fills my dreams." He sat up and pushed back his hair. Armand crossed himself, and William's eyes narrowed in wry amusement. "I only wish that that could close it, dear Father."

"H.H., must you go on with this?" asked Haakon, stropping the prince's razor.

"Yes. The more I learn the more I am convinced of the necessity." He splashed cold water on his face, settled into a chair. Haakon lathered his cheeks and chin and drew the razor carefully up his throat.

"I'm glad I trust you," muttered William. "One quick cut, and—" His voice broke, and he huddled over his knees shaking.

"What? What is it, my son." The priest knelt at his feet, chafing the young man's hands.

"He mutilated de Coulan, and forced me to be part of it."

"Mere dreams," scoffed Haakon in a hearty tone.

"No, I was there. I saw it."

"How?" asked Armand cautiously.

"We travel out of body. In the space of a thought you can be anywhere. Oh God, I'm afraid."

Lindel roughly pulled William back in the chair and resumed the shave.

Pulling a chair near William, the priest held the boy's shaking hand and coaxed gently. "What is it you fear, my son? For your immortal soul?"

"No, Father, for my miserable life. The more I learn the more vulnerable I become."

"Would you stop talking!" grumbled Haakon, blotting at a nick.

Armand frowned. "How can that be? Surely the more she teaches you the more powerful you become?"

"True, but only people with a predisposition to magic may use it. You have that predisposition, Father, as do I. I could ensorcell you with very little effort, and you me. But if I tried the same on Haakon it would exhaust me, and likely yield no result. His mind is blind to the other realms."

"So where's the problem?" grunted Lindel, wiping the last of the lather from around William's ears and mouth.

"Magic users leave a . . . a signature. When I'm working I feel as if I glow like a meteor. Each time I use magic I become more easily located by other magic users."

"By your enemies?" asked the priest softly.

"Yes."

"There's no way to block them?"

"I can guard myself from their attacks. I cannot hide from them."

"So what's the good of it?" asked Lindel. "Each time you use these powers you are weakened physically, and now these sorcerers on the other side can find you. We should put our trust in good honest cannon."

"But good honest cannon cannot close this gateway. Only weak and fearful flesh."

"So what exactly is this magical gimcrack that we seek in Nuremburg?" asked Haakon as they trotted down the Neckar Valley.

High, wooded hills loomed on either side. On one sat the

walled fortress town of Dilsberg. Smoke rose from its chimneys, blue gray lines drawn against the sky. Smoke also seemed to be rising from the four riders as their breath steamed in the frigid December air.

Sagitta shot William a warning glance and jerked her head toward Armand. The prince frowned and shook his head. "He has a right to know."

"Perhaps 'twere better if he knew aught of our plans."

"We either trust one another, or we end this now," shot back William.

Aggrieved, the priest asked, "Why do you distrust me so?"

"Because you will not study with me," snapped Sagitta.

"I will not endanger my immortal soul," he flared.

"Peace, both of you!" ordered William. "I do trust you, Father. So I will tell you that what we seek in Nuremburg is the *Heilige Lance*."

"The Holy Spear," translated Haakon for the puzzled Frenchman.

"Also called the Reich's Lance, the Spear of Longinus," said William.

"The Spear that pierced the side of our Savior," whispered the priest.

"Yes."

He looked at the girl. "I thought you said we would not serve in the name of my God?"

"There is but one power in the world, Father, though it bears many names. Your new faith grows upon the foundations of the Old Religion. Despising it, but nonetheless partaking of it. The Spear has power, for it drank the blood of a sacred king. More important is the prophecy which surrounds it. That whosoever claims it, and solves its secrets, holds the destiny of the world in his hands for good or evil."

"Good or evil," repeated William and shuddered.

"If the legends are true it is a dangerous talisman to bear," Armand said. "Let it fall and it is an augury of tragedy and death. Charlemagne allowed it to fall from his hands while returning from his final victorious campaign. Frederick Barbarossa died at the very moment the spear fell from his hands."

"You are well-informed, Father," said Sagitta with a quelling glance.

"I am a student of the mystical. And you should not hide

from the prince the dangers attendant to bearing so sacred an object. His heart and mind must be pure. He must put aside fornication—"

Sagitta chuckled. "Dear Father, sex is the ultimate creative power. Your faith's rejection of that principle will be its downfall."

William, his face hot with embarrassment, spurred Barbarossa into a gallop. Haakon pounded along at his side. They drew rein only when the other two were far behind.

"Sex as power. Sex as evil. Sex is sex," grunted Haakon, and William gave a brief spurt of laughter. "That's better. Why regret the having of a mistress, H.H.?"

"It seems so strange. Since I have outgrown nurses I have lived in a completely male household. Now, to experience her, it's like . . . like quicksilver and cashmere, roses and the bite of lemon. She's—"

"She's a woman."

"But is she, Lindel. Is she?"

"Does she behave like a normal one between the sheets?"

William's face was flaming again. "We've never fully consummated."

"God's blood, no wonder you feel so horrible! We'll find you a wench, lad, just as soon as we reach Nuremburg."

"I can't. I can't waste it."

"Waste it?"

"It's too embarrassing and complicated to explain."

Haakon drew his crop thoughtfully through his fingers. "Willy, are you in love with the chit?"

"I don't know. *I don't know!* She never talks to me. I know nothing of her. I'm a child to be trained and instructed." He bowed over Barbarossa's withers. "I *want* so much."

Haakon laid a hand on the young man's shoulder. "So do we all."

The prince straightened. "And only in death do we find contentment."

"Lowering thought. Is there to be no happiness in life then?"

"I think not. Each moment of joy must be paid for by a moment of equal pain."

"You Dutch merchants, always keeping the books in balance. Do you see God as an accountant?"

William smiled slightly. "If he is he's a shockingly bad one. I'm more than due for some joy."

Haakon caught Barbarossa's reins near the bit and drew the two chargers to a halt. "Then find it in the moment, H.H. Find it in the moment.

Eight

I am a thorn:
beneath the nail

"Oh Lord, spare me," murmured William, and the other guests at the table sent up a great shout of laughter.

William watched the automaton's approach with the air of a hare beset by snakes. Haakon, his face ruddy with drink and an enormous meal, clapped a hand over the bosom of the girl seated on his knee. He thrust his fingers deep within the cleft between those soft white mounds billowing above the bodice of her gown. She shrieked and landed a half-hearted box to his ears.

The automaton completed its pentagonal pattern down the long table and came to rest before the prince. With a sigh William removed the head from the stag and lifted out the chalice it contained. The chalice held enough wine to drop a sailor in his tracks. Stalling for time, the prince studied the slender sculpture of Diana seated on the stag's back, leaned in to Sagitta, and said,

"She looks like you."

"I'm somewhat better clothed," she said with asperity, eyeing the naked female figure.

"Stay in this company much longer, and you won't be."

"Drink it! *Drink it all!*" roared Graf Henry von Solms-Braunfels.

William rose and, with a nod to his host, and the gentlemen

and . . . *ladies*, tipped back his head and drained the cup in a long swallow. Cheers rocked the hall. William swayed, drew a hand across his brow, and gave them all a slight bow. More would have toppled him face-first into his plate. He settled back into his chair and, turning the automaton in his fingers, inspected the intricate movement which ran it.

"The man's a master," confided Solms-Braunfels, sending a gust of alcohol-laden breath into William's face.

"Is he a watchmaker?"

"Indeed yes."

"I confess a fascination and love for clocks."

"Why?" asked Sagitta.

"There is something so reassuring about a device which echoes the movement of stars and sun and planets."

"To seek to understand the spheres is to dull their music," said the girl softly.

"I don't agree. The better one understands, the more one can appreciate," replied William.

"God's blood, get a few drinks into the child, and he waxes philosophic," laughed Solms-Braunfels.

"The Holy Father has declared such researches to be heretical. It is not for man to invade the cosmos," said Father Armand primly.

"That's because Kepler's and Galileo's researches have revealed the error of church doctrine," shot back William.

"Untrue!"

"Then why the ban?" Armand frowned down at his plate. William waved an unsteady but admonitory finger beneath his nose. "You see, Father, you can think of no good reason. Where lies the danger in truth? I think we live in the most fantastic time since the glory of Greece. My secretary's son—Christiaan Huygens, he's in Paris right now—has done unmatched work in mathematics, and with his brother they have developed lenses of such power and clarity that it cannot be believed. I have seen the ring about Saturn . . . discovered by Huygens," the prince added with a slight belch. "I have gazed at the structure of a leaf. From the greatest to the smallest I have seen such wonders . . . such wonders."

"What magic is this?" asked one young German thickly.

"Not magic. Science. Preferable to magic."

"Oh really?" said Sagitta in a freezing tone, and William blushed.

"You yourself have said there are very few people with the talent of magic. Science is open to all."

"When knowledge ends only faith remains," said Armand.

"So we should abandon the pursuit of knowledge lest we diminish faith? That's stupid," said William belligerently.

"The simple folk of village and cottage are happier if they're not confused with things beyond their understanding," declared Sagitta.

"Sagitta, how do we *know* it's beyond their understanding?"

"Because if it weren't they wouldn't be common," cried Solms-Braunfels, and there was another shout of laughter from the table.

William clipped his lips together and turned the automaton between his fingers. Haakon leaned across the table and gave him a rap on the knuckles.

"Drink makes you dour and testy. You should avoid it."

"No, this company makes me testy," he muttered in an undertone. Pushing back his chair, he rose and bowed to Solms-Braunfels. "Graf, I thank you for your hospitality, but I find myself fatigued by my journeys and the lateness of the hour. So I will take my leave of you and see you in the morning." He spoke in German and was not surprised to see that Sagitta understood. He rather suspected that there was not a human tongue unknown to her.

She rose and shook out her skirts. "I will accompany you."

"It's not necessary."

"Nonetheless."

"Ho, ho, enjoy yourselves, children." Their host leered.

"And *that* was *precisely* what I was trying to avoid," gritted William as they left the dining room.

"Why should you care? He thinks you are a splendid fellow for possessing a mistress of such beauty and refinement." Sagitta swept him a curtsy.

She crossed the hall and pushed open a set of double doors. William followed her out onto the snow-covered balcony.

"Does it not bother you to be so categorized by a drunken, rollicking German lordling?"

She looked back, surprised. The stars formed a net for her golden head. "Why should it? It is no sin to be your mistress."

"It's no great honor either."

"Don't you think you should allow me to be the judge of that?" They locked eyes. Surprisingly hers dropped first. Sagitta walked away, trailing her hand in the snow on the balustrade.

"I thought it was just something you did. A way to waken my powers."

"It is . . ."

"I see."

"And it is more."

"What more?"

"Don't ask me that. I should be no more than teacher."

"Will your White Lady object should . . . should it prove to be more?"

"*Your* White Lady as well."

". . . Yes." And he knew she hadn't missed his hesitation.

"You are not an easy tool to fit to the hand, Willy."

"I resent the implication."

"You see what I mean."

"What do you want of me? You and your Mistress?"

Her eyes were downcast, fingers playing in the powdery snow. "Perhaps my Mistress and I do not share a complete unity of purpose where you are concerned."

He lifted her hand and chafed the tips of her fingers until they turned pink with returning circulation. "Oh?"

"I'll say no more."

"Very well." He dropped her hand. "If you won't tell me what you think, at least tell what your terrible queen requires."

"That you halt this menace which threatens us all."

"I'm doing my level best. I study with you to the detriment of my health. I have come as a thief, albeit a royal one, to Nuremburg. What more do you want?"

"A sense that you have given yourself over totally to us. That you embrace my Lady, and will serve her unquestioningly."

"It's not in me to serve anyone unquestioningly, Sagitta. I'm sorry," he added, at her evident distress. "I can't be aught than I am."

She briefly dropped her face into her hands. "And what you are is admirable . . ."

"But?" She looked inquiringly back at him. "I hear the but even though you do not speak it."

"William, this mechanistic way is not the proper path. My

Mistress is the representation of all living things. One lives in harmony with her. One does not seek to tear her mysteries from her."

"Sagitta, I cannot believe that your Lady is a proponent of ignorance. If she is, then where lies the difference between her and the foe we oppose? Both would represent death."

"No, no, she is—"

He swayed and caught himself on the balustrade. "Oh, please, I'm too tired and fuddled with drink to continue this debate."

"Would you to bed?"

"Aye, and let them," he jerked his head back toward the dining room, "envy me my beautiful and refined mistress."

They awakened to the sound of weeping. Sagitta's leg was a warm weight across his thigh, and her hair filled his mouth. William sat up, raked away the clinging strands, and realized, when full consciousness had returned, that the crying had stopped.

"What?"

"You didn't hear it with your ears." She was scrambling from the high-canopied bed, wrapping a sheet about her body.

"*What*?"

"It must be the priest. He is the only one to whom we are both attuned."

William groped for his shirt, slid his sword from his scabbard, and padded after her. The floor was burning cold beneath his bare feet.

"Wait!" William ordered, as Sagitta laid a hand on the knob.

He stepped past her, turned the knob, and shoved open the door. Nothing emerged, and he relaxed from his tense *en garde*. Armand's moans were loud in the frigid darkness. Propping his sword against one of the beveled posts supporting the bed's canopy, William leaned in on the thrashing priest.

"Father! Armand! Wake up."

The Frenchman came upright with a terrified cry. One flailing hand struck Sagitta. She gripped it and chafed the chilled fingers.

"Hush, you're safe now. Willy and I are here."

He buried his face in his hands, shoulders heaving. "Oh God preserve me."

"What did you see?" demanded the girl.

William glared at her. "Give him a moment. Can't you see he's mad with fear?"

"His power is to show us the future. Your life may depend upon what he sees, and how we respond to his visions."

"*No!*" The single word seemed to ring in the darkened room. "I'll have no part of these spells and magics." Armand ripped his hand from Sagitta's grasp.

"You have no choice, Father, they come to you unbidden. Wouldn't it be better to have control over them?" asked Sagitta.

"No, I shall drive them out," he panted.

"How? With a hair shirt and a scourge? Fasting and prayer? If you tore out eyes and tongue you would no longer be able to tell of your visions, but they would haunt you within the confines of your skull. Only death will release you, and even that is no promise of peace when you walk our paths." Her tone was harsh, biting.

"I know. I know," Armand groaned. "Hell is beckoning me. I will spend eternity damned."

Sagitta shook back her hair in irritation. "I'm not speaking of that fairy tale known as heaven and hell. I'm speaking of the dead walking." Armand recoiled and crossed himself, and William found himself offering up a quick prayer. "Father, what did you see?" Her small hands gripped his shoulders, and she gave him a slight shake to punctuate each word.

"Stop it, woman, you're scaring him half to death." William pulled her hands from the priest. "Father, you need not speak if it distresses you."

"He can help!"

"Let him help to the limits of his strength, and in ways which are pleasing to him. What good is forced service in a cause like ours?"

Sagitta threw her hands in the air, made a sound like an enraged kitten, and flounced away. Her dignified retreat was somewhat marred when her trailing sheet tangled about her feet. She stumbled, the sheeting pulling down to her waist. With an oath she yanked it over her breasts.

"Your Highness was sleeping upon a stone," said Armand slowly. "And there were black birds circling. Someone was weeping. That's all I remember."

"That's all right." William stroked the hair off the priest's forehead. "Go back to sleep."

Armand's hand shot out and grasped William by the wrist. "I will not do this again."

"I understand. That's fine."

"You can't stop the visions," snapped Sagitta.

"I can keep them to myself. I should have done this in Paris, then I would not now be traveling with—" He folded his lips, stopping the flow of words, but William could provide any number of possible endings to the sentence.

"Father, I don't believe I'm evil."

"You are a Dutch heretic."

"True, but not, I think, a devil." William rubbed at his tail bone and glanced down at his feet. "No sign of tail or hooves yet."

That drew a small smile from the priest. "No, my son, I think you are only misguided. I will pray for your soul, and your conversion."

"All men need prayers, but a conversion?" William shook his head. "Unlikely. Now sleep. Tomorrow I will need your help exploring the St. Lorenz Church and deciding how to obtain the Spear."

"That you will carry such a sacred object comforts me, sir, and to that end I will aid you."

"Thank you. Good night."

"Absurd," snapped Sagitta as they stepped back into the corridor. "He'll be a thief, but not a mystic."

"You play games with words. You're not asking him to be a mystic, you're asking him to use magic."

She blushed, closed her teeth briefly on her lower lip, then shot him a challenging glance and said, "And as for conversions, you're not even a Christian anymore."

He froze. "*I most certainly am!*"

"You're not!"

"I am!"

"You serve my Lady, who is a goddess."

"I *serve* her. I don't worship her."

She elevated her small, tipped-up nose. "There is *no* difference."

"There is to me," bellowed William. Sagitta stalked away,

trailing the sheet as a queen trails ermine. "And one could argue that I'm doing her a big favor."

"She saved your life!"

William charged after her. "I'm saving the world."

"Because *she* asked you to."

Gripping her shoulder the prince spun her around. "Because *she* can't do it herself!"

They were nose to nose, lips compressed, bodies shaking with anger. Suddenly Sagitta gripped his head and pressed a hard kiss onto his mouth. He tried to resist her, but his mouth softened and their tongues fenced. He almost forgot the bitter cold creeping up his legs, and his numb toes.

"It was a foolish fight," whispered William into her fragrant hair.

"You're not a Christian."

"Don't start."

"The chancel screen is carved in rosewood and details the temptation of Christ. The work was overseen by an Italian, Giani Batiste, in 1132, and is considered to be the finest example of his work. Passing through, we see the high altar."

Armand glanced surreptitiously at Sagitta. She was looking particularly fetching in a red dress with gold embroidered banding. The white underskirt held a pattern of snowflakes, as did her white lace collar. The hood of a white wool cloak framed her lovely face.

"I will not wail away in a puff of sulfurous smoke, nor be struck to salt," she growled at him, and he had the grace to blush.

"Forgive me, verger, but I am especially anxious to view the treasure house," interrupted William. "I am told St. Lorenz contains many sacred objects."

"Oh yes, indeed yes. If you will follow me."

They crossed the transept of the church, Armand and the verger, Herr Kress, pausing to genuflect deeply before the altar. William inclined his head politely. Haakon's fingers beat out an impatient tattoo on the hilt of his rapier. A single pillar with a chiseled Tabernacle rose to support the choir superstructure. Armand stopped and lightly touched the stone, then swayed and would have fallen but for a quick grab by Sagitta.

"Fire from the skies. So much will be destroyed. This alone will save this church," he muttered.

Sagitta cast a nervous glance at the supercilious verger, but he and William and Haakon were already starting down the stairs into the crypt.

"Hush. Are you so anxious to be burned?"

The soft brown eyes slowly refocused, and he gasped, "Dear God, I've never had a waking vision before."

"Let me teach you control before it is too late. Please, Father, I beg you."

He removed her hand with fastidious fingertips. "No."

"You're such a *fool*," she called bitterly after him.

The door to the treasure house was propped open with a heavy brick. Inside a priest copied lists; he spared the visitors a single bored glance. On the desk before him rested a two-foot-long key that looked to weigh twenty or thirty pounds. Slowly the travelers circled the room while the verger pointed out a vial of Mary's milk, plate and chalices of gold and silver overlay, a finger reliquary containing the finger of John the Baptist, and finally, in the midst of all this gleaming clutter, an iron spearhead, black with age, resting in a leather-bound case.

William, his stone face securely in place, spared it only a glance and passed on. Haakon paused to gape, and Sagitta threaded her arm through his and urged him on.

"A little less obvious, please."

"Will you distract that yammering fool," said the soldier, with a nod to the verger. "I need to talk to H.H."

"Yes?" asked William, bending low to eye with repulsed fascination an arm reliquary.

"Have you looked at that door? That monster must be two feet thick, and a lock on it like an elephant's asshole. We're also *below* ground, so we can't knock out a wall."

"Just as well . . . might be a little noisy."

"So how are we going to get this thing?"

William smiled at the verger and muttered in French from the corner of his mouth. "I don't know."

Thirty minutes more, and they escaped from their eager guide. The sun was out sparkling on the layer of ice crystals which had formed on the snow. Their boots crunched loudly, mingling with the cries of sellers in the market, the screams and shouts of children, and the jangle of bit and harness as coaches and wagons rumbled past.

They stopped at a tavern across from the Nassau-house. Haakon teasingly asked if they were relatives, and William shortly replied "undoubtedly." The Norwegian's suggestion that they stop by for a visit drew frowns, and he subsided into his flagon of beer. A plate of sizzling sausages was ordered, Armand shuddering expressively at the mounds of sauerkraut which accompanied them.

"So, what do we do?" asked Haakon.

"The treasure house is locked at night. I thought to ask," said Armand virtuously.

"Steal it by day?" suggested William, his mouth twisting on the word "steal" as if it tasted bad.

"There's always a monk on duty in there," said Sagitta. "That *I* thought to ask."

"Ask for it?" asked Haakon. "Tell them the good father here" —a hard dig in the ribs—"is supposed to take it to Rome for some damn reason or another?"

"No, no." William massaged his temples.

Silence lay over the table.

"We got to piss in a quill sooner or later," grunted Haakon.

"I'm thinking. I'm thinking."

"So what are we going to do?"

"You keep asking that."

"It is the pertinent question, is it not?" After a suitable interval had elapsed Haakon added: "I don't suppose you two could just magic the door open?"

"No," said Sagitta. "The Lady's magic doesn't work on cold metal or mechanical devices. Which is why we disapprove of them," she added in a sharp aside to William.

"The door is wood," said Haakon, tamping tobacco into his white clay pipe.

"And bound by metal," Sagitta replied repressively.

"Remove the lock, the door opens," said William.

"Are you planning to saw through that monster? We'll be there until winter passes into summer, and the good fathers may notice."

"No, we'll burn through it," replied William, and a spark leaped from his fingertips into the bowl of Haakon's pipe.

* * *

A burst of boozy song echoed down from the sacristy.

"I only hope our little father can get out of there under his own power," whispered Haakon as he stood guard at the end of the long hall leading to the treasury.

William, his face tight with concentration, ignored him. A tiny tendril of smoke drifted from a point just to the left of the lock. Stretching out a hand William coaxed it like a snake charmer. It thickened and lengthened. Sagitta, resting her hands on his shoulders, added her power to his, and a spot the size of a guilder began to glow like an ember.

The glow ate its way deeper into the wood, and William cautiously led it around the lock.

"God's teeth!" ejaculated Haakon. William jumped, and the flame collided with the lock and died. Acrid smoke rose from the seared wood, blackening William's and Sagitta's faces and setting them to coughing. William staggered to his feet, eyes streaming, and unlimbered his sword.

"What are you doing?" asked the soldier.

"What is it? What startled you? Someone coming?"

"No, no." Haakon sheepishly pointed up. "I just heard the bawdiest refrain it's ever been my pleasure to listen to. Everything they say about monks must be true."

"You interrupted me for that?"

"You didn't have to listen."

"I thought something was wrong!"

Haakon jerked a thumb over his shoulder. "Get back to work."

A torrent of Latin profanity poured from William's lips as he stormed back to the door. Haakon folded his hands piously on the hilt of his rapier and rolled his eyes heavenward.

"God will be no more pleased with profanity—"

"You cannot convince me that you speak Latin."

He grinned. "I know a cuss word when I hear one."

"Haakon, go to hell and pump thunder."

Forty minutes later the lock dropped out into Sagitta's hands. It weighed more than she expected, and with a clang like a tolling bell it hit the stone floor. All three conspirators froze. There was the sound of an interrogative from upstairs. Armand's breathless reply. The singing resumed.

"Would one of you *move it* and get that thing?" hissed Haakon.

William, using the door for support, pulled himself to his feet and tugged on the door. It didn't budge. Gasping, he rested his cheek against the rough wood, and dashed away tears of weakness and vexation.

"Haakon, I can't. So tired." Deep wheezes punctuated each word.

Haakon ran to them, fanning away smoke with his hand. In the close quarters beneath the church the smoke hung like a funeral pall. Heaving open the door, he darted into the treasury and swept up the Spear.

Juggling the case in one arm and his rapier in the other, the soldier dithered between the two magicians. "Which one of you gets this?"

"Give it to His Highness." Sagitta was slumped on the steps leading into the treasury.

"I hope one of you can walk, because I can't carry both of you and the damn magic gimcrack as well."

"Magic," muttered William, swaying as he stood. "Really takes it out of you."

Haakon caught him as he fell. "Wonderful. Then what the devil good is—"

The urgent frustrated whisper died in his throat at the sound of approaching footsteps. Armand's voice drifted down to them, pleading and cajoling.

"There's fully half a bottle left. Why leave the fire and come down here to shiver our—"

"I tell you I heard something," slurred the monk.

"Quickly," hissed Haakon, and led the stumbling Sagitta among the sarcophagi in the crypt. "He's going to spot the door. And then the Spear, or rather he *won't* spot the Spear, and then we're well and truly in shit."

Haakon laid William and the Spear behind a tomb. He eyed the effigy figure sleeping for eternity in stone.

"Smoke! Do you smell it, Father? 'Tis plaguy uncanny. A fire in a church of stone."

Sagitta whimpered. The monk, with Father Armand still expostulating, drew near.

Suddenly Haakon arranged himself on top of a sarcophagus, rapier in hand. Then, with a hair-raising wail, he sat bolt upright, slid to the ground, and advanced on the horror-struck priests swinging his rapier and sobbing hysterically.

With a scream of terror the monk bolted for the stairs with Armand in close pursuit. Haakon plunged after them and caught the Frenchman by his soutane.

"Quickly, while we've the chance."

"*You!*"

"Of course. You don't really believe in ghosts, do you?" The soldier's teeth gleamed white in the darkness.

Armand jerked a thumb toward the stairway, and the sound of rapidly retreating footsteps. "He'll raise the alarm."

"We've got time. He won't stop running until he reaches the bishop's palace in Cologne." Haakon chuckled.

"And when they smell the wine on his breath they'll take it for a foolish dream," added Sagitta weakly, clinging to a pillar.

Armand crossed himself. "I have ruined a good man."

"You have helped us with a necessary task," Sagitta replied.

"God forgive me."

"Here." Haakon thrust the Spear of Longinus into the priest's arms. "Carry this. Maybe it will make you feel better."

"His Highness?" gasped the priest, noticing for the first time William's absence.

Haakon retrieved the prince from behind the tomb, slinging him over one shoulder. "Exhausted, no more. Now come, we must be ready to exclaim at the uncanny doings of this night over Solms-Braunfels's breakfast table."

They reached the street unobserved, but once out of St. Lorenz, Armand stumbled to a halt. Throwing back his head he cried, "Oh, Father, I am so confused. I do evil, but for a noble cause. Is this reason enough for my actions?"

"Father." Haakon gripped him by the upper arm. "Don't agonize. We don't have time for it. Or at least don't agonize here. And remember, there are those on our tails who do evil for an evil cause. Who would you rather have the Spear?"

Nine

I am a tide:
that drags to death

Icy water dripped onto his face. Haakon opened his eyes and stared aghast into the dead-white face of the thing crawling through the window of the river barge. Lank hair hung dripping on its bare shoulders. Its eyes were shark-gray smeared with a white film.

The Norwegian screamed in terror and flung himself off the bunk. The corpselike thing landed on his back, clinging with a horrifying strength. Haakon lumbered about the tiny cabin, cracking his head on the beams overhead, slamming his unearthly attacker against the walls. Its grip on his throat tightened. He plunged up the ladder onto the deck. The sleepy boy nodding at the tiller let out a howl and flung himself overboard. The soldier's eyes widened as a clawlike hand gripped the gunwale, and another drowned corpse pulled itself onto the barge.

Merchants, sleeping by their wares, awakened, stared in consternation at the deadly fight, and ran for the rails.

Haakon gasped, "Would somebody *help*! I'm in a little trouble here." His voice emerged as a barely discernible croak. Black spots danced before his eyes.

William erupted onto the deck and drove his sword into the creature's back. It snarled, drained a foul-smelling black substance onto the deck, and continued to cling like a limpet to Haakon's back. Sagitta, flames dancing on her fingertips, raced up the ladder.

"*No!*" screamed William.

She flung the fireball, then gasped when she realized what she had done. William gathered some snowflakes, formed them

100

into a blanket, and flung the glittering creation over the fire. It died in a hiss inches from Haakon.

"I'm sorry. I'm sorry," she screamed.

"What do we do?" the prince screamed back.

"What ever it is could you please do it fast?" croaked Haakon.

Two more creatures climbed aboard. Sagitta bowled them over with a fireball. The captain of the barge stuck his head through the hatch, screamed, and fled once more below. William, racing down the ladder, sent the man sprawling. He ran unceremoniously across the captain's broad back and into his cubbyhole of a cabin, and ripped the Spear from its case and raced back on deck. Haakon had dropped to his knees. Sagitta was weaving a net of flame about her slender body. Once more she flung fire at Haakon, and William cried out in dismay.

The drowned thing died with a ghastly sizzle, and Haakon lumbered to his feet. William gaped.

"Silly, silly. Magic can't hurt him, remember?" Sagitta laughed wildly.

"Look out!"

William leaped past her and drove the Spear into the side of a new attacker. Real blood gushed from the wound. The creature sighed as if in relief. For an instant William saw the face of the girl it had been, and then it was gone.

Swinging wildly William charged across the deck. Each time he connected, red blood spurted and the thing vanished. But the prince felt as if it was his blood which was being given to free the souls of these damned creatures. His knees wobbled, and he doubled over, catching himself on the knuckles of his left hand.

Haakon ran up, rubbing at his throat and coughing.

"Here, give it to me!" He grabbed the Spear and with a mighty swing hewed the head off one creature. It kept coming. Haakon goggled from Spear to creature and back again.

"You can't use it," shouted Sagitta. Her hair hung like witch-locks about her face, and she looked like a mad woman. "It resonates only with the prince."

"Scheisse."

From behind them they heard a frenzied muttering—Father Armand, rattling off prayers. The creatures were unimpressed. William lurched to his feet, snatched back the Spear, and staggered once more into the battle. The deck was burning where

Sagitta's arcing fire had landed. Smoke and snow blended in a blinding curtain. The horses, tethered at the stern of the barge, were screaming and plunging in terror.

Nails like a hawk's talons bit deep into William's thigh, and he screamed and fell back. Green pus bubbled from the wounds, and a burning agony shot up his leg and into his groin. The prince cursed, swung, and lopped off the hand. Red gore was added to the bilious green poison staining his leg.

A final swing, and the last creature died. William dropped the Spear and, holding himself, collapsed to the deck writhing in agony. Sagitta stumbled to him and fell on her knees at his side.

"*What the hell were those?*" bellowed Haakon, jerking like a maddened marionette as he tried to keep a watch in all directions.

Sagitta ripped off a long piece of her petticoat and tied it tightly about William's upper thigh.

"What can I do to help?" asked the priest, dropping down at her side.

"I must have hot water and a knife. The poison . . ."

"Mary, Joseph, and Jesus!" muttered Haakon. He seized a bucket and began dousing fires. With a soft bump the bow of the barge ran into the bank, and they stopped. "Where is that cowardly captain?" He stomped away.

"I'll return shortly," said Sagitta, smoothing back William's hair.

"Am I dying?"

"No. I won't let you."

She ran below and unearthed her crystal knife, a needle, and some stout thread. The priest was on deck when she returned. Steam curled from the surface of the water in a pewter basin.

"You must hold him down."

"Wait," called Haakon. He shoved the trembling German bargemen toward the tiller, then hurried to where the horses' tack lay piled. He cut off a length of rein.

"Bite on this," he instructed William shortly. The prince's dark eyes were wide with fear.

"Strip him," ordered Sagitta curtly, laving her hands in the steaming water.

"You hold his legs, Father, I'll hold his shoulders," said Haakon, tossing the blood-and-pus-stained breeches over the side.

Sagitta fished her knife from the water. It flashed down. William groaned and fainted. With more strips torn from her petticoat the girl cleaned the wound with hot water. When the blood at last ran clean she poured brandy into the wound and sewed it closed.

She brushed back her wet, matted bangs with a trembling hand and noted the priest staring at his palms. She crawled to him and pulled his hands down. The soft skin of his palms was red and blistered.

"What did you do?"

"I didn't think. I lifted the basin directly from the galley fire."

"And continued to carry it?" asked Haakon.

The priest looked at William. "For his sake."

"Poor hands." Sagitta bent and kissed each palm. Embarrassed, Armand drew them away. "Haakon, carry H.H. below. Father, I have an ointment for your hands."

"And then?" asked the priest.

She sighed. "And then we must make some hard decisions."

Even after they had left the barge and taken accommodations in a Mainz posting house, the debate continued.

"It is now more imperative then ever that we reach London," argued the sorceress. "The second talisman must be obtained."

"Look at him! He can scarcely walk. How is he to ride?" demanded Haakon.

"Don't discuss me as if I'm not present," said William wearily.

Haakon turned on the priest. "Father, help me to convince this mad woman."

Armand seated himself on the bed next to the prince. "Sire, what do *you* want to do?" Sagitta and Haakon exchanged glances and had the grace to blush.

William's dark eyes were on Sagitta. "I know time is of the essence. But I'll do your Mistress little good if I die. I must have rest." Deep wheezes punctuated each word.

"Where? Where can we be safe?"

"Nowhere," snapped Sagitta, and took a nervous turn about their room.

"I have relatives littered all across Germany," said William with a wan smile. "In some public court they're not as like to come upon us. Thus we can make our slow way home."

"*Home!* May I remind you they tried to kill you at home," said Sagitta.

"True, but that was then, and this is now, and the situation has changed. Now I *know* they are trying to kill me, and I have the three of you to guard me, not to mention Hans, and Baruch, and John Maurice, and—"

"I think we get the point," sighed Haakon.

Mazarin sat within a circle of mirrors. On one silvered surface was reflected the delicate features of Henriette-Anne, Duchesse d'Orleans, and Charles II's best-loved sister. In another reclined the languid mistress of King Louis, Françoise de Montespan.

"All is in train, Madame, for your journey to England?" asked the sorcerous cardinal.

"Indeed yes, though my husband was loath to let me go."

"Monsieur must realize that *my* bidding takes precedence over his sulks and tantrums. And the treaty?" asked Mazarin, pulling himself from irritated contemplation of the sodomite brother of the king.

"Charles will sign."

"Excellent."

The prelate shifted to another mirror, where the fat, dissipated features of George Villiers, Duke of Buckingham, gazed out. Seated next to him was a lush, overblown woman who wore her sexuality like a revealing gown.

"The Prince of Orange makes his slow way toward The Hague. He will find the letter waiting?"

"Indeed yes. I urged the King to write it myself, and stood by as he did so."

"Then Orange will soon reach you."

"We'll be ready," promised Buckingham.

"But our weapon must be readied. Call the circles for tonight. It is time the good father suffered some prophetic dreams. Let the white bitch think she has defeated us by her feeble wards about the prince and the girl, and by selecting a blockhead as paladin, we—"

"We shall slip below and sow betrayal within their midst." Barbara Villiers laughed, setting the tiny dark curls falling across her high forehead to jiggling. Mazarin frowned at the interruption.

"Orange has obtained the first talisman. He must not obtain the second."

"He won't," grunted Buckingham. "You may depend upon it."

"Good. I don't find disappointment to be an agreeable emotion."

The hushed and sacred interior of St. Peter's Basilica. Sagitta dancing a slow and languid measure before the altar. William, kneeling humbly, head bowed in prayer. The music quickening, taking on Moorish overtones. Sagitta shedding clothes like a tree losing leaves. William, his fair face twisted with lust, ripping off his own attire. They copulate like animals atop the altar. Flames rise about them, stones crack and fall. Sagitta, mouth stretched in wide, frenzied laughter as the dome of the basilica falls.

Armand awoke screaming . . . swept back his sweat-matted hair . . . pulled the chamber pot from beneath the bed and retched desperately.

They will destroy the true faith.
But the Holy Mother bade me seek and join with them.
So which is the true vision?
The priest slept no more that night.

Sleigh bells rang in the night. Spinoza closed his book and hurried to the window. Torchlight splashed across the glass. He lived in one room on the top floor of Hendrik van der Spyck's house, and he had to crane to peer down into the snowy street. A great party of armed men and horses stamped and swirled about a large sleigh. Fear took him. Had it been discovered that he had helped the prince to escape? Had the Netherlands abruptly renounced their tolerance of the Hebrew race?

There was furious knocking on his door. Squaring his shoulders he stepped through the clutter of books, papers, and lenses, and threw wide the door. And was nearly bowled over by a small missile masquerading as the Prince of Orange. The youth landed on his chest, hugging him fiercely.

"Highness. Great God, what have you been about?" Spinoza said, noting the prince's wan face and sunken eyes.

William limped to a chair. "I've been ill."

"I apprehend that."

"Come to the palace. I've so much to tell you."

"This winter weather is terrible for my consumptive lungs—"

"Not to worry," boomed Haakon. "We've enough furs to keep you toasty all the way to Norway."

"Who the devil are you?"

"Haakon Lindel," said the prince. "He saved my life in the North Sea."

"Then you're back from England."

"I never got there." William opened his mouth, closed it again, considered. "It really is a long story. Come to the palace."

"I suppose I shall have to. I may die of consumption, but if I don't go I shall surely die of curiosity."

Out in the street Spinoza realized that the troops were the personal guard of Prince John Maurice of Nassau. The old man himself rode with them, Bentinck at his side. A dainty little lady was curled in the furs in the sleigh.

"Heer Spinoza, I've heard so much about you."

"Good God."

"I took your advice," said William.

"What?"

"You know, natural science."

"Good God!"

"And my dear friend Father Armand du Lac." William indicated the priest. He was a mound beneath a pile of furs, with only his plump face showing.

"Good God!"

"Since your induction as First Nobel of Zeeland last year you have taken upon yourself adult responsibilities. Your grandmother has formally ended your minority, so it is time that you took over the management of your household and private estates."

Johan de Witt's tone was dry and precise, but William was accustomed to the style. De Witt had taken his responsibilities toward his "ward of state" very seriously, and had spent a portion of each day with the prince since the boy was fifteen. Irksome to the prince, but perhaps proof, mused William, as he sifted through the piles of correspondence on his desk, that the Raadspensionary had not been behind the poisoning attempt.

"Your grandmother, whatever her other virtues, is not a manager. The books are in a hopeless state, debtors remain unpaid, King Charles owes your house a vast sum, and the King of Spain has yet to make a payment against the loan made to his father. That sum now stands at several million—"

"My uncle Charles has invited me to visit."

All conversation ceased in the busy office.

"What?" asked de Witt.

"I shall go," said William. Haakon's eyes met his for a brief but intense moment.

"I would prefer that you not," said the Raadspensionary.

"Your protest is noted."

Bentinck burst out. "*He* doesn't want you to go because he wants no reminder of the close ties between families of Orange and Stuart. The fact that you are a Prince of the Blood Royal." De Witt flushed. "*I* say nay also, but for love of you, Highness. Consider, your mother, and the Queen of Bohemia, both died within a few months of going to that evil country. Poison, mayhap—"

William met this outburst unmoved and unimpressed. "Hans, one can meet poison . . . anywhere." Bentinck's mouth shut with an audible click.

The Queen of Heaven, the blue of her mantle like a summer's sky. She smiled gently down upon him. He fell at her feet. Bending she cupped his face between her hands. Kissed him. She now wore Sagitta's face. Suddenly she was naked, and she pulled his face between her legs. And rottenness poured from her womb. Gagging, Armand fell back.

He was running down endless passages seeking the prince. To warn him. He found William in Haakon's arms. The prince smiled, and beckoned to him. Armand fled.

Shivering, the priest rose and splashed water on his heated face. He had seen little of William since their return to The Hague. William had been gentle but firm—while his supporters were agitating for him to be given place in the Council of State it would not do for him to be too familiar with a Roman priest. The Netherlands were liberal—but there were limits. Sagitta slept in his bed, Haakon rode at his side, but for Armand there was no place.

The priest dressed and made his way through the corridors of the old palace. And was nearly bowled over by Sagitta hurrying past with a coat clutched in her hands. Armand shrank back against the wall. Sagitta took another few hurried steps, then stopped and looked inquiringly back at him.

"Is aught amiss, little father?"

"No." Visions of her naked body suddenly danced before him. "*No!*"

She held up a placating hand. "All right." Another step, but she paused again. "Are you quite sure?"

"Yes."

"I can't stay. William wears this coat today, and it had been torn."

"Today?"

"He makes his first entrance into the Council."

"I'll return to my room."

"No, come." She took his hand, her eyebrows rising in surprise as he quickly snatched it back. "I know he wishes to see you."

"Now that I am no longer a threat to him."

"Expediency is the god of princes, you must know that."

"Then they blaspheme."

"Armand, I'm out of time."

He shrugged and followed her.

William, his chin pointed toward the ceiling, jigged with impatience as his valet struggled to tie his cravat.

"You damn fool! How shall I speak when you tie it so tight?" He dealt the man a ringing slap on the ear.

"Steady. Easy," warned Spinoza.

"I beg your pardon," William forced out. The valet bowed.

The room seemed filled with people. Haakon, a foot resting negligently on a chair, watched with some amusement. Sir Constantine Huygens, the prince's secretary, was shuffling nervously through the sheets containing His Highness's maiden speech, while his son, Constantine the Younger, looked gloomily on. Bentinck was reverently laying out William's orders of knighthood: the Garter, the Danish Order of the Elephant, and the Cross of the Knights of Malta.

There was a knock.

"Come," shouted Haakon, and van Gent entered.

He swept a bow to William. "You sent for me, sir?"

"Yes." William shrugged into the coat which Sagitta held for him. "You're sacked."

"Wha . . . what?"

"You heard me. I expect to have you out of my house by the time I return."

"But . . . but you can't."

"I just have."

"I'm your governor."

"I've attained my majority. I do not require a governor." He turned his back on the gasping van Gent.

"Johan de Witt will hear of this!"

"I'm sure he will." The man left. "God's blood, I'm in a foul mood today," William said suddenly, and with an embarrassed smile.

Spinoza ruffled his hair. "It's the prerogative of princes."

"You are quite sure you won't accompany me to England?"

"Quite sure. You will cause quite enough comment without including the dreadful atheist Jew." He cast a humorous glance at Sagitta and Armand.

The priest stepped forward in surprise. "Then I am to accompany you?"

William took him by the shoulders. "Of course. I must have my chosen companions. I have not forgotten my duty in the midst of all this political maneuvering."

"Mission? Duty?" asked Huygens, his nose twitching rather like an observant rabbit's. The old man loved gossip and intrigue better than almost all else.

"To serve God and protect my nation," said William glibly.

"Worthy goals," grunted Haakon. "But now we must serve a sterner master."

"Which is?" asked William.

"The passing time. Have you primped enough? Are you ready?"

"I was not primping, and yes, I'm ready."

The party swept out, and Father Armand fell into step with the younger Huygens.

He said cautiously, "His Highness has certainly been raised in an exclusively male household."

"Yes," the man replied, with a sideways glance at the priest.

Armand paused, feeling his way delicately. "Is there . . . resentment over the presence of Mistress Sagitta?"

"There are certainly some pretty boys who were sorry to see her come," drawled the young man.

"I see. Then His Highness . . ."

"Seems to enjoy a good deal of private time with handsome soldiers such as your friend Lindel."

Armand dropped back. Perhaps his nightmares were not mere phantoms of a disturbed mind, but true visions after all. And if such were the case. . . . He wrenched his mind from a contemplation of evil, and what he might do to stand against it.

It had been a foul crossing, but at last the coast of England lay gray green and misty before them. William, wrapped in a cloak and with Haakon's arm draped over his shoulder, stared expressionless at the approaching shore.

"What are you thinking?"

"That my mother died in yonder country."

"Premonitions, or did Hans get to you?"

"Neither, just reflecting. I think she always loved my uncle more than me. And she certainly loved England over Holland. I shall now see if that fascination works its spell on me, or if I shall remain as I have lived—a Dutchman to my core."

"Bentinck's very jealous of me," said Haakon, in an abrupt change of topic.

"I know. I do what I can, but you are my paladin, and knowledgeable of the world beyond the seen. I cannot involve my sweet Hans."

"Do you also, perhaps, like me just a little for my own sake?"

"Oh Haakon, can you doubt it! In truth I love thee well."

"Just wanted to hear it. You're a far cry from the half-drowned stripling I pulled out of the waves aboard that tumbling old scow. Now I travel in a princely retinue with a hundred retainers, and I go to meet a king."

"Charles is a good man, and I remember him with fondness, though it has been nigh on ten years since last I saw him."

Then, with a flash of that pragmatism which delighted or repelled so many of his followers, the prince added, "Though I hope the matter of his debt to me may be resolved. My family paid to place my Uncle Charles once more upon his throne. I hope he understands that my princely house is in so great a need that without payment I shall be hard-pressed to subsist."

"Let Sagitta bearjaw him. I swear that girl could send the dead in flight. Damn, what a tongue she has!"

"And I take it you've been receiving the rough side of it?"

"A minor spat. She thinks I'm not serious enough."

The prince laid a hand against his cheek. "You're not, and I bless you for it. Sometimes I long for relaxation, and an end to tension. She never stops reminding me that the fate of the world rests upon my shoulders. God's eyes, I find the fate of Holland almost too much to bear." He turned and looked up into Haakon's weathered face. "Certainly I bear too heavy a burden, one that my shoulders are not strong enough to carry—and without God's amazing help I know well that I should succumb."

"Ah, but which God? The Catholic God or the Protestant God? Or is he actually God*dess*? I confess my theology is all at sixes and sevens since we began this mad adventure."

"I remain true to my faith."

"Despite all this magic?"

"I reconcile it."

"I'd love to hear how—if you can convince me, you've the precision and slippery reasoning of a Jesuit. But I wish you'd talk with Armand a bit more about God and all that rot. Include him in your devotions."

"Why?"

"He's been plaguy long-faced recently."

"I doubt he would attend a Calvinist service."

"Invite him anyway."

"What's worrying you?"

"I don't know. I'm just concerned."

"Perhaps Sagitta was too quick to deem you head-blind."

"I hope to God I am. All this magic gives me the headache, and the only remedy for the headache is copious amounts of ale and schnapps. If you turn me into a sorcerer you turn me into a drunkard."

Thomas Butler, Earl of Ossory, who had been sent to escort William to England, came on deck, and Haakon and the prince's private moment was over.

They passed the night at a posting inn in Rochester, and the next day boarded the royal barge and began the slow voyage up the river. William had buried Sagitta and Armand among his retinue, but the girl stood out like an exotic lily in a field of pedestrian daisies, and the priest was a source for much muttering. William put about that the Frenchman had been retained as an auxiliary secretary to old Huygens, and was further an expert on matters concerning art, and had been brought along to advise the prince on any purchases he might desire to make. William then prayed that no one would engage the priest in an artistic discussion, for Armand couldn't tell a Holbein from a Rubens, and would soon be unmasked.

At Whitehall Stairs William was received with the honors due a Prince of the Blood, and found it a heady experience. From powerless schoolboy and virtual prisoner to Stuart prince in seven short months. But he was not lost to all caution despite the warmth of the reception. He kept his wards firmly in place and scanned the crowd of welcoming nobles for any agents of unearthly power.

He was then conducted with great ceremony into the presence of his uncle, Charles II of England. A hush fell over the assembled courtiers as William knelt to kiss his uncle's hand. But Charles rose, and raised up the young man.

They made an odd contrast as they stood side by side beneath the royal canopy. William, inches shorter than the lanky Charles, was dressed elegantly but soberly in a suit of white with orange ribbons, his orders flashing on his breast. Set against this was the brilliance of the king's red suit, picked out with blue ribbons and a great blue sash pinned with a number of glittering honors. His jet-black wig, curling black mustache, and saturnine features dimmed William, making the Dutch prince seem very young and rather colorless by comparison.

Then Charles, with tears sparkling in his brilliant black eyes, kissed and embraced William many times, like a father greeting a long-absent son. A great cheer shook the assembled nobles of England and Holland.

It was an auspicious beginning.

So Haakon figured there was only one direction for things to go—straight to hell.

Ten

I am a wind: *on a deep lake*

"Odd's fish, sir! Will you come poaching upon a king's preserve?"

William, walking across the bedewed grass from the stables toward the palace, heard his uncle's voice roaring out. There was a sharp rasp as a window was thrown open, and a young man came leaping out, his clothes clutched to his bare chest. He crashed through a grape arbor and landed hard on his side.

William drew back, shocked and more than a little curious, and shocked by his own curiosity. Becoming suddenly concerned for the bare-assed leaper, the prince ran to him and touched one heaving shoulder. A merry face, bright red from the gentleman's efforts not to laugh aloud, was turned up to him.

Charles thrust his head from the window. "Ho, nevvy, seen you an ill-favored rogue lacking in clothes just recently emerged from this window?"

William glanced at the young man whose luminous blue eyes were both wide with alarm and sparkling with mischief. His blond hair lay tumbled over his shoulders, and his square, manly face was the handsomest William had ever seen. The man held a finger to his lips. William hesitated for an instant, realized the man was shielded by the leaves of the arbor, then called,

"Nay, uncle, I've seen no *ill*-favored rogues."

"Hmmph." The window slammed shut.

"My thanks." The young man hopped on one foot, pulling on

his long stockings. "Well, I'm safe now. Old Rowley will be exercising the weapons of love, and have no time to search for an errant soldier." He held out a hand. "John Churchill of the King's Regiment of Foot Guards."

"William, Prince of Orange."

"Oh Lud!" cried Churchill, pressing a hand dramatically to his heart.

"I won't tattle."

"You surprise me. You seem such a sobersides. Rochester has even writ a poem to your graveness." Seeing William's frown he hastened to add, "I intend no disrespect, sir. Indeed, some argue that this merry court needs a few more men of serious and honorable mien."

"Mien?" asked William, his grasp of English not being sufficient to this word.

"Uh, face? Manner?"

"*Je comprends*," said William, switching to French.

The young Churchill asked in the same language, "Have you breakfasted?"

"Nay, I've been riding."

"How energetic. I have but recently *risen*." Churchill grinned.

"Tell me," William hesitated.

"Yes?"

"Who rests above?"

"Ah, the fair Castlemaine. She is a fine woman though she is near thirty, and she has prodigious great appetites."

"The King's mistress."

"*Former* mistress. I think the fair but rapacious and temperamental Barbara has exhausted the royal patience and the royal purse. The pert and pretty Nelly currently holds sway over the royal cock, but there is a new contender for the King's affection—Louise de Keroualle. She came over in the train of the Duchesse d'Orleans, but many say she was sent by Louis XIV on purpose to ensnare the King, who is easily taken with that sort of trap."

William stiffened at this mention of the French king, and decided he would give the fair Louise a wide berth lest she prove to be more than a pretty whore. Churchill either missed or chose to ignore the prince's silence, and continued to rattle on in a merry, if improper, fashion as they made their way into the warren of Whitehall Palace.

"I was going to ask you to sup with me, but Princes of the Blood do not dine with penurious soldiers."

"Perhaps another time, Captain Churchill."

They parted, and William sensed that the young soldier had wondered at finding a prince without escort, but William's upbringing had been simple in the extreme, and to suddenly find himself with a retinue of a hundred people was a little overwhelming. At times he craved privacy, and his early morning rides had provided that. He had also found that the fogs and smokes of London were playing havoc with his asthma, and that only a hard gallop helped to ease his breathing.

Hans was waiting in the cockpit, one of the finest sets of apartments in Whitehall.

"They call me sobersides," remarked William as he lowered himself into the steaming water.

"They also claim you will melt, so often do you bathe," replied the page. "Though the Lord knows they could all do with a bit more water. Pah, how this palace stinks! What will Your Highness wear?"

"Oh, I don't know. Something suitably . . . sober."

The connecting door opened, and Sagitta tripped in. Bentinck frowned.

"Good morning."

She knelt at the side of the tub and, wetting a sponge, squeezed hot water down the back of William's neck. Huygens entered, followed by Zuylestein and Haakon. The older men looked shocked at the presence of the diminutive lady in her pale pink dress. Haakon merely grinned.

"I wish I could come tonight," sighed Sagitta.

"So do I, but my impression is that this is to be a cock party. Buckingham, Lauderdale, Rochester, Sedley, others of the so-called 'Wits,'" grunted William.

"Are they?" asked Sagitta.

"What?"

"Wits."

Haakon shrugged and quoted, *"Nor are his high desires above his strength. His scepter and his cock are of a length.* Judge for yourself."

There was an explosion of unintelligible sounds from the listeners.

"What?" demanded William.

Grinning, Haakon explained. "Rochester commenting upon the King's instrument of love."

"I scarcely think these are proper topics for a prince's chambers," said Huygens a little primly.

"Why not? They seem to be the sole topic of conversation of this bawdy court. Does no one ever govern this country?" asked Haakon rhetorically.

Sagitta stepped aside to allow Bentinck to wrap the prince in a large sheet. But she could not resist lightly touching the scar on his thigh. She flushed at his quick indrawn breath. William began dressing with cheeks as red as hers.

Huygens read from a sheet covered with his precise handwriting. "Tomorrow Your Highness visits Parliament. The day after the Duke of York has arranged a fox hunt. There is to be a grand ball in your honor. The day after that you dine with the Lord Mayor—"

"Enough! Remind me each day where I must be. Zuylestein, how go the negotiations?"

"Well enough, but I doubt we shall receive the full amount owed Your Highness."

"Even a portion would be a help." William shook out his shirt sleeves where they emerged from beneath the great embroidered cuff of his coat, and picked up his hat. "Gentlemen, I give you good day. Today I wish to go exploring. Madam." He offered his arm to Sagitta. "And Lord Lindel, will you walk with me?"

"With pleasure, Highness."

"Where is Father Armand?" William asked as soon as the door fell shut behind them.

The soldier shrugged. "Praying in his rooms I suppose. Though he's been given a kinder welcome than I would have expected in this Protestant country."

"For a Protestant country it has a plaguy Catholic court," said William dryly.

Sagitta gave her head an impatient shake, setting the knots of curls over each ear to dancing. "What does any of this matter? Catholic, Protestant. Only the Lady represents the true faith."

"Sagitta, I am *not* a pagan. Try though you might I shall never renounce my faith."

"You cannot serve the Old Religion and the new."

"I'm making a pretty good stab at it. Now what is this second talisman we're seeking?"

"A painting."

"Lovely," drawled Haakon, eyeing a heroic scene of Ulysses being drawn up to Olympus. The canvas literally covered one wall of the audience chamber through which they were passing.

The girl glared at him. "A very *small* painting."

"That's a mercy."

"So where is it?" asked William.

"I don't know."

"You don't—" began Haakon.

"*Yet*. I'll know it when I see it, as will the prince."

William stopped and gathered up her hands. "Sagi, lovey, there are *two thousand* rooms in this palace."

"Then the sooner we begin the sooner we'll finish." She flounced ahead, leaving the men to follow.

"Glad I left this an open-ended visit," remarked William to Haakon. "Though my uncle may begin to wonder when I stay for oh . . . two or three years."

Haakon laughed, and Sagitta's slender back stiffened.

"Father," cooed the lady who reclined on a settee. Her gown of canary yellow with an underskirt of deep green was cut low across her bosom, and an emerald necklace nestled in the valley between her breasts. She held out a hand. "Barbara Castle-maine."

"Madam."

He bowed over her hand, and as he rose from the salute Armand found himself staring into the silvered surface of a strange concave mirror. For an instant he thought he saw eyes staring out, but the disturbing fancy passed as he crossed himself.

"I have sent for you because I am wishful of making my confession, but if I am indeed so evil that you must needs cross yourself while greeting me . . ." Her voice trailed mournfully into silence.

"Madam must forgive me, it was not her soul or her person

which offended. Merely a wicked thought. But madam, have you not a personal chaplain?"

"Yes, but alas the wretched creature is down with the flux."

"I would then be happy to oblige, madam."

Beyond one of the doors of the elaborate Castlemaine suite, Armand could hear the merry cries of children. Five of them—all sired by King Charles. Yet the priest maintained a grave and serious mien as he listened to the woman confess to a number of venial sins. He assigned penance which she very prettily performed, and then, shaking out the folds of her gown, she rang for refreshment and confided chattily, "I converted six years ago, and it is such a comfort."

"Yes, to know that one has embraced the true faith removes all fear and doubt."

She cast down her eyes. "I know, Father, that many hate me, calling me the great whore. And I know that I have sinned in lying with the King, but men have needs which must be met, and better that he lie in my arms than others less loving." She clasped her hands at her bosom and cast her eyes up. "I have always felt that it is my destiny to bring His Highness back into the bosom of the church. So perhaps Heaven will forgive my indiscretions."

"Such feelings do you credit, and remember, madam, that St. Augustine himself was a sinner. In God there is forgiveness."

They talked for several hours, and as he left Barbara pressed his hand fervently between hers.

"It has been long since I have enjoyed so pleasant a visit. Please come again. In fact, by your leave I will include the Duchesse d'Orleans. She is the King's favorite sister, and shares my hopes for His Highness's ultimate conversion."

"I would be honored to meet the Duchesse."

"It shall be arranged."

William with customary cautiousness asked Haakon to accompany him to Buckingham's dinner. The dining room in the duke's sumptuous suite was filled with gentlemen. Hat plumes swayed and bobbed as they talked. Yards of ribbon adorned their elaborate suits at shoulders, elbows, and knees. Orders and medals flashed on chests, and rings sparkled beneath falls of lace. Pipe smoke mingled chokingly with candle tallow. William glanced longingly out of a small mullioned window at the bright June day.

"Welcome, welcome, Your Highness," boomed Buckingham.

The French fashion of embraces between men had invaded the English court, and William endured the salute without enthusiasm. The stink of sweat and cologne washed off the duke's body like an almost observable mist.

"I thank you for your hospitality, Your Grace," replied William in his stiff English. He had learned the language at his mother's knee, but found it came rusty after so many years of disuse.

"Shall we speak French?"

"Perhaps a mixture of both, Your Grace. I would like to practice my English, but Lord Lindel has none of the tongue, and it would be dull work for him to listen to a strange language."

"Fair enough."

They began a slow circuit of the room, the duke making introductions to those courtiers the prince had not yet met. William acknowledged the obeisances with proper grace, but his eyes kept straying to the walls, searching for a certain picture.

"James, Duke of Monmouth."

William recalled his wandering attention and stared in frank curiosity at this eldest and favorite of Charles's bastards. The young man bowing before him seemed to be of an age with William, and there was a surprising resemblance in the shape of the eyes and face. But where Monmouth wore an elaborate periwig echoing the black of his own hair, William wore his own hair the candlelight pulling sparks of red from his chestnut curls.

"I would know you for a cousin, sir," he cried, breaking his usual reserve.

"Aye, the Stuart stamp." Monmouth laughed. "And 'tis said we Stuarts stamp not only on the face, but in the blood." Buckingham frowned almost as if in warning, and William noted and filed the remark and the duke's reaction.

"Wine for Your Highness?"

"Please."

Buckingham waved over a servant.

"Ho, George, come settle a dispute," cried Lauderdale. "Killigrew here claims 'twas you who cut off Coventry's nose—"

"Nay, nay," called Monmouth. "'Twas me. The cheeky fellow had given offense to my royal sire."

He and Buckingham walked away, and William, sipping thoughtfully at his wine, went to listen to the small orchestra playing softly in an alcove. He wondered why Monmouth had felt it necessary to stress the point of his relationship with the king—then realized the young man had been making the point to *him*. After all, only the Duke of York and his fragile daughters Mary and Anne stood between William and the English throne. Perhaps Monmouth meant to suggest that he too held a claim.

William gave an irritable shake of his head at the emotions the thought had roused in him: resentment of Monmouth; a flare of interest at the thought of ruling this island nation.

"Don't be greedy," he said quietly to himself in Dutch. "You should be satisfied to obtain the station which *is* yours, and not hanker after others."

Haakon, a foaming tankard clutched in his hand, leaned against a wall, listening to Sir Charles Sedley. The poet had one hand laid at his breast, the other raised in graceful declamation. William joined them:

> Phillis is my only joy
>   Faithless as the wind or seas;
> Sometimes coming, sometimes coy,
>   Yet she never fails to please.
>   If with a frown
>   I am cast down,
>   Phillis, smiling
>   And beguiling
> Makes me happier than before.
>
> Though, alas! too late I find
>   Nothing can her fancy fix;
> Yet the moment she is kind
>   I forgive her all her tricks;
>   Which though I see,
>   I can't get free;
>   She deceiving,

> I believing,
> What need lovers wish for more?

"Bravo." Haakon laughed, applauding. "Though I normally have little taste for verse."

"'Tis far less frank than other verse I've heard here 'bouts," said William.

"Aren't you glad Sagitta is not so inconstant a lover?"

"Hush." William frowned him down.

"Highness," came a new voice. William turned to see Rochester, his pale blond periwig flowing on his shoulders, and a wicked light in his eyes, grinning down at him. "Pray, do not preach morality in the bawdiest court in Christendom. Particularly when you come with a whore in tow."

"Madam Sagitta is *not* a whore." It was said with fine stiffness, and despite his lack of inches William managed to gaze down his nose at the earl.

Servants began carrying in the first course, and the gentlemen drifted to the table. The silver plate before William must have weighed fully four pounds, and he wondered what the entire table setting must have cost.

The table was filled with four soups, and as many meat dishes: a saddle of mutton, Scotch collops, a great roast awash in its own juices—a profusion of food.

Suddenly the double doors opened and in strolled the king, one of his little spaniels cradled in his arms, and a pack of five more twining and yapping through his red-stockinged legs. With a rush the guests rose and bowed low.

Charles waved a negligent hand. "Sit. Sit. Thought I'd join you."

"Honored, Majesty."

Buckingham bowed, and offered his chair. An extra chair was brought, and the table rearranged. William found that he and Haakon had been separated by the length of the table. Monmouth was on one side of him, Buckingham on the other. There was a prickling along his scalp, and he shrank in upon himself.

The dinner began, the Dutch prince watching in fascination as several of the spaniels lay upon priceless embroidered chairs, chewing noisily on scraps and bones. Another trotted away and lifted its leg against the heavy damask drapes.

The second course began. Brawn, chicken cullis, pasties. William found the food to be bland and heavy, but he politely ate of the lighter dishes. It seemed to be raining beer and wine, and his host was careful to see that William's glass never long remained empty. He knew he was drinking far too much of the heavy red wine, but felt it would be churlish to refuse. Still, as he watched the men about him he began to sense that perhaps he was engaged in a drinking contest with some of Whitehall's more seasoned topers.

Blearily he glanced over and noticed that the servants were serving each dish to the king on bended knee. Charles caught his glance and explained:

"They wait on me on bended knee as a mark of respect, nephew."

It must have been the wine talking, breaking down the rigid reserve with which William normally held himself, but he heard himself saying, "I thank Your Majesty for that explanation. I thought they were begging your pardon for serving you so bad a dinner."

There was a roar of laughter from the table, Charles laughing as hard as the rest. Only Buckingham looked momentarily stung.

"Odd's fish, nevvy, I had no notion there was a wit hidden beneath that sober Dutch exterior. We'll make you a merry prince yet."

William rose and bowed. "If I could emulate Your Majesty's charm of manner I would consider myself to have done well."

There were shouts of "here here!" and tankards were pounded on the table. The white-linen tablecloth was spattered and stained, and food littered the floor. The little dogs raced about in a frenzy of excitement.

Haakon, far down the table, watched in alarm as Buckingham continued to fill the prince's glass. After so many months with the boy, Haakon knew William had little head for liquor, and from the way the gentlemen watched the group at the head of the table, Haakon had begun to fear that there was a joke afoot, and that William was to be its butt.

The third and final course was brought. Sweetmeats and puddings, and a syllabub. The centerpiece was a pastry stag who bled red wine when the arrows in its sides were removed. William laughed and clapped with delight. His normally pale face was bright red, and his bangs had been rubbed into sweat-matted disorder.

Buckingham passed his hand over William's glass. Haakon, who had had as much as he could hold, shook his head, leaned forward, and tried to decide if the duke had really slipped something into the prince's wine.

The meal dragged on. They had by now been sitting at table for almost five hours. Haakon was feeling like a particularly well-stuffed Christmas goose, and he propped himself in his chair, blinked blearily at the company, and listened to the songs and conversations swirling about him.

"Ladies of high rank go masked to the theatre and, indeed, are known to sit downstairs amongst the naughty women," Rochester said, laughing.

"Aye, but ladies masked like a covered dish give a man appetite!" riposted Sedley, and the king laughed with delight. William's husky little chuckle carried through the room and, loosening his lace cravat, he reached again for the wine.

"But there are no ladies present here, which I call damn poor hospitality," cried Monmouth.

"So let us find some," called Rochester, raising his glass and baptizing his neighbors with wine.

"He who returns with the prettiest lady shall be Lord Misrule for the evening," Sedley said and giggled.

The courtiers streamed from the dining room. Only Buckingham, the king, and Haakon remained. Charles sat absently pulling the ears of a spaniel through his fingers. Buckingham lay back in his chair with eyes closed. Haakon, stifling a yawn, wondered if mine host had fallen asleep before his king and his remaining guest. But as he studied the older man he realized that there was a tenseness about the jaw. The Norwegian felt a sudden flare of unease and concern for his tipsy prince. Pushing back his chair, he froze as Buckingham's eyes snapped open. The man pinned him with a cold and calculating glance.

Haakon hiccuped loudly and shuffled for the door. "Must piss or I'll explode," he slurred in French.

Once out of sight of those reptilian eyes he gave his head a hard shake. Then moaned, for it seemed to send the fogs roiling about the confines of his skull, and his stomach gave a heave.

*William. Where by all that was holy could he be found in this
rabbit warren of a palace?* Haakon picked a direction at random and set off, ducking under low lintels, wandering the maze
of crooked hallways.

Suddenly from overhead he heard feminine shrieks, and the
shouts of men. Forcing himself into a lurching run he followed
the noise, burst out into the June evening, and found the knot of
courtiers giggling at the foot of an ivy-covered wall. Glass littered the grass.

"The prince?" he croaked.

Rochester thrust upward with a finger. "Above."

"Apartments of the Maids of Honor," someone else said.

"God's blood! Sedley." He gripped the poet urgently by the
shoulder. "For the love of Heaven help me with the child."

" 'Tis rare sport." Monmouth guffawed.

"Buffoon," muttered Haakon beneath his breath, and with the
poet in tow he ran back into the palace and up the staircase.
Several other gentlemen, having been recalled to propriety, followed.

The girls were fleeing like pretty, nodding flowers for the
farthest apartment. William had one little lady by the fold of her
gown and was pulling her determinedly toward him. Screams,
tears, and laughter filled the room with a horrible din. Haakon
caught the prince by the shoulders and got punched in the eye
with a wildly swinging fist.

"That does it!" Pulling back a fist he hit William neatly on
the jaw, then caught him as he collapsed. "Excitement's over,
ladies. Your virtue is safe. Presuming you had any to safe-
guard." One tall, saucy-eyed girl with glistening black hair
launched a vase at him. Haakon blew her a kiss. "Thank you,
my sweet. I'll come back to properly thank you for that token of
affection," he called as he backed out the door, William held
tightly in his arms.

"Highness."

"Oh, go away!" William rolled onto his side and buried his
head among the pillows.

Bentinck looked desperately at Huygens and Zuylestein.
"Highness, you must get up."

"I'm sick! Can't you see that? Leave me in peace!"

Haakon uncrossed his arms and pushed off from the wall he

had been propping up. Grasping the blanket, he twitched it aside. "What you are is embarrassed, and the only cure for that is owning up and facing the music—however disharmonious it might prove to be."

William scraped his hands through his tangled hair, then sat up with his elbows propped on his knees. The assembled members of his suite gazed at him with varying degrees of censure and concern—and, in the unregenerate Haakon's case, amusement.

The prince didn't feel very amused. Shame was like a bad taste on the back of his tongue. There was also a niggling sense that his actions had not been his own on that disastrous night. His magical wards felt stretched and even tattered, and he seemed to sense that another will, secret and whispering, had driven him to behave so abominably.

But was that not perhaps mere wishful thinking? A chance to excuse himself from actions which were essentially inexcusable? Most likely. He decided to say nothing to either Haakon or Sagitta. Perhaps Father Armand might be understanding, and comforting. . . .

He plucked himself back from the brink of self-pity and said with a firmness he didn't feel, "Have my bath drawn, Hans. I will rise."

"Lord be praised," quavered Huygens, raising gnarled hands in an attitude of prayer. "But only if Your Highness is certain you feel adequate to it?"

"No, I feel rather like something those blasted hounds of the King's have vomited into a corner, but I shall live—and not enjoy the experience."

"Just punishment for overindulgence, I'd say," said Zuylestein. He had served as William's governor from the prince's ninth birthday until his replacement by the unmentionable van Gent, and he stood on little ceremony with the young man.

At that moment the door to the bedchamber flew open and King Charles entered, surrounded by a sea of those self-same blasted hounds. With their tails waving gracefully over their backs they flowed across the room and proceeded to settle onto every available chair. Several joined William on the bed.

"Good morning, nevvy."

"Good morning, Majesty."

"Feeling a bit out of curl, are we?"

"I fear so, Majesty."

"Well, I'm something of an expert in such matters." He dropped one heavy lid in a profound wink to the others. "Though it rebounds little to my credit to admit it, and I've come with the makings of a cure."

"I'd welcome it."

The king pulled out a covered goblet containing a thick brown liquid.

William reared back. "What is it?"

"Eggs beaten in milk and chocolate." The prince grimaced, but took the goblet and drained the odd potion. "I hope there are no hard feelings?"

"No, no hard feelings," William said with as much grace as he could muster. "But I think I'll not attend any more of His Grace's dinner parties."

"Nephew, if I might speak with you in private of certain personal and familial matters?"

"Of course, sir."

William waved out his retinue, and then, feeling at a disadvantage in his nightshirt, he shrugged into an elaborate Turkish robe and seated himself opposite his uncle.

"So, how are you finding your visit?"

"Most enjoyable, Majesty."

"Not ready to return home yet?"

"No, sire, though I confess a certain longing for home."

"For that flat, dull land? Nephew, you surprise me."

"It is my home, sire, I was raised there. And for the most part I have been happy."

"Oh, aye, I doubt it not, but you lack your rightful place."

"Yes, and it rankles, but by being installed as First Noble of Zeeland I have taken an important step toward attaining the Stadholderate and protected myself against . . . well, other dangers."

Charles rose and took a turn about the bedroom. "The Dutch have given me little cause to love them, William Henry."

"Indeed, sir? And in what way have we offended?"

"By denying you your rightful place." Charles turned the full power of his slow smile on the prince. "And by being damned interfering in our trading interests."

William shrugged. "We are both seafaring nations, sire."

The king dropped back into his chair. "But you're happy, lad?"

"As happy as any man can be 'til he be gathered to glory."

"Hmmm. Religion is a great comfort."

"So I've always found."

William shifted irritably. Was there a point to this disjointed conversation? Also, after two days of hoping he never saw a plate of food again, he was now feeling decidedly peckish.

"Ah, the Stuart blood. Perhaps there *is* something about it . . ."

The grumblings of his stomach were forgotten. William leaned forward intently. "Yes?"

". . . Which leads us onto contrary paths. My father, your grandfather, shed his blood to preserve and return to this nation her soul."

"Soul," repeated William, once more losing the drift and direction of this slippery conversation.

"Nevvy, I have always felt that a faith which has stood the tests of time is more to be trusted than some new-fangled religion," said the king, turning a stern eye on William.

Hands gripping the arms of his chair, William cautiously asked, "You refer, sir, to the Old Religion?"

"Oh, aye."

"You serve the Lady?"

"I'm . . . leaning toward it."

Now it was William's turn to rise and take an agitated turn about the room. "It alarms me, uncle. It bestows strange powers. Perhaps there is good cause that the memory of the old ways has faded from the world. So few can practice it. Might it not lead them to evil?"

He faced Charles and found the king eyeing him in perplexity. "Er . . . interesting questions, nephew, but all I'm saying is that I wish you would take more pains and look into these things better and not be led by Dutch blockheads."

"*What?*"

"Talk to Father Armand. He is a worthy and pious man."

"*Oh!* You're talking about Catholicism."

"Yes, what did you think I was speaking of?"

"Nothing."

"I would like to see you in your proper place, nephew, and I, together with others of your royal relatives, might be able to aid you in that . . . if you're willing to give us something in return."

Frigid hostility clipped the prince's words. "I thank you, uncle, but I'll do naught if it goes against the foundations of my republic."

The king fell back exasperated in his chair. "William Henry, you can be a most difficult young man. Are you being deliberately obtuse?"

"I beg your pardon, Majesty. Perhaps it's due to my *long*, *close*, and *fond* association with those Dutch blockheads that I'm unwilling to betray them now."

"I give you good day, Prince."

"Majesty."

"Dutch blockheads," mused William, twirling the goblet where it rested on the bedside table. "Well, I've certainly shown myself to be one. Putting my trust in a merry drunkard and secret Papist. What the hell was this conversation all about?" he inquired of the ornately painted ceiling. "Dear God, I'm becoming as bad as Haakon, babbling to myself. So shut up and find that painting."

Eleven

I am the tomb: *of every hope*

"Indeed, Minette, I find him so passionate a Dutchman and Protestant that there is no bearing him!"

"Sit, Charles," soothed "Minette"—Henriette-Anne, Duchesse d'Orleans—patting coaxingly at the settee next to her. "Such heat in summer weather does you no good. If the wretched boy cannot see that you act in his own best interests —well!" She shrugged with pretty expressiveness.

"Perhaps I should leave," faltered Armand, closing his missal and sliding toward the door.

"No, no, Father," cried Barbara. "Pray, stay with us."

"Yes, stay," added Minette, turning the full force of her startlingly blue eyes upon him. "You have confided some of your fears to us. I think it is time you heard how we strive to banish those terrors."

Charles glanced sharply at his sister, but she gazed back with an expression of limpid innocence, and he sighed, smiled, and sat at her side.

"My presence in England is no accident, good Father," continued the delicate little Duchesse. "I have come to help weld a bond between two great kings. My brother"—here she paused to hug the king's arm tightly—"and Louis, my brother-in-law. I carry a treaty which will enable them to rework the shape of the world."

"Ah . . . just so."

"But such political and military maneuverings can be of no interest to a man of God such as yourself. Of greater import is that my brother"—again she gripped Charles's arm, and she laid her head against him; the bright, chestnut curls mingled with the green ribbons at his shoulder, and the king stroked them gently—"being convinced of the truth of the Catholic religion, is resolved to declare it and reconcile himself with the Church of Rome." She clapped her hands like a delighted child, and Charles, smiling fondly, laced his fingers through hers. "And, even better, he will in good time bring our beloved nation once more back to God."

"As the welfare of the nation permits, dearest sister," the king demurred. "Such things cannot be undertaken lightly. I am unwilling to risk crown or head by too quickly forcing my ofttimes troublesome subjects."

"And where stands the Prince of Orange in all this, Your Majesty?" asked Armand.

"Quietly I hope. My brother Louis and myself are willing to place him upon his throne once the Netherlands have been conquered."

"Holland as a puppet state," breathed Armand.

"Well, yes," admitted the king. "But William will have his throne, and I will have neutralized a strong trading competitor. But the wretched boy seems determined to resist."

"I think the Prince loves his country very much, and he may be wary about trusting to the good offices of the French king.

He has told me that he believes King Louis to be behind several assassination attempts."

The lines about Charles's mouth deepened. "Nonsense. Utter nonsense! Kings may make war upon one another, but they do not hire secret killers."

"But . . ."

Armand's voice trailed into silence, and he frowned, remembering the killers who had attacked the prince in that French inn, and the warrants they had carried. But his dreams—those awful, terrifying dreams—suggested that William was a cunning and devious foe. Might he not have *arranged* to be attacked? Planted the warrant? It had been many weeks since the priest had enjoyed an uninterrupted night's sleep. He shook his head wearily, trying to marshal his tumbling thoughts.

Charles rose and helped himself to a glass of wine. "I'm beginning to fear that my nephew suffers from brain fever. He babbled on in the most alarming manner yesterday about great powers and great evil. When he asked if I served 'the Lady' I thought he referred to our Blessed Virgin, but on reflection I think he meant something quite different."

Armand suddenly found himself the focus for two pairs of feminine eyes. Both Barbara and Minette were staring intently at him, as if trying to communicate without words.

"I . . . I think his mistress exercises no good effect over the Prince, Majesty," said the priest hesitantly.

Charles laughed and set aside the glass. "Father, *no* woman exercises a good effect upon a man." La Castlemaine frowned blackly, but the king's focus was on his sister. "They are the most dreadful yet fascinating rogues and devils." He leaned down and lightly kissed his sister on one pale cheek. "Ah . . . um . . . good Father, I hope that I may trust you as completely as my sister seems to?" Armand bowed. "It would disturb me to find that word of my secret design had come to the ears of the Dutch. Or, God forbid, even to my own subjects. Consider this conversation to have been somewhat in the nature of a confession."

He swept from the room with a rustle of brocade and a sharp click of heels upon the wooden floor. Barbara followed and, after taking a cautious glance down the hall, quickly shut the door. She laid her arms across the portal as if blocking out evil with her plump white arms. The action lifted her magnificent bosom, and she turned her full, sparkling eyes on the priest.

"Father, the time has come to speak frankly and openly of matters which have too-long lain hidden." She gathered herself and announced dramatically. "We know that the Prince of Orange is practicing black and pagan magic!"

Armand stared shocked at Barbara. "How? How could you—"

"God grants power to those who would resist evil," spoke up the Duchesse d'Orleans. "Both here and in France there are people determined to stop the Prince. Among them a prince of our church."

"How can I trust you?" He dropped his aching head into his hands and groaned. "How can I know which among confused visions are the truth?"

With a rustle of skirts Minette dropped to the floor at the priest's feet and gathered his hands into hers. "Father, my brother thinks I am mad to have trusted you with the news of the secret treaty, but I have done so because *you* are our only hope. I have revealed secrets to you, praying that you will see that my brother and brother-in-law are the bulwarks to stand against not only the Protestant heresy, but against a return of pagan evil."

"What . . . what do you want of me?" Armand shrank back in his chair, but there was no escape there either, for Lady Castlemaine had come up behind him.

"We must separate William from the sorceress who has so blinded and tempted him. You must bring him alone to where the guardians await."

"And then?" whispered the priest.

"He will be stripped of his evil powers and cleansed," said Barbara, leaning in over Armand's shoulder.

"But his powers must be dampened before he is brought to us, lest he destroy us with fires summoned from Hell."

"I cannot believe he would . . . harm those who sought to help . . ." His voice trailed away into nothing, and Armand recalled William's face thrown into sharp relief by the flames which flickered on his fingertips. He shuddered.

"Father, you have been granted a gift from God to see the future! What have you seen?"

"I don't know. I don't know! In what can I trust? How can I

know the truth? I have seen Louis as Antichrist, and so also have I seen Orange."

"Have you ever witnessed or heard tales of Louis practicing black magic?" pressed Henriette-Anne.

"N . . . No."

"Have you witnessed such acts by the Prince of Orange?" asked Castlemaine.

"Yes." He hung his head in defeat.

Barbara dropped gracefully to the floor at the Duchesse's side and reverently crossed herself. "Father, we have placed in your hands knowledge which could destroy a king. Is that not surety enough? What can we do to ease your mind?"

"Pray with me," he whispered.

The creature has herself said she is no Christian. How then can I hesitate? The boy is young. Freed from Sagitta's evil influence he will turn his face once more to God and, perhaps, guided by a wise and loving uncle, find the true faith.

What greater service could he do his prince?

"He will not be harmed?"

"I swear it so."

"Then what must I do?"

"He is never alone save when he rides," grumbled Barbara. "To seize him from his chamber is well-nigh impossible."

"So place men in a tree and blow his head loose from his shoulders," said Buckingham.

"You are a fool," hissed Mazarin. The duke shrank back from the mirror as if fearful that the cardinal would reach through and seize him. "A ritual killing will wed his power to ours. He must be killed in circle."

"Sometimes," said the Duchesse d'Orleans. "That which is done in public is least seen."

"What are you suggesting, madam?" asked Mazarin.

"The priest is ready to serve, and the drug he will use not only lowers wards, but enfeebles the limbs. The prince will have to be escorted to his chambers—"

"But that Norwegian monster will no doubt accompany him," objected Barbara.

"And the witch," added Buckingham.

"But not if they are otherwise occupied."

"Occupied how?" sneered Barbara.

Minette gave the other woman a brittle little smile. "A pity that the gallant Lindel did not find your charms to his taste. Then *you* might have occupied him." Barbara flushed. Her failure to seduce Haakon had not sat well. "But failing that I think the ball will do nicely."

"It will all depend upon the priest," mused the cardinal.

"He is clever, my master, and the prince trusts him." Minette shrugged. "And if we fail we will simply try again. No man can be protected forever."

Oddly enough, he was suddenly afflicted by shyness. The footmen flanking the great double doors eyed him questioningly, but William waved them back. He nervously turned his hat in his hands. Beyond the doors he heard the murmur of the crowd, like the voice of the sea grumbling over distant rocks. The sweet strains of the orchestra ran beneath. Behind him, his retinue coughed and shifted. Sagitta lightly touched his wrist.

"All right?"

He hunched one shoulder. "All those eyes."

"You've been on display since the moment of your birth."

"It doesn't seem to get any easier."

Haakon stepped to his side and ruffled his hair. Huygens gave a loud hurummph of disapproval. "What is it, whelp?"

"I . . . I don't know. I have a presentiment. . . ." The prince's eyes sought out Father Armand, standing silent and pale in the midst of William's entourage.

"Your Highness will be fine," said the priest in a colorless voice, and William realized with a flare of guilt that he had sadly neglected Armand during the past weeks. It was no wonder he seemed stiff and withdrawn.

With a determined nod, William faced the doors and stepped through as a footman called in stentorian tones:

"William Henry, by the Grace of God, Prince of Orange, Count of Nassau, Count of Katzenellenbogen, Vianden, Dietz, Lingen, Meurs, Büren, and Leerdam, Marquis of Ter Veere and Vlissingen, Lord and Baron of Breda, of the town of Grave and the lands of Deist, Primbergen, Herstel, Cranendonck, Warmeston, Asley, Moseray, St. Vith, Doesburg, Polanen, Willemstadt, Niervaart, Isselstein, Steenbergen, St. Martinsdijk, Geertruidenberg, the Higher and Lower Swaluwe and Naaldwifk, Hereditary Burgrave of Antwerp and Besançon, Hereditary Stadholder and Governor of Holland, Zeeland, Gelderland, Utrecht, and Overijssel."

"Oh, *well* done," said Haakon to the footman, laughter edging the words.

William flushed with pleasure at the inclusion of the Stadholderate, for the Perpetual Edict had supposedly removed that position forever beyond his reach. He thought he saw the fine, firm, and loyal hand of Huygens in its inclusion, and he flashed a smile at the old secretary. Several women, seeing that sweet, hesitant smile flicker across the sensitive mouth, suddenly rethought their earlier sniffing dismissal of the prince as far to grave and formal and disinclined to flirt.

Charles and his sad little queen (whom that merry and unregenerate sovereign had once characterized as looking like a bat) were seated beneath a royal canopy. The king was very fine in a suit of crimson and black. Catherine of Braganza wore a short string of very fine pearls clasped about her throat, and more draped the bodice of her pale-green gown.

Sagitta and Haakon, walking a few paces behind the prince, made a striking couple. Her silver-light hair had been arranged in the new French fashion: parted in the center, flat on top, while the sides of the hair were curled and puffed and brushed out in a mass of small ringlets. The back was worn long, and a single gleaming ringlet fell over one white shoulder. Her gown was the pale blue of arctic ice, and a shimmering silver underskirt rippled like moonlight on a frozen lake.

Haakon, a hand resting lightly on his rapier hilt, was a resplendent figure in deep midnight blue, with much gold lacing. He wore a shoulder belt of the same gold, and, with his flowing gold hair and strong chin with its small cleft, he provoked more than a few tremors in feminine hearts.

William wore dove gray with black breeches and silver embroidery and ribbons, and a black hat with gray feathers. The buckles on his high-tongued shoes were studded with diamonds, and the new garter insignia which Charles had bestowed upon him sparkled with diamonds and enamel work. But all in all he seemed a small and subdued figure among so many exotic birds of paradise.

Charles greeted him with a kiss to each cheek, then languidly waved to the orchestra to resume. Black pages and a few fancifully dressed dwarfs circulated through the ballroom bearing trays of sweetmeats. Nearby an elaborate fountain shot streams of wine into the air.

Charles and Catherine began the dancing. Ladies sat on small chairs, the gentlemen standing in attendance. After the king and queen came the Duke of York and his enormously fat wife. Then, as the next-highest-ranking people in attendance, William led his vivacious little aunt, Henriette-Anne, Duchesse d'Orleans, onto the parqueted floor.

With his hat held at his side he led her gracefully through the intricate steps of the gavotte. They made a charming couple, with their bright chestnut curls and slight builds. The ordeal over, William pressed a handkerchief to his heated brow. Though he had been well-drilled in dance, with a predominately male household and a strictly curtailed social life he had had little opportunity to lead out an actual female. And had he stumbled, or taken an embarrassing misstep before all those watching eyes . . . he pressed the handkerchief to his lips.

He was already beginning to wheeze under the onslaught of hundreds of candles, the press of bodies, and an acute case of nerves. Sagitta rubbed him between the shoulders, trying to ease his labored breathing.

It was close on to two hours before the well-born had displayed their terpsichorean skills, and the set dances could begin. Haakon, with his eye on a pert and pretty little lady, went charging across the room, only to be cut out by John Churchill.

"Try my sister, Arabella," the soldier counseled with a grin.

Haakon bent his gaze on the tiny lady. "Ma'am, will you take this pup over a seasoned fellow such as myself?"

"Pray, sir, the more seasoned are likely to be tough. I shall dance with Captain Churchill."

"Spiked, by gad, by a sharp-tongued filly. Might I at least know your name, cruel charmer?"

"Sarah Jennings," she threw laughingly over her shoulder.

"What about your sister?" called Haakon, as the sets began to form up.

"Ho, Bella," shouted John. "Come and dance with this great northern ox."

"Captain, I don't know whether to challenge you for the insult, or bless you for the partner," said Haakon, studying the lovely face of Arabella Churchill.

William hurried across the room to where Sagitta was holding at bay seven admirers.

"Dance, ma'am?"

"Delighted, Highness."

As they took their place in the set, William paused to send his hat skimming to old Huygens. The secretary snatched it out of the air, and they bowed to one another. The ballroom rang with laughter, and soon hats were fluttering through the air like demented birds. Sarah Jennings caught one and pulled it down over her bright curls. It hung over her eyebrows and made her look like a particularly fetching rustic. Soon other ladies had secured their partners' plumed hats, and the dance began.

"You seem in prodigious good humor," remarked Sagitta as she and William minced toward one another and bobbed heads like courting birds.

"I am. I feel that we'll find that blasted painting."

"Premonition?" asked the witch sharply, as she circled gracefully at the end of his hand.

"No. Perhaps just wishful thinking. If you want a premonition go to Father Armand."

William turned to face the gentleman on his left, and they sided. He gripped Sagitta's hands across the set, and they romped two hands around. Spinning her under his right arm they progressed down the line, and began anew with a new set of partners.

Armand advanced on Barbara.

"All prepared?"

His hand slipped nervously into his pocket. "Yes."

"And don't forget to bring it."

"I won't."

Monmouth and Buckingham sided, the older man asking as they passed, "The word has gone out?"

"They will be waiting."

The Duchesse d'Orleans circled lightly with Armand. "'Tis a pity we haven't learned the location or design of the second talisman."

"It's a painting," said Armand shortly.

"Oh!" She glanced about the ballroom. Her mouth drooped. "Oh."

Thirty minutes later the dance ended. William's labored breaths sounded like the doleful cry of an ancient bagpipe. Sagitta led him to a chair.

"You shouldn't dance anymore," she scolded, fanning him with her lace fan. The diamond chips on the sticks flashed in the candlelight.

"One normally does."

"What?"

"Dance . . . at a dance."

"Wretched boy! You'll be laid down for days."

"Boy," he mused. He caught her gloved hand. "Sagitta, how old are you?"

"Like all women I'm eternal."

"That's not an answer."

"It's all the answer you're going to get. I'll bring you a drink."

"Wait." One pale brow arched inquiringly. "I have something for you."

He reached in his pocket and pulled out a small box wrapped in silver paper and tied with orange ribbons. Her hand trembled slightly as she accepted his gift. Her ice-blue eyes fluttered nervously up to meet his.

"Open it!"

Hesitantly she tore away the paper, then lifted the lid of the silver gilt box. A diamond rolled into her hand. The faceted stone, framed in gold, lay sparkling against the white material of her glove.

"Dear heaven!" she said faintly, and dropped into the chair at his side.

"It was my mother's. She pawned it to raise money for Charles. It took me a long time, but I finally bought it back. It's called the Little Sancy." Her continued silence was alarming him. He added nervously, "Thirty-seven carats." And then he concluded sadly. "You don't like it."

"No! No! That's not it. I . . . I . . . William, are you in love with me?"

"God's blood! Spare me! I suppose . . . falling—" A sharp coughing jag shook his slim frame.

"I'll open a window."

She rushed away with an agitated rustle of skirts and bumped into Armand approaching with a goblet of wine.

"Is that for the prince? Good, he has need of it." She forced open her hand, noting that so tightly had she gripped the diamond that the frame had pierced the glove and drawn blood from her palm. "I have done as I must, Father. His love is both his glory and his bane."

"You're babbling," said Armand, and Sagitta was too agitated to notice the sharp suspicion and dislike which edged the words.

She released the frenzied grip she had on his coat cuff. "Go to him. Go!"

Haakon, Sarah, and Sagitta tripped lightly through a complex hay. A pale, misty figure of a woman, mouth stretched wide in terror, eyes two dark holes in infinity, swooped through the air and coiled like smoke about the body of Sarah Jennings. Sagitta gave a cry of fear and fell back. Haakon, well-lubricated by a great many glasses of wine and ale, and intent upon admiring Sarah's neat ankles, slammed into Sagitta and went sprawling. The dance stuttered to a disorganized halt. Sagitta, her pale eyes wide with fear, held out her hands as if to fend off a blow. Her eyes flicked from place to place in the room. Haakon, frowning, tried to follow her gaze and saw nothing.

"The Spear! The Spear is drawn! William!" Her voice rose in an ascending wail.

Haakon, with a smile so brittle that it seemed like to break, caught her by the shoulders. "You're going to get us burned," he whispered while continuing to beam and nod at the gathering crowd.

The room was filled with floating specters invisible to all but Sagitta and apparently King Charles who rose from his throne, staring in confusion at the empty air. He abruptly crossed himself. A ghost flitted past, and suddenly its features melted into a skull. Sagitta clutched her side and collapsed on the floor, like a flower shattered in a killing wind.

"What is it? Can I help?" asked John Churchill.

"I . . . I don't know." Haakon knelt helplessly at the girl's side, supporting her lolling head against his shoulder.

"John," ordered Arabella. "Carry her from this crush and these prying eyes. I'll bring some ass's milk."

"Ah . . . that won't be necessary," demurred Haakon, becoming aware of what Sagitta's alarming ravings meant.

". . . Blood of a king. . . ."

"Bit of air . . ." he muttered, backing for the door, Sagitta clasped in his arms.

". . . We die. *Ah!*" With a final shriek the girl came to frenzied life, struggling wildly in his arms.

Haakon bolted.

Outside, he set her on her feet, gave her a hard shake, a ringing slap, and demanded, "It's H.H., isn't it?"

"Yes."

"Can you find him?"

"Our blood is mingled. When his is shed I feel it—"

"*Can you find him?*"

"No. His mind is closed to me. I sense only shifting confusion. They have physicked him with some foul drug to drop his wards and close his mind."

"What the *hell* good is magic, save to bring us trouble and danger!" He slammed his fist into the wall, breaking the skin across his knuckles.

"He is lost," mourned Sagitta, dropping to the floor. "We are all lost."

"Come on!" Sucking on his bleeding hand the Norwegian pulled her to her feet and ran down the corridor.

"Where . . . what are you doing?"

"Using my wits, something which you sorcerers seem to have in short supply. Ho! You there! Fellow!"

The servant paused and looked back questioningly. Haakon drew out a gold louis d'or, and the man's eyes widened. "This and a good many more like it are yours, my man, and any of your fellows, if you can tell me if you saw the Prince of Orange passing, and where he went."

The man's tongue peeked out and nervously wet his lips. He gave Haakon an ingratiating but uncomprehending smile.

"God's nigs!" cursed Sagitta and, seizing the coin, repeated the question in English.

The servant bolted below stairs, and Haakon gave Sagitta a reproachful look.

A moment later the man returned with a red-nosed ancient

who bobbed and bowed, and wiped beer foam from his upper lip, and bowed some more. "Aye, your La'ship. I saw the poor young prince a staggerin' along with that Frenchie mumble-matins."

"Where did they go?" cried Sagitta, pressing the coin upon the old man.

"Down in cellars. The gentry morts play at in-and-in with the gentry coves, and raise all manner of stinks and noise."

"Can you show me?"

"Aye, take you to stairs, but I'll nay go down. Don't hold with uncanny goings on, real or no."

The old man seemed to sense their urgency, and he broke into a shambling trot. Haakon tossed a coin over his shoulder to the first man.

"Down yonder."

Haakon drew his rapier, kicked off his shoes, and went cat-footed down the creaking stairs. Sagitta, her skirts bundled in her arms, crept after.

They found Armand huddled at the foot of the stairs. A single candle threw a pool of light onto the packed-dirt floor, and at the edges of the light they could distinguish the bulk of tumbled furnishings and leather-bound crates. Another stairway leapt up into shadowed darkness. In the distance they heard the low murmuring of voices.

"You son-of-a-bitch," gritted the soldier, leaping down the last few steps.

Armand rose and stretched out his arms as if to block their way. The tip of the rapier lay in the hollow of his throat, but he neither flinched nor retreated.

"No, you shall not pass. Soon he will be free from your influences—"

"Soon he will be free from ours or any influences," Sagitta cried. "They are killing him!"

"You will not trick me again. My eyes have been opened to your evil."

"Kill him," ordered the sorceress curtly, and darted nimbly past Armand.

The priest grasped at her and caught a fold of her gown. The rapier slashed down, cutting the material free.

"You cannot pass," Armand cried triumphantly. "The power of God closes their circle against your evil. Even I, tainted as I am, could not enter." Then his eyes widened as the girl raced through the low archway.

"You stupid fool. You believed anything they told you, didn't you," raged Haakon.

He drew back his arm for the killing thrust, arm shivering with strain. Stared down into the shocked brown eyes of the priest. Hesitated. Remembered fond moments on the road as the foursome would sing, or tell tales, or jape one another. He tightened his grip on the hilt, toughened his resolve, and then with a muttered oath shoved Armand aside and ran through the door.

William lay naked on a makeshift altar. Blood ran from a deep wound in his side, staining the wood of the table. The Spear of Longinus, it's tip gleaming wetly with the prince's blood, lay forgotten on the dirt floor. Dark-robed figures circled William like carrion birds, but some had drawn back in alarm. Sagitta glimmered like captured starlight in the dank cellar. Directly across the circle stood a masked woman. William lay between them—the prize over which they fought.

And it was clear that power was building. Red fire seemed to lick at the folds of the black-clad woman. An answering white flame formed a nimbus about Sagitta.

"Jesus, Father forgive me! It's real," shrieked a terrified young man, and Haakon recognized the voice of the Duke of Monmouth. The Norwegian stepped aside as the bastard came bolting out the door.

A man moved, twitching back the folds of his robe, reaching for his sword. Sagitta, her full attention bent upon the black sorceress, was unaware of her danger. Haakon lunged and spitted the man through the throat. The man collapsed bubbling and gurgling, and with a yelp of terror several more members of the coven bolted for the door. Haakon let them pass.

Twin fires lanced out, met, and struggled in writhing lines of power which lit the low room. The masked woman shivered with strain and fell back a step. Suddenly she threw up her arms and cried out in a strange language. There was a crack, and the door lintel sagged.

"Jesus! I'll not be trapped down here," bellowed a man, and ripping off his robe the Duke of Buckingham fled, almost bowling over Armand, who clung to the doorjamb, swaying like a drunkard. A torrent of Latin prayers fell from his white lips.

There was an explosion of fire at Sagitta's feet which lapped over onto Haakon. He tensed for the pain, then his jaw dropped when he felt *nothing*.

Mind blind. Magic couldn't touch him.

He threw back his head and shouted out, "Thank you, Jesus!"

Sagitta reached out, cupped the flame in her hands. The color faded from red to white, and with a cry she flung it back. Her opponent staggered under the blow—then drew back her lips in a snarl, and fire rained from her fingertips onto the helpless body of the prince.

Several things happened simultaneously. Sagitta, her white-gloved hands flying, sought to form a ward and fling it like a blanket over William. Haakon in desperation threw his rapier at the woman, and Armand, moving with a speed surprising for one of his bulk, flung himself across the room, covering William's body with his own. His thin, tearing screams were horrible to hear.

The masked sorceress was building for another assault. Fire pulsed about her body like a soap bubble trembling above a washerwoman's tub. Sagitta gestured, and the flames sank through the folds of her opponent's robe. For the briefest instant the woman stared horrified at her hands, which were glowing as if a fire had been lit beneath the skin. Then, with a throat-tearing shriek, she collapsed.

The rest of the coven ran like a covey of terrified quail breaking from cover.

"Now for it!" bellowed Haakon, leaping across the room to recover his weapon. He spared not a glance for the fallen witch. "What the devil!" he grunted as he stared down at Armand, whose clothes had burned away and whose skin had blackened and split under the fiery assault.

The priest had thrust his fingers into the wound in William's side, and in an agonized whisper he was praying. Haakon stared in amazement as the bleeding slowed, then stopped, and the wound closed. The burns across William's chest faded, vanished. Armand toppled sideways, a burned husk lying shriveled upon the floor.

"He . . . he healed him."

"Yes," said Sagitta, sparing only a glance before she stripped the robe from the sorceress, revealing the Duchesse d'Orleans.

"It can be done. At what cost you have observed." She swept up the Spear and wrapped it in William's clothes, which she had found thrown in a corner.

"Is she . . ." Haakon nudged Henriette-Anne with a toe.

"No, but what damage has been done internally I cannot say. Now let us hurry before these hell-born curs recover some dunghill courage and return."

"What about Armand?"

"Let him lie."

"By gad you're a cold bitch."

"And I thought I told you to kill him?"

"Well for us I didn't—H.H. didn't seem like to survive that wound they had given him."

They paused at the foot of the stairs, listening to the sounds of hurried footfalls from above.

"They'll try to kill us before we reach the populated parts of the palace," whispered Sagitta.

"Let us try another stair," replied Haakon, and shifting William higher onto his shoulder he ran back into the dim-lit cellar.

They took the second stair, Sagitta running lightly in the lead. She fumbled with the heavy knob of the door at the top, but it was locked from the other side.

"Stand to side." Haakon balanced precariously on one foot and drove his heel into the door. He grunted as pain shot up his leg, and the door scarcely trembled. "Damn! How about that fire trick from Nuremberg?"

"We don't have the time," muttered Sagitta in a nervous singsong, listening to their now fast-approaching pursuers.

"Hold him." Haakon shoved William into her arms, backed three steps down the stairs, and with a roar charged at the door. The door crashed open, the bolt tearing completely through the jamb.

"Impressive," remarked Sagitta, dragging William through the door. Haakon stood blowing like a winded horse and rubbing at his sore shoulder. "A triumph of brawn."

"Your brains weren't counting for much, sweetling," he growled, and swung William over his shoulder.

They ran.

Their desperate flight carried them through a series of offices, the speed of their passage whirling papers from cluttered desk tops.

"*Wait!*"

The sudden shriek out of what he had believed to be an unconscious burden so rattled Haakon that he jumped, tangled his feet, and fell in a heap. William crawled cursing from beneath him.

"*What? What now! God's blood!*"

"There it is," said William bemusedly, and pointed to a small painting.

Twelve

I am a salmon: *in a pool*

Haakon gaped, drew nearer, and peered at the tiny painting. He reached to take it.

"No, no!" scolded William. "Leave it, and let us go on."

"What?"

"Don't argue!"

"Leave it he says. Toss across twenty—be damned—miles of brine. Put up with this stinking court—bawds, drunks, and rakes, and now *witches*, for Christ's sweet sake—and he says leave it!"

The music from the ball filtered down the hall, and William slowed to a quick walk. "You're talking to yourself again."

Haakon glared. "I'm surprised I'm not raving, made mad as a weaver by all this."

They stepped through the doorway into the prince's apartments.

William fell into a chair. "Safe."

"Good, then perhaps H.H. would deign to explain a few matters to a Norse blockhead."

"You said it." Sagitta giggled, leaning wearily against the wall. "He didn't, but if the name fits . . ."

William took her gently in his arms and guided her to the bed. "Sit, rest, gather your strength, for we must go back."

"Back? Go back where?" erupted Haakon.

"To the ball. Help me dress."

"Zounds," sighed the soldier.

William suddenly paused and gave the older man a fierce hug. "Thank you, thank you both."

Haakon shook out the prince's shirt. "Why didn't we take the painting?"

William glanced up from where he had been inspecting the tender pink skin on his side. "Because if we had been captured the enemy would have two of the talismans."

"But how are we—"

"Patience." The prince settled his coat more comfortably on his shoulders. "Please, I have little memory of events after Father Armand called me from the ball. While we walk tell me what in hell happened."

Sagitta and Haakon, their voices tripping over each other, described the apparitions in the ballroom, their frantic search, the fight. Haakon demonstrated several of his passes, using Sagitta's fan for a rapier.

They reached the great double doors of the ballroom. A drowsy servant looked up from his mug of ale and grinned blearily. Haakons took hold of the knob.

"So are we going after these bastards?" he asked.

"No." said William.

"I've sworn to have them."

"Then you are doomed to disappointment. We play a great game here. Our personal outrages must be set aside."

"You leave a hedge of enemies at your back!"

"I cannot cut a swathe through my uncle's court, leaving a trail of bodies like a passing plague." He laid a soothing hand on Lindel's cuff. "Haakon, we cannot let poor Armand lie—his body might be used to discomfort me. Pray, gather him up and see him buried with all rites of his church."

"And what shall we say?"

"I'll leave that to your imagination."

"Be careful in there."

"I shall."

The Norwegian bent a stern eye on Sagitta. "Keep guard over him."

"I don't need a reminder!" She flounced past.

Lindel loitered by the door, anxious to see the reaction of the various plotters. He suppressed a grim smile at the terrified expression which flickered across young Monmouth's face as the couple swept into the ballroom.

William bowed before the Duchesse d'Orleans. Fingers trembling, she pressed a handkerchief to her lips.

Ah, madam, perhaps heaven will exact the vengeance which I am denied.

"Today sad tidings have come from France. My sister—" the king's voice broke, and he drew a hand across his mouth. "Dearest Minette died in convulsions on June 30th. God rest her soul." There were murmurs of sorrow and assent from about the table.

"So, Sagitta did cook her innards," muttered Haakon.

"Hush," warned William.

"And today we learn that we are to be bereft yet again, for our beloved nephew, William Henry, Prince of Orange, says that he must now return home. Dearest nephew, in memory of these merry weeks which you have spent at our court we make you a gift of twenty fine horses, and various deer and rare birds for your parks and aviaries. May the ties of love and loyalty which bind the house of Stuart never wither or be betrayed."

William rose and bowed low, and Charles embraced him. "I thank Your Majesty for the hospitality which you have shown me. May our two nations ever live in peace and harmony. And I grieve for your loss. It was an untimely death." He resumed his chair.

"True," muttered Haakon, "It should have happened weeks earlier." William kicked him.

"Is there aught that we may give you, nephew, to make complete your visit at our court?"

"Your kindness and hospitality have been greater than I ever expected or indeed deserve, Majesty, yet . . ." He hesitated with pretty confusion.

"Speak, Willy."

"Well, sire, since you command it, there is a small painting by my countryman Hieronymus Bosch which hangs in your offices. It would please me mightily to receive it."

Charles frowned. "And what would you do with this painting?"

"Hang it in a place of honor."

The king leaned in and said in an undertone. "Willy, lad, it's a fair disturbing bit of paint daubing. Sometimes it has seemed to me that the image on the canvas has changed, showing other realms and landscapes."

William looked ingenuously up into his uncle's face. "If it will show me pictures of your court, then I would thank it, uncle, and feel that I have never truly been separated from you."

"Hmmmmmm." Charles fell back in his chair, fingers drumming on the arms. Suddenly he ordered, "Ossory, go and fetch the picture for His Highness. You know the one."

The nobleman bowed himself out of the room. William studied his nails. He felt a suspicious gaze upon him and looked up to meet the black gaze of Buckingham. He looked blandly back.

Minutes later Ossory returned with the tiny six-by-four-inch painting on his palm. With a bow he offered it to William. The prince accepted it, rose, and kissed Charles's hand. He and Haakon withdrew, leaving the king with his ministers.

"That's it! That's all we had to do? Just ask for it?"

"Apparently so." William thrust it deep into a pocket and gave his coat a satisfied pat.

Haakon began cursing. Lowly, monotonously, continually, in five languages. William listened in amazement, then said, all sweet innocence:

"I never knew there were that many cuss words."

Haakon kept going. He broke off only when they entered the Cockpit, and he found Huygens gazing at him with shocked disapproval.

"Sir Constantine, Hans, Zuylestein, could you all withdraw save Lord Lindel and Madam Sagitta. I have matters to discuss with them."

As soon as the door closed behind the retinue William drew out the painting. Eerie, long-snouted creatures crawled among exotic plants of strange design. As William gazed at the canvas, the creatures stretched, writhed, awakened. Suddenly a strange wind arose, tossing the plants and tumbling the creatures toward the right edge of the picture. In his mind William fancied he could hear frightened cries and wailings. A new landscape rolled into view, with a sky of lemon yellow and small buglike creatures scurrying across a broad, empty plain. One drew near, and the prince realized it was a mechanical object like a coach built of metal. Another great storm blew them away, and he saw a forest glade—and Sagitta pouring blood from a crystal goblet onto the thirsty ground. With a shiver he thrust the painting away.

"In my Father's house there are in truth many mansions," he murmured softly.

"What did you see?" asked Haakon, curious but unwilling to take a peep into the magic picture.

"I don't know. Other worlds?"

"And times," said Sagitta softly.

"See anything useful?" William shook his head. "Can he control this thing?" the soldier demanded of Sagitta.

"Probably not. But he may see something which will be to his benefit."

"He might also grow a gray beard down to his belly button while he waits for that to occur."

The girl looked at William. "You must also be cautious and use the painting sparingly. Too long among its alien landscapes could drive you mad."

Haakon gaped, then shut his mouth with an audible snap and blurted out. "Unbelievable! I've said it before, and I'll say it again—"

"And no doubt yet again," murmured William, with an expressive roll of his eyes.

"But this magic seems to be far more trouble than it's worth. It's gotten to be nothing but a botheration. You wear out the body practicing it. You can scramble your brains." He flung his hands into the air.

"*I* defeated La Duchesse," said Sagitta curtly.

"And I could have spitted her." The woman blinked at him. "Well? Couldn't I have? Are you afraid to answer for fear I'll stick you some night while you lie sleeping?"

"*Haakon!*"

"Well, I wouldn't. I'm loyal to my friends, but God help them if they prove to be false."

"You have no reason to threaten or warn me."

"Enough of this!" ordered William. "What's next, Sagitta?"

"A Venus figure. A representation of my Lady."

"Fine. Where is it?"

"In Paris."

Haakon flung himself into a chair. William goggled at her.

"P-Paris?"

"In the Louvre."

"Better and better," grunted Haakon.

"Can we just bribe someone to steal it?" asked William. She shook her head. "Of course. I have to do it personally, correct? How do you propose that we enter the stronghold of our enemy?"

"I don't know."

"Like I said, magic and magicians—useless," muttered Haakon:

"Our enemies seem to be exceedingly dim when it comes to outguessing us. This painting was hanging in full view, available to all, and Buckingham or Monmouth could have swept it up at any time," mused William.

"Well, we are not so fortunate this third time. They know full well what they possess, and they keep the figure well-guarded. Within it is a large part of my lady's strength. Free it from their bonds and wards, and she comes one step closer to the boundaries of this world."

"This is *good?*" murmured Haakon, sotto voce.

She spun on him. "You distrust my Lady? You who have been honored by her as no mortal man in living memory?"

"Sagi, sweet, I'd distrust God Almighty when we're talking about this much power. It is the rulership of the world that hangs in the balance, no?"

"We are discussing God Almighty, but in the true form as Goddess."

William flung out a hand. "Hush, both of you. You blaspheme."

"You will see, William," said Sagitta.

"Fine. I'll see. Right now we lack the time for a religious and philosophical discussion. How are we going to get into the Louvre and at this figurine?"

"Get hired to empty the honey pots. Slip in, steal the statue, run like hell."

"Very funny, Haakon."

"I thought it was appropriate. We're in so much shit already—"

"Hush!"

"Get into the household in some capacity. Not so lowly as servants, but not so high we rouse suspicion . . . musicians?" suggested Sagitta.

"Nice idea but I can't play a note," said Haakon cheerfully. "I might be able to master the Jew's harp."

"Singing?" suggested Sagitta.

Haakon threw back his head and let loose with a torrent of sound that was reminiscent of a rutting elk.

William took an agitated turn about the room. "If we enter secretly we can be removed in secret. None would ever know our fate."

"Sagitta becomes Louis's mistress. She wears him out with serious fucking. We're lurking in the garden wrapped in our cloaks. She throws open the window. You swarm up the wall, steal the figure. We all run like hell," offered Haakon.

"This is silly. I'm the Prince of Orange, for Christ's sweet sake."

"Highty tighty," sniffed Haakon. "I was willing to empty chamber pots in the interest of humanity."

Sighing, the prince dropped into a chair. "Sometimes I forget that this is not some intriguing game, but the opening skirmishes in a deadly war."

"Forget and you will die. And with you all living things," said Sagitta.

"Oh, thank you so *very* much," grunted Haakon, and pulled his hat over his face.

Late in the day John Churchill stopped by to say farewell. Wine was poured, and William, smiling over the rim of his goblet, asked, "Have you ever managed to attract my royal uncle's attention by something other than poking his mistress?"

"Not yet, but war gives a man opportunity for notice and advancement."

"War?"

"There are always wars, and rumors of wars, and as soldiers we all fret for them." He took a long pull at the wine. "But speaking of la Castlemaine, she will soon be gone."

"Gone?"

"Indeed yes. The King has apparently become so weary of her greed and tantrums that he is packing her off to France. He is said to have told her to 'make the least noise you can, and I care not who you love.' But there are other rumors."

"Yes?" nudged Huygens, who had a weakness for gossip.

"'Tis rumored that she has taken a leaf from the book of Madame Montespan, and has practiced black magic to keep a hold on the King."

There were murmurs of "no," "shocking," which ran about the room.

"I would offer you a position in my personal guard, Captain Churchill, if you wish it," offered William.

The young man rose and smiled down. There was a glitter in his blue eyes, and an intensity about that tall form. "Thank you, Highness, but no, I prefer to be on the winning side."

There were murmurs of confusion and outrage, which William waved down. "I see."

"Though I expect you will do well enough, you are the nephew of a king."

"I am a Dutchman first and always."

"And so susceptible to being led by Dutch blockheads."

William started and shot the soldier a sharp glance. "Captain, you begin to interest me very much."

"There are many things going out of England and into France, Highness."

"Thank you, Captain, I believe I understand." William crooked a finger, and Bentinck hurried over.

"Bring me a purse," he said in Dutch.

"Sire, it's a waste to pay for a courtier's idle and, yea, even insulting gossip."

"Humor me, and I think it goes beyond that. I think Captain Churchill is giving me a message. Let us see if we can further loosen his tongue."

The officer shook out several of the coins and gave William his blazing smile. Tossing them lightly on his palm, he mused, "It's an odd thing about money. Kings as well as penniless soldiers require it. Sometimes kings will pay it to other kings in the interest of . . ." He paused, considering.

"In the interest of . . . many things," suggested William softly.

"True enough, but I know you also enter into your uncle's calculations."

"No king can afford to overlook a single decimal when he is counting."

Churchill bowed himself out.

"What by all that's holy was that all about?" burst out Zuylestein.

"Leave me, I must consider. All of you," he added, with a sharp glance at Sagitta.

For a long time he paced, rubbed his fingers up the length of the Spear, withdrew the Bosch painting, and studied it's shifting landscapes. He gleaned very little but a headache, but as he was about to set it aside he saw a tent furnished with the accouterments of war. *He*, William, looking old and rather frail, stood in the center of the tent. At his feet knelt a much older John Churchill. The vision faded.

He sent word requesting audience with Charles, and summoned Huygens and Zuylestein to accompany him. It had to appear to be a legitimate negotiation, and—with a pang—the prince decided that he could forgo some of the debt owed to him if it would help convince Charles.

The king sat with one of his bitches on his lap, her pups tumbling on the floor about his feet.

"Well, Willy, how come the plans for departure?"

"Well enough, Majesty, but I confess I am loath to depart."

Charles glanced from the young man's sulky countenance to the frowning Zuylestein. "Oh? I had thought you to be pining for those wet lowlands."

"While it is true I miss Holland, I do not miss my life there. God's wounds, uncle, I will be nineteen come November! I am a man grown, yet when I return home they will once again treat me as a witless schoolboy."

"I share your suffering, nephew, but I'm uncertain what I can do to ease those sufferings."

"I am a Prince of the Blood Royal, uncle, can you not kick sense into the Loevensteiners? You and other of my . . . royal relations?"

Charles smoothed his mustache, pulled the bitch's ear

through his hand several times, then leaned forward, his dark eyes intent.

"Some weeks ago I broached these matters with you and received rudeness and bluster for my pains."

"I know, and I'm sorry, uncle. I was too quick to reject your offer. I behaved like an ill-bred boy."

"If such is the case it may be that I can be of some service to you, Willy my lad, but if you are indeed a man then you must know that men bargain."

William extended a hand, and Huygens laid a sheaf of papers in it. "Uncle, I have contended that the sums owed to me were 2,400,000 guilders. You claim the amount is 1,800,000, I am ready to accept that figure as accurate . . . if certain *accommodations* can be reached."

So abruptly did Charles rise that the little bitch tumbled with a yelp onto the floor. "The time has come for private speech."

Their various entourages withdrew, and nephew and uncle sized each other up.

"You know that the Netherlands have been a thorn in my side for more years than I care to recall."

"Yes."

"You also know or should at least guess how badly my brother Louis resents the interference of your nation in the war of 1668."

"Yes."

"He wishes to see these cheesemongers taught a lesson."

William squeezed his hand so tightly that he felt the nails biting into the soft skin of his palm. But he had spent a lifetime perfecting the art of dissimulation. None of his anger showed on his face.

The king continued. "I have signed a treaty with France. A secret treaty. I had wished to have you present at the signing, but you bit my nose off when I tried to give you a little hint," complained Charles.

"I've said I'm sorry."

"But even after your churlish behavior I had your best interests at heart. I insisted that a clause be inserted in the Treaty of Dover guaranteeing that you would be made the ruler of the United Provinces."

"I thank you, uncle." He was amazed to hear how steady his voice remained.

"Yes, well, be that as it may, the treaty is signed, but I fear me that Louis will not trust you after the reports I and Minette sent."

"Then perhaps, uncle, I should travel to France and reassure my royal cousin?"

"Johan de Witt, and the others who rule your nation?"

"They will be delighted. The Raadspensionary has always viewed Louis as his friend and ally."

"He's about to find out differently, eh?" Charles gave a crack of laughter. "So you would go to Paris?"

The long lashes fluttered down over the soft, liquid-brown eyes. When William raised his eyes to Charles's face, they were filled with humble admiration. "If *you* would smooth my way, Uncle, I think all would be well."

Charles flicked a long, careless forefinger across the young man's cheek. "Flatterer. You look much like your mother right now. And I loved her well. As I love you. Very well, I will write to Louis." Lifting a quill from the desk he looked back and added, "But you would do well not to make such a business about your religion."

"I won't. And in many ways I think King Louis and I are serving opposite sides of the same coin," said William a trifle dryly.

"It's a shame about that priest. It would have sweetened you in Louis's eyes had you arrived with a French father in your entourage."

"Indeed, no one regrets the death of Father Armand more than I." William stared down at the backs of his hands, sighed, and pushed to his feet. "He gave me a great gift."

The mobile brows arched, and Charles stared intently at William. "Do you mean . . ."

Clasping his hands piously William cast down his eyes and prayed God to forgive him for dissimulation. "Yes, uncle, the gift of life."

"God love and preserve you, Willy," cried the king, crossing himself.

"And you, dear uncle." Gritting his teeth he formed the sign of the cross, and waited to see if he exploded in flames. To his vast relief nothing happened.

But he wondered if God were keeping count. One lie too many, and *bang*. His righteous wrath would lance out and pin William like a bug.

It was not a reassuring thought.

Thirteen

I am a hawk: *above the cliff*

Wraithlike, the white-clad figure drifted into the room in the Louvre palace. Quiet sobs shook the slim form, and its arms were cradled, holding something wrapped in the folds of its chemise.

William sat bolt upright, drew his pistol from beneath his pillow, spun the wheel, and leveled on the apparition. His wards snapped into place, and he summoned his power, ready to blast and burn should a magical attack be forthcoming. Sagitta sat up sleepily and scraped her hair back out of her face, then tensed when she saw the intruder.

"Oh gods and little fishes," sighed William. He thrust the pistol away, swung his legs out of bed, and hurried into a wrapper.

"I'm sorry. I'm sorry," sobbed Louise de La Vallière.

"What on earth?" asked Sagitta, and frost rimmed the edges of the words.

"Madam, what is wrong? How may I serve you?"

William was now close enough to determine that the cradled object was a small, pudgy dog. It wheezed alarmingly as it sprawled on its back in Louise's arms, and it regarded the prince out of protuberant brown eyes.

"I am so miserable," sobbed the king's mistress.

Haakon came cat-footing through the connecting door, rapier in hand. He was completely naked, and la Vallière gasped.

"What the Christ?" he demanded as he took in the scene:

William patting and urging a nightgown-clad woman into a chair, and Sagitta throwing a cloak about her pale nakedness.

"Haakon, put on some clothes, you're alarming Madame de La Vallière," said William.

"Alarming her? How can I be alarming her? She's Louis's whore." La Vallière dropped her face into her hands, and her sobs rose in volume. "She has to have seen a man before."

"Go! Go!" With a gesture like a woman herding geese, Sagitta drove the soldier back through the door.

He returned a few moments later to find La Vallière sipping weakly at a glass of wine while William squatted by the chair patting her hand. Sagitta was a figure of disapproval, posed against the bedpost. The dog was snoring before the embers in the grate.

"I'm so sorry to have disturbed Your Highness," said Louise in her soft pretty voice. "But you were kind to me, and I am in misery."

"I'd like to know what form this *kindness* took," Sagitta whispered icily to Haakon as he joined her.

Haakon was rummaging through the gossip that a week at the Louvre had gleaned. Louise de La Vallière had been a lady-in-waiting to Henriette-Anne. (Not a good thought, that. Could it be that she was a part of the coven, and her presence here was an attempt to lure the prince?) She had caught Louis's roving eye, and had become his mistress about nine years ago. She had borne him several children. But last year Françoise Athenais de Montespan had enamored the king, and poor Louise now drooped about the court like a mourning dove. She had several times begged the king to allow her to retire to a convent, but Louis kept refusing. Apparently he liked having the old mistress and the new mistress in close proximity.

William asked quietly. "What has happened to so distress you, madam?"

Her eyes slid to Haakon, then the lashes fluttered down and a blush rose in her thin cheeks. "While it is true I am the King's mistress, I am ashamed in my position. I love the King. Though I suppose it is scant excuse for my sin."

"It is a reasonable one," said William.

"Tonight the King came to my chambers. I was filled with joy thinking he had once more returned to me. But he was merely passing through on his way to *hers*. And . . . and . . ."

Her delicate baby's face worked, and she burst out in a sob. "And he threw his dog at me as he passed."

"Oh dear."

"And . . . she's a very . . . unpleasant little dog, too."

Haakon choked on a laugh, transformed it to a cough, and shrugged apologetically as William glared.

"Madam, what would you have of me?"

"Oh, I don't know. You listened to me when we met at Versailles three days ago. You liked my horse. You seemed kind, and I have no one with whom I can talk. There is no kindness at courts, only greed and lies and pain," she concluded bitterly. "Have you seen my little girl?" she asked abruptly.

"Yes. She's very lovely."

"Yes, I think so too. I think she is proof there is a God, for she shows me that even out of evil good can come. I worry for her. 'Tis said that Madame de Montespan practices black magic to hold the King's affection." She drooped, and Sagitta stirred briefly. "However she accomplished it, she has taken that which I most desired in the world. But surely she would not hurt my baby, my little Marie-Anne."

"No, I'm sure not," said William, still holding her hand, but his gaze was locked with Sagitta's. "Madam . . ."

He tugged at an earlobe, trying to think how to phrase the question. Finally he decided candor was the simplest. He asked, "Louise, there is a statuette which I am interested in seeing. But the Louvre is so vast that I fear I shall never locate it. It is possible that the King keeps it in his chambers. It is a small, female figure, primitive in design and execution." He looked to Sagitta for amplification.

"Carved out of stone, its legs are fused together beneath a swelling belly like that of a woman big with child. There is only the suggestion of a head," continued the sorceress.

La Vallière frowned, her head cocked to one side like an inquisitive bird. "Oh, *that*. Madame de Montespan has it."

It took an hour of soothing, petting, and talking before the young woman was sufficiently revived to leave. Haakon had firmly led Sagitta from the prince's bedchamber, for it was obvious that the gentle La Vallière wilted beneath Sagitta's cold eye.

Once Louise had been sent back to her lonely bed, William tapped on the connecting door, and all three of them piled into the big, canopied bed, with the prince in the middle. Though it was only September the nights were already cold, and the stone walls of the Louvre seemed to exhale a constant cold breath. The heavy tapestries covering the walls helped, but not much.

"Well," gusted Haakons, propping his arms behind his head. "It's a hell of a note when it seems that most of European history is being written by whores. The ground is littered with current whores, and out of favor whores, and no doubt future whores as well. We're forced to haul that virago Barbara Castlemaine to Paris because Charles is too cheap to pay to be rid of her. Now H.H. becomes the comforter and confidant to a waning whore while the waxing whore plays at black magic. Lovely."

"Plays at black magic, I wonder?" mused Sagitta. "Rumor about the court indicates that de Montespan is close with Mazarin." She turned her head to regard William. "And you know that as I am to you so Mazarin is to Louis."

William pleated the covers between long fingers. "The Duchesse d'Orleans was part of the circle. Castlemaine too, and now I've brought her to Paris where she can lend power to Montespan and Mazarin. I wish she'd fallen overboard."

"We do have our heads in a noose, no doubt about that," grunted Haakon.

"How did you meet her?" Sagitta asked suddenly.

"Who?"

"La Vallière."

"During that self-aggrandizing outing where Louis led us all out to Versailles to show off his glory. The landscape designer Le Nôtre was droning on about the gardens while cartloads of dirt trundled up to fill that swamp. I slipped away to shake some of the fidgets out of Barbarossa, and came across Louise also riding alone. She's a cracking good horsewoman."

"Hmmph."

The covers rustled as he shifted to face her. "Are you jealous?"

"No."

"Yes," said Haakon in the same breath.

Sagitta thrust a finger beneath the Norwegian's nose. "You be quiet!"

"No! There are a few things I'd like—"

A stertorous snore interrupted him. The trio all looked to the hearth, where the dog lay like a furry sausage. She was on her back with all four legs thrust rigidly into the air. They burst out laughing.

"Oh, no, and now you'll have to return that abomination to the King," said Sagitta.

"And won't he wonder how you got it," chortled Haakon.

"Yes." William smiled slowly. "I think I'll take it with me to our first meeting tomorrow. I've been nervous about these negotiations, but what an icebreaker Piddle there should be."

Haakon started to climb from the bed. William clutched at him.

"No, don't leave. I feel safer with both of you here."

"All right, but you get to sleep. You'll come down with the croup if you don't get enough rest." The soldier's tone was gruff.

After the prince was asleep Haakon gently brushed the hair from his forehead. "Aye, you sleep. Though we lie among enemies I'll keep you from harm."

And though he couldn't understand why, he drew William into his arms and away from Sagitta's encircling arm.

"Now heed you well," said the prince to his entourage. "We begin negotiations today with a powerful and wily foe. Say little lest we give away too much, and speak no haughty word. Louis is proud and quick to anger, and we lie within his power."

Piddle hung in William's arms, groaning softly with each breath.

"King Louis will want land concessions to give him control of the Rhine," said Zuylestein.

"That is not negotiable."

"But Highness, in return he'll make you Stadholder—"

"No."

"What Louis cannot seize at the bargaining table he will take by war," warned Huygens.

"So be it."

"But, Highness," burst out Bentinck. "I would readily see a dozen of the States hanged if the country had peace, and you were sovereign of it."

"No! The people of my country have trusted me, and I will never deceive or betray them for any base ends of my own! We will hear no more of this."

"Then why the devil are we here?" demanded Zuylestein.

"For a private reason which I swear to you bears directly on the security of our beloved country."

"But King Louis thinks we've come to negotiate," wailed Huygens.

"So negotiate. Tie them up for a week or so. I doubt I'll need longer than that."

Haakon hung back from the discussion, allowing William to handle his bewildered courtiers. His thick golden brows were knitted, and he stared at the heavy tapestry on the far wall as if the hunting scene held some secret message. Once the black circle discovered that the talisman was missing they would instantly suspect William. And then no amount of diplomatic folderol would protect them. Somehow they had to escape from Paris and France before the theft was discovered, and Haakon doubted that a diplomatic mission could gather itself and fly with unseemly haste. Though the mission was reduced from England it was still seventy souls—none of whom William would abandon to the tender mercies of an outraged black magician.

A week at the Louvre, and Haakon was beginning to feel the strain. He and Sagitta together with the faithful Bentinck and old Huygens made certain that William ate or drank nothing which they had not first tasted or prepared. Someone accompanied him at all times, though the prince had clearly shaken off his irksome escort at Versailles when he met La Vallière. But it was exhausting to have the sense that one was surrounded by invisible enemies.

They passed through high double doors into a council chamber. A long table covered with green-baize ran the length of the room. Bottles of wine, ink stands, sheafs of paper stood ready. The French were already assembled, but the large chair beneath an ornate canopy stood empty. Haakon scanned the chairs on the Dutch side and folded his lips tightly together when he noted that there was no comparable chair for William.

Haakon strode to William's side. "Highness, that chair looks low for you, pray try it."

"Oh, Haakon, please," the prince said in an undertone.

"Do it."

"Oh, very well." William sat, and found himself with his chin almost level with the table. There was a titter from the

French. "Er . . . perhaps if I sat on a book, or several books," William said mildly, but his dark eyes were sparkling.

"Not necessary, Highness. I see just the thing." And throwing a grin at the prince Haakon circled the table, seized Louis's thronelike chair, and carried it to William.

There was a furious outburst from the French, laughter and a few cheers from the Dutch, and the entire meeting was delayed twenty minutes while a chair was obtained for William. At last all was ready, and Louis made his entrance.

He was dressed with stunning sumptuousness, wearing a coat of dark teal blue, the color almost completely obscured by gold and silver embroidery in a pattern of leaves and flowers. The folded cuffs of the sleeves were picked out with red bands, and the wrists of his silk shirt where they thrust out from the coat were also tied with red ribbons. Red stockings, red feathers in his hat, gold-embroidered breeches, a walking stick, and a flowing embroidered cloak completed this astounding ensemble.

William noticed one other anomalous feature—a hand mirror clipped to the king's belt, like a lady's fan. The prince's eyes were caught by the silvered surface, and his stomach gave a heave. *So that is how he keeps in contact with his demon*, thought William, and raised his eyes to his cousin's.

Louis was not much taller than William, perhaps half an inch or so, and his black eyes were small, and he kept his lids lowered over them, which gave him a cunning look. A tiny black mustache perched on his upper lip, and the curls of his black periwig reached to his breastbone.

The courtiers of both countries bowed low, while William inclined his head slightly. Louis stretched out an exquisite white hand to his cousin. William grasped it, forced it around, and gave it a hearty shake. Louis's nostrils pinched slightly at the snub, but he said nothing—he merely arranged his cloak to his satisfaction, and seated himself.

"Well, cousin. We are pleased to receive you."

"I thank Your Majesty, and I hope the reason you could not receive me earlier had nothing to do with ill health or diplomatic or other . . . setbacks."

Louis waved this aside with a negligent hand. William, who was perched on the edge of his chair, slewed around and gathered up Piddle, who had fallen fast asleep on the cushion.

"Oh, Majesty, I almost forgot. You seem to have lost this. I'm pleased to return it to you."

The king's eyes flicked from the dog to William and back again. William, with his added sight, could see the anger crawling and coiling like flame-colored serpents all about the figure of the French king, but Louis was a consummate politician. Nothing showed in that faintly exotic face.

"Why thank you, cousin. Though we wonder how you came by that animal."

"Perhaps I can satisfy Your Majesty's curiosity at a more convenient time."

William, angered by the constant use of "cousin" in lieu of his titles, tossed the little dog across the table. Piddle, finding herself bereft of her new friend, sent up a doleful howl, squatted, and lived up to her nickname. Louis's face tightened in anger and disgust, and he lashed out with a backhand slap that sent the dog sprawling to the floor. Her howls of fear and pain echoed through the chamber.

William came half out of his chair, then sank back and said softly, "If the dog no longer pleases you, sir, I would be happy to take her."

"Oh God," groaned Haakon, propping his head on his hand, for he found Piddle to be a most unprepossessing bit of doggie-dom. He then added, under his breath, "Make that seventy courtiers, and one ugly hound." William kicked him, though he gave him a puzzled glance.

Piddle was removed, and the meeting came to order. Demands and counter-demands were made. The parameters of the negotiation having thus been set, everyone prepared to adjourn. But Louis held up a hand.

"Cousin, you are, I think, coming to the age when men think of marriage, and to that end I wish to offer you a bride."

"You do me too much honor." Louis gave William a thin smile which seemed to suggest that he agreed.

"I therefore offer you my baby daughter, Marie-Anne."

William stiffened, pushed back his chair with a scrape, and rose to his feet. "*Cousin*, in my family one marries the legitimate daughters of kings, not their bastards!"

"*How dare you!*"

"It would quite *astonish* you what I dare! I think this meeting has accomplished all that it can. Bentinck, Huygens, Zuylestein, Haakon, attend me!"

They stalked from the chamber in a fine show of outraged dignity, with Haakon providing a monologue as they went.

"Speak no haughty word. Oh no, we wouldn't want to do that. That's such *good* advice. So who goes and—"

"Stow it, Haakon!" gritted William.

"Yes, Highness."

"Hoy, old knight of the quill," called Haakon.

Huygens looked up from his letters and smiled. "You're a merry rascal, Lord Lindel, though I confess I like it well. Now, what may I do for you?"

"Your son Christiaan, sir, is in Paris, *n'est-ce pas?*"

"Yes, he is a member of the Académie des Sciences," said the old man, with justifiable pride.

"Do you suppose he could arrange for an astronomical viewing on Thursday next?"

"Why . . . certainly."

"Somewhere *out* of Paris."

Huygens laid aside his quill. "Lord Lindel, what is this all about?"

The soldier swung out a chair and straddled it, arms folded along the back. "You've known H.H. a long time."

"Since his birth. I served as secretary to his father. I drew up the plan for the Prince's education. Yes, I have been with him a long time, and I love him dearly. Does that answer your question?"

"More than." Haakon laughed. "Then I'll tell you true. I think he's in danger here, and I wish to have all of us assembled and ready to flee if . . . if it should become necessary."

"What! From an outing? We'd lose all our baggage."

"Huygens, what matter goods if you come safely out of deep water?"

"Hmmm, you do make your point, Lord Lindel."

"Who knows, maybe I'll set up as a philosopher when I'm done with soldiering."

"Stick with soldiering, Lord Lindel," replied Huygens dryly, and resumed his writing.

* * *

A small orchestra hidden among a grove of beeches and chestnuts spilled music into the night and created the illusion that the trees themselves were singing. The night sky seemed littered with stars. As William stared up at them their twinkling seemed like distant laughter, as if they mocked the puny efforts of earthbound humans to comprehend their natures.

Huygens helped his son fine-tune the setting on the impossibly long and narrow telescope. Haakon and Bentinck had led the horses into a secluded dell. Sagitta was in the midst of a bevy of court beauties. De Montespan as well as La Castlemaine were there, and William released a sigh of relief. Two less to worry about. Louis, resplendent in white, red, and gold, sniffed a pomander and allowed himself to be instructed by Christiaan's assistants, and was only seen to yawn twice.

William's heart was jumping, so to ease his tension he inspected the contents of the long buffet table: roast suckling pigs, candied rose petals, sorbets, champagnes, elaborate pastries. William briefly closed his eyes as he considered the cost of this entertainment. He only hoped this statuette proved worth the price. Quickly he popped a sugar plum into his mouth, and thrust several more into his pockets—then flushed, and wondered where he had come by this parsimonious streak.

Piddle was groaning, her fat little body shaking with desire as she watched William's hand travel from table to mouth. He gave her the candies in his pockets.

"Your Highness."

"Christiaan," said William with real pleasure, and gripped his former tutor's hand.

"It was good of you to include me in your entertainment for the King."

"You were not *included*, you are the focus of the evening. I also thought it would do Louis no harm to recall that, though the Netherlands may be small, they have many men of genius."

"Yes, but alas our genius seems to be for science and commerce, and in these dangerous times we will need a military leader of genius. And I don't think Johan de Witt qualifies. The States would do well to make you Captain-General before it is too late."

"And I was about to say that I too have no genius for warfare."

"No, what you are is untested and too young for the test, though I fear it is coming."

William's eyes darkened. "Be assured it is coming."

"I have a gift for you," said the scientist, in an effort to lift the melancholy mood which had fallen over the prince. And from over his shoulder he removed a brass telescope.

"Thank you, it's beautiful," said William, leveling it first upon a distant hill, and then upon the river of stars overhead. He slung the strap over his head, the telescope falling like a rifle across his shoulders.

"It is a new design, perfected by my friend Isaac Newton. It is a *reflecting* telescope, utilizing a mirror."

"Oh."

Huygens laughed. "I am bewildering you."

"A little, yes."

Huygens started away, and William caught him by a sleeve. "Christiaan, one thing. After supper, when you begin your demonstration, pray be as enthralling as you can." He spoke quietly and in Dutch.

"All right," said the physicist slowly. "I'll do my poor best."

"And . . . and don't be surprised at what may happen."

"Father has already given me some hint of strange goings-on."

Haakon returned and told William in an undertone, "The first batch are away."

"Good. Hans understands the timing?"

"He's a bright lad. You can depend on him."

"I do, but I depend on you more."

"You still want me to come despite Sagitta's objections?"

"You're coming."

Supper was served, and Louis was pleased to be pleased. The moon set early, and in the darkness Christiaan's soft voice began his quiet but fascinating lecture about the wonders the court was about to witness. William, Haakon, and Sagitta slipped away to where Bentinck waited with their tethered horses.

"You will be careful, Highness," the page said, in a frenzy of worry.

"Yes," said William curtly, thrusting Piddle into Bentinck's arms.

"Please, please, can't I come with you?"

"No, I need someone here I can rely upon. Remember, you must all be gone by midnight, for I'll not return. We'll be mak-

ing straight for the border. Have faith, we'll meet again at The
Hague."

"God go with you."

"And you, Hans."

Piddle howled.

"He should wait with the horses."

"No."

"I don't know you in this mood. You're being stubborn."

William whirled. "*I'm* being stubborn? You have consistently
refused to consider my reasons for including Haakon in—"

"Because he can be of no use!"

"I don't agree. You say the statue will be warded and no
doubt guarded by Mazarin, since he wasn't at the fete. But
magic can't affect the mind blind, and Haakon is blind as a
post, so let him get the statue while we handle Mazarin."

"I am your teacher," cried Sagitta, as William boosted himself onto the wall around the Louvre.

"I think this has more to do with jealousy than sound magical
advice." His hat vanished as he dropped onto the far side.

"And I'd say there's no answer to that," remarked Haakon, as
he cupped his hand to assist Sagitta with a leg up. She glared at
him, but accepted the help.

They were soon in the palace and hurrying toward de Montespan's apartments. The servants paid them little heed, and the
few courtiers they met were of such lowly status that they were
not likely to recognize William or his companions. All the
same, the prince released a pent-up breath when the door to the
mistress's bedchamber finally closed behind them.

Mazarin's black eyes glittered in the candlelight. William
gasped and recoiled, treading upon Sagitta. She yelped. Haakon
leaped past, his sword drawn for a killing thrust.

The cardinal continued to lie slack-jawed and staring upon
the bed.

"God's breath, is he dead?" whispered Haakon, as if fearful
Mazarin would awake.

"I-I don't know." William found that his teeth were chattering, and he locked his jaw.

Sagitta said, "The force which animates him has withdrawn."

Here in this room which fairly crawled with magic, Sagitta
suddenly seemed a lot less human and very fearsome. Uncom-

fortable, William turned away and inspected the chamber. Against one wall stood a strange concave mirror. In its silver yet distorting depths was reflected a beaten silver table set round with black candles. And in the center stood the Venus. Ugly, squat, and gray, she seemed to hang like a hapless fly in a web of nauseating green power lines.

"Then let's hurry, before it decides to return," grunted Haakon. The scrape of his rapier being sheathed broke the spell which held William, and he pointed silently to the table.

"Black candles," snorted Haakon, reaching in and closing his hand about the Venus.

In that moment several things happened.

A gust of that chilling cold which William had not felt since his first out-of-body experience so many months ago issued from the mirror. Spinning, he stared into a surface which no longer gave back an image of the room, but instead a swirling gray maelstrom. Instinctively he sensed that where his picture was a tiny window into other worlds, this was a gateway. With legs gone limp with terror he retreated by halting steps. *Something* was issuing from the mirror.

Sagitta stretched out her hands, power weaving from fingertip to fingertip. She thrust the cage at the creature. Its horrible red eyes flashed, and the cage shattered. Sagitta screamed and collapsed.

Haakon spun, the Venus swallowed up by his great fist. "What the devil!"

"Haakon, go! Run!"

"And leave you? Not bloody likely!"

If Sagitta can't stop this thing . . . how can I possibly? Time's running out. It's almost through the gate. . . .

His thoughts seemed to be spinning like birds in a whirlwind. William heard Christiaan's dry and faintly pedantic voice saying, *"Light, I believe, is a wave, and see how it can be reflected by a mirror and, when shown through a lens, seems to increase in potency."* A much younger William watched with fascination as a black burn appeared on a block of wood.

Reaching back, William jerked the telescope off his shoulder. With fingers that trembled with haste and terror he unscrewed the caps and shook out the mirror and eyepiece.

Would magical light behave the same way? Surely yes. Even magic seemed bound by the most basic natural laws. Calculating quickly, William found the focal point for the ward which had guarded the Venus. Holding the mirror by its edge he dropped it into the vortex, careful to keep his fingers clear of the power. The lines struck its polished surface and shot across the room into the face of the concave mirror. The creature squealed, withdrew, and then, as if pushing against great pressure, began again to emerge. With his left hand William held the eyepiece in that line of light. The beam, strengthened by its passage through the glass lens, struck the creature, and what appeared to be gouts of steam— parts of the body of this mist monster?—blew away.

"Oh, well done, Willy! Well done!"

"Well, thank you, but . . . er, we've got a little problem here."

Haakon stared from William, whose arms were beginning to tremble with strain, to the mirror and back again. "Ah, yes, I see the problem." He pushed back his hat and scratched. "If I pull over another table to put the eyepiece on?"

"That might work, if it's the correct height, but this mirror is not going to balance on its edge." Sweat was crawling down his cheek, and William was wild to wipe it away. "Well . . . look . . . maybe you should just cut on out of here."

"No. Look, you're the one who can use all this magical trash. What say I take over holding the mirror, and you take the Venus and cut on out?"

"No, I'll not leave you."

"Stalemate."

They stood considering while the seconds crept past. "Just a thought, and a damned unpleasant one," said William. "But what if he"—a jerk of his head toward Mazarin—"has another of these mirrors stashed about the place?"

"*Scheisse.*"

"See if you can rouse Sagitta. Maybe she'll know what to do."

Haakon's methods were direct and effective. He emptied a pitcher of water over the sorceress's head. Sputtering, she clung to his coat. Tiny shudders shook her body, and she seemed blanched and diminished by her encounter with the creature. But her quickness had not deserted her. In moments she had taken in the situation and climbed to her feet.

"I'm weak, but I think I can close this door. At least for a while."

"And if he's got another?" asked Haakon.

"One problem at a time," pleaded William, whose shoulders now felt as if hot pokers had been driven through the joints.

Sagitta muttered and waved her hands, creating a web very similar to the one which had guarded the Venus. Stepping back she said, "Let's try it."

William pocketed the lens and mirror, and shook his hands to return circulation. Nothing emerged from the mirror.

"That's it, let's go!" urged Haakon. He ripped down the bed curtains, opened the window, and quickly lowered William and Sagitta to the ground. He tied the material to the leg of a heavy marquetry chest, gave a quick prayer that it would hold his greater weight, and slung a leg over the sill.

Suddenly the door burst open, and, though nothing appeared to enter, Mazarin stirred, sat up, and leveled a terrifying look at Haakon. For an instant they both looked equally bewildered when nothing happened, then the cardinal swept up a cup and launched it at the Norwegian. It clipped him on the side of the head, knocking away his hat and sending him backwards out the window. He managed to keep enough of a grip on the velvet curtains to somewhat break his fall, but he still lay on his back gasping like a fish, while Sagitta plucked at him and hysterically ordered him to "come along, come along."

"A moment, I . . . I can't . . . breathe."

"None of us are going to be breathing for much longer if you don't hurry!" cried William.

Haakon rolled onto his knees and pushed himself to his feet. He paused to recover his hat, then stooped again for the cup.

"Now what?" hissed William, already running for the garden wall.

"Souvenir," came the laconic reply, and Haakon pocketed the lapis lazuli cup surmounted by a figure of Neptune in silver. "*Scheisse!* I should have spitted Mazarin while he was lying there on the bed. I'm an idiot!"

"Too late now," said William, and quickly led them away from a party of armed men that was flowing through the gardens. The Louvre was stirring like a disturbed anthill, and the companions were being driven from the palace walls back toward the palace. They ducked in a side door and paused, panting.

"They'll find our horses. Oh, Barbarossa," mourned William.

"What now?" asked Haakon, surveying the so-far empty hall. His rapier was out.

"Put up." The prince laid a hand on Haakon's wrist. "They'll know us for sure if they see you waving that about. Sagitta, was La Vallière at the entertainment?"

"No. Where are you going?"

"To test a hunch."

He led them quickly to the former favorite's chambers. The lady was there, reading her Bible.

With a hand to her swanlike neck, she fell back a step. "Highness!"

"Madam, I have little right to ask this of you. Only the friendship which we have felt for each other, and my belief in your goodness and piety have brought me here, but, madam, will you hide us?"

"From what do you flee?"

"Evil. There is black magic afoot in this palace. Even now it stretches out its hand to take us—"

"De Montespan?" she asked.

"We have come from her chambers, where we have seen horrors."

"Have no fear. You will be safe here."

"We have horses tethered on the west side."

"They will be found and secured for you."

"And, madam, we must be out of Paris tonight."

"It will be done. You may rely upon me."

"You are good to do this."

"I do it not only for you, but for the sake of the King and his immortal soul." She hurried from the room.

"Can we trust her?" asked Sagitta darkly.

"Yes, for she is a good and devout lady," said William calmly. He was turning the Venus over in his fingers, inspecting the unprepossessing figure.

"It has often been the case that religiosity does not equal goodness."

"Your constant disdain for my faith is beginning to grate upon me," said William, struggling to keep the anger from his voice.

"More evil has been done in the name of your Christian faith than—"

"And none was done in the name of your Old Religion?"

"The old grandmother used to tell that kings were sacrificed to appease the—" began Haakon.

Sagitta interrupted. "Not quite true, and, anyway, is this the time for a religious discussion?"

It was close on an hour later before Louise returned.

"It was touch and go, but your horses are safely stabled with mine. The search is still continuing, but Eugene is keeping watch, and when it eases we will slip you to the stable and away."

William lifted her hand and kissed it. "Madam, you are too good, and I am forever in your debt."

"Free my lord from the evil which surrounds him, and I will consider myself repaid."

William busied himself with reassembling his telescope. Haakon, like the old campaigner he was, snored in a chair. Sagitta stared out the window. The prince would have given much to know what she was thinking.

"You should leave that," said the witch abruptly.

The prince drew his hand lovingly down the telescope's length. "Not on your life. It saved us when magic failed."

"It didn't fail—"

"Oh, Sagi, please. Why are we fighting so much recently?"

"Perhaps because you don't heed me as you ought."

William held up a hand. Footsteps approached the door. A discreet tap, and Eugene entered.

"Now is the time," said La Vallière simply.

They gathered up hats and cloaks. Just before William passed through the door, Louise gave him a fierce embrace and whispered.

"God has given you both wisdom and intelligence. Trust to them, and His guiding mercy."

"Never fear, I shall."

"And give me back my King."

"I shall try. I swear it upon my honor."

Fourteen

I am the blaze: *on every hill*

There is a Terrible joke about the Dutch going round, read William, squinting a bit to decipher Louise de La Vallière's childish scrawl. *Holland is a countess of about a hundred years old; she is very ill, she has two doctors at her bedside: They are the Kings of England and France. The King of England says, Show me your tongue . . . Ah! what a foul mouth! The King of France feels her pulse and says, She needs a good bleeding!*

I worry every day about you, dear Prince, remembering your kindness to me, and despairing of your fate.

William threw the letter across the table with a violent gesture. "The former mistress of the king of France knows that war is coming, but the Raadspensionary refuses to see it. 'Sdeath! The man's a fool."

Spinoza picked up the sheet and peered through a magnifying glass at the wandering hand, while Haakon read over his shoulder.

With a sigh Baruch said, "As you know, I have long been an admirer of Johan de Witt, but I fear me that your assessment is correct. When the cannon balls begin to whistle past his ears he will then be brought to realize that France is our enemy."

"And that will be far, far too late," said Haakon, stretching out in an armchair. "It takes preparation to fight a war."

William ran an agitated hand through his hair. "The States are struggling to select a commander in chief. Zeeland is naturally proposing me, but that has scant hope of passing so long as de Witt and the Loevensteiners continue to hide behind the veil of legality that conceals their hatred of me and my house."

"What legality?" asked Haakon.

"It was determined back in the '50s that no one can be ap-

172

pointed as Captain-General before he has attained his twenty-second birthday. I'm a long way from that."

"So who have they got if not you?"

"Prince John Maurice."

"Who has not seen active service in years," broke in Spinoza. "He's near seventy, and infirm at that." The philosopher sighed. "This little country has been at peace for twenty-odd years. I think maybe we have lost the talent for war."

"Well, we'd best get back into practice, because we're by God going to get a bellyful of it whether we're ready or not," said William, lifting his head from his hands.

A gloomy silence fell upon the room. The only sound was the pop and crackle from the burning logs in the fireplace, and the muted roar as the heated air and smoke rushed up the chimney.

"Your Highness, may I inquire . . ."

"Yes?"

"Why did you go to France? When I bade you farewell in Zeeland you were fleeing for your life from French assassins. Why then put your head in the noose?"

"It's a little complicated." Haakon and the prince exchanged glances. Finally William gave himself a little shake. "Well, you see, it all began with a milk-white horse, and an ancient goddess . . ."

" . . . So after being smuggled to the stables by La Vallière we rode hard for the border, being pursued by every imaginable foe, but being armed with Spear, painting, and statue—"

"And being able to shoot straight in a pinch," interrupted Haakon.

"We held them off, and so reached The Hague two weeks ago. And now a frightening lull has fallen. Sometimes I sense Louis and Mazarin probing about me, but why do they hold off?"

"Because, spooks or no spooks, you don't start a campaign in late October," grunted Haakon.

But Spinoza, lying back in his chair with a hand covering his eyes, seemed not to hear. "I am unmanned," he said faintly. "All my life I've sought truth, rationality, and now you tell me that magic exists."

"Well, in a word, yes," admitted William.

"And you are instructed to fight Louis to . . . to . . . ."

"To preserve first my country, and, if the Lady can be believed, life itself."

"And when you have won you will found a great kingdom based upon these powers?" William stared uncomfortably down at his hands. "Ah, I see you are not yet settled upon that."

"I'd say our first concern is to survive the coming months. Religion and philosophy will have to wait upon the harsh reality of war," grunted Haakon.

"I consider that a dangerously narrow view, Lord Lindel," said Spinoza softly.

"That's your privilege, sir."

There was a soft tap, and Constantine Huygens the Younger stuck his head apologetically around the door. He had taken his father's place as William's secretary the day after the prince's return. The old man had said that at his age a man should retire gracefully, quoting Horace's retiring gladiator: *"fixis as postem armis."* ("With arms hung up on the pillar.") To which William had quickly replied with Vespasian's dying speech: *"Imperatorem stantem mori oportet."* ("An emperor should die on his feet.")

But Huygens had rather tartly responded. "On his feet, aye, H.H., but not with saddle sores on his bum from jouncing across France on some madcap venture. I'm too old for this. If you're going to have adventures you had best have a younger man."

William had humbly begged the old man's pardon for putting him through such stress, but secretly he didn't think much of the son's ability to stand up to the pace either. Constantine the Younger seemed mostly preoccupied with the state of his bowels, and interested only in gossip, which meant that William could not trust him to keep his secrets. It was going to result in William having to write much of his own correspondence, a thing which he viewed with no keen enjoyment.

"Sir, I hesitate to interrupt you, but there are several trivial matters which need to be resolved." Huygens consulted his notes. "The steward of your house at Bodegraven desires your help in settling a breach-of-promise suit, then there are a number of bills which need your personal attention. Your long absence has left things rather in a muddle."

"Are you suggesting that I owe you an apology?" asked William, torn between amusement and pique. "Lord Lindel."

Haakon paused with his hat halfway to his head. "Sir?"

"Pray give me three days to sort out these household matters, then hold yourself ready to ride."

"I am at your command and disposal, sir. May I ask to where, H.H.?"

"To make an inspection of the fortifications."

Huygens gaped. "De Witt will have a fit," he promised solemnly.

"He will, but he was overruled by their High Mightinesses, the States. I forgot to mention that while they debate about making me Captain- and Admiral-General, they have decided that I should visit the fortifications on the Rhine and IJssel, to see if they are in a good state of defense."

"Will wonders never cease!" said Spinoza.

"Proof that there's a God, eh?" teased William.

"Or a Goddess," quipped the Norwegian.

Late that night, when William sought his chambers, he found Bentinck waiting for him, ready to assist him into bed.

"Hans, find me some quick and promising young lad and make him my page. You are far too useful to me in other roles."

"Sir?"

"You will be one of my aides-de-camp when this pestilential war begins, and if I'm ever given command."

"Then it is coming?"

"Oh yes, you may be sure of that. In fact, I ride out with Lord Lindel in three days. I wish you also to accompany me."

"Honored, sir, but for now let me help you." He smoothed the hair back off William's forehead. "You look so tired."

William grasped the hand and pressed a kiss onto it. "Hans, I love you so much. Love me always." There was something pleading in the voice and the soft, dark eyes. Bentinck hugged him close.

"For always."

Sagitta entered dressed in a wrapper, her hair falling like a river of white gold down her back. William kissed her then went to the wash basin, while Bentinck busied himself with the hanging of the prince's coat. Seating herself on the bed, she picked up a scrap of paper which lay on one pillow.

"What is this, Bentinck?"

"Oh, Heer Spinoza left it several hours ago. He said to tell His Highness that the words writ there might give guidance."

Water dripping from his chin, William raised his head out of the basin and called, "Read it, Sagi."

"'The last end of the state is not to dominate men, nor to restrain them by fear; rather it is to set free each man from fear, that he may live and act with full security and without injury to himself or his neighbor. The end of the state . . . is not to make rational beings into brute beasts and machines (as in war); it is to enable their bodies and their minds to function safely. It is to lead men to live by, and to exercise, a true reason . . . The end of the state is really liberty.'" Frowning she added, "There is a postscript. 'I could substitute *superstitious* for *brute*, but I think you catch my drift, H.H.' What is this about, William?"

"An ongoing debate."

"Between you and Spinoza?"

"Between me and my soul."

"What do you fear, dear one?"

Her breast was soft against his cheek, and he could hear her heart beating. Suddenly he was sobbing. The tears scalded his throat, and he dug his fingers into her shoulders, pulling her closer, trying to crawl beneath her skin. Anything to banish the dreadful aloneness.

"Sagi, my country is in such desperate danger."

"Shhh, you will save her."

"What if I can't? What if they make me Captain-General, and *I can't do it?*" Their eyes were locked, blue to brown. Strain and exhaustion had etched deep lines on either side of his mouth. Sagitta kissed away the tears which had gathered there.

"Come to bed."

William heard the soft *snick* of the closing door as Bentinck slipped away. She soon had him stripped and beneath the covers. His teeth were chattering, yet his skin felt fiery hot where it rested against her cool flesh. Already his erection was a painful presence. And that made him sob all the harder, for the thought of enduring another agonizing bout of coitus interruptus was more than he could bear.

Warm kisses, as soft as a feather's touch, drew a line from his collarbone to his hip. Her tongue flicked across the head of his cock, and he gave a *whoof* of surprise as fire shot from his groin to the top of his skull.

Sagitta straddled him, her knees pressed firmly into his sides. Passive and supine William lay back and waited for her to mount him. Instead she gripped his shoulders and, giggling, pulled him over. Their faces were only inches apart. A few wisps of white gold hair lay damply plastered against her cheeks.

"Don't look so shocked," she whispered.

"What are we doing?"

"Making love."

"This isn't another ritual?"

"Of sorts." Her eyes darkened, and her grip tightened on his shoulders.

It was bliss to actually consummate. After the last, shuddering release he lay atop her savoring the languid sense of well-being which filled every corner of his exhausted body. Laughter came bubbling up, and Sagitta's eyes snapped open. She had been playing with a strand of his hair, and now she gave it a hard yank.

"Oww!"

"Are you laughing at me?" she asked.

"No, at me. I guess I'm now—finally—technically not a virgin anymore."

"My poor love. We should have done this long before."

Leering, he said, "I quite agree." There was a shadow in her eyes and, sobering, he pulled her close. "What? What's wrong? What have I done?"

"You, nothing. But I, I have . . ." Her voice trailed away, and she shook her head.

"Your Lady, will she . . . object?" he asked, picking the word with care.

"Let me just say she will not be pleased."

"Because I am a mere man."

"No, because, in your arms, I am a woman."

They lay in silence, and William realized from her regular breaths that Sagitta had fallen asleep. Gathering her more securely in the crook of his arm, he said softly to the darkness.

"I can have her. I will have her. You can guide, Lady, but I'll not be driven. Not by any man. Not even by a goddess."

The darkness gave back no answer.

Somewhere high on the wall a lone trumpeter blew a sour fanfare. William pulled his hat further down over his eyes. Throughout the Gelderland fortress the royal party heard doors slamming, the slap of running feet. The governor of the fort rushed out, wiping his mouth with the back of his hand. It was evident they had caught him at his dinner, for his breeches were loosened and a napkin flapped at his neck. He was soon shivering, as the cold December wind cut through his shirt.

"I'm here to inspect the fort, governor. Kindly put on your coat and escort me," barked William.

But Everard van Tichelaar was made of sterner stuff than the forgotten and rudderless outpost captains Haakon and William had been intimidating over the past weeks. Drawing himself to his full height, he sucked in his paunch and demanded.

"By whose authority, Highness? I had no word of this from the Raadspensionary."

"Johan de Witt is not yet the sole ruler of the Netherlands. The States still hold a role, and it is they who have given me the authority."

"Authority? Ha!" He snapped his fingers beneath Barbarossa's muzzle. "That for your authority."

"No." Haakon laid a restraining hand over the prince's. "Allow me to handle this. *You disrespectful bastard! You want authority, I'll give you authority!*" And, whipping out his sword, he spurred Thunderer toward Tichelaar and laid him low with a heavy blow across the back with the flat of his blade.

A crowd of ill, ragged soldiers had gathered, and from back in the ranks came a thin cry of *Viva Orangie!* The call was taken up by others until it became a roar. Tichelaar rose groggily from the ground, his teeth chattering.

"P-pardon, Your Highness. I . . . I had not grasped the full . . . full import of your visit."

It was soon apparent that Tichelaar had no more idea of commanding a fort than William had of shoemaking. Exasperated, the prince burst out, "Is there no one in this pestilential fortress who knows one end of a cannon from another?"

A whip-lean man in his late fifties stepped forward. "Captain Pedro Ronquillo, Highness, at your service."

"What the devil are you still doing in Holland," drawled Haakon. "There have been better pickings in any number of armies."

The Spaniard shrugged. "I have a Dutch wife. I'll escort Your Highness, but you won't like what you see."

They climbed onto the battlements and stared despondently at eight ancient cannon resting in rotting carriages. William walked to the parapet, looked over, and fell back with a muffled oath. The ditch which he thought encircled the fort in fact had been filled in on the eastern side, and was now an orchard and garden.

A disdainful forefinger pointed. "This?"

"Tichelaar's idea, to cut costs."

"Brilliant, and the most likely result will be to end up with cut throats," grunted Haakon.

"This all has to be dug out." William shook his head.

"We'll try, sir, but the first hard freeze will stop that, and we only have one hundred and fifty men."

With narrowed eyes William scanned the walls. "In a fort that would require two thousand to properly defend it. Well, lead on."

"To?"

"The armory. I may as well see the worst all at once, and then fall into a single fit of hysterics."

They crossed the parade ground, with a gaggle of curious and adoring troops at their heels. William nodded and smiled. Despite his fury and despair, he knew that the life of his country would depend upon these men and how well they would fight for him. Though he still held no official position, he did not doubt that when the onslaught of war broke across the land his country would turn to him, placing its faith in the House of Orange, as it had always done. So he was gracious now, though the effort made his face feel as if it would crack.

In the armory Haakon lifted one of the heavy, obsolete *lontslot* muskets. "No *snaphaan*?"

"No, sir."

"Powder," asked William.

"We have enough for each musketeer to fire seven rounds, and still have powder for the cannon."

"Gunners?" William asked his voice tightening with strain.

"There are eight at Maastricht, I'm one, and there's one other."

"Along the *entire* Rhine frontier?" Haakon's voice spiraled almost into the soprano range.

"Yes, sir."

"God preserve us, we're all going to die," said Haakon. And no one had the heart to dispute him.

"God preserve us, but there is virtually no powder, lead, or matches to be had anywhere in the country!" cried de Groot.

Johan de Witt wheeled sharply on his heel and stared from beneath lowered brows. "What!"

William raised his head. Exhaustion lay like a smothering blanket across his chest, and his eyes burned in the feeble glow of guttering candles. He and the Deputies of War had been meeting since eight the preceding night. It was now close on four in the morning.

"He's quite correct. Through the treachery of an Amsterdam banker, Louvois has been able to buy up our stores. The French Minister of War has been our biggest customer. Dutch soldiers are going to die under a hail of Dutch shot."

"Are you accusing me of treachery or wrongdoing?" asked de Witt in a low voice.

"No, it's just another symptom of a trading nation too intent on profit to look to her own defense."

"So what do we do?" asked the Deputy from Overijssel.

William slewed around in his chair. "Make me Captain-General!"

"Don't be absurd," snapped de Witt. "You're but nineteen. The Perpetual Edict bars you until your twenty-second year."

"What a pity Louis isn't going to wait for me to attain twenty-two."

"Do you honestly consider yourself capable of commanding an army?" Scorn was thick in the Raadspensionary's voice. "You are completely inexperienced. You may have some knowledge of military theory and parade-ground exercises, but you have never in your life heard a shot fired in earnest."

"What you say is absolutely true, and I'm the first to confess that I would give anything to serve an apprenticeship under some experienced commander, but we don't have one. *And we're running out of time.*" William brought his hand down hard on the table. "We must muster men while we still have a chance."

"We have sufficient men."

"We have possibly thirty thousand, and I'm being generous."

"Nonsense! We have one hundred thousand on the rolls."

So violently did William come to his feet, that the chair fell with a clatter behind him. "And they don't exist anywhere but on the rolls, and in your head!"

"You forget yourself!"

William rushed on, ignoring the outraged murmurs of the Deputies. "I've spent the past three months riding from one end of this country to the other. We have a dead-pay scandal that I doubt could be matched by any other nation in Christendom. Officers put their valets in uniform, or borrow troops on muster day from other units. This is no army! I know. I've counted. Can you claim as much?"

"I think it best if your elders continue this discussion. You are obviously distraught, William Henry. You will feel better after you have rested."

"Go ahead, talk. You'll still be talking when the French come to bury us."

"Highness!"

"Hans, dear God, breathe, dear fellow." William threw his book aside and helped his friend into a chair.

"T-the States! They've voted to make you Captain- and Admiral-General."

"Dear God!" William dropped heavily into a chair.

Drawn by Bentinck's shout, Sagitta and Haakon hurried into the study.

"What, what is it?" asked Haakon.

"It's happened," said William faintly.

"Well, I haven't told you quite all," said Bentinck, shamefaced.

"What's wrong? What have they done?" asked the prince.

"It's only for one campaign."

"*No!* I refuse!"

"*What?* This is what we've been fighting for for four pissing months!" bellowed Haakon.

"Think, Haakon. If I accept these terms and fail, I'll be discredited forever!"

"And if you do not take command, your credit or lack thereof will be the least of your worries," broke in Sagitta. Her aspect was upon her, and she seemed somehow both more and less than human. "*Remember for what we are fighting.*"

William paced jerkily away and stared out a window at the snowy February day. Humiliation lay like an aching lump in his throat. *To be treated like a troublesome, unruly, and untrustworthy boy . . . no, they could all go straight to hell!*

But as his breath misted the window panes, and tears blurred his eyes, he remembered crisp days skating on the frozen canals . . . the riotous wonder of spring and the tulip fairs . . . a day's hunting in the woods near Bodegraven, pausing for a cup of fresh milk from a friendly and pretty farmer's wife . . . the horny hands of old gaffers busy carving wooden shoes for their plump and rosy grandchildren.

"They're my people. To set my own wounded vanity before them is to fail them," he said quietly to himself. Straightening his shoulders he turned to face his companions. "Hans, pray tell their High Mightinesses that I accept their terms."

A huge bonfire in the courtyard of the Binnenhof flickered in the windows and threw a ruddy glow across the faces of the diners. Despite the snow, hundreds of people were holding an impromptu dance in the courtyard. The sounds of singing and cheering came faintly through the heavy walls of the palace. Inside the dining hall several hundred delirious Hagenaars watched while their beloved prince ate his meal.

William had always found the ritual of the public meal to be a trial. Today, after the strain of appearing before the States to take the oath as Captain-General, and his worries now that the responsibility had at last fallen upon him, he found himself with less appetite than usual.

Staring grimly into space, he turned a walnut between long, slender fingers. Suddenly a child's crying cut through the crowded hall.

"What is that?" asked William.

Zuylestein left to investigate and, returning, reported, "A little orphan boy from Leiden has lost his hat in this chaos. I've had him removed."

"Poor baby," said the prince in a low tone. "Bring him to me. He shall have a ducat."

The child arrived, wide-eyed, but still snuffling slightly. He stared in mute terror and wonder at his prince, and drew his sleeve across his sticky face. He had obviously been enjoying the sweetmeats which William had thrown to the crowd earlier in the evening.

"I hear you lost your hat."

"Y-yes, sir."

"Well, tonight is very special for me as well for the Netherlands, and I'd not like to think that someone was unhappy tonight. So here are two ducats. Buy yourself a new hat, and when you wear it think of me, and wish me well."

He folded the chubby hand about the coins, patted the child on the cheek, and sent him out with a soldier for escort.

"You like brats, don't you?" asked Haakon.

"Yes. Perhaps it's a function of being lonely for so much of my childhood. But if God spares me in the coming confrontation I'd like someday to marry and have a house full of babies." His eyes were upon Sagitta as he spoke, but if she was aware of it she gave no sign.

The spectators were removed, a heavy, sweet dessert wine was set out on the tables, and William's household drew near. Sagitta bloomed like a fragile lily in the midst of so many men. They ranged in age from their late teens to old Prince John Maurice, but one thing they all had in common—the uncommon grimness of their expressions.

"La Vallière reports that Louis is deep in negotiations with various German states," said William softly. "If he succeeds we will be left without a friend in the world save Spain, and her aid will be more symbolic than real."

Haakon pulled a letter from his pocket. "I have a comrade with whom I served who is now fighting for France. He managed to get a peek at a report prepared by Louvois on the state of the army. According to Edvard the elite troops number almost 8,000 men. There are in addition 25,000 horse and 86,000 foot, and some number of miscellaneous foreigners. In all somewhere between 105,000 and 120,000 troops."

"They'll be well-enough supplied," grunted Prince John. "And brilliantly led . . . Turenne, Condé, Luxembourg."

A walnut shattered with a loud *crack* beneath William's fingers. "And to oppose all that we set a Captain-General with no experience, and very few to advise him. God must come to our aid!"

"She will," said Sagitta, so low that only William heard her.

And for some unaccountable reason he felt a chill close about his heart.

Fifteen

I am a flood: *across a plain*

A fortnight later, booted and spurred, William met with Johan de Witt in the Raadspensionary's office.

"So." De Witt laid aside a sheaf of papers. "I told you several months ago that I would oppose your appointment for as long as I could, but that if you were appointed I would support you faithfully."

William propped himself on the corner of the desk. "Is this a somewhat oblique way of telling me that you intend to abide by your word?"

"Yes." De Witt folded his hands precisely in the center of his desk. "You have instructions, Captain-General?"

"A few. Please make heroic efforts to obtain me powder and shot. Otherwise we shall be forced to hurl insults at the French. I'll also need the conscription of every man between the ages of eighteen and sixty."

"Harsh."

"But necessary if we are to survive."

"Where do you anticipate the first blow will fall?"

"Upon the east. Louis will cross the Rhine. That way he can flaunt his great army beneath the noses of the German princes, and keep them quiescent."

"The IJssel Line must be held."

"I will do my uttermost to see that it is." William slid off the desk and settled his hat. "I ride for my hunting lodge at Dieren. From there I can coordinate the defense of the Doesburg fortresses. It is one of the key forts along the line, and the best place to make our stand."

"God go with you, William Henry."

"And keep you, sir."

* * *

"Louis declared war on April 8th. He states he has long been displeased with the conduct of the Dutch, and now he owes it to his glory to chastise us . . . blah, blah, blah." William handed over the letter, which had just arrived from de Witt. "And my dear Uncle Charles preceded him by a few days. It is indeed true that kings have no relatives."

"Louis is sure to march soon, but when?" Haakon drove a gloved fist into his palm. "*When*? Our intelligence is hopeless when it's not nonexistent."

"William and I will handle that," said Sagitta, spurring up beside them.

She was dressed as a man, in a sober coat of gray with a gray hat. In her saddle bags rode the Spear, the painting, and the statue. She and her burdens were a constant reminder of just how much rested upon the tiny army drawn up outside of Doesburg.

And tiny it was. Where the States had promised eighteen thousand men, William and his field deputies found fewer than eight thousand waiting. And not all the eight thousand were worth having. Sickness ran rampant through the ranks, and men deserted in droves when their pay continually failed to arrive. Haakon had resorted to harsh measures to prevent desertion. But it was not much of an army that required another army to guard it.

"Where to today, H.H.?" asked Haakon, deliberately ignoring Sagitta's reference to esoteric powers. Now that he was back in the familiar surroundings of a military camp the Norwegian found the whole business rather distasteful.

"I want to check repairs along the IJssel Line, and I mean to make time, so we'll take only a few of my personal guard."

As they trotted out of the fortress, the dust kicked up by their horses' hooves hung heavily in the air and only reluctantly settled back to earth. William could feel sweat breaking out beneath the brow band of his hat. At IJsseloort they paused to contemplate a handful of flat-bottomed boats, lying like despondent hogs in a rapidly drying wallow. Their crews threw dice on their scrubbed decks, and occasionally stared curiously at the martial troop drawn up on the river's bank.

"Even Heaven seems determined to thwart me," muttered the prince. "Without water we cannot move supplies, and without water the Water Line is going to be as useless as the IJssel Line.

Why, this year of all years, do we have the driest spring in living memory?"

"You know the answer to that," said Sagitta in a low tone. "He uses his power while you continue to refuse. Do you not now see your folly?"

"He has the luxury to break his health by spell-throwing. I have to be in the saddle from dawn 'til dusk, and then labor over paperwork 'til midnight. When do you suggest that I make magic?"

"Sooner or later you must make the sacrifice, or we will be lost."

William had gone white around the nostrils. "I don't think anyone can question my willingness to *sacrifice!*"

"Then use the gifts you've been given!" She jibbed at her horse's mouth, pulling the animal back on his haunches, then spun and cantered away.

"Bitch," remarked Haakon.

"Be silent," grunted William.

The next day they had reached the end of the line. All along its twenty-six-hour length men had labored to dig ditches, place palisades, build walls. None could doubt the earnestness of the effort—nor its futility.

At dinner, William industriously mashed a turnip into mush with the prongs of his fork, while Huygens searched fastidiously through his plate for some edible bite. Haakon, after wiping clean his plate, had passed on to a liquid diet of dark ale.

William skimmed the plate away with the tips of his fingers, leaned back, and pinned Haakon with a grim glance. "Well?"

The mug hit the table with a dull crash, and Haakon shifted to face the prince. "We can hold it with a hundred thousand men."

"We have perhaps twenty-five thousand in all the country."

"Then the IJssel Line cannot be defended."

Silence hung like cobwebs in the sweltering dining room. The screech of William's chair being thrust back cut like a blade, and Huygens upset his plate, so violently did he jump.

"We start back?" asked Haakon.

"No, I have matters to attend to. In the morning."

"We're going to lose six hours."

"Tomorrow, Lindel."

"Yes, Highness."

The governor of the fortress at Nijmegen was more than

happy to prepare a bedchamber for the prince. Sagitta helped William remove his boots and loosen his neckcloth.

"We can cover more territory if I accompany you."

He caught her hand. "You won't know what you're looking at. No, it's better if you stay here and guard my body. Keep me breathing. I may be gone a long time."

"Keep your wards up. You're vulnerable in the astral world. Both Louis and Mazarin, or any of those bitches in Paris, could attack you."

A wan smile. "How very encouraging."

Her lips were soft against his. "Come back to me."

"I will." A convulsive grip of his hand on her upper arm kept her close. "And let's not fight so much in the future, Sagi. I do. . . . " He cleared his throat. "Love you."

"Go."

The astral world was disturbed. It was less like flying through a silver sea, and more like laboring through canyons and valleys of crystal and steel. It was as if the very fabric of this overreality was being stretched and torn. It was with relief that William dropped out of it onto the battlements of the fortress at Maastricht. A gunner leaned against his cannon, whittling on a stick. William's heart rose as he viewed the quiet efficiency of the fortified city. Men drilled, great stacks of fodder and supplies lined the walls.

Then, hunching his shoulders as if against a blow, he turned to look outward, and his breath caught—for where he had hoped, prayed, to see the French invasion force he saw only a small covering force. Louis, not willing to lose an entire campaign, had moved on.

William flew down the Rhine. French flags snapped in a freshening breeze over the forts at Orsooi and Burik, and before Wezel lay a besieging force. And on the far bank of the river lay the vast bulk of Louis's invasion force. Drawn despite himself, William drifted, a voiceless bodiless ghost, through the teeming camp—closer and closer to the great golden tent pitched near the river, where flies and the stench would be less likely to offend the royal nostrils.

Somewhere deep within him a little voice was yammering at the top of its little lungs that what he was doing was *insane*, but he was fascinated, like a moth by candlelight. He hovered gaping and bemused when he realized that Louis had come to war with not only his queen in tow, but with his mistress as well. And in that moment he was nearly lost. Only some sudden prick of impending danger sent him tumbling away, frantically jerking the silver cord which linked his astral form to his body—away from the terrifying *clash* of snapping jaws filled with iron teeth, champing, biting, pursuing, ready to sever that fragile link between life and disembodied death.

Sweating and gasping he fell back into his body, rolled to the edge of the bed, and vomited while Sagitta held his head.

Groaning he lay back and forced past a raw throat: "Call Huygens. We cannot stay here and let Holland be lost! We must fall back behind the Water Line."

"Mazarin and his sorcerers haven't left us enough water to create a wading pond," said Sagitta, dipping a cloth in water and laying it across his eyes.

He peeped out from beneath the cloth. "You and I are a match for any ten of them?"

"Why don't we forget the bombast, and concentrate on making it rain?"

"Well," gusted Haakon, settling down onto the battlement with William and waving a bottle in the prince's direction. "This will be the real test."

Haakon looked startled when William took the bottle, wiped the mouth, and took a long pull. "Of what? And what is this shit?"

"Wine."

"Could have fooled me."

"A test of all this magical bullshit. God rot this foul rain!"

"I worked hard for this rain," remonstrated William, but with a youthful grin which Haakon hadn't seen in a long time. "Don't be ungrateful."

"How do you do it?" the mercenary asked, watching the water run from the brim of the prince's hat.

"Sagi says I think too much, and that that's deadly with magic, but I can't help it. I just can't reach out and herd the pretty clouds, so I start with the ocean. I picture the clouds sucking up water like great sponges, then releasing it over my unfortunate Holland. Between that and opening the sluices and cutting the dykes, we are indeed a sad and soggy little nation."

Haakon grunted. "Better that than a sad and *conquered* little nation. I just wish the plaguy peasants would stop working for the French," he added.

"Who can blame them?" said William with a sigh. "They watch us flooding their ripening fields, and they see hunger, perhaps starvation, come winter. Of course they close the sluices." William hung his head, and Haakon wondered if the moisture on the prince's face was entirely due to the rain. "War makes men very hard," William said suddenly.

"No, command makes you hard. If you're just a soldier your main concern is preserving your butt. You don't have to make the difficult choices."

"Ever since my birth my people have loved and adored me. It is due to their stubborn loyalty that I am Captain-General, and I repay them by ordering them shot when they try to preserve their homes and fields."

"H.H., you're trying to save their goddam country—and, believe me, if a French army rolls over them they're going to learn the meaning of bestiality. Your shooting orders will seem like love pats. Besides, you've got bright peasants. It won't take many executions for them to get the message."

"You're such a strange person, Lindel. Don't you ever analyze? Your actions? Your soul?"

"I never fret, Willy. I just put my hand to the plow and drive to the end of the furrow. And Sagitta's right . . . you think too much."

"You said this would be a test of magic. How so?"

"If we can hold Muiden with five hundred troops, and your magic gimcracks against the Marquis de Rochefort and his four thousand troops, I'll be a believer."

"But will I?" said the prince, so softly that Haakon had to strain to hear him. "These men know that we guard the main sluices. If we fall the Netherlands are lost. Will it be magic, or their own valor?"

"Or your presence, sire," growled Prince John Maurice of Nassau.

William and Haakon rose and hastened to assist the old man up the final few stairs onto the battlements.

"I was remarking that it would take magic for us to withstand Rochefort."

"Willy, never explain yourself. That's a prerogative of princes," said the old prince to the young one. "And personally

I care not if you dance naked by firelight if you think it would do any good. Thunder in hell, I might join you."

Haakon covered his eyes with a hand. "God, what an appalling prospect."

"Don't eat a bullet, Lindel. I want the pleasure of shooting you myself," remarked the old man, as he unlimbered his telescope and eyed the French.

The sound of the crowd was like the waves of a great sea rising and falling as it mumbled and grumbled at a rocky coast. Each time the sound increased, the worthy magistrates of Dordrecht started and paled.

William, seated at the long table in the Peacock Inn, crumbled a piece of bread between his fingers and tried to school his features into something approaching amiability. This visit to Dordrecht had carried him away from his headquarters at a critical moment, and only the pleas of the magistrates—that if they returned to the city without him they would be killed—had overcome his objections. As he sat looking down the table at the troubled faces of the good burghers of Dordrecht, he suddenly remembered Prince John Maurice's assessment of the situation in a recent letter: *The government lost its head, the people its heart, the country its hope.*

In the two weeks since the French invasion, the country had collapsed like a sad soufflé, great areas lay beneath water, and riots had erupted in many of the major cities. The people, searching for someone to blame for this *Rampjaar,* had turned on de Witt and the Loevensteiners. Earlier in the day, William had learned of an attack upon the Raadspensionary which had laid him low with a knife wound.

Suddenly he murmured aloud to Sagitta. "We're *Dutch.* We're sober, hard working, decent, and cheerful." He gestured toward the outer wall of the inn. "So why then are we acting like maddened Frenchmen?"

"They're in a panic."

"And my noble presence seems to have done nothing to quiet them," he said sharply. "This was a fool's errand."

"Sir," asked one wan-faced older man. "What hopes for peace?"

"None, I would say. Over my strong objections de Witt has

sent an embassy to Louis, but he refused to see them. He thinks we are nearly beaten. Why should he offer terms?"

"Now, H.H., be fair," sang out Haakon, sniggering a bit into his beer. "Louis was a very busy man. He had to hold a dress rehearsal for his splendid entry into The Hague."

There came several cries of "What?" and "You can't be serious."

Haakon raised a hand. "So help me God, he rode with great pomp into Utrecht just six days ago. There he was, all in gold on a big white charger, with the rain pelting down and pretty girls flinging sodden flowers at him." The Norwegian's face hardened. "And he's going to learn to his pain that he's just made a major military blunder. If he'd pushed on right after his Rhine crossing, nothing, humanly speaking, could have stopped him." He wagged his eyebrows significantly at William and Sagitta, and the prince glared. "But by lazing about in Utrecht he's cost himself the war."

"Lord Lindel," cried one magistrates. "Do you truly believe we can stand?"

The soldier rose and raised his glass to William. "With His Highness the Prince of Orange leading you, I know you can."

William felt the blood rush into his cheeks, and he awkwardly accepted the toasts of the assembled magistrated.

"Sirs, I thank you for your hospitality, and I'm sorry I could do little to quiet your good citizens, but now I must return to my headquarters."

The coach was brought round, and it pushed its way slowly through the crowds surrounding the gate of the inn. Suddenly a sweating, red face was thrust in a window, and the man bawled, "Highness! Highness, are ye yet Stadholder?"

More people were now clinging like ticks to the sides of the coach.

"Good people, I am content as I am." —

"But we are not, until we see Your Highness Stadholder," screamed the crowd, and, seizing the horses by their bits, they forced the royal party back into the inn.

The mob now filled the courtyard of the inn, and a pair of spokesmen told the magistrates bluntly that they would not be permitted to leave until they had declared the prince Stadholder. Paper and pen were brought, and a trembling magistrate drafted the resolution offering William the Stadholderate of Holland.

William's lips were clipped tight shut with annoyance, and climbing onto the top step of the coach he called out:

"Good people, I thank you for this display of love and devotion, but I have taken an oath not to accept the Stadholderate of any province even if it is offered to me. I am still bound by the Perpetual Edict, even if these gentlemen are not." He raked the terrified magistrates with a cold eye.

A clergyman stepped from the crowd. "Sire, this pestilential Edict was forced upon most of the States against their better judgment. We place our faith where it has always rested—in God and the House of Orange. I absolve you from your oath."

Still William hesitated, and Sagitta, leaning in close, hissed:

"Take it, William, take it! It is what my Lady and I, and others who love you, have labored for for so long."

And with a slow nod, trying to disguise the elation which filled him, William acquiesced.

August 20, 1670

Dear Grandmama,

Pray forgive the length between letters, but events in this Unhappy country have moved with Bewildering speed. After the good folk of Dordrecht forced the magistrates to declare His Highness Stadholder, the news spread like Wildfire, and on July 4 Willy was declared Stadholder and Captain- and Admiral-General of the whole Republic for life.

That same day de Witt, but newly risen from his bed of pain, Resigned. So ends an era, and all hail the New age! My little prince showed but little emotion when the news was brought him of his elevation, and perhaps that is right. It is a fine thing to be master of one's country—as much of it as is not in French hands or Under Water.

De Witt has been importuning H.H. with whining letters asking His Highness to clear his name of the imputation that he has Neglected the army. He also asks that the Prince silence the pamphleteers who lampoon him at every opportunity.

One of Willy's first acts was to issue a statement
exonerating all the Regents from responsibility for the
military Disaster, so I don't know what more that ass
requires, but William did—

"Haakon, where the devil are you? I ride for Woerden with or
without you!" called William.

"Coming, H.H." Haakon put down his pen and hurried out,
buckling on his sword. "God's blood, there's never a moment to
catch your breath or take a shit in this outfit!"

"You have to do it on horseback." Bentinck grinned.

The young men swung into their saddles, and Sagitta offered
a stirrup cup to the prince.

"You're certain you won't come?" William asked.

"I can serve you better here. We must have some small victory to give heart to the people, and pause to the French. Somewhere there must be a French force small enough for us to
defeat." Her smile took some of the sting from the words, but
only some.

"Very well, scout, but scout cautiously. De Montespan almost
spotted me last time."

The party clattered away, and Sagitta had started back for the
house when a lone rider on a foam-flecked horse galloped
through the gate.

"The Prince. The Prince," he gasped, falling rather than dismounting from the horse.

"Ridden to Woerden," Sagitta said, soothing the trembling
mount. "What's toward?"

"I bear a letter from the Council in The Hague. The de Witts
are trapped by an angry mob in the Gevangenpoort prison, and
their High Mightinesses beg that the Prince bring troops to restore order." The man glanced down the road. "Perhaps if I ride
hard . . ."

"You would never catch them. They left hours ago, and your
horse is spent. We have no remounts," she lied, in answer to the
question in his eyes. "But I will see that the Prince receives the
letter upon his return. Return now to The Hague, and tell them
the Prince will come when he can."

Tapping the letter thoughtfully against her teeth, Sagitta
watched man and weary horse trot back down the road. Then,

with an abrupt nod, she vanished into the house. Several minutes later she emerged wearing her boy's clothes. In a short time she was on the road to The Hague.

"Where's Sagitta?" asked William as he seated himself at the table.

With a shrug Haakon lifted a cover and peered suspiciously beneath it. "Hell! Trotters again."

"What do you expect? Pheasant and asparagus? We're at war, Haakon." A bowl of barley soup was placed before the prince, but he had no more then lifted his spoon when a messenger burst into the room.

"Highness, the de Witts are dead! Torn to pieces by a maddened mob in The Hague!"

The chair was thrust back, and Bentinck leaped to William's side, for the prince had gone deathly white.

"What madness is this?" he whispered.

"Madness indeed, sire."

In a few terse words the messenger described the day's events: Cornelius de Witt's imprisonment, accused of plotting to murder the prince; his trial and interrogation under torture; the judges' determination that there was no evidence to support the charge, but fearing to release him lest the angry mob turn upon them; Johan joining his brother in the Gevangenpoort; the cavalry called in to maintain order; the rabble beginning to disperse; then inexplicably the cavalry being ordered away and the mob suddenly going wild, attacking the prison, forcing the door, and dragging the brothers into the street, where they were felled by musket fire and then torn to pieces.

The man shuddered. "I saw a woman running by clutching a bloody bit of cloth for a souvenir. Her nails were red. A message was sent to you to bring troops to restore order—"

"I was in Woerden much of the day." William turned to Huygens. "Bring me my correspondence!" They searched through the letters, but no message was found.

The man trembled, seeing the anger on the prince's face. "I swear to you, Highness, a message was sent."

"I don't accuse you." Turning to Haakon and Bentinck he added, "There is I think little point riding to The Hague tonight. Tomorrow I will consult with the states, though I know not whether to proceed against the culprits with vigor. From what has been said half the city was involved, and this thing has been done by the foremost burghers."

"If you don't act you will be accused of complicity," said Haakon.

"I'm not a dictator. I can't simply ride into the city and mete out summary judgment. But I fear me you are correct, Haakon, and I will rue this day's work long after the bloodlust is forgotten."

It was late that night when William awoke as Sagitta slid into bed beside him. Pushing up on an elbow, he combed his hair out of his eyes and asked blearily, "Where have you been? I was worried."

"Riding. I needed the deep woods."

"Terrible things have happened. The de Witts are killed."

"Is this so terrible? They have been your foes from the moment of your birth, and though out of power would have continued to conspire against you."

"Sagi, if we must needs kill our opponents then civilization is a chimera. Governments are formed so that men may disagree without murder, and I tell you true, I loathe a mob more than anything."

"They acted out of love for you."

"That does not comfort me."

Raindrops chased one another down the window panes and hammered with a throaty roar on the roof of William's headquarters at Nieuwerburg. Spinoza, Prince John Maurice, Bentinck, Zuylestein, Haakon, and Sagitta all listened as the prince outlined in an unemotional voice the terms upon which Louis and Charles were willing to offer peace.

"The ceding of the United Provinces as a territory of France, an indemnity of sixteen million guilders a year, and each year an embassy to be sent to the Sun King commemorating our gratitude for his kindness in so graciously spreading the mantle of his glory over our unworthy and undeserving nation."

"Outrageous!"

"Unbelievable!"

"Unthinkable!"

"And the English terms?" grunted Haakon, after the Dutch had vented their feelings.

There was a rattle of papers as William fished up the letter. "An indemnity of a million guilders, trading concessions, the Zeeland island of Walcheren, and ten thousand pounds a year to be paid by us annually for the right to fish in English coastal waters."

"Modest by comparison with Louis," remarked Spinoza.

"And my uncle is so certain of my agreement that hard on the heels of this incredible missive he sends a special embassy. Arlington and Buckingham are due here this day."

"Buckingham!" exclaimed Sagitta.

"Quite."

Haakon, William, and Sagitta locked gazes for a long moment.

"There is no question of making peace on any of these terms," said Zuylestein.

"I agree."

"Then, since peace must wait 'til the next life, those of us in this one must pursue the war," gusted Prince John. He pushed to his feet and slapped the hilt of his rapier. "I'm for Muiden. Who rides, and will accompany me on part of the road?"

"I," said Zuylestein. "I fear to leave my troops for as much as a day without their papa, lest they melt away."

William embraced them.

"I suppose I must saddle my horse and paddle back to The Hague," said Spinoza. "What a shame one cannot ride ducks."

"Stay, I wish to discuss something with you."

"Yes?"

"I would wish to make you a councilor. I have need of your wisdom, Baruch."

"I'm a dabbler in theory, Highness."

"Nontheless, I would welcome your advice."

Spinoza gave a gracious and graceful little shrug. "Then I shall of course serve you to the best of my poor ability."

A young aide stuck his head in. "Highness, the English emissaries are here."

"Send them in. Sagitta, you, I think, had best withdraw."

She swept him a curtsy and left through a side door, but Haakon thought her expression was sour, and he tugged thoughtfully at his lower lip.

The discussion had been going on for hours. William polite but intransigent, the English envoys increasingly furious and frustrated.

"Your uncle loves you well and seeks only your best interests," burst out Arlington.

"Oh, of course, that explains why he makes war upon my poor country."

"He would see you king."

"I thank him, but I like better the position of Stadholder, which the States have given me, and I believe myself obliged in honor and confidence not to prefer my interest before my obligations."

"Highty tighty! Your people are weary of this war, Highness, and wish peace with England, and if you persist in your misguided policies you may meet the same fate as the de Witts."

William, slamming his hands onto the desk, almost levitated out of his chair. His dark eyes were blazing. "Don't imagine, Lord Arlington, that your threats to have me torn to pieces by the people frighten me—I am not in the least fainthearted by nature!"

Now also on his feet, Buckingham burst out in amazement: "Surely you see that everything is lost?"

He could not control the slight tremor which shook his words, but William kept his gaze steady and his chin up as he said coldly, "My lord, my country is indeed in danger, but there is one way never to see it lost, and that is to die in the last ditch."

The door slammed shut on the heels of the furious emissaries. William sank trembling back into his chair.

"Well," said Haakon. "Now all that remains is to select the appropriate ditch."

Sixteen

I am a spear: *that roars for blood*

It was carried on the wind: the smell of sodden ash, and, over all, a sickly sweet odor. Several horses plunged and blew, their steel-shod hooves ringing on the frozen ruts of the road. William's magic had brought the rain. Louis's had frozen it. The Water Line had become a highway, and the Hollanders' Christmas gift of

1670 had been the full force of Luxembourg's troops sliding and marching into the heart of their country. The French general's orders to his troops had been, "Go, my children, plunder, murder, destroy, and, if it be possible to commit yet greater cruelties, be not negligent therein. Let me see that I am not deceived in my choice of the flower of the king's troops."

The sudden freeze had forced William to lift the siege of Charleroi, and he and his weary troops had tumbled willy-nilly back into Holland trying to stem the hemorrhage. They were now two days behind Luxembourg, and Haakon hoped they wouldn't catch him. They were hopelessly outnumbered, and Willy's prestige would not bear another defeat.

The younger men muttered and held handkerchiefs to their faces. Haakon, his square-jawed face expressionless, watched William. Alone among these puppies, only the Norwegian knew the scent. It was the smell of roasted human flesh. Haakon had smelled it in Poland. He had hoped to never smell it again. Certainly not in this country of quiet farmers and tradesmen.

William shook out the reins, and Barbarossa pushed through the hedge at the side of the road. The flat, fallow fields of Holland lay before him, and beyond that the village of Bode-graven. But no village stood. Instead, charred rafters and walls thrust out of the snow like black teeth from white gums. Far back in the column someone gave a sob.

Grimly William rode on. On the outskirts of the village had stood one of William's many homes. It was a blackened ruin. They pushed on into the central square, Barbarossa stepping daintily around unburied bodies lying in the snow or hidden in the debris of their homes. Only three houses were standing. The wind sighed around exposed rafters, and soot rained like black tears onto the trampled and bloodstained snow. The only sound was the harsh call of crows, and the clap of their wings as they rose, disturbed, from their gruesome feast. It was New Year's Day, 1671.

Mutters and curses ran through the column. William's face was a white mask showing nothing. Only his eyes betrayed his fury and anguish. Suddenly he raised a hand, calling for quiet, and then Haakon heard what had attracted the prince's attention: the sound of an infant crying.

William swung down, and a foot soldier rushed to hold Bar-barossa's reins. Haakon followed the prince into the house and up narrow stairs. The wails died as the echo of their footfalls reached the child. She was lying in a crib in one corner of the bedroom. Tucked about her was an embroidered quilt. Haakon wondered if the hands which so lovingly prepared that cover were now frozen clay. The baby whimpered softly and sucked at her fingers. William with gentle hands scooped up the child and wrapped her in a fold of his cloak.

"She will be fostered in my household," he said.

Haakon drew a finger down one newel bedpost. "We're alone here. You can let it out."

"I'll let it out on the battlefield. Come."

They returned to the column and rode on to Zwammerdam. It was a repeat of the massacre they had found in Bodegraven. A few people who had managed to flee the fury of the French had begun to creep back to their shattered homes. Despite the horror of their circumstances, the terror-stricken Dutch greeted their Stadholder with cheers, and cries of relief. Women clung to his stirrup leathers and kissed his boots, and a number of the men offered to enlist at once.

William with a gentleness and a patience far beyond his twenty years calmed and soothed them. He promised help and a supply train, and he urged that the surviving women and children travel at once to The Hague or to Amsterdam.

"We may be sending them from the frying pan into the fire," said Haakon.

"Please," gulped Bentinck.

"What?" growled Haakon.

"They burned them in their homes. Civilians—"

"Welcome to war, Hans William," came the brutal reply. Tapping his crop on his boot, Haakon leveled his gaze at the prince and resumed: "Luxembourg is like to fall upon The Hague in fury, and whether the city can long withstand a siege with so many peasants flooding the city—"

"No, he won't."

"Eh? Won't what?"

"He'll never reach The Hague. I'll see him drowned in a ditch first."

"Well, better him then me," grunted Haakon, and spurred after William.

* * *

"We must have a thaw."

"You're mad."

"You're the one who is always telling me to use magic."

"Not when it will destroy you!"

"It is a risk I must take. The duty of a ruler is to rule, or die in the attempt."

"But not to throw his life away needlessly!"

"Sagitta, help me or hinder me, but weary me no more with words. While you talk, Luxembourg marches, and my country lies helpless before him."

Only a single candle lit the room, and Sagitta's deep-burgundy gown blended with the heavy draperies, creating the illusion that her face, framed by silver-light hair, swam disembodied in space. She nodded slowly.

"Very well, we will go together in search of the sun. But we must make this effort in a place of power."

"Are there such in Holland?"

"Yes, but they are difficult to find. Magic lies but lightly upon this land. The stones and trees no longer sing to the Goddess. You practical, somber folk have buried the memory deep."

"Perhaps it is better so."

"Do not scorn what has given you a throne."

"No, the love and loyalty of the Dutch people have given me the Stadholderate."

"Do not be so sure," came the cryptic answer as Sagitta swept from the room.

"I know this place," cried William in amazement, over the boom of the surf. "It was here I came to myself after meeting with your goddess."

"Yes, it is a place of power." She slid from the saddle, then looked back inquiringly when William did not dismount.

Leaning on the pommel, the prince asked, "Sagitta, satisfy a curiosity. Were you the white mare that appeared at the Binnenhof?"

"What should it matter?"

"It does, so humor me."

"All right, yes, it was me."

"Being not completely human, can you bear my child?"

Her back stiffened. "How dare you! You forget yourself."

He spurred in close, yanked back her hood, and tangled his fingers in her hair. "How? In what way?"

"You're a man. The mysteries are not for you." Her expression was cold, the words flat and emotionless, but a pulse was beating frantically in her throat, betraying her.

"We're not talking mysteries. We're talking about what lies between us."

She averted her face. "Don't. There are other matters which must concern us."

"You have loved me as a woman to a man."

"And paid for my weakness," she cried.

"What are you saying?"

"My Lady..." Her voice ran down into silence, and she averted her face.

In a violent motion he swung to the ground, huddled in on himself. "Am I so unworthy?"

"I am her handmaiden."

William slewed around, hands pressed to his breast. "And I am your lover!"

"Why when you learned of sex did you not find some mortal woman, and lay with her?"

"Because I'm not a rutting beast! When I join with a person it must be with love." He stumbled away through the deep sand.

Sagitta ran after him, the hem of her habit catching on the frozen blades of grass. Gripping his shoulder she jerked him around. "What is it you want of me?" she cried.

"The reassurance that you love me."

A faint and illusive expression flickered briefly across her face, then was gone. He frowned down at her, trying to recapture the moment, trying to quiet the sudden nervous fluttering which invaded his stomach. He shook his head, shrugging off nameless fears, and he cursed magic, and the raw sensitivity which allowed him to read levels upon levels in every word she spoke, the flutter of her fingertips, the shrug of her shoulders. She murmured into his shoulder, "My love is not something you should want."

Hands tightening on her arms, he gave her a hard shake. "I will take that risk."

Covering her ears Sagitta cried, "Stop it! Don't you know what you risk? Don't you see the danger?"

"Sagi, you frighten me—"

Her head snapped up like a coiling snake's. Her face was cold, repulsive, alien. "I should. I *should*!"

"How is he?"

Spinoza looked up from his book. Haakon had thrust his head around the door, and the lines of his big face dropped like a saddened hound.

"No change," said the philosopher, and his eyes flicked to the big canopied bed. Haakon hesitated, twisted a lock of golden hair about a finger. It was an oddly coquettish gesture, when the finger was the diameter of a belaying pin. Spinoza realized that the younger man was worried and frightened, and, like most healthy young animals, desperately uncomfortable in the presence of illness.

"Come in, come in. I could do with the company."

"You sure I won't . . ." Haakon jerked his chin toward the silent bed.

"You won't disturb him. He's far too weak."

"Damn . . ." The roar adjusted to a hoarse whisper at Spinoza's wince. "Damn her, I wish she was choked!"

"She suffers too."

"Still," muttered Haakon sulkily.

Spinoza smiled, and stretched out a hand. "Come. Come sit."

The Norwegian tiptoed into the room with much jingling of spurs, the ring of his scabbard against various pieces of furniture, and the discovery of every squeaking floorboard in the room. With a sigh of relief he lowered his bulk into a chair and stared at the bed.

"What did they do in that cold, lonely place?" asked the Jew, as he nursed his pipe to life.

"Magic. And, I have to say, it worked. Or maybe there really is a God, and he took pity on these poor Dutch beggars. Whatever, the thaw is almost complete. I rode out three days ago to scout, and could have laughed. All these poor French bastards staring nervously down as the ice cracked beneath the hooves of their horses. And the expressions on the foot soldiers—they were about to shit. The weight of the horses was breaking through the ice, but it was going to be their frozen butts that got to wade. The horse boys might wet their toes, but little else. I saw soldiers marching with their muskets held over their heads, in freezing water up to their necks. And Luxembourg—"

"What about Luxembourg?" came a reed-thin voice from behind the tightly drawn curtains.

"Highness!" Spinoza yanked back the curtains, and caught William as he struggled up onto an elbow.

The dark eyes were burning in the white, drawn face, and he repeated with growing agitation, "What about Luxembourg?"

Haakon replied, "Rumor had it that he was pitched from his horse and broke his leg. Alas, rumor exaggerated, he had only caught a bad cold. May it go into the croup and kill him."

"No, that task is for me. Alas for my people in Bodegraven and Zwammerdam. He will—must—pay for that." A sudden desperate coughing shook the frail body. Spinoza supported the prince against his shoulder and held a handkerchief before his mouth. "A . . . drink," William panted.

Haakon sprinted for the wine which stood mulling on the edge of the fire.

"Mix a little honey with it. My mother used to do so, and it eased the throat," instructed Spinoza.

"How . . . is . . . Sagitta?"

"Well enough. Whether it was exposure or magic or both, you and the girl were very ill when you were brought in." Spinoza coaxed a drink down the boy's throat. "Thank God your horse had more wits than you, Highness—becoming hungry and cold he trotted home like an obedient beast, and the alarm was raised."

"But it worked—that is all that matters."

"Oh yes," said Haakon. "It worked. Luxembourg is out of Holland."

Another coughing fit shook the prince. He lay back exhausted against his pillows while Spinoza rubbed his chest. "How can Louis be doing it? He must be an empty husk, sucked dry by sorcery. Haakon, I must have a victory of arms. I can't take much more of this," he whispered.

"It will come," Spinoza soothed, but Haakon frowned from beneath knotted brows.

"By God, we'll force him to fight. We'll pick the moment, and we'll win."

"And if you lose?" snorted the Jew.

"Then we'll pick another moment and win *that* one."

* * *

"Ho, these rascally Dutchmen are as superstitious as Frenchmen, don't let anyone tell you otherwise."

"*Haakon!*" cried William, and spurred Barbarossa for the big figure trotting nonchalantly at the head of three thousand men.

As the big charger slid to a halt on his haunches, the prince kicked loose the stirrups and launched himself at the Norwegian. Haakon rocked back under the impact, but managed to keep a grip on horse and prince.

"That glad to see me, are you?"

"Yes, oh yes!"

The soldier helped William slide to the ground, then dismounted himself. "Bivouac those men," he bellowed to his second. "And reassure them that the sky isn't going to fall. The Prince of Orange won't let it." He dropped an arm across William's soldiers. "Now me for some wine, and a chance to get out of this wet. God's teeth, I need webs between my toes."

They were soon gathered in the prince's tent; Sagitta seated on the floor at William's feet, her skirts spread about her like a fall of rose petals; Spinoza comfortable in a camp chair, his face more deeply lined than Haakon remembered it from January, but with that catlike smile still in place; Bentinck, sturdy and faithful, serving wine.

Haakon drank deep, gusted a sigh, and smacked his lips. "Ah, that's better. Now what are you doing blundering about the Spanish Netherlands, H.H.?"

"Supporting my Spanish allies," said William.

And Bentinck muttered at the same time, "Blundering is absolutely the right word." He blushed to the roots of his red gold hair when he found everyone's eyes upon him. "Oh, not through any fault of the Prince's! It's the fault of these *allies*. Everyone squabbling over prerogative, and those Spaniards not knowing their asses from a ravine. You'd think after ruling these lands for years they'd have decent maps!"

"My Hans is irritable," said William, with a little wink and a smile. "But how went Naarden?"

"Well enough. A little stretch of the muscles for my troops. We broke their backs with six days of easy siege. Luxembourg pulled out with his tail between his legs, and has now also withdrawn from Utrecht. We marched in two weeks ago, and then the storm hit. Worst thunderstorm I've ever seen. Destroyed the cathedral, leaving only the belfry standing. The troops seemed to think it was some kind of comment from God."

William sat aside his cup and gripped Haakon's hands. "I'm glad you're here, and your three thousand will help. Condé is camped near Seneffe. I hope to draw him out and finally get down to the matter. One pitched battle, and—"

"Which we'd better damn well win," grunted Spinoza. "We can't afford a big loss."

"And I can't afford this war of attrition, Baruch. That they *will* win. They have more men and arms. No, we must fight, and place our faith in God."

"And other things," said Sagitta abruptly. She rose, shook out her skirts, and left.

William shook his head in frustration. "There, I've offended her yet again. I seem to do that more and more frequently."

"You've got greater things to worry about than the tantrums of a girl," said Bentinck. He too left the tent.

William reached into his pocket and withdrew the squat Venus figure. "He's right, you know. I have to worry about the woman who stands behind her." And closing his fingers tightly about the stone carving he walked to the tent flap. "I'm going to check on the men."

"Fine."

The flap fell closed behind him, and Haakon looked at Spinoza. The rain pounded on the tent top.

"How is he?"

"Tired, under more pressure then a young man—than any man—should bear. Torn between magic and faith."

"Is there any real difference?" asked Haakon cynically. "It's all praying to an invisible God."

"It's not just faith in his Calvinist Lord. There is also faith in mankind."

"I don't think I understand."

The secretary laid a hand on the soldier's shoulder. "Don't worry, I'm not sure I do either." Spinoza paused to tamp tobacco into his pipe. "I'm glad you're here. Try to keep an eye on him when at last this battle is joined."

"Reckless is he? I'd heard rumors."

"Wisdom or folly? I'm not sure. He rides in the van. Always galloping to where the action is hottest. His officers have pleaded with him to take more care for his safety, but he only replies that his men fight best when he leads them. And against that there is no argument—it's the truth. I think he has no fear."

"*Scheisse*. Well, I'll have plenty for the both of us." Haakon levered himself out of the chair. "I'm going to see what intelligence has been gleaned." He grinned back at the Jew. "Sharpen your pen, Heer Spinoza, there'll be a battle to record soon enough."

They had slipped through a thick belt of woodland lying to the south of Seneffe. The Spanish, with their uncanny ability to always do the wrong thing, had stubbornly decided to take a short cut and discovered too late that it led them directly beneath the French sentries. Condé was now off harrying the unfortunate Spaniards. More unfortunate than the dismay of the Spanish allies was the loss of the baggage train. That loss had left William very low on cannon.

But he was not to be deterred. He would fight with or without artillery. The army was now drawn up in order of battle in the open meadows around Seneffe, and the prince, Haakon, and Sagitta were all three present. Each seemed to sense that today's battle was to be the turning point.

William stood impatiently by Barbarossa while Bentinck refastened his breast and backplate. Suddenly he tensed and, lifting his head, seemed to test the wind.

"Louis is yonder," he said, pointing with his chin toward the little village.

"Come to gloat over our destruction?" snorted Haakon. "Well, it may be a little premature."

Sagitta, dressed again in boots and breeches, unbuckled her saddle bags, and drew out the Spear, painting, and statue. "You must carry these today. This battle will be settled not with iron alone."

William glanced down at Bentinck's red head. The young officer was arranging the prince's broad orange sash and securing it at William's hip. Bentinck looked up. "Highness, it's all right. I know you're using magic. I don't care. I'd go to Hell with you if that's the only way I can serve. And I don't think God would be so cruel."

"Oh Hans!" William flung his arms around the young officer and hugged him close. "Pray with me."

Haakon moved to Sagitta and lifted the case containing the Spear from her hands. Her expression was bitter.

"Here, H.H. This is a sacred object. Mayhap God will hear us better."

William lifted out the blackened Spear, then knelt and set it point down in the moist earth. Shoots of tender June grass caressed the pitted blade, softening its harsh, sharp-edged appearance. Bentinck, his fresh face screwed up tight with concentration, knelt beside the prince with William's hand in his. His lips moved silently. William seemed a statue, and Haakon, as he gazed at him, felt a thrill of fear, for the prince's face looked as serene and motionless as the face of an effigy. The officers of the prince's army noticed the little tableau and also dropped to their knees—Prince John Maurice, stiff and halting, Waldeck and Ouwerkerk grim-faced, Henry Casimir shivering with suppressed excitement. To the east, a priest who rode with the few remaining Spanish troops blessed his flock. Haakon swallowed a lump in his throat—he had thought of Armand for the first time in many months.

"If there is an eternity," he said in a gruff whisper, "and you can hear me . . . well, keep an eye on him. You died to let him live. Don't let it all go for naught. Pass it onto God, won't you? I feel more comfortable asking favors from friends."

William rose, and, removing a pistol from one of his saddle holsters, he shoved in the Spear. He unlaced the breastplate of his armor and thrust the picture and the Venus into his shirt.

"Not very comfortable, that," said Haakon.

William winked. "Maybe they will stop a bullet."

"You're going to need all the help you can get." The Norwegian flicked a forefinger across the jeweled Garter emblem where it rested on the prince's right shoulder. "Must you wear this?"

"How else can my men locate me in the thick of battle?"

"And how else can the French marksmen shoot you without a target?" Haakon smacked a hand against his forehead. "God's blood, and I'll be riding with you! And them being only Frenchies, and not able to shoot straight, they'll no doubt aim for you and hit me."

There was a roar of laughter from the young officers. Perhaps it partook more of nerves than humor, but it went far toward relieving the tension, and many of the men, hearing that gay

laughter, laughed themselves, and prepared with better heart to
face the arrival of the French.

It was not long in coming. At nine o'clock Condé and his
army arrived, and found the allies waiting for them. He quickly
arranged his troops and drew up his artillery on a small knoll.
William, having picked the place and the moment, was in
slightly better position for an artillery barrage. But a cannonade
was not going to settle this battle. The torrential rains of May
and June had made the roads virtually impassable to the heavy
artillery wagons. Both armies were limited in firepower.

A little before ten the cannon began belching and roaring.
Balls sang overhead and buried themselves deep in the moist
earth, sending up great gouts of mud and grass. Barbarossa
danced, and William controlled him with one hand. His other
rested lightly on his hip, gripping his baton. Some younger
soldiers flinched at the high-frequency screaming from the sky,
but William disdained to acknowledge the incoming fire, and in
time his example calmed the fears of his troops, or at least
shamed them into a sturdy endurance.

Smoke billowed across the meadow, crawled in the hollows,
and clung to the trees like tattered remnants of white and gray
finery. The acrid scent of gunpowder stung the eyes and nose.
William handed his baton to his equerry, unlimbered his telescope, and tried to sweep the length of the French line. He cursed
the masking smoke, and, lifting a hand, he created a hollow in the
center of the meadow. The winds came rushing in to fill the void,
and the smoke blew aside. There sat Condé, a resplendent old
figure on a big gray horse, coolly sipping wine from a bottle.

"He plays a waiting game," said William, massaging his
aching temples. That brief flare of magic had pinpointed him to
Louis and his circle, and the prince felt them probing his wards
and shields. "Well, I'll wait no longer. Folly or not, 'tis time to
come to grips." Wheeling Barbarossa he stood in his stirrups
and roared over the din of the cannonade:

"Guards advance, cavalry in formation one hundred yards
ahead. Strike the center. Walenburgers hold hard, and close on
the left flank when they attempt to encircle us. Count de
Souches, to the right, but only after we've joined." He turned to
his equerry and scribbled out a message. "For Prince de Vaude-
mont—he must hold the Spanish in reserve. The French out-

number us, so we must be thrifty with our men. Go." The young man dug in his spurs and rode hard for the Spanish.

Rising again in his stirrups William cried over the din of cannon and the murmurs of men. "Hollanders! With me!"

They advanced at the trot, Haakon on his left, Bentinck on his right. He could hear the jingle of harness, the squeak of saddle leather, the ring of sword on stirrup iron, and, in the distance, the suck of hooves in muddy ground as the French cavalry rode to meet them. William peered through the veiling smoke. The French were perhaps sixty yards ahead. He called the charge, and his own cavalrymen rocked into a slow, collected canter. Balls whined past like a flight of beetles on a summer's eve. The Dutch cavalry gave answer. William fired off both pistols, then dropped them and drew his sword, an enormous, heavy-hilted Pappenheim. A ball struck the blade of the saber, setting up a weird harmonic vibration that echoed in his head.

The French line seemed solid. Then, suddenly, as if by mutual consent, gaps appeared. The two lines merged, the riders cutting and thrusting as they passed. William saw a saber descending and lifted his to meet it. The blow landed near his hilt, and the shock vibrated down his arm. With a twist he threw aside the enemy blade, then slashed. His sword grated down his opponent's armor, bit deep into the man's thigh. Then the prince was into the second rank, where the entire episode repeated itself. Only this time his blade found no target.

The Hollanders reformed and rode again to meet the French horse. They made one more pass, then the French cavalry wheeled and galloped out of the skirmish. William found himself in a sea of advancing French infantry, and with no time to ponder the withdrawal of the French horse. *Possibly the advance of Waldeck?* he wondered, then hacked away the hand of the man gripping his stirrup.

The two sets of infantry had now engaged. Both sides fired their every musket and pistol, then lunged forward with pikes. For a long moment there was much thrusting and slashing, but well beyond the distance where anyone could be struck. Then abruptly the French drove forward. What had been fairly discrete lines became a surging, shouting, screaming, bleeding mass.

Off to his left William saw Ouwerkerk, streaming blood from a wound in his head, hard-pressed by foot soldiers.

"Come on children!" he screamed to his men, and spurred Barbarossa into a run. They hit the French with such force that the troops broke and ran under the onslaught.

"Hot work, Highness," the young man gasped as Haakon knotted a handkerchief over the wound.

"True, but we'll—" A tongue of deep-red fire arched through the overcast sky. William flung up a hand. The tumult of battle died around him as he turned inward and strove frantically to deflect it. It touched his breastplate. The polished surface seemed to brighten suddenly, and the blade of flame was deflected. It became a writhing, shuddering sheet of fire that fell upon a great oak tree with an explosion of sound. The tree burst asunder, tiny tongues of fire licking among the green leaves and the shattered limbs.

There were cries of "lightning" from the troops, French and Dutch alike. William spit out a mouthful of bile and said softly, "Sagi, thank you."

"This cannon is killing us," screamed Haakon over the din. "Let me take some men and see if I can take them."

"Yes. Good. Go."

Bellowing, driving the plunging Thunderer down the line, Haakon gathered a column of infantry, and perhaps fifty cavalrymen. They toiled away through the deep mud. William scanned the field, trying to get some sense of the battle. He saw old John Maurice heavily engaged with foot soldiers, and rode to his aid.

Barbarossa was flecked with foam, his flanks heaving. The deep mud was exhausting man and horse alike. William didn't know whether to curse the mud or bless it, for it also blunted the effect of the cannon balls. . . . With an evil whistling, another ball came in. It landed on the hindquarters of the horse just ahead, crushing and mangling the legs and haunches. The poor beast went down screaming, trapping its rider beneath. The man's screams joined those of the horse. Barbarossa's hindquarters tensed, and he lifted over the fallen horse and rider. The backs of French infantrymen were presented to the prince. He drove the point of his Pappenheim through the nearest. The man collapsed, wrenching the sword from William's hand. This sudden assault from the rear dismayed the French, and they fled. The old prince and the young leaned on their pommels, gasping for breath, their faces grimed with smoke and mud. A young soldier recovered

William's sword, wiped it on his breeches, and respectfully presented it. William remembered seeing him from the first.

"Your name?"

"Walther Halewijn, sire."

"You'll be a lieutenant at the end of this day Walther Halewijn." William suddenly realized that he was screaming, but there was no need. One set of guns had fallen silent. "Haakon! He's done it!"

He spurred toward the French lines, straining to see. Haakon, tall on his great black horse, was waving a standard over his head. The great swathe of material rippled and snapped in a freshening, rain-filled breeze.

The French were regrouping, preparing to retake their captured guns. Suddenly Thunderer shuddered, staggered, went to his knees. Haakon kicked out of the stirrups, swung his right leg over, and stepped to the ground. The big charger rolled onto his side. Haakon spared not a glance for the fallen beast—he was looking to the rear. Shouting, waving his sword, he gathered the Dutch, and they came flying back off the knoll. On the crest of the tiny hill appeared a marching line of French troops.

William led his men forward to cover the retreat. As he rode he caught a witless running horse by its bridle and brought it along for Haakon.

"Should have thought of this—*stand still, damn it!* Many of Condé's troops have been off—*whoa!*—harrying dagos. *God rot you!* They're going to keep marching up in waves." The horse was continuing to spin in circles about Haakon each time he tried to get a foot in the stirrup. Lifting his foot Haakon gave the brute a hard kick in the stomach. It sat back, eyes rolling, then relaxed and stood docilely while the Norwegian mounted. "Short little shits, these Frenchies," he remarked as he sat with his knees practically under his chin. He kicked loose his feet, and tightened his knees on the horse's sides. "As I was saying, maybe we should withdraw."

"No. Here I stand and here I fight." William whirled Barbarossa, and returned to the battle.

"But it's not a ditch!" shouted Haakon, as he cantered after.

The sun lay on the horizon like a gleaming white disk floating in a milky sea. William chewed on a piece of stale bread, washing it down with sour wine. His body ached, but his mind was strangely clear.

"Wonder what o'clock it is?"

"Six-thirty, seven?" guessed Bentinck.

"Wish I had my watch. It has that new pendulum movement perfected by Christiaan. 'Tis most wonderous to see the wheels go round."

"The men are tired, hungry," said Prince John Maurice.

"So are theirs. And he can't have anymore in reserve."

"So we continue?" asked Haakon.

"Aye."

"Then I'm for my men," grated Maurice. "To tell them they must continue to stand and be slaughtered."

"You criticize me, cousin?"

"I merely regret the necessity of war, that so many good men will return no more to Holland. But no, I don't criticize you. I, alas, see the necessity of continuing this pestilential battle."

Night came, and thick clouds boiled out of the south. Bentinck, slumping in his saddle, rode up. "Highness, this is hopeless. We can scarce see hand before face, much less the enemy."

"There's a moon up yonder," muttered William, more to himself than in answer to Hans.

"And ten thousand Frenchmen out in the darkness," muttered Haakon. His voice was hoarse with fatigue.

"We must see them to kill them." William's eyes glittered in the darkness as they were lit now and again by the muzzle flash of pistol, musket, and cannon.

Tears, perhaps? wondered Haakon, then sank once more into exhausted lethargy.

William rose in his stirrups and held the Spear aloft. "All right, you bastard," he screamed. "Here I am! I pit my Moon Lady against your darkness. *Let there be light!*"

For a long moment there was silence as even the shouts of the soldiers, the cries of the wounded, and the sound of the guns fell mute. Suddenly a howling wind rushed through, filled with the scent of the sea. The clouds parted, and a full moon swung pale and serene overhead. The pale rays fell on a scene of horror. A groan went up from the French. William swayed, and Haakon steadied him. Stiffly he turned in the saddle.

"Hollanders, to me."

With the suck of hooves pulling from mud, they advanced

again, but at a walk. The horses and men could give no more. Steel beat on steel, and then came a trumpet's call. The French began to withdraw, and the stunned and exhausted allies watched them go, too weary to hinder or pursue. The legendary Condé, the greatest general of an era, was withdrawing, leaving a twenty-year-old general in possession of the field.

William pitched from his horse, sprawling facedown in the blood and mud.

Bentinck leaped down and raised the prince to his shoulder. Haakon stared up at the moon.

"And this is a victory?"

Seventeen

I am a boar:
ruthless and red

William unbuckled his sword and threw it onto the table. Several elaborate candelabra tottered and fell with a crash. Pulling his breeches from his sore bottom he winced slightly, then cautiously seated himself in one of the big chairs. The former commander of the fort at Rocroi seemed to have had a taste for the classical, judging from the chairs, which would have been more at home in ancient Rome, and the rape of the Sabine women commemorated and glorified in the gilt bases of the candelabra.

"Usual orders about looting, and offenses against the civilian population," he said to Haakon, who leaned in the doorway.

"That's not going to be a popular order. The French didn't show that kind of restraint against our men's wives and mothers. They're going to want a little revenge."

"I don't deal in revenge. I deal in war, and I hope to God this is the last gasp for this one."

"H.H., these men are just that . . . men, not Calvinist saints. If Calvinists have saints."

No smile relieved the grimness of the younger man's expression. "My order stands, Haakon. Any rape or looting, and I'll personally see the man hanged."

"As you command, sire."

"Oh, sit down, do, and stop being so stiff. Somewhere in this pleasure palace masquerading as a fort there's bound to be some beer."

"We're in France now. It'll be wine."

William waved it aside. "Whatever."

Haakon dragged a chair around to face the prince, and settled down with his long legs stretched out before him. Locking his hands behind his head the Norwegian tapped William's toe with his. "So where to now?"

"I don't know. Seneffe shouldn't have had this profound effect. All of Louis's armies are tumbling willy-nilly over the border, with their king and his ménage in the lead. I wish I knew what had happened."

"You could use the painting, or fly around in your spirit body, or whatever it is you do."

"Each time I use the magic they pinpoint me, and frankly I'm too tired to fight off another of their assaults. Let them hire a sniper to shoot me. I'm tired of magic."

"Just like you're tired of war." Haakon hunched a shoulder in inquiry. "So what's left?"

"How about diplomacy? It worked to get my uncle out of the war."

"No, Dutch naval victories, the news of *your* victories, and the fact that Charles is flat broke got England out of the war."

"So perhaps Louis is broke, and devastated by our victories."

Haakon made a rude noise. "I thought the plan was to squash Louis."

"Whose plan? Sagitta's? I just wanted the French off my soil."

"But all this magic hoo haw?"

"You said it yourself, Haakon. It's pretty fucking useless in most circumstances. Did gunpowder and the bravery of my troops win this war, or a bag full of magical gimcracks? I don't know."

"If you hadn't melted the ice last December we wouldn't be sitting miles inside France. Louis would be dining at The Hague, and you know it."

William threw up a hand. "All right. All right. We'd better

have a conference about this. Sagitta was picking a bedchamber for us. We'll meet there."

"I'll catch up with you. Your orders have to be delivered, and I'm by God going to find something to *drink!*"

But Sagitta was not in the room. The servants had carried in the baggage, but it lay jumbled on the floor, chairs, and bed.

"I'm starting to look like Louis," muttered William. "Traveling to war with half the palace."

He was tired, but he began to gather clothing in an effort to clear a chair—and discovered after his arms were filled that there was no convenient armoire. Inspecting the paneling he soon discovered the trick—hidden closets. He also discovered that several of the panels swung open to reveal mirrors or *highly* suggestive paintings. Cheeks burning, he quickly hid the portrayals of lascivious and disporting classical figures, and began hanging coats. One gray coat crackled when he gripped the pocket. Automatically his fingers fished out the sheet of paper, and he cast a bored eye over its contents.

The remaining coats slid unheeded to the floor. William walked to the bed and sat. He read the letter again, and his fingers closed convulsively on the crackling paper. Breath coming in short wheezes, he lay back against the pillows and fought for control.

"Whoa! Easy now! Don't juggle that bottle like a burping baby. My Dad told me about this vintage . . ."

The door opened.

"Haakon, you live for your gut," said Sagitta scornfully.

"Madam, an army marches on its stomach and its cock—"

"That must be pretty damn uncomfortable—"

"And who am I to be more saintly than the men I lead?"

William stood with his back to them. He studied his reflection in a mirror. Was he really so inscrutable? It seemed incredible that his anguish should not be written on his face. For an instant the prince mourned for the youth who would have displayed his grief and betrayal. When had this hard-faced man taken his place?

He turned, hands clenched tightly behind his back. Something in his expression made the others fall silent.

"We face a difficult choice. And I choose to make the decision with only the two of you to advise me. If I debate with my generals and the allies there will be only confusion. But we must choose wisely." Haakon proffered a glass. William waved it aside. "The French are out of the United Provinces and have been driven from the Spanish Netherlands, so I have discharged my duty to my allies—"

"France lies supine before us," interrupted Sagitta. Her voice stuttered into silence at the blazing glance that William bestowed on her.

"*Don't interrupt me!*" He resumed in a more normal tone, "If I press on for Paris the French will be forced to fight. More men will die. And for what? Vengeance? My glory? I have all I wish. The Standholderate . . . my country free."

"Forget not your destiny, William Henry, to close the gate," snapped Sagitta. "And for that you will be rewarded. At the moment of your birth three crowns appeared above your head. Even then the Lady blessed you."

"Or suspicious midwives saw spots before their eyes when the candles were so suddenly extinguished," he replied sharply and a little bitterly. "You are like the ignorant fortune-tellers at a kermis festival, using the words of the customer to quickly fabricate a tale."

"It is no fabrication. It happened. And there are three crowns. You now have the Stadholderate for life, and it is guaranteed to your male line."

"Yes." William had to force the word past the loathing he felt.

"You stand third in line for the English throne, and through your mother's line you can make a legitimate claim on the throne of France. More so if you back that claim by right of conquest."

William looked to Haakon. The soldier shrugged, drained his glass, and refilled it. "Don't look at me. I'm just a simple soldier. Kings and magic are beyond me."

Sagitta rose, crossed to William, and dropped onto the floor at his feet. Her skirts billowed gracefully about her. That beautiful face was uplifted to his. "You can have everything."

"It is not right that a man should have everything."

"Ordinary men, maybe, but you are special. The power sings in your blood. You will found a dynasty."

"With you?" The question was sharp.

She hung her head. "Perhaps. If I'm permitted. You know I would do anything for you."

"Obviously."

The paper fluttered to the floor between them. She scanned it, raised strained eyes to his implacable face.

Haakon inquired, "Am I missing something here?"

"Tell him," William ordered. Sagitta mutely shook her head. William glanced to Haakon as if he could no longer bear to look at the woman kneeling at his feet. "Do you remember, oh, over a year ago when a messenger was sent with a letter warning me of the danger to the de Witts, begging me to restore order in The Hague? And how we searched, after the dreadful news of their murders had reached us, but no letter could be found?"

"Vaguely."

"Well, there lies the letter. And where do you think I found it?" He bent his gaze on Sagitta. "In your pocket. When did it arrive?"

"Only moments after you had ridden for Woerden."

"So I could have saved them?"

"Why would you have wanted to? They were a danger to you. They would only have continued to agitate against you. I acted out of love for you, and in your best interests."

"You have stained me with their blood," he cried. "And my good people who, whipped to a frenzy, behaved like maddened animals. I should have realized when I heard the manner of the de Witt's deaths—torn to pieces. It is a tradition with your Lady, is it not? If you could not think of me, could you not at least consider the effect on these ordinary folk who must now live with the nightmare of their bestiality?"

She shrugged. "It is sad, but unavoidable. At times the great must use the simple."

"That's disgusting."

"You do the same with your universal conscription. The simple do not wish to leave their peaceful fields and fight, but the great see the necessity." She looked away and added softly, "And I did it for you."

"I don't believe you. It's true, your terrible Mistress holds your full loyalty."

"Is that not how it should be? She is the goddess. And are you so pure? Have you not done murder?"

"*No!*"

"Seventeen thousand dead at Seneffe? French and Dutch."

"Soldiers, fighting in a war."

"We were at war with the de Witts."

"A convenient sophism."

She waved her hands impatiently before her face. "None of this matters. What matters lies to the west. It awaits us in Paris. So long as Louis lives the gateway between the dimensions lies open."

"And so long as I live the gateway for your Lady also remains open."

"No, William!" Haakon cried, lunging out of the chair.

"*Calme*, I'm not contemplating suicide. I'm merely exploring the parameters of this maze in which I find myself."

"Advance on Paris. Conquer France. You owe it—"

"To who? You? Your Lady?" He turned away, composed himself, and faced them. "Leave me. I will give you my answer in the morning."

"Hans, the Prince wants you."

Haakon's face glowed eerily in the darkness, lit only by the light of a single candle. Bentinck scrubbed at his face.

"What o'clock?"

"Near three, I think."

"God's blood. Has the prince rested at all?" he asked as he pulled on his breeches and thrust his bare feet into his shoes.

"No."

"And you've sat with him all night?"

"Much of it. I drank. He prayed."

Bentinck grunted. "Sounds right."

A branching candlestick at Williams's elbow threw a pool of golden light across the desk. The scratch of the quill was loud in the room.

"Sir," said Bentinck.

William didn't look up from his writing. "Hans, I wish you to carry this letter to Paris. Give it directly into my royal cousin's hands, and await his answer."

"You sue for peace?"

"I have no desire to be a modern Alexander."

Haakon folded his arms across his chest. "And what of . . . those other matters?"

"My letter addresses that."

The Norwegian grunted. "It better be a hell of a letter."

The pepper of the sand on the page, and the soft exhalation as William breathed across the drying ink, was loud in the silent room. "I pray God it is."

Haakon lifted the sheet before William could seal it. He scanned it briefly with Bentinck reading over his shoulder.

"Do you really think this will work?" asked Hans diffidently.

"I don't know. But can I do less? Sagitta was right in one respect—how many more deaths must be laid to my conscience? If at all possible I will stop this war."

"Somehow I don't think the White Lady's going to think she got her money's worth," said Haakon.

William suddenly smiled. "Oh, Haakon, do you sell yourself so cheap? Surely a night of playing at in and out with you should be enough for any woman be she goddess or not."

Haakon slapped his thigh. "By gad, you're right! I had not properly considered the matter." Crossing the room, he lifted the drape and peered out. "'Tis a bright night."

Bentinck bowed. "Then I'll to horse at once, sir, and have this answer back betimes."

"Take Barbarossa, Hans. I know he will bear you safely back to me."

Bentinck paused at the door. "We've had some times, haven't we, H.H.?"

"High ho, here's a pretty state," said Haakon. "We'll reminisce of old glories when we're old men."

"Aye, you're right." Bentinck saluted briefly, and left.

William sat huddled, listening to the retreating footfalls. Suddenly he was on his feet, running to the door and flinging it open with such violence that it crashed against the wall. He flew down the hall, tears brimming in his great, dark eyes. Bentinck caught him in a tight embrace, felt the hysterical sobs shaking the slender body.

"Here, here. What's to do?" he soothed.

"Hans, I love thee well!"

The prince kissed Bentinck lightly on the lips.

Haakon, leaning in the doorway, quietly slid back into the room.

Clouds boiled like a brooding frown in the west, and the sun drew fire from them as it sank burning and orange into their billowing embrace. A party of horsemen approached out of that dying fire, leading a familiar bay stallion. Haakon stiffened, seized a glass. For the space of a heartbeat he studied the approaching figures. Then with an oath he flung the glass at the sentry and ran for the prince's chambers.

A great crowd gathered about the gate of Rocroi. The five riders, dressed in the red and blue of Louis's personal guard, reined up a hundred yards from the gate. They bore a flag of truce.

"We bear a message from His Royal Highness, Louis XIV. Here is your reply, Orange."

The officer brought his crop down hard across the big bay's rump, raising a weal and drawing blood. The stallion squealed and plunged. The lead was dropped, and the horse galloped wildly for the gate. William stopped him with a shrill whistle. Snorting, blowing, his eyes showing white, the big horse minced toward his master. He bore an awkward bundle wrapped in a black cloak.

William laid a hand on the material. It was stiff with dried blood. Flies buzzed about the bundle, and the stench for rotting flesh hung sweet and heavy in the hot August air.

"Willy, no," cried Haakon, thrusting between horse and master.

William flung him aside, ripped at the knots with shaking fingers. Nails tore and blood stained his hands. Cursing he drew his sword and sawed at the swollen ropes. The bundle slid to the ground, spilling Bentinck's naked, tormented body onto the cobbles. The soles of his feet had been beaten until the skin burst. His fingers were burned away. His eyes were empty bloody sockets, and his manhood had been hacked away.

"*No!*"

It tore like a scream from his throat. William spun to face the gate, but the French party was already trotting away, mission discharged, on the road to Paris.

His breath coming in short sharp pants, the prince seized Haakon. "*A gun! Give me a gun!*"

Prince John, his old face weary and grave, gripped William by the shoulders. "Cousin, no. We do not shoot men under a flag of truce."

"They do! They murdered my envoy." He dropped to his knees beside the mutilated body and rocked back and forth in misery. "They murdered my Hans. Oh, my Hans."

Prince John laid an arm across his heaving shoulders. "All the more reason that we show we are Christian gentlemen."

William ripped free and ran through the gate. Sagitta, who had been standing silent and impassive, rushed after him. She could see the power gathering, flickering like tongues of flame about his body Then, abruptly, she stopped and watched as he cast the spell. Watched it wash harmlessly off the oblivious soldiers. William collapsed in the dust of the road.

With Haakon supporting him on one side, and John Maurice on the other, they brought him back into the fort.

"I told you," said Sagitta. "Now will you do as I say?"

"*Get out of my sight!*"

"You no longer have a choice," she called to his back.

William pivoted slowly to face her, his expression terrible. "I know that."

Rich and lush, the Île-de-France lay before them: ripening fields, peasant villages, a haze of smoke marking the sight of the city Soissons. William, armored, his baton clutched in his hand, stared across the tossing wheat that rippled like the golden manes of running horses.

"Burn it."

Prince John Maurice came stiffly around in his saddle. "Beg pardon?"

"Burn it. Burn everything. Fields, houses—"

"People?" asked Haakon cruelly.

The lines about the prince's mouth deepened. "The men may do as they will."

"I don't deal in revenge. I deal in war," sang out Haakon in a mocking little voice. "Brave words, Highness, with no moral strength."

"*You*. You talk to me of morality?"

"Willy, the purpose for war is to make your enemy want to stop fighting, not to commit atrocities."

"Child," said John Maurice gently. "You can flood these fair fields with blood, and it won't bring back Hans."

"Punish the guilty, William, not the innocent. Do you want to be remembered as a Luxembourg?"

The prince bent over his pommel, but when he straightened

the narrow face was as cold and as implacable as death. "Carry out my orders."

"Spinoza." Haakon entered without ceremony, and Baruch sent a blot of ink flying across his page.

"Damn you—"

"We must stop him before he takes Soissons. If he massacres that town . . ." Haakon shook his head helplessly. "If he acts now out of hate, he will destroy himself later for penance."

"I know, but what do you propose?"

"He thrives on philosophy the way other men thrive on meat. Talk to him."

"I want to, but he refuses to see me."

Haakon drove his fist several times into his palm. "Oh, he'll see you."

Alarmed by the Norwegian's expression, Spinoza asked, "What are you going to do?"

"Beat sense into him, and then you're going to talk sense into him."

"Do you really think that's going to work?"

"I have no idea, but I can't come up with a better one."

"Haakon, he has not wept. Not mourned once for Bentinck. We must drive out the passionate hatred with a stronger and more vital emotion. He must find release."

"Oh, he will. I'll let him work out a little passionate hatred on me."

"Haakon, that's not what I meant," Spinoza cried to the soldier's back.

They were bivouacked in the castle of a petty noble. Five miles away was Soissons. As Haakon hurried through the halls he could hear the thunder of the cannon. The assault had begun.

Haakon paused before the door to the prince's bedchamber, drew a deep breath to steady himself. He wished he were at Soissons taking part in the bombardment. An assault on a city he understood. The battle for a man's soul was frightening and alien territory. He entered.

"I'm busy, go away."

"Get out," Haakon ordered Huygens. The secretary rose half out of his chair.

"Sit down! We're not finished," ordered William. Huygens dropped back into the chair.

"*Get out or I'll kick your butt from here to The Hague!*"

Huygens scuttled from the room like a terrified beetle.

William was on his feet, nostrils pinched, fingers tightened like claws about the back of his chair. "I will not remand my order."

"Yes, you will. Because if you don't I'm going to be standing in the gate of Soissons, and your Hollanders are going to have to cut me down to get at the people."

Shaking his head in bewilderment, William relaxed from his tense pose. "Have you gone mad?"

"No, but you have. No man is worth this."

"*How dare you!* My Hans was—"

"Your Hans was a nice boy. He probably would have gown up to be a nice man." Haakon shrugged. "But I've seen a lot of nice boys not make it to old age."

"You have no heart. How can you be so cruel to me, seeing how I suffer?"

"Everybody's been patting your little cheek. It hasn't worked, and I'm frankly bored with it. You're not a prince— you're a brat, and a spoiled one at that."

The rasp of steel was loud in the room as William swept out his sword. Haakon's lips skinned back in a parody of a smile as he drew and dropped to the *en garde*.

"Yes. Good. Spit me. Run me through like the dog I am. I'm going to wallop your butt."

With a cry of inarticulate rage William lunged. Haakon parried easily and swung around behind the desk, thrusting the chair at the prince. William kicked it aside. They joined, the ring of steel on steel loud in the room. Haakon's heavier rapier easily beat down the small sword, but William was blindingly fast. From down the hall came the pounding of running feet, the clank of weapons.

The two men were locked *corps à corps*, their breath panting into one another's face, the smell of their sweat strong in each other's nostrils.

"Bentinck's dead," rasped Haakon. "You can't bring him back."

"I . . . can . . . avenge him."

"Would . . . he . . . want . . . you . . . to?"

The door opened with a crash, and the prince's guard tumbled through.

"*No!*" cried William. "Leave . . . us . . . be."

Haakon flung off the smaller man, brought around his rapier, and hit William hard in the face with the hilt. The prince staggered back, hand pressed to his face. Haakon drove in and slammed William across the ribs with the flat of his sword.

"Believe me. I'm only doing this because I *love* you." He punctuated the word love with another blow.

William drove his sword point-down into the floorboards, leaned back against the wall, and began to laugh, gasping out, "Then God help the woman you marry."

· Suddenly the laughter dissolved into tears. Sobs shook the slender body, and Haakon put an arm around the prince's shoulders. Spinoza pushed through the gaping guardsmen.

"I stand ready for Your Highness's order," said Haakon.

"William Henry, when you were my student you honored me by noting down my words and philosophical mauderings. What said I on the subject of hate?"

"A strong man hates no one, is enraged with no one," whispered William.

Spinoza continued. "He who lives under the guidance of reason endeavors as much as possible to repay hatred with love and nobleness. He who wishes to avenge injuries by reciprocal hatred will live in misery. Hatred is increased by reciprocated hatred, and, on the contrary, can be demolished by love."

William straightened and mopped at his wet face with his sleeves. "Lindel."

"Highness."

"The usual orders on looting and rape."

The presence of an army at her gates had struck Paris like a thunderclap. For a few days hysteria had reigned, as there was no king to reign in its stead. Hiding his annoyance and irritation beneath an impassive mask, William had sent out troops to reassure the carters so that the city would not starve.

But now Paris was beginning to return to life. Vendors wove through the streets. Carters cursed and whipped their horses, and sedan chairs were trotted briskly through the piles of garbage and excrement. William noticed a pair of glowing brown eyes regarding him through the narrow window of a chair. Dainty fingertips thrust through, and a lacy handkerchief dropped at Barbarossa's feet. William raised his hat politely and rode on.

Dear God, did they think he was Louis, to be flattered by such blatant seductions?

No, he amended. The problem was that Louis had completely lost face with the fickle Parisians, and they had chosen to love their conqueror. It was not surprising, for when at last William approached the Louvre he found the court flown, and the palace filled with looters—Dutch, Spanish, and French. He had hanged them all, placed the mayor in charge of the abandoned palace, and returned to his bivouac on the Mont des Martyrs. It had not required magic to locate Louis. Intelligence alone suggested his whereabouts. People had never seemed to matter very much to Louis. Only one thing held his heart. Versailles. Sooner or later William would have to ride for the half-completed palace and root Louis from his lair. But now he had one final call to make.

He drew up at the gates of the Carmelite convent in the Rue d'Enfer, listened to the deep, sonorous ringing of the gate bell. As he waited in the austere receiving room he compared the luxury of the Louvre to these bare stone walls. The only furniture was a plain wooden table and two straight-backed wooden chairs. A crucifix hung on the eastern wall. Through a narrow lancet window he could see a pretty herb garden. He spun at the turning of the door handle.

"And what would the Protestant beast with us?" asked the mother superior in a dry voice. Her face within the wimple was heavily lined, but the skin still possessed a flawless, glowing quality.

William swept off his hat, knelt and kissed her ring. "Your servant, ma'am."

"So the beast has manners, and some understanding of our ways." She motioned to him to rise.

"Ma'am, I am neither a boor nor a barbarian. And during my campaigns I have frequently slept in convents, and the sisters had nothing to complain of."

"I hope you did not lie too comfortably among the sisters, and that their gratitude had nothing to do with prowess." She chuckled at the sudden blush which washed into the young man's cheeks. "And so the beast proves to be a baby." She seated herself, hands folded serenely in her lap. A rosary was wound through her gnarled fingers.

"You have a sister among you whom I wish to see. She befriended me when she was of the world, and I wish to be sure that she was not forced into this life by the King."

"You refer to Sister Louise de la Misericorde, and I can assure you, Highness, that she was not forced to take the veil. In fact, she fled to us on one cold winter morning, and we had to lock the gates against the King's troops."

"You reassure me, madam." William fidgeted. "But I would still wish to see her."

"Why?"

"For friendship and love's sake."

"Worthy reasons, my child. I will inquire if she will see you."

She left with that peculiar floating gait of the long-time nun. A few minutes later, and La Vallière entered. If anything her delicate beauty was enhanced by the severe garments. William's eyes flicked down to her little bare feet. They were rough now, and a little sunburned on the tops.

"Louise."

"Highness." She carefully inclined her head as if fearful her neck would break.

"Are . . . are you happy?"

"Oh, yes. My soul is so content, so tranquil, because I worship the goodness of God."

"I had thought to ask you of tidings of the court and the King. Then I discovered you were here."

"I can still give you tidings. Many are dead. De Montespan, La Castlemaine."

"Dead? How?"

"You would know that better than I, Highness. I fled to this place of peace because of the evil which crept through the court. My lord is trapped in a web of sorcery. I pray for him each day.

William's mouth was a grim line. "I'll do more than pray for him. I'll send him to God for judgment if I can."

"And in so doing judge for God," came the sharp reply.

"Louise, what else can I do? He killed my dearest friend, who had come to parley. And more than killed. They tortured my Hans ere he died. He will be revenged."

"Highness. Willy." She clapsed his hand in hers. "Do not blacken your soul with an act of vengeance."

"First Haakon and Baruch and John, and now you. I spared the people, may I at least not have the King?" She made no reply. Irritably he strode away, turned back to face her. "You know that black magic holds sway in the court?"

"Yes."

"And yet you still counsel me to hold my hand?"

"Save my lord. Give him back his humanity and spare him."

"I don't know if I can do that."

"Why? Because you would rather hate?"

"No, I don't know if it's possible." He took another nervous turn about the room. "What became of de Montespan and Barbara Castlemaine?"

"They weakened and died. Toward the end they were like shrunken and empty wineskins."

"He used them to cast his spells," mused William, "thus leaving himself strong. And I am fearfully weary."

"Must it be a duel of magic? Can you not put your faith in God?"

"I tried that when I sent a letter with Hans. My most noble cousin's reply was the broken body of my friend. I still have faith in God, I just think I have none in man. We are born to evil, live and die in it."

"No. There is much good and beauty in man, and he is greater than the angels, for he can choose—good and evil, God or the Devil. Help my lord to choose. Please, Willy, I beg you. Punish him if you must, but spare him so he may find salvation."

William sighed. "You ask much, but as I owe you my life I will grant your wish." He lifted the cross from her breast. "I swear I will try to save him." He kissed the cross, and for the briefest instant he felt her fingers brush lightly through his hair. "Ah, Louise, if your daughter is as sweet and virtuous as you, mayhap I should have married her."

That drew a little smile. "She's too young for you, Highness." She suddenly drew the simple cross over her head and gave it to William. "Give this to my lord, and remind him that I love him . . . always. And perhaps it will protect you as you walk in shadow."

William bowed and left. He did not look back.

Eighteen

I am a stag: *of seven tines*

Water fountained over the bows of the replica of the galley *La Reale*.

"Left," said William tersely, as he watched through his glass.

The cannon roared again, and this time the ball struck amidships. Masts tumbled on the galley, and she began to list. Debris from the two yachts which had also floated in the grand canal littered the water. William lifted his glass and swept the face of Versailles. Scaffolding obscured one wing, and great cranes stood like dormant giraffes. And in place of the army of workmen there was indeed a true army dug in about the palace. They were currently dug deep, for William had been blanketing the palace with a continuous artillery barrage for almost a full day. Rubble lay at the feet of the chateau, and the walls were pocked by hits.

"We fire on glass and stone instead of men," said John Maurice, riding up. "A useless exercise, for it is the men we must fight."

"I doubt it will come to a fight, cousin."

"I hope you're right." The old man hooked a knee over the pommel of his saddle and lit his pipe. "I presume there is some purpose to this bombardment?"

"Yes."

"Terse and to the point." John Maurice sucked on the stem of the clay pipe. "But if Your Serene Grace would vouchsafe a more detailed answer?"

William chuckled, and the old man cuffed him lightly.

"Louis cares very little for humans, cousin, but this palace is the envelope for his soul. Each crash of the cannon and each fall of plaster bites like the loss of ten thousand to you or me."

The sun sank behind them, turning the canal into liquid gold.

228

William slung his telescope and swung into the saddle. "I'm going to chase the fidgets out of Barbarossa before supper. Dine with me, cousin?"

"Aye, happily. Take a guard," he bellowed after William. "You're in France, dammit. Louis would pay much for your ass."

"Louis's not that type," shot back William, and spurred Barbarossa into a gallop.

Despite the strenuous efforts of thirty thousand men, the valley in which Versailles lay was still a dank and marshy place. As the evening advanced, mold and leaf began to exhale a thick white fog. It rose around the big stallion's knees, making it seem that horse and rider were swimming in a milky sea. Overhead a silver moon sprang up. William became aware of tinkling bells. Heart racing, he reined in and waited.

Out of the swirling mist stepped the White Lady. She was dressed as he recalled, but this time, in honor of late summer, she bore a sheaf of wheat.

"William, you stand at the moment. Why do you delay?"

The prince folded his hand about the simple gold cross which Louise had given him, and faced the goddess. "I choose my moment, lady."

"The gate remains open. Delay is danger."

"I am weighing how best to close this gate."

"You have the talismans. Use them. They, together with your blood, will defeat your enemies."

"Your enemies too, lady."

"I do not forget it." She stretched out one gleaming white arm and pointed toward the distant palace. "There lies Louis and his demon. There also lies a place of power. Meet them, face them, destroy them."

"I have made a vow to a lady dear to me to spare Louis."

"You have made a vow to *me*!"

"No, lady, I promised you nothing. And I have done nothing that I would not have done without your presence."

"Without me your blood would lie dormant."

"True. I suppose I should thank you for that."

"Act, William Henry."

He cocked his head to one side, considering. "Close one gateway, and open another. I'm not certain how I feel about that."

Turning Barbarossa, he rode away. Power beat on him, but

this time there was no paralyzing sense of awe and dread. Her handmaiden had trained him. He could now resist the mistress.

Sagitta seemed to spring up out of the mist. Her face was all angles, white and strained. "What have you done?"

"I've been insolent to your lady."

"Oh mercy."

"It's not your fault. She can't hold you responsible because I'm a churlish mortal."

"Willy, you *must* face Louis and Mazarin."

"Why? We're winning with gunpowder—why add magic?"

"Your blessed guns will not close the gate."

"Louis can choose to close the gate."

"He never will. He is too closely controlled by Mazarin."

"What a pity I'm not so well controlled by your lady, eh?"

"I didn't say that."

"You didn't have to. Sagi, don't you think it's time to be completely candid with me?"

"William, open the way to my Lady."

"And if I do?"

"She will give you three crowns. You will rule over a golden age which has been lost for an eon."

"And if I don't?"

"You doom mankind."

"In what way?"

"You condemn them to strife, hunger, war. Remember the burned children of Bodegraven. Remember Hans!" The prince paled, and his grip tightened on the reins, setting Barbarossa to dancing. Sagitta resumed in a quieter tone. "If the Old Religion reenters the world, we will protect and cherish the humans. We will find the magic ones—like yourself—nurture and train them, and they will rule with wisdom and grace. Under their guidance man will again live in harmony."

"Harmony. You always use that word when you're chastising my interest in science."

"William, my Lady is a goddess. Man should not seek to harness her mystery. William, your way will lead to weapons of terror. Ours to peace. Consider the world you would rule. Rich fields tilled by peaceful and contented peasants. Farmers, fisherfolk, craftsmen making humble libation to the Mother. Not tearing life from the earth, but accepting her gifts. And the great ones—like you—studying the mysteries."

"And how will this eternal peace and prosperity be purchased, Sagitta? Surely so much good cannot come forth without some suffering."

She held out the painting.

Dismounting, he accepted the talisman, looked on the two faces of the future . . . a vast white chariot rising on tongues of flame into a dawn sky . . . the writhing shadow of a man, frozen in a wall . . . Sagitta. Her eyes grew to dominate her face: great pale blue moons. Behind them lay not the face of the Maiden or the nurturing Mother, but the implacable face of the Hag. Visions rushed past. William saw himself riding deep into the woods. He studied the face with wonder, noting the deep lines about the mouth, the graying hair. Women awaited him—Sagitta, ageless and beautiful. Her hand gripped the crystal knife. He lay back on a stone altar. She cut his throat and gathered the hot blood in a crystal goblet, dripped it into the thirsty, ravenous earth.

A long line of his sons, each waiting to pay the price of fertility. . . .

He thrust the painting into his breast.

"Sagitta, I am a Christian man. That blood price was paid for all eternity to wash away our sins."

"You are a sacred king." They regarded each other in a silence so profound that it seemed to stretch to eternity and back. "William, is not the result worth the sacrifice? You've always said you're willing to sacrifice for your people. And during the intervening years you would have so much."

"The contented bull to slaughter. Yes, I see." He ran a hand over his mouth.

"William, please. Heed your heart."

He thrust his foot into the stirrup. "No, it's a singularly unreliable organ. I think I'll use my mind, and . . . consider." He swung into the saddle.

"Do not consider too long. Death will pass through that gateway. It must be closed."

"I agree." He shook out the reins, and Barbarossa walked a few paces. Suddenly the prince slew around in the saddle. "Oh yes—would I be given you?"

She hung her head. "If you want me."

"Sagitta." He held out a hand, and she walked to him. Bending low in the saddle he softly kissed her lips. "Remember, I love you. For always."

"Do you hate me for what I've done?"

Spinoza's head jerked up, and he stared wildly at the door where William stood like a child about to be punished. So engrossed had he been in Vespasiano da Bisticci's *Lives* that he had not heard the prince enter.

"Hate you? What mad humor is this? You're overwrought. Sit. Listen to the bees." He gestured toward the window of the little inn in the village of Versailles. It was practically obscured by a climbing rose, its branches like twisted tendons, its flowers themselves an explosion of color, drenching the room with their heady scent. "Watch the sun play tag with the dust motes."

"I'm not overwrought. It's a serious question." William straddled a chair opposite his old tutor, folded his arms along the back. "I have made war. You are a man who hates war."

Spinoza stroked his chin. "How goes the bombardment?"

William hunched a shoulder. "I abandoned it."

"I see. Why?"

"It was an exercise in spleen. I was revenging myself for Bodegraven and Zwammerdam."

"The boy makes war on plaster and wood while his enemies revenge themselves upon the innocent, and he asks if I hate him. God grant me patience."

"I'm serious."

"So am I." The older man leaned in intently. "Yes, I hate war as the most hideous of all human endeavors, but I am also not such a fool that I advocate lying down in a ditch and waiting for the marauders to slit my throat. You've made war because war was waged upon you." He watched the subtle play of emotions across that young face. He stretched out a hand coaxingly. "But tell me what really oppresses you."

The chair went flying as Williams fell on his knees before the philosopher and buried his face in his lap. "Oh Baruch, my father, I am afraid."

"Afraid?" He stroked the chestnut curls. "What are these fears and alarms? Afraid? When half your generals and all their

High Mightinesses beg you to have greater care of your person?"

William's dark eyes strained up at Spinoza. "The death of the body is nothing. I fear the loss of my soul."

Baruch caught William's chin in his hand. "I would say such confusion is unavoidable when you practice magic yet call yourself a Christian."

"I have been offered all the kingdoms of the world. I have been shown a world of peace and tranquillity to be purchased by my death and the death of other sacred kings. A small price maybe? But is it really peace or is it stagnation?"

"Cease to speak in riddles, and be plain with me."

Springing to his feet, William paced the room. "There are apparently a multitude of worlds lying in close proximity with one another. Certain people, disposed by blood, can open the gateways between these worlds. So Louis has done with aid of his magical advisor. So I have done with Sagitta."

"And what seeks to enter through these gateways?"

"For Louis's part, a vast, life-devouring evil. Or perhaps I wrong it to call it evil. It is mindless and passionless. But if it enters, all life on this earth ends."

"And through your gateway?"

"Through my gateway comes the White Lady—the ancient goddess of a pagan faith. A goddess of earth and woman. Of intuition and magic."

"That doesn't sound so terrible."

"But I think it *is*. The White Lady has said that her foe hates humans for our random creativity, but I think she fears us too. She has shown me a blissful vision of a peaceful pastoral kingdom—contented peasants tilling bountiful fields, ruled over by wise magic-users, all worshiping the mother goddess. But such bounty must be purchased by blood sacrifice. The price of fertility is death."

"And you're the first candidate."

"Yes. So, I am afraid. I don't want to die. Not that way. Yet is that evil and selfish of me? If my blood can buy peace should I not willingly make the sacrifice? And I would have my years of glory and honor. She would make me a king with many crowns and a multitude of nations beneath my wise and benevolent rule. She would give me the woman of my dreams." He gave a sharp bark of laughter. He turned back to Spinoza. "So what should I do?"

"I have no idea."

"Heer Spinoza!"

"I can't make such a decision for you. But I can point out one thing. You embody an interesting balance. A synthesis, if you will, between all these competing powers."

"Meaning what?"

"Meaning that, unlike most men who spend their lives bowed over their plows, tilling a single furrow, you stand at a crossroad. Many paths lie branching before you. You have the luxury of choice."

William paced, nervously washing his hands. "I know. I know. And I *can't* choose. What if it's the wrong choice? Is it right for me to make such a decision for all mankind?"

"William, a man must have the courage of his convictions. The fact that your choice may have broader implications is meaningless. The decision you make must be a decision for yourself. Beginning and ending with yourself. Now, tell me. What do *you* want?"

For a long moment, William stood with bowed head. Then, squaring his shoulders, he walked with decision toward the table. He laid a hand upon the philosopher's microscope.

"*This.*"

"Then find a way to accomplish *that.*" Spinoza opened his book and resumed reading.

They rode down a long boulevard lined with whispering beeches and chestnut trees. The crescent moon was tangled in their topmost branches, and it seemed to William's fevered mind that it followed him like a glowing blade. Haakon's face, bitter and confused, seemed to float before him.

"*But why can't I come? You let me come at the Louvre when she didn't want me to.*"

"*I can't Haakon, not this time. Your loyalty does you credit, but this I must do alone.*"

"*H.H., Willy, please!*"

"*No.*"

The delicate tinkling of water returned the prince to his surroundings. The avenue debouched into an open glade. The horses' hooves crunched on the gravel which ringed an elaborate fountain. Apollo, enthroned in his chariot and surrounded by dolphins and mermen, seemed to burst from the pool. The moonlight turned the gushing waters to molten silver.

The figures in the pool wavered, became transparent, solidified again. William drew a hand across his eyes, but the world continued to phase in and out.

"The boundaries between the dimensions are very thin here," said Sagitta quietly. "Now remember, you must first destroy Louis, lest he and his demon open the gateway and call forth the death. We will then channel our power against the demon Mazarin, and so close the way."

William caressed the cross.

Down a path leading from the battered palace they came walking. Louis resplendently attired as always, the silver embroidery on his black coat catching the moonlight; and Mazarin, his scarlet robes like dried blood in the night. Suddenly a familiar, burly figure leapt from the trees, pistol in one hand, sword in the other. Louis spun away, and Haakon's shot went wide.

William stretched out along Barbarossa's neck and spurred him into a gallop. Drawing his sword, his gripped it by the blade and swung the hilt smartly across the back of Haakon's head.

"*Ooowwwww! Scheisse!*"

Yanking Barbarossa back on his haunches, William pulled the war-horse into a canter-pirouette, kicked his foot loose from the stirrup, and slammed his boot heel hard into Haakon's jaw. The big Norwegian dropped like a stone and lay groaning on the gravel.

"Kill him," said Louis. "You have violated the agreement."

"No. If you win the coming encounter, *you* kill him. I won't care anymore."

The prince rode back to Sagitta, and they dismounted. He noted with a kind of distant pride that his hands were steady as he unpacked the talismans. The shining face of the pool separated the combatants. Between the misting waters of the fountain, and the strange power of the place, William found it difficult to focus on his enemies. But one thing he could see clearly—a cord of flame running from Louis's gut to the gut of the cardinal. Frowning, William summoned the sight and saw a similar cord of silver connecting him with Sagitta.

Louis cried aloud, and the waters of the pool began to burn as if they had been replaced by oil. Feeling Sagitta's gaze upon him, William stepped forward. The heat of the flames scorched his face. Resting the point of the ancient iron Spear on the fountain's rim he brought his boot heel down with all his force. The pain, shooting through arm and leg, and Sagitta's wild scream shocked him, and he lost his balance. But it was done. The Spear lay broken, the blackened point wavering beneath the disturbed waters and leaping flames of the fountain.

Drawing a knife, William frenziedly slashed at the painting. The creatures writhed once, then lay still. The Venus was in his hand. Screaming, Sagitta launched herself at him. Hands forming claws, she raked at his face, drawing blood, her nails digging deep into his wrist as she fought him for control of the tiny statuette. He clipped her across the chin with the hilt of his dagger. She collapsed in a heap at his feet. Laying the statue on the rim of the fountain, he ground it to powder beneath his heel.

"What have you done? What have you done? You have killed us all!" shrieked Sagitta.

William drew his pistol and spun the wheel. Leveled it at Mazarin.

"That won't work. You've destroyed the only things which might have reached him!"

"Let's just try this, shall we?" He shifted his aim to Louis. The Frenchman flinched, and the flames in the pool died. "You animate him. You or him, cousin. I offered you a choice in my letter. You repaid my generosity by killing my Hans, and for that I would love to kill you. Instead I offer you the choice again. There will not be a third chance." There was a note of hysteria in the light young voice.

Louis suddenly reached for his belt. William threw himself down, expecting the king to emerge with a pistol. Instead he ripped the intricate mirror from its cord and smashed the glass on the fountain's edge. Flinging aside the bent frame, he turned to face Mazarin. The cord of fire darkened, brightened, darkened again. An unholy whistling erupted from the thing which wore Mazarin's envelope—a sound of terror and fury. The fire linking human to creature burst into desperate flames. Louis's face contorted. The cord withered and died. The king tottered a few paces to the right and fell on his face in the gravel.

Sucking in a breath, William released it halfway, held it, and squeezed the trigger. The explosion was deafening. Blinking spots from before his eyes after the intense muzzle flash, William ran through the acrid black smoke and stared down at Mazarin.

Shreds of rotting flesh clung to the skull which grinned up at him. The smell was revolting. A thing long dead had been left too long above the ground. Green putrescence oozed from the staring eye sockets.

"Good God, the rumors of his death in '61 were not exaggerated."

Sagitta's voice jerked him from his fascinated contemplation of the corpse. "Louis," she croaked. "Kill him."

"No."

Their eyes met, and she began falling back, step by frightened step. Slowly they circled the Apollo pool.

"William, what are you doing?"

"Freeing the world."

"You're going to kill me also?"

He stopped, shook his head. "No. I love you. There is another way."

"Why, Willy? We can give you so much."

"Because the price is too great."

"All men must die."

"I prefer to die in bed." He resumed his careful stalking.

The girl fled from him, crying, "You are selfish. Think of your people."

"I am. You fear humans, Sagi."

"Whatever are you talking about?" But her voice was jumping.

"We are penetrating the mysteries of the cosmos, and the secrets of life at its smaller levels."

"And it is wrong. You must grasp the purity of the whole, not tear from the Goddess the secrets of her heart."

"Spinoza says that the more we understand individual objects, the more we understand God. I think that is a very profound statement. Why does your goddess fear what my God does not?"

"The mechanistic path has led mankind to terror and suffering."

"No, ignorance and hatred and intolerance have led mankind to terror and suffering. And not all of our discoveries lead to death." He drew out the watch which Christiaan Huygens had sent him. "Look at this. Is it not a wonder? It keeps the time so that sailors can more closely know whence they sail. And a *man* has built this thing of wonder. No magic involved, just intellect." He tapped a finger against his temple. Suddenly he abandoned the hunt and began pacing nervously, his hands gesturing in the air before him. "Did you know that even the body yields to a mechanical interpretation? Physics and chemistry bound in flesh. Huygens told me. How the blood passes from the arteries into the veins through hairlike vessels. Marcello Malpighi has called them capillaries. How fascinating it all is. How miraculous!" He whirled to face her. "Do you understand?"

"You will only confuse them. Man needs little to be happy."

"Is there bliss in ignorance, Sagitta? Somehow I don't think so. No, I don't think I like your world. A world where peasants —no matter how happy—live in ignorance. Where the great ones, the magic-users, live in fear of the advances of the human mind. We would begin a new Inquisition, and burn the Newtons, and the Huygens, and the Malpighis. No, it must end now. The magic must withdraw."

"You cripple only yourself!" she cried. "You will face your foes with only these . . . these *things*." She snatched the watch from his hands and flung it to the ground; ran to Barbarossa and ripped the telescope from the saddlebag and slammed it against the bole of a tree. The mirrors and lens shattered, a sound like brittle tears. "These *useless* things!"

"Then that will be my sacrifice."

He settled onto the ground, his back propped against the fountain's rim, and entered the astral world. It was a risk. He knew it. She could easily kill him while his physical body lay helpless in the vast gardens of Versailles. But somehow he didn't think she would. That much love at least remained.

The overworld was a place of billowing clouds. Better to hide from him? He stretched out with all of his senses . . . heard the delicate ring of silver bells. Sagitta came wailing onto the astral plain. Her silver-light hair blew about her anguished face, fell across her soft, white bosom. Her dress was askew, and one pale pink nipple drew his eyes. *The taste of her mouth, the brush of her fingers across his cock. . . .*

Furious, he hardened heart and mind against her, plunged into a looming bank of mist. A mare shrilled in terror, the sound echoing the girl's cry of despair. Whirling, the mare bolted, her tail whipping across William's face, drawing tears. Silver hooves flashed dangerously near his head. He leaped in pursuit, but was brought up short by a dragging weight clutching at his legs. He staggered, almost fell.

Sagitta clung to him. "William, I *beg* you!"

"Don't grovel! I cannot bear it! And I cannot trust it!" His hands closed on her shoulders, and he shook her wildly. "Hate me, fight me, revile me!" He realized his face was wet with tears. With a groan he threw her aside, covered his face with his hands. Her sobs tore at him.

The clouds roiled wildly as an icy wind swept the astral world. There was a hysterical ringing of bells. Seven white mares circled him, flashes of white, silver, and blue in the obscuring mist. Drawing on his power he withdrew streams of silver and plaited them into a glittering rope.

The rotting face of his long-dead mother screamed out of the clouds. Contemptuously he ignored it. The White Lady might seek to terrify, but she had no power over him. He kept his focus on the running mares. One of them was the magical avatar of Sagitta, and far more real than the human envelope which sobbed at his feet. Swinging the lariat lightly, he suddenly flashed his arm out. The first mare continued her frenzied run. He checked his throw, and tried the same trick with the next one. This one checked, and shied sharply to the right. He was after her in an instant.

The mare's head wove in snaking circles as she tried to avoid the rope. William let her panic, and watched the rise and fall of the hindquarters, the bend of the hocks. Timing it carefully, he dropped the lariat over a hind foot, jerking it up tight around the fetlock. The sudden yank pulled the mare off her feet, and she tumbled forward, somersaulting on her atlas. The force of horse meeting the end of the line also pulled William from his feet. Nursing an aching shoulder, he leapt to his feet and ran to the sprawling mare. She was just lurching to her feet. Twining his fingers in her flowing mane, he vaulted onto her smooth back, muffling a yelp of pain as his strained shoulder complained.

The mare's head came up violently, and her atlas cracked the prince in the jaw. His head swam for an instant, and he tasted blood as his teeth snapped down on his tongue. Desperately he tightened his grip on the mane and wrapped his legs firmly around the horse's barrel. She screamed, and plunged forward in a series of spine-jarring, stiff-legged crow hops.

When that failed to dislodge him, she tried a monumental, twisting buck, sunfishing wildly. William pulled off his hat and slapped her hard across the rump. With a squeal she leaped forward into a gallop. Their speed seemed to tear the breath from his mouth, and William hunched on her withers, face buried in the whipping mane.

Her head was dropping for another buck. William drove both heels hard into her flanks. She grunted with surprise and outrage, and continued to run. The next time, she ignored his punishing heels and did her worst. He had begun to lose all feeling in his fingers. That, at least, could the Goddess do for her handmaiden. The storm winds which rocked the astral plane now carried a stinging snow. The prince's breath was coming in short gasps, and his entire body ached as if clubs had been hammering upon his shoulders. The material of his breeches grated on raw patches on the insides of his knees. The mare stopped, head down, blowing exhaustedly.

"Run you bitch," he muttered past stiff lips, forgetting it was Sagitta to whom he spoke in the extremity of the fight.

The words seemed to sting her into action. Planting her front legs, she bucked with everything she had. William's head snapped back and forth like a flower whipped in a high wind. His knees weakened, and he began to slip to the side. The mare gave a great neigh of triumph and rose clawing to the air with her forefeet. That she was headed over backwards there was no doubt. Frantically, William clutched at the mane and swarmed like a terrified monkey up her long neck. He was practically sitting on her head when his weight overbore her and brought her crashing down on all four feet. He fell once more onto her back and, screaming like a banshee, he kicked, and beat at her rump with the flat of his hand. She staggered into a run. He kept her at it until foam drenched his breeches, and saliva ran from her gaping mouth. Great shuddering breaths heaved her sides as she finally came to a shivering stop.

With a whinny that was almost a sob, she swung her head around and pressed her velvet muzzle against his knee. It was surrender. William slid to the ground. Passed out. . . .

Sagitta lay across him with her cheek pressed against his knees. William noticed with head-swimming detachment that she looked transparent: a glass filled with candlelight. Leaning forward stiffly, he reached out a hand to stroke that beautiful hair which lay like a cloak across his legs. Sagitta raised her head. Her eyes were clouded.

"I loved you."

His hand brushed at nothing. A wind sighed away to the north, carrying the sound of ice bells.

There was a low, nervous whicker from the trees. William, blinking back tears, staggered to his feet. A flash of white among the boles of the trees. He stumbled into the woods. The mare waited for him. Cupping his hands about her muzzle he stared into her eyes. Liquid brown, they stared back, filled with trust and a touch of confusion. Dark hooves—she ran no longer on feet of silver.

William pressed his face into the hollow of her neck, and wept as the stars wheeled overhead, and the crescent moon sailed into the west.

Weak-kneed, he tottered back into the clearing. The mare followed, dropped her muzzle into the Apollo pool, and drank deeply. She watched, water slobbering from her lips, as William knelt beside Louis.

"Wake up, cousin. You bastard." The sharp slaps echoed in the darkness. Louis groaned.

William crept like an old man to the pool and filled his hat with water, and dumped it over the king's supine body. Louis sputtered, coughed. William assisted him to a sitting position.

"Cousin?" asked Louis.

"Cousin," affirmed William.

"You're on my grounds."

"I'm in your goddam country with a goddam army! Don't get uppity with me!"

Louis shook his head, the curls of his black wig swinging heavily as he tried to clear his mind. His gaze fell upon the rotting corpse of Mazarin. He retched, shuddered.

"Did you . . . did you . . . ?"

"Kill him? No, not technically. I think he was already dead."

William assisted Louis to his feet, handed him a handkerchief to wipe at the vomit which stained his leg. The king walked to the pool and stood in the water of the fountain, beading his hair and face with water.

"I don't know if it washes away that easily."

Louis turned to him. "What?"

"Blood."

Louis hawked, then spit a glob of phlegm into the water. "I've been such a fool."

"No argument there." The dark eyes which were raised to William's held a question. "No, I'm not going to kill you.' William retrieved the broken pieces of the Spear, the shredded painting. Of the Venus figure only dust remained. He blew lightly, and it vanished. He straightened. "Because, as despicable as you are, as useless, pompous, and vainglorious as you are—you're human. And as flawed and sinful as we humans are, I've discovered in myself a deep love of mankind."

Louis splashed toward William where he stood on the rim of the pool. The prince raised an admonishing finger. Louis stopped, eyed him warily.

"One more thing. A word of caution—you attack my country again, and next time I won't let you keep your crown." And, planting his foot firmly in his royal cousin's chest, he shoved. Arms windmilling wildly, Louis fell backwards into the water. "And now I'm going home. Oh yes." William pulled the cross over his head. "This is for you, from a woman who loves you better than you deserve."

Louis was still fishing for the cross as William transferred his tack from Barbarossa to the white mare. Grunting with strain he heaved Haakon across the bay's back. Then, leading the stallion with his limp burden, William rode slowly toward his army's lines. The crescent moon sank into a line of purple clouds on the western horizon. Passing by a farmhouse, he heard the eager clucking of chickens and the clear, arrogant call of a cock. Streamers of gold and purple light fountained joyfully in the east, outriders for the rising sun.

As they reached friendly lines, Haakon groaned and swung astride Barbarossa. "You've broken my head and busted my gut."

"You're lucky I don't kick your ass! What did you mean by disobeying my orders?"

"I've never taken orders well."

"This was a matter of honor."

Haakon snorted. "Honor, hell. Winning is the important thing."

"You are an uncouth northern barbarian. A prating fool—" William flung an arm around Haakon's neck. "And I love thee well."

"So what now, H.H.?"

"We go home."

"Home! But we have France."

"I don't want it. I want to go home."

"You are a Dutch blockhead."

"Probably."

"Where did you get the mare? A present from your royal cousin?" William busied himself with untangling the silken strands of her silver mane. "What happened to Louis? What happened to Mazarin? What happened to *the goddam war!* You clout me in the head, and when I come to it's all over!"

"Yes, that pretty well sums it up."

Haakon gave an inarticulate scream of rage. "William Henry, by the grace of God—and assuming I don't kill you in the next three seconds—Prince of Orange, tell me—"

Dismounting, William thrust the mare's reins into his friend's hands. "Haakon, give the order to break camp. And see to her. She's very precious to me. I think I shall ride to many victories on this mare."

William gave her a pat, then walked swiftly toward his tent. He could feel Haakon's eyes drilling holes in his back every step of the way. Stripping off his gauntlets, William entered. Spinoza closed the book on a long forefinger. Arched an eyebrow.

"All settled?"

"All settled."

"Nothing to report?"

"No. What's for breakfast?"

The book flew across the tent, pages fluttering like frightened birds.

"God*damn* you, William Henry!"

"What? What did I do?" A boot hung from one hand.

"You ride away filled with grim determination to face the battle of your life, and you ask me what's for *breakfast!*"

"You're just an old lover of gossip. All right, what do you want to know?"

"This great threat?"

"Is gone. The gateways—both of them—are closed."

"And that miserable Louis?"

"Probably being allowed to eat his breakfast in peace, back at the palace."

"And Mazarin?"

"Destroyed."

"And Sagitta?"

"Gone." He sat with bowed head for an instant. "To wherever handmaidens of the White Lady go."

Spinoza tamped tobacco into his pipe. William pulled off the other boot and cocked one knee over the other. The older man thrust his pipe between his teeth. Muttering around the stem, he asked:

"And you?"

"Just the plain, simple Prince of Orange."

"So the magic passes from the world," mused the philosopher. "A melancholy thought perhaps, but inevitable in the end."

Spinoza groped for a flint. A sudden flame danced on the tips of William's fingers, then arced across the room to land burning in the bowl of the pipe.

"With a few added features."